# PRAISE F(

"Every American citizen should read this deliciously disturbing novel. They don't get much more hard-hitting than this plausible river of darkness from which we all might drink."

— REAVIS WORTHAM, TWO-TIME SPUR AWARD WINNING AUTHOR OF THE RED RIVER SERIES.

"Dissolution is fast-moving, unpredictable, and frighteningly, often feels prophetic."

— JOHNNY D. BOGGS, WISTER AND SPUR AWARD-WINNING AUTHOR

"Dissolution repeatedly blurs the line between fiction and non-fiction in a way that only a master storyteller with a keen understanding of human nature and an appetite for research could do."

— STEVEN HORN FRANKLIN, AWARD-WINNING AUTHOR OF *THE PUMPKIN ROLLERS*

**FROM WESTERN WORD-SLINGER AND ANTHROPOLOGIST W. MICHAEL GEAR, THE THIRD INSTALLMENT IN THE BESTSELLING CONTEMPORARY APOCALYPTIC WESTERN SERIES, *THE WYOMING CHRONICLES*!**

In the aftermath of Sam Delgado and Breeze Tappan's ambush of the posse at Slickside, tempers flare in the Bighorn Basin. During an attempt to stop unchecked violence from breaking out, Governor Agar faces death, saved only when Lauren Davis shoots first, prompting Lauren to join the Governor's security detail.

After the Collapse, insulin is in short supply. Word comes down there's a lab north of Boulder, Colorado, that can make enough insulin to keep people alive. Governor Agar handpicks a team–The Fallen Eagle convoy–to retrieve the scientists and their lab–at a cost some will consider too high.

In the midst of violence, road blocks, and gangs, Fallen Eagle faces head-on the depths of human barbarity and a seemingly unstoppable cunning adversary. It all comes down to Sam and Breeze. One of them will have to make the supreme sacrifice… Or, in Sam's words, "Never bring a pickup truck to a snowplow fight."

Written with the wit, tension, and action readers of the bestselling *Dissolution* and *Fourth Quadrant* have come to expect, Michael Gear's *After the Eagle Has Fallen* takes the Wyoming Chronicles series to the next level.

# AFTER THE EAGLE HAS FALLEN

## The Wyoming Chronicles: Book Three

## W. MICHAEL GEAR

WOLFPACK
PUBLISHING
— EST 2013 —

**After the Eagle Has Fallen:**
**The Wyoming Chronicles Book Three**

Paperback Edition
Copyright © 2023 W. Michael Gear and Kathleen O'Neal Gear

Wolfpack Publishing
9850 S. Maryland Parkway, Suite A-5 #323
Las Vegas, Nevada 89183

Paperback ISBN 978-1-63977-730-3
Hardcover ISBN 978-1-63977-729-7
eBook ISBN 978-1-63977-731-0

*To*
*Walter Earnest Perry*
*Who told a little boy*
*Marvelous stories*
*And*
*Opened the doors of imagination.*

# AFTER THE EAGLE HAS FALLEN

# YOU CAN ASK WHY

*Why the hell am I still alive and breathing? I should be dead. Killed in Colorado. Taken a bullet at Buffalo Camp. Died on The Line. And I never should have survived the events at Marsy Ranch. If some bullet or explosion had taken me out, I would have considered it justice given the things I've done.*

*Maybe that's what goaded me to pick up a pen and start this journal. Well, that, and my old friend Breeze told me it was important to write everything down. When a world dies, there should be witnesses.*

*I guess that's what I am.*

— Excerpt from Lauren Davis' *Journal.*

# CHAPTER ONE

*I DID THIS.*

The stench filtered up the tree-covered mountain in western Wyoming's Owl Creek Range. Something about the cloying smell of decay couldn't be mistaken. And it lingered. Seemed to cling to the inside of Samuel Michael Delgado's nose. Dense fir, spruce, thickly packed lodgepole pine, and the occasional cedar clung precariously to the steep mountain slope. Borne by warmer air rising from the valley below, noxious odor mixed with the summer scent of evergreen. Drifting and eddying, it rose around outcrops of stone and through tangles of deadfall.

Where Sam crouched over his rifle—partially hidden in the shadow of a towering fir—the smell made a mockery of the otherwise serene morning. He endured, his stomach queasy. Sam had picked a spot downhill from the section of backcountry trail known as "Slickside." To reach it, he had been forced to pick his way down the precarious slope with its treacherous footing.

Rotting corpses—both men and horses—desecrated what should have been pristine wilderness.

Desecration? Maybe that was the human in him. Some creatures reveled in the largess. Ravens and magpies cawed and flitted from one conifer branch to the next—not to mention the swarms of flies. Carrion beetles scurried. A local grizzly sow and her cubs had been gorging themselves on the carcasses, mostly hitting the dead horses.

Crouching hurt. Sam's ribs were healing. His still-mending hips—the doctor said it was a cracked pelvis—ached from the ride up from the ranch. But he wanted to be here. Hidden. Out of sight of the searchers combing the forested slope.

From his vantage beneath the fir's low branches, Sam could see the ravaged remains of one of the dead horses. Wasn't more than thirty yards across the slope from his hide. Given the orientation of the carcass, the mare had been sliding, back first, as it plummeted from above. The horse had slammed into the tree, bent backwards around the trunk, snapping the backbone. There it had wedged, caught in the narrow V created by the vertical trunk and steep pitch. Something big—probably the grizzly —had torn the gut cavity open. Ravens and magpies had crapped white streaks down what was left of a tan-brown hide. A horseshoe rusted on a desiccated hoof where it stuck up at a tragic angle; strips of hide hung from the bleaching canon bone.

Sam didn't need to scramble his way over there to know what remained had to be crawling with balls of maggots. Not given the way the camp robber jays kept darting down to snap up bites.

The poor horse was just one of the animals that had fallen from above. The others—along with the men who'd ridden them—were scattered down the mountainside. Screened from his view by thick timber and gray tangles of deadfall.

Sam leaned his head back, gazing up through the needle-thick branches. Gray skies hung low. Sullen. How long since he'd seen a clear day? What he could see of the smoke-filled air above looked dirty and dull. At this elevation, the sky should have been a crystalline blue. Instead, a constant haze hid the rugged high peaks of the Owl Creeks and Absarokas. Seemed like the heavens brooded, somber and depressing. Speculation was that the overcast came from burning cities and forests on the West Coast—and maybe all the way from China.

Sam dug his heels deeper into the duff to keep from sliding, his outline masked by one of the dead branches. What used to be called "squaw wood" in a less culturally sensitive age. Some part of his brain wondered what it might be called now. "Dead and desiccated lower branch, easily broken off the tree trunk and used for firewood in the mountains?"

Didn't matter. That progressive world—the one filled with such idealistic hopes for social justice, historical retribution, and progressive revolution—was just as dead as the one once inhabited by right-wing nationalistic zealots. All the haters on either side, snuffed out…along with a couple hundred million other Americans who'd awakened one Friday morning in May to discover that the impossible had happened: the banks had been hacked. Credit had been destroyed in a matter of hours— along with the value of the dollar. Genius, really.

As it had been described to Sam, all the hackers had to do was corrupt about ten percent of the account balances. Doing so had ruined confidence in the system. If American Express, VISA, Mastercard, and the rest couldn't process and trust on-going withdrawals and deposits, credit card purchases were immediately declined across the board.

The American economy had stopped in an instant. Even then, it could have been saved. The system could have been back-dated. Reset once the malware had been purged.

But people panicked.

Americans hated other Americans.

Already on the frayed edge, divided by the two self-righteous political parties, ethnicity, religion, abortion, gun control, class, income, privilege, and every other thing, Americans turned on each other. Long-suppressed frustration, stewing anger, festering distrust, and all the other pent emotions exploded over that Memorial Day weekend. What anthropologists call "deprivation theory" had unleashed its ugly chaos across the country.

Sam reached up and swept back a lock of black hair that hung down from under the liner on his gray western hat. Not that he was a cowboy. Just a Latino city kid from Hempstead on Long Island in New York.

He'd come to Wyoming as an anthropology graduate student to work on his dissertation in archaeology. By now, he would have been finishing up field work on the high-altitude site known as the "Penthouse." Instead, the Collapse—as people were starting to call it—had left him and his fellow students stranded.

"Up here!" a voice called from behind the screen of timber across from Sam's position.

He cocked his head, shifting the .44 Marlin rifle on his lap. Magpies squawked, and from the direction of their flight, Sam could pretty well place where the searcher was located—maybe fifty or sixty yards across and slightly downhill. Magpies. Such pretty black-and-white birds shouldn't be eating rotting flesh and maggots.

For a guy who'd grown up bussing tables and washing dishes in The Yucateca—his parents' Mexican Restaurant back in Hempstead—he'd had a hell of a crash course on wilderness skills.

Lots of creatures, he'd discovered, ate carrion. The searchers had already driven the grizzly sow and a couple of badgers off the carcasses below.

"Is it Bradley?" another voice queried from down in the timber.

Too many trees to see who the speakers were. Six men and three women were scrambling around on the treacherous slope. A "recovery" party. Looking for the remains of their lost relatives and friends.

Sam cocked his head, hearing rocks and dirt tumbling as someone scrambled for footing.

"Yeah," the call came from across the way. "At least, I think." A beat. "Shit! Yeah, it's Bradley's belt."

Sam took a deep breath, cut it short when the stench tickled his nose.

His heart began to thump, drum-like in his chest, the image of that day still so clear. He could see it, feel it. How he shouldered his rifle, picking a spot on Edward Tubb's shirt as the line of riders crossed Slickside. That's what they called the narrow and precarious ledge of a pack trail etched into the steep pitch. Tubb had ridden just behind Bradley Cole, the outfitter who was leading the posse.

In his memory, Sam triggered the Marlin, watched Ed Tubb jolt in the saddle. Breeze's M4 had been blasting beside him. She'd killed Bradley Cole. On the narrow thread of trail, the panicked horses had done the rest. Bucking and grunting, they'd tumbled down the near-vertical drop to bounce, fly out, and slam into the timber, jagged rock outcrops, and deadly tangles of deadfall.

To end here. Lodged against tree trunks, jutting rocks, and spears of downed timber.

Sam sucked in his lips, squinting. At the time, he'd been horrified. Now? A numbness—an anesthetic of the soul—left him without feeling. Once, he'd been a compassionate human being. The notion of murder incomprehensible. Beyond abhorrent.

But that had been before the Collapse. Before Edward Tubb and Director Edgewater. Before the battle of Clark Ranch.

Before they'd murdered his Shyla.

*Shyla.* He clamped his eyes tight—ground his teeth against the grief and hollow ache.

The sound came from behind and above. Where no one was supposed to be. Someone was coming, cascading stones and dirt in a cautious descent. Sam shifted, clicking the Marlin's safety off. He craned his neck, ready to defend himself from whomever had discovered his hide.

Sam let out a breath as Breeze Tappan eased her way down from the timber above.

Breeze carried her M4 carbine, using it for balance as she artfully descended the slope, digging her boot heels into the lose scree. A western Rand's hat was clamped low on her head; her long brown hair swayed as she scrambled for balance. The Levi jacket and faded Wranglers she wore might have come straight off the set of a Taylor Sheridan production.

Ducking, she scuttled under Sam's tree, shifted, and used her boots to gouge out foot holds in the thick duff as she settled beside him. "What are they doing?"

"How'd you find me?" he asked in a low voice that wouldn't carry.

She gave him what Sam called her "Tappan look," that hard-eyed and evaluative stare that seemed to bore right down into his soul. Part of it was her eyes, common to the family—tan shading to hazel and ringed by a darker brown. Sam wasn't sure why, but they reminded him of a wolf's eyes. That same predatory look.

"Followed Old Tobe to where you tied him up at the switchback," she told him in a whisper. "Picked up your tracks. Might say I followed in your footsteps." She was staring out over the slope, past the dead horse where it wedged against its tree. As she did, another gray jay fluttered down to grab maggots before flying off. "Doctor told you to take it easy on those ribs and hip. Riding up here? You're lucky you didn't rebreak something."

Damn. Didn't he know? He'd almost passed out when he had stepped down from Old Tobe. The pain didn't matter. He'd needed to come.

"Why are you here?" Sam ran nervous fingers along the smooth wood on the Marlin's stock.

She spared him another squinty look. "Same as you. I needed to be here while they collected the last of the bodies."

Breeze turned her gaze to the slope; the sound of people gasping for breath, muttering, and cursing could be heard as they fought their way up the incline. The sound of stones, kicked loose, carried as they went tumbling down to hit deadfall with hollow *thunks*.

"Thought if something went sideways, and they started a war, I didn't want you fighting all by yourself." She gestured with a tilt of the head. "Lot of anger bottled up in those people. They catch you up here? Alone? No witnesses? The ravens and magpies will be feasting on you next, Delgado."

Sam kept his attention on the screening trees. "*Nynymbi* led me here."

She shifted her gaze his way again. "Hate it when that Shoshoni spirit helper of yours makes an appearance. Someone always seems to end up dead."

"Yeah." Sam swallowed dryly. "They brought down five bodies yesterday. Edgewater's men I guess. Tubb, Cole, and that Sheriff Kapital are the last ones. Just heard one of the searchers call that they'd found Cole."

Breeze pursed her lips, eyes thinning. "Grandpa couldn't deny the families access to the trailhead behind the ranch. Couldn't tell them no. But, Sam, if they've found Bradley, they're going to know he was shot. Even scavenged like he is, they're going to see the bullet holes in bones, his shirt. Maybe find the flattened slugs under the skin on his off side. The same as they've seen in deer and elk after all these years of packing out game animals."

"And they'll know you shot him." Sam reached out to tap her M4. "You and Lauren are the only people in the county carrying those. And Lauren was in Cheyenne."

Breeze sucked her cheeks in, emphasizing the smooth lines of her jaw. Sam had always thought she was an attractive woman. Maybe not the gorgeous knockout that his Shyla had been, but Breeze possessed a presence that drew the eye. Fit and vibrant. A fact that Breeze herself seemed completely unaware of.

"County's split right down the middle," she told him. "Doesn't matter that we exposed Director Edgewater for the piece of shit that he was. But the Sheriff? The people who thought they were doing the right thing? Being patriots? Believing in the government and its authority?"

She gestured at the dead horse wedged in the tree. "We killed people here, Sam. People with families. Old friends. People who thought they were just doing their jobs. Someone's got to pay for that."

"Yeah, well it won't be Tubb or Edgewater." He glanced down at his hand where it rested on the rifle. Slowly bent his index finger, as if feeling it against the trigger. How the gun went off. Tubb, he'd killed here, on Slickside. Edgewater, he'd shot in the Park County Courthouse up in Cody. He'd used Governor Agar's personal pistol. Bang. Bang. Bang.

He'd been looking Edgewater straight in the eyes. Hadn't thought twice about it. As if killing a monster was just another job to be done. Who the hell was Samuel Delgado these days?

The clatter of loose rock came to an end as a second person reached the first. "Damn," the newcomer muttered. "That him?"

"Yeah, this is Bradley," the first could be heard to say. "Or what's left of him. Let's get him in a body bag."

Another voice called from lower on the slope. "I found Hank Kapital. Bear's been at him, but his duty belt's still on his hips." A pause. "And, sure enough, here's his coat. Badge on the pocket."

"Is he shot?" another voice called from much lower on the slope.

"Not that I can tell."

Then from where Cole's body lay: "Well, Bradley sure is. Got a bullet hole in his upper arm bone. Two-twenty-three if you ask me."

"If that's true, Tappans are gonna pay!" an angry voice bellowed from below.

"Five'll get you ten, that's Breeze's work," one of the women called from still lower. "People saw her. She was carrying a black gun when she left town with that Mexican kid the day before the posse got shot up."

"Tappans will get theirs. My word on that." The voice had gone strident.

"That's Corwin," Breeze whispered. "Bradley's brother."

"God, who's gonna tell Sandra?" the woman downslope asked. "And then there's the kids to think of."

"Sandra is Bradley's wife," Breeze supplied. "He's got three boys, one's diabetic."

"It's one thing if Brad died from a fall," Corwin's voice, though barely audible, reeked of rage. "Another when it turns out he was shot by Breeze Tappan."

Breeze muttered, "Well, shit. That just cuts it." She rose. "Come on. We need to get to the house before they get these bodies off the slope. I think we'd better be set for a war."

As if on cue, the ravens circling above cawed in what could have been raucous laughter.

# IN THE BEGINNING

*Sitting on the porch at Tappan Ranch, deep in the mountain heart of Wyoming, I can look back. It might have been fated. My road to this place was anything but certain. I don't know how long it's been since the Collapse—that Friday morning before the Memorial Day Weekend when the Chinese hacked the banks. I haven't seen a calendar since the day I left Colorado Springs. Time is a weird thing. Since that morning, I've lived in constant chaos. An eternal roiling boil of "now." Right up to the afternoon when Breeze and Brandon wheeled me out of the Cody hospital, installed me in Breeze's old room at Tappan Ranch, and made me the "queen of the front porch."*

*I'm still convalescing. The shrapnel in my lungs hurts every time I inhale a breath. That's what happens when you're blown up in an explosion. Bones broken, eardrums burst. They dug most of the metal out of my left lung. I'm told my body will mend.*

*No one talks about the rest of me. I never really understood PTSD. I thought it was just depression and nightmares...*

*It's more.*

*There are moments when the world in front of my eyes vanishes, and I'm there again. On The Line at Buffalo Camp. There's a horde trying to climb into the back of the truck with me, carrying guns, knives, clubs. Two of my friends are dying just feet away from me, and I know I'm next. It's not a nightmare. It's real. I'm terrified, so terrified I can't breathe, ready to shoot anything that moves.*

*Odd things trigger the shift. A heavy step behind me. Someone drops a cup...*

*I can't control it. I'm so broken, I'm a danger to everyone around me. And I know it.*

— Excerpt from Lauren Davis' *Journal.*

# CHAPTER TWO

BREEZE'S GELDING, Joker, picked his way carefully down the trail, ears pricked. The descent here was tricky and steep, the trail a narrow gouge cut into the damp black soil, the bottom crisscrossed with roots. Occasional rocks and poor footing added their own hazards. Around them, branches on the fir and spruce hung in bowed green. Tufts of moss grew on the north side of the bark. Deadfall piled in a mess back in the forest's dim recesses. Breeze heard Sam ask, "We're not going to run smack into them, are we?"

She glanced back to where he clung to Old Tobe's saddle, a hand on the horn. The way Sam was riding, half crouched with his knees jammed in the swells, she could tell his ribs and hips were bothering him. Watched the guy wince every time Old Tobe took a jarring step. Sam wasn't that long out of the hospital after having a Polaris land on him over at Clark Ranch. Took guts to ride with knitting bones.

Joker didn't need her help as he led the way down the narrow switchbacks below Slickside; tall firs crowded close on either side, the branches almost touching overhead. This was primeval forest, dark and moody. A mountainside of silence.

Sam had been quiet on the climb back up to where the horses were tied. They both had been. Seeing that slope, that half-rotted and scavenged horse, had sobered them. For Sam, it was a reminder of the day he stepped over the line to become a killer. But for her? After the terror she'd lived getting out of Colorado? After killing those men on Willow Creek Pass, and the bits and pieces of herself that she'd lost at the I-25 checkpoint and on The Line down by Cheyenne?

Breeze—her M4 across her saddle bows—kept scanning the trees to either side, her sleek brown pony tail flipping back and forth as she did. A chickaree squirrel chattered at them from an upper branch in one of the towering firs. The familiar trail felt somehow ominous, partly because just over there, beyond the screen of black timber, people who had once been friends were struggling their way down the slope with the ravaged, rotted, and maggot-infested corpses of their loved ones.

*People I killed.*

To answer Sam, she called back, "They had to go up the Creek Trail to reach the bottom of the slope. Their horses would be tied off maybe a half mile below the place where they'll have to bring the bodies down, and it's all steeper than a cow's face. Not to mention having to clamber over the deadfall and through the black timber. Unless they sent a runner down the canyon, we should hit the ranch a couple of hours ahead of them."

Still, that didn't ease her worry. That horrible image stuck in her mind: Bradley Cole, in her sights. The moment the trigger broke, her three-round burst hitting him. How he juddered under the impact. Never knew what hit him as the 5.56 rounds tore through his chest.

*He was riding with the enemy.*

She watched a nuthatch scurry around behind one of the spruce trunks as she ducked a branch. Somewhere back in the timber, she heard elk banging and crashing as they fled.

Sam half-growled under his breath, "It ought to matter that Tubb raided the ranch the day before. They were going to take Shyla, Danielle, Ashly, and the rest of the women. Arrest your mother and Meggan. Hell, Tubb bragged he was taking the ranch for his own. 'Confiscating' it for the 'common good.' That was how Edgewater and all his *cholo* bastards called it."

Breeze swayed with Joker's rolling gait as the horse minced his way down a rocky section, shod hooves striking on stone. She glanced back to be sure Sam made it. His face was pain-set, jaws clamped against what had to be agony as he swayed in the saddle. For a guy who'd barely been out of New York, he'd come a long way. The surprise was that he was doing this well after being blown up.

The trail widened as they hit the colluvial fill at the bottom, and Sam urged Tobe up next to Joker. He had a pinched look, a sour twist to his lips when he said, "Our people were just defending themselves."

That made her chuckle humorlessly. "Think justice is objective? Those people over there are carrying the stinking and critter-scavenged remains of a father, husband, and brother down that slope. Who's going to remember that Tubb's people started it? And what about the sheriff's friends and family? Good old Sheriff Hank, as he liked to be called. Pus-gutted piece of work that he was, he was still doing what he thought was his duty, right? Following orders given by the DHS director. And Steve

Fallow, the FEMA guy, was in on it. All part of what Kapital thought was the government." A beat. "That's how they see it, Sam."

"But we proved that Edgewater was setting up his own little empire in the Bighorn Basin. Taking and raping young women, robbing businesses, looting."

"Maybe he was." She continued to frown. "Fact is, when they came to the ranch that day, our side shot first. People are going to remember that."

"Some choice," Sam muttered. "Be abducted at gun point to be raped and have your ranch confiscated or shoot the mother fuckers first. They killed Shyla, and Pam damn near died. It's a miracle your mother's still alive." A beat. "Still makes my blood boil."

Breeze ground her teeth at the memory of her mom propped in the hospital bed, barely clinging to life with a bullet-punctured lung. That sight of her, pale, drugged, and limp, had shaken Breeze to her roots. But Pam had been strong enough to warn her that Tubb and the sheriff were putting together a posse to hunt down her brother Brandon and the rest of the women.

She resettled the M4 where it rested across the saddle. "Boiling blood? Rage? Desperation? That's the line where, if we fall too far, we'll never get back. Never save that bit of civilization where the rule of law has value."

Now, knowing that Bradley Cole's family was bearing his remains down the mountain, she wondered if boiling rage wasn't the reason she'd killed him. She'd been half crazy. Fatigued and depressed. Ragnovich had relieved her of her duties as a Line rider. She'd been desperate, hopeless, and maybe a little berserk.

Sam was giving her a knowing squint from beneath the wide brim of his secondhand Resistol hat. Asked, "What are you thinking, Breeze?"

"Wondering if I'm just as much a monster as the rest of them." She tapped slim fingers on the cool metal of the M4's receiver. "Killing becomes second nature. Instinctive. Maybe I don't know when to stop."

"Killing is okay when it's about justice."

She grunted in response. "Is it? I would have told you so after I shot those three guys down in Colorado. They killed Felix. Would have gang raped me before putting a bullet in my head. After that I was on The Line." A thoughtful pause. "In the beginning, when the extent of the Collapse still hadn't sunk in, Governor Agar used President Brown's 'No unnecessary travel' order to close the Colorado border. Agar established The Line, that whole string of observation posts to keep people from crossing the border. Made the decision that he'd save Wyoming, even if it meant condemning hundreds of thousands down in Colorado to starvation."

"Yeah, but there were what? Eight million people south of The Line?

He couldn't feed them all." Sam watched a hawk circling overhead, its colorful feathers muted against the background of gray sky. "If this weather doesn't warm up, if we can't grow more food, we may not be able to feed the half million who are in Wyoming now."

Breeze shifted in the saddle, Joker walking easily down the trail, his ears rotating to the sounds of the forest. A chickadee was calling in the fir trees off to the left. She made a dismissive gesture with her hand. "You've heard about The Line? What I did down there?"

"Yeah, the I-25 checkpoint? Where you stopped it from being overrun?"

She tilted her head, her hazel-tan eyes narrowing. "I didn't think, Sam. They were coming in a horde. Some of the men were shooting, killing our Guard people. It was instinctive." A beat. "Syms went down. Shot through the head. Skull makes a crack-snap sound when a high velocity round shatters it. Blood. Brains. Bone. Shit gets blown every-where. Syms hit the pavement like sacked meat."

She tapped the M4 again. "I grabbed up his weapon. This same M4. Flipped the fire control…and ran through the whole magazine. Never shot a fully automatic weapon in my life. I just leveled it at the crowd and mowed those people down. Like swathing hay. Didn't think. Had no clue what I was doing. Men, women, mothers, their children…"

She shook her head, trying to rid herself of the image.

"What I heard was that if they'd overrun the checkpoint, a flood of people would have followed. That they'd have swamped Cheyenne. Would have been a bloodbath." Sam slapped a hand to his thigh. "That's the weird math of all this. Figuring how many you kill, and how many will live as a result."

She shifted her gaze from the trail to where her hand grasped the battered M4. Wondered if she could fix all the blame on her hand. Convince herself that it had acted on its own when it pulled the trigger. They did that way back in history. If thy hand offends thee, chop it off?

Yeah, sure.

They rode in silence as they descended the last quarter mile to the fork in the trail. Breeze reassured herself that all the shod tracks led up the Creek Trail, and none had come down since she'd taken Joker up.

Turning into the old burn where a forest fire had played hell back in 2010, Sam surprised her by saying, "We've got to fix this."

"Fix what?" She gave him a glance, aware, not for the first time, that he had a nice jaw, straight nose, and bronzed cheeks. Would have made a great Latino movie star with those gleaming dark eyes. The battered cowboy hat, the strands of black hair hanging down to just above his collar, gave him a dashing look.

Sam shifted in the saddle, made a face, and gasped from pain. Then he gave an expansive wave. "All of this. Slickside, Clark Ranch. All the boiling blood."

"I'm not following you."

He spared her a desperate look. "Breeze, I was there. In Cheyenne. At that meeting with Dr. Holly and Governor Agar. The whole eastern part of the country is gone. Maybe EMP all the way west to the Nebraska border. Any place with a large urban population has fallen into barbarity. We know that at least one Chinese army—and maybe three—are on the West Coast. The only places left with infrastructure are in the Rocky Mountain West. Here, the Dakotas, Montana, parts of Idaho and Utah. Maybe Nevada, rural Arizona, and New Mexico. But who knows for sure?"

"I thought Agar was sending out scouts."

"I heard that, too." Sam lifted his hat, ran a sleeve over his forehead. "What we can't let happen is for people to start taking the law into their own hands."

"Excuse me?" She spared him an incredulous look. "You been paying attention to your recent past, Delgado?"

He nodded, chewing on his lower lip. "Seriously, Breeze, we've got enough trouble without going to war with the Coles and good old Sheriff Hank's family. Or those people up in Cody who sided with Edgewater. Governor Agar was very specific. His quote was 'However you pacify the Bighorn Basin, I don't want a homegrown *Game of Thrones* up there.'"

"Yeah, well, you and I are smack dab in the center of just about every potential blood vendetta in the Basin."

"How do we stop it?" He kept giving her that sober look.

"Guess we could go back, ambush the trail as they ride out. Shoot them all, drag the bodies off into the aspen grove, and claim they mysteriously vanished into the mountains. Lot of wilderness area up there. Grizzlies and things, you know?"

He moved stiffly, as if trying to find a position that didn't hurt. "Seriously."

She took a deep breath as Joker stopped at the creek crossing to drink. When Old Tobe joined him, she tilted her head back, stared up at the haze-heavy sky. Speculation was that the whole world was burning, and maybe some of it was nuclear fallout, although according to sources, background radiation was only a little higher. The summer temperature highs and lows were about five degrees cooler so far. Snow kept falling in the high country. The trails they had taken across the Owl Creeks to Boulder Ridge were now impassable. The worry was for the sugar beets, corn, barley, wheat, and other crops down in the basin and throughout Wyoming's farming belt. A mid-summer or early fall freeze could mean famine for thousands.

"Hell, Sam, I don't know. People are dead." She considered him. "When Thomas put us through that healing up in *Puha* Cave, the dead forgave us. The problem is, the living might not be so understanding."

Just the mention of the Shoshoni healing ritual sent a shiver down her back. In the dream she'd had, Water Ghost Woman, the Shoshoni spirit, had promised her the strength to endure. Had given her the power of life and death, and the stricture that she use it wisely. Had warned her of hard days to come, of pain, and sacrifice.

*As if I haven't already had enough of that shit,* she thought.

Sam was right, of course. Corwin's voice had been filled with anger and promise. As she sat there on Joker, the man was struggling his way down the precipitous side of the mountain. As he wrestled his brother's rotted and ravaged remains over deadfall and slippery talus, he was pondering Bradley's murder. And, knowing Corwin as she did, he was an eye-for-an-eye kind of guy.

If his blood was boiling hot enough—as Sam would say—she wouldn't put it past Corwin to shuck a rifle and start shooting the moment he rode into the ranch yard. Get it over with right there.

"I think," she told Sam, "that we'd better give some thought to how we're going to handle this. If they come down the trail in a mindless rage, we're going to have dead people scattered all over the ranch yard."

# THE WEAPON

*I had a fiancé that I loved. Lieutenant Tyrell Ramirez. He was stationed at Fort Carson in what he called "The Unit." What the mostly ignorant public called Delta Force. Officially, the Army said it didn't exist. Not that they were fooling anybody.*

*Ty was competent, strong, and fearless. He's dead.*

*On the day the country collapsed, he came to me and told me to leave Colorado Springs and get as far from civilization as I could. He asked me to head here, to Tappan Ranch. So many things would have been different if I'd done what he told me to. Instead, I went to Cheyenne. To The Line. More than anything, the unrelenting terror turned me into what I am now. By the time Captain Ragnovich pulled me off The Line, I was a shattered, unreliable weapon.*

*If Ty were alive, he wouldn't know me.*

*But, then, neither do I.*

— Excerpt from Lauren Davis' *Journal*.

# CHAPTER THREE

THICK WITH KNEE-HIGH brome and timothy grass, the creek pasture was normally used by the Tappans for winter graze; it covered maybe ten acres on the other side of the fence and spanned the valley bottom west of the ranch house. To Sam's right, Tappan Creek ran close against the base of the south-facing slope, most of its course obscured by willows.

Sam had taken a position at the pasture gate, not more than fifty yards from the Tappan ranch house back door. Braced against the post, he kept his right leg straight, bearing most of his weight. He wasn't sure where the crack had been in his pelvis, but it still hurt to keep weight on his left leg.

And then there were his knitting ribs. He tried to keep his chest just so. If he stretched, it hurt like sixty. Bending or twisting brought the kind of pain that crossed his vision and brought tears to his eyes. And God help him if he sneezed or coughed. Damn, the ride on Old Tobe had left him on the verge of passing out a couple of times. But the notion that if he did, first, it would hurt too frigging much to fall off the horse, and second, he'd couldn't bear the idea that he'd do it in front of Breeze. That she'd consider him unworthy.

Something about her—that hard gaze, or the way she just radiated competence—left him achingly aware of his own inadequacies when it came to being a man. Maybe, now that it was the end of the world, it was some weird genetic atavism poking up from his Pleistocene ancestors? Some artifact of his education in anthropology concerning a male's role in a fragile and vulnerable sociocultural situation? Or maybe it went deeper? Something Darwinian?

Whatever. He could always chalk it up to too much Latino machismo heritage in his genes. Thinking of Breeze, he fixed his gaze on the trail where it emerged from the willows on the far side of the pasture. She should have been here by now.

Reaching the valley bottom, they had split up where the Slickside trail branched off the Creek Trail. He had ridden ahead and taken on the task of warning everyone at the ranch. Spread the word that Corwin and his party might ride in demanding blood. Breeze had stayed back, keeping an eye on the trail in order to provide a last-minute warning.

Funny how his world had changed. It all came down to protecting this place and these people. The ranch house itself was a low-roofed log structure, a rambling kind of affair. A wing of bedrooms had been added to the main structure back in the sixties; then the big commercial kitchen with its screened porch had been built on in the 90s when backcountry outfitting had been at its peak.

On the south side of the yard, the imposing barn had to be three stories tall; attached corrals and pens had been built on the east. The grassy mountain slope rose immediately behind it. Across the road and on the north side—backed against the base of the slope—were the three small guest cabins, storage sheds, an outhouse, and beyond them to the east, open-faced equipment sheds. Opposite them, with a small patch of grassy lawn, was the bunkhouse where most of Sam's fellow students lived. Or what was left of them.

Out of the original field school that had traveled to Tappan Ranch to survey, map, and test the Penthouse site, only Jon Brimmer, Danielle Cory, Ashley Tempest, and Shanteel Jones remained. Well, and Court Hamilton. But he was in Cheyenne working with Governor Agar's planning team.

Others had left at the beginning of the crisis, while some—like Amber Sagan and his Shyla—were dead.

*And me? What have I become?*

Seemed like he'd never had much time to think about the changes. Barely had time to accept that his parents and family back in Hempstead were dead. Mom, Dad, all the cousins. Tio Luis. Rubio, Dedos, and all the rest. Maybe incinerated in a nuclear blast. Or, if they were unlucky, killed in the aftermath of chaos, rioting, and radioactive fallout. Radiation poisoning sounded like a horrible way to die. The same with his friends. All the people he'd known from that life. Hundreds of them. People he'd gone to school with. Passed in the street. Teachers.

Just...dead.

The Yucateca—if it still stood—would be nothing more than gutted ruins.

Hard to get one's thoughts around that.

Sam studied the two-track road that led back across the pasture and then up the valley bottom, across several creek fords, to the old burn where the Tappans cut their firewood. Timber rose thick on the north slope, a dark green mass of conifers. While the south-facing slope across the valley was dotted with limber pines and junipers interspersed with patches of bunch grass, currants, and brush.

His .44 Marlin over his shoulder, Sam shifted to ease the pain in his hip and ribs and stared up at the glowering dark haze. Wished for clear skies. A real sunset. His good hip braced against the gate post, he let his gaze follow the barbed-wire fence that ran up the slope and into the pines. The wire was tight, the T-posts perfectly vertical, the line straight. Looking at it, Sam wondered if it was a metaphor for the Tappans: strong, upright, and tough.

Then he returned his attention to the two-track trail where it disappeared into the narrow-leaf cottonwood and willows beyond the far pasture fence. Yes, there. Something moving by the creek crossing. Breeze seemed to pop out of the willows, trotting Joker as she emerged from the shadows and passed through the far gate. She cantered the horse across the grass-thick pasture, and Sam had to admire how she seemed so perfect in the saddle. He saw poetry in motion when Breeze rode—a unity of rider and mount. Flowing grace in movement. It spoke to something deep within him. Elemental.

Sam turned, winced at what it did to his ribs, and called, "It's Breeze! Bet they're coming."

"We're ready!" he heard Bill's wife, Meggan, call from the screened back door.

Only the sounds of the crickets, birdcalls, and the burble of the creek vied with the cadence of Joker's shod hooves as Breeze rode up and pulled to a stop; she twisted around in her saddle to look back up the trail.

"They're not five minutes behind me," she told Sam. "You got everything ready here?"

"Yeah."

Sam hitched around on his good leg in time to see old Bill Tappan, Breeze's grandfather, as he stepped around from the front of the house and stumped his way to the middle of the road. There, he took a position, stuffing his thumbs into his belt.

Old Bill was in his early seventies, rail thin, and a fourth-generation Wyoming rancher. He'd served his time in Vietnam—and with his first wife, Betty, raised four sons. Only to watch three of them turn their back on the ranch in pursuit of different dreams. Even Betty had given up, divorced Bill, and left for Sun City. Not a word had come from any of them after the Collapse.

Only Frank remained. Bill's youngest, he'd married his rodeo sweetheart, Pam. Had three kids, including the twins, Breeze and Brandon, and a third daughter who lived in town. Frank now ran the ranch.

Not that Bill had ended up alone. Meggan, in her fifties, had come into his life. She, along with Pam, were the ranch matrons.

And then there was the Shoshoni elder, Thomas Star, and his grandson, Willy. Both of whom had sided with the Tappans when the shit came down.

Sam turned, limping along behind Joker as Breeze led the way to where Bill had taken a position. He stood where the road met the graveled ranch yard. The old man gave his granddaughter a crooked smile, then turned his brown-ringed tan eyes on Sam. Given his bow legs, flannel shirt, and battered western hat, old Bill could have been a cliché. Sam had heard it said that Bill Tappan had bullets for eyes. The simile fit, and now there was no give behind them.

"We're ready," Bill said as Breeze rode for the barn to take care of Joker.

"Everybody's in place?" Sam asked, the fluttery feeling turning queasy in his stomach. He tightened his grip on the Marlin's wrist, the wood and metal reassuring. He liked the rifle. Didn't matter that it was an old-fashioned lever gun. He shot it well, and while it wasn't a long range weapon, the blunt .44 magnum slugs had never let him down. Pray to God he wasn't going to be shooting it tonight.

"Thomas and Willy are behind the cabins," Bill told him, pointing across at the guest cabins. "Brandon and Shanteel in the loft in the barn. Lauren Davis is on the porch with her M4...told me I'd have to break her legs to get her to stay inside."

"She's barely out of the hospital," Sam protested as he glanced at where the young woman sat in the shadowed porch glider.

Bill muttered, "Says she's healed enough to shoot."

"She got blown up down at Marsy Ranch. They took a chunk of metal the size of a quarter out of her right lung, and half the bones in her body were broken. She shoots that M4, the recoil's likely to shatter her into pieces."

"You tell that to the Queen of the Fourth Quadrant," Bill grunted. Shook his head. "These girls all think they're tougher than old boots."

"Maybe because they are."

The old man just squinted his bullet-hard gaze in reply.

Sam heard the crack of a hoof on stone, turned to face up the canyon. The flutter in his stomach went runny. "Here they come."

"Yeah," Bill said through a weary exhale. "Hope this don't go south."

"You got your 1911?"

"Stuffed in my waistband at the small of my back. Didn't want to look provocative." The old rancher chuckled. "Hope we don't play hell."

The first of the horses to come trotting across the creek pasture was a big white one, what the Tappans called a gray. Sam didn't understand that. But then he didn't know why, at the age of eight, Old Tobe was called old. Horses were a whole new world to him. And what the hell was a piebald? He wondered if he'd live long enough to get the chance to learn.

There were nine horses and two mules that emerged from the willow-thick Creek Trail, the latter now following on lead ropes. They came across the pasture in single file. Sam could guess what lay under the manties that draped the bundles laid across the mules' pack saddles. He took a deep breath, trying to still the frantic beating of his heart, his mouth gone dry.

He kept glancing at the shadows, half expecting to see the ghostly shape of *Nynymbi*, his worrisome Shoshoni spirit helper. But nothing moved in the gloom.

"Find 'em?" Bill called, nothing in his voice reassuring.

"Found 'em," the man in front assented, words clipped as if bitten off. "Bradley's got bullet holes in what's left of him. You know anything about that, Bill? Like, maybe I ought to ask Breeze about it?"

In the dim light, Sam could see the rifle across the man's lap, the muzzle pointed Sam's way. He laid his thumb atop the Marlin's hammer. All he had to do was cock the rifle and pull the trigger.

"Corwin," Bill started, "this whole thing has gotten way out of—"

"My brother is *dead*, Bill. Don't try running none of your bullshit on me or any of the rest of us."

"Yeah!" the cry came from the open barn door as Breeze strode out, her M4 hanging from one hand. She was headed across the yard in a striding gait, slim body looking tense as a strung bow.

Sam heard Bill mutter, "Oh, shit."

"Bradley was leading that posse, Corwin." Breeze walked up, the M4 held by its pistol grip. Sam figured all she had to do was rotate it and loose a burst.

In the fading evening light, he could see the expressions on the other riders, five men and three women, all looking very unhappy, mad, and scared. The horses stamped irritably, anxious to be taken home to food and rest.

Sam stepped painfully forward, raising a hand. "Tubb killed my Shyla. When he did, he took any reason I had to live. I mean…there was nothing, you know?" He tipped his head toward the little knoll on the southern slope. "That's where they buried her. Shot through the heart. Because Tubb and Edgewater were going to kidnap her for gang rape. Add her to their collection of sex slaves. And she wouldn't have it."

"Breaks my heart," one of the men behind Corwin muttered angrily.

"Put a sock in it, Stew," Corwin ordered as Sam stiffened, fought to keep his expression from tightening. The heat began around his heart. The anger beginning to burn.

"Hey, now," Bill was motioning for calm with both hands as if he could press the anger down. "You all were there in the Hot Springs High School gym. You heard the testimony from those girls we rescued. Now, I'm sorry about Bradley. Sorrier than you could ever know, but—"

"He was just doing a job!" Corwin almost spat the words.

"He was riding with the enemy," Breeze snapped. "I stood there. Over my mother. Shot through the lung. Dying in a hospital bed. And for what? She told those assholes that if there were charges—"

"Hank had warrants!" another of the men, a guy in a gray hat, barked. "She was resisting arrest!"

"Bullshit!" Sam said, grip tightening on the Marlin. "They were taking her against her will! That piece of shit—"

"Watch it, Beaner," one of the guys in back called. "That's about enough out of your mouth."

The anger burned free, hot, consuming. "All right, mother fucker, let's finish this. Fill a bunch more of those body bags!" Sam brought the Marlin up, thumbing the hammer back.

Sam started to take a step forward to get a better shot, was stopped by Bill's iron hand on his arm. "Thought you were the one wanted to keep this from burning out of control?"

"You hear them?" Sam cried as guns were raised all around. "They're backing Edgewater and Tubb! The people who *murdered* Shyla. Shot Pam. These people, Bill! They think taking young women and raping them is just A Okay! They've declared that they are on the side of sick trash like Edgewater!" He swallowed. "They're *evil!*"

"Whoa, boy." Bill's hard eyes were burning into Sam's.

Corwin spat off the side of his horse, his AR 15 pointed straight at Sam's chest. "You're the one who shot Bradley? Got all those neighbors and friends of mine killed?"

"I *did!*" Breeze cried, stepping forward. "It was them or us."

"I say we end this." One of the men in the back shouldered a bolt-action rifle, the safety clicking off.

"Hold on here!" Old Bill thundered. "You're on my place, damn it!"

"And, first one of you that shoots, you're all dead!" a new voice called from the side.

Sam turned, surprised by the hunched figure that hobbled forward from the porch. He could see the raised outline of the black carbine. Made out Lauren Davis's blanket-draped shape as she made another awkward step, her weight braced on a crutch.

"Who're you?" Corwin asked.

"Lauren Davis. The hero of Buffalo Camp. Line rider. The bitch that broke the Marsy Ranch siege." A slight pause. "And the ghost-haunted witch that will kill you all dead." She took another awkward step. "You might notice? I'm here on your nine o'clock? Got you from what the

Guard calls the flank. The term they give it is 'enfilading fire.' Very effective."

She braced her M4 on the crutch to steady it. "And Thomas and Willy are over yonder, which puts you in what we call a crossfire. Any of you that might make it out past the house will be shot dead by Brandon from where he's got you covered with a scoped rifle."

"Lauren?" Breeze asked. "What are you doing?"

"Haven't killed anyone since Marsy Ranch." Lauren had her cheek weld on the M4 so she could aim the red dot sight. "What's another five or six when I'm already damned?"

The riders were now looking worried, the horses—aware of the tension—shifted, stamping. Eyes rolling.

Sam took a deep breath, shook Bill's hand off. His heart was still hammering as he stepped over to Corwin's horse, ignored the muzzle that now was but a hand's breadth from his chest. He looked up into the angry man's eyes. In a weary voice he asked, "What are we doing here, Mr. Cole? Edgewater did this to us. He's still using us against each other. Even from the grave."

"My brother's dead."

"So's my Shyla." Sam nodded toward the muzzle of Corwin's AR. "Go ahead. Shoot. If killing me gives you peace, pays you back for your brother's life—"

"Damn, Sam," Breeze exclaimed from where she had her M4 up. "What the hell are you doing?"

But Sam just stared up into the man's hard eyes. "My wife's dead. Your brother is dead. You kill me, Lauren will kill you. And on, and on. We going to kill each other? Or find a way to live together? If it's the first, you pull that trigger, and get it over with."

He saw it in the man's eyes, the moment Corwin made his decision. "Come on," he called, spurring his white horse off to the side. "Let's get these bodies out of here. We've got people waiting on us in town."

Sam stepped back as the riders circled wide, kicking their horses to a fast walk. The stares cast his way were anything but happy. The brewing anger apparent in the hard set of their mouths or the rage in their half-throttled curses. One of the women spat in his direction.

Sam closed his eyes, feeling sick. Wondered what the hell had come over him. He heard Breeze step up beside him as Bill wandered off, muttering under his breath about "Crazy sons of bitches."

"That was about the stupidest thing I've ever seen, Delgado," Breeze told him.

"Yeah." Sam swallowed hard. "Problem was, I lost it. Nothing mattered but killing that guy."

"Maybe he needs killing," she told him, eyes on the line of horses as they trotted eastward toward the trucks and trailers parked just beyond the ranch cattle guard.

"How do we keep the Basin from destroying itself, from becoming that *Game of Thrones* Governor Agar's worried about, if I'm no better than the rest of them?" Sam thumbed the hammer back and lowered it to half cock. Funny thing, he could feel the pain in his ribs and hips now. Hadn't realized it had gone away in the mad.

"Excuse me?" Lauren called weakly. "Little help here?"

Sam and Breeze turned, seeing the young woman, propped now on her crutch. She looked like she was about to collapse. Her M4 was hanging by its sling.

"You never did know when to stop," Breeze chided as she hurried over to take Lauren's arm. Sam followed on his aching hip. Slung Lauren's over arm over his shoulder and relieved her of the M4. Blazes and hell! That hurt! He tried to ignore the pain in his ribs as he took her weight. Awkwardly, they hitched their way back to the porch.

Getting Lauren resettled in the glider, the woman gasped in relief.

Sam laid her carbine down, braced his Marlin against the log wall. Sucked a breath of relief as he tried to ease the agony in his ribs and hips.

He turned, hearing the distant call of voices, the banging as horses were loaded into stock trailers. Thought about the look he'd seen in Corwin Cole's eyes. Promise had been there.

"Yep," Lauren quipped, her face looking slack in the dim light. "Soothing place you've got here. Just perfect for rest and convalescence."

# RECONCILED

*Living at the end of the world is a simple and uncomplicated thing. You understand that any future you have is short. That you've done things you can't take back. Monstrous things that seemed right in that split second you were given to take action. Unlike before the Collapse, you are the only person passing judgment on yourself. No officer of the law, no court, no jury to second guess what you might have done. Just you.*

*The only thing that matters is being alive after the bodies are lying on the ground. No right. No wrong. Just that one metric: I'm still breathing.*

— Excerpt from Lauren Davis' *Journal.*

# CHAPTER FOUR

THE NIGHTHAWKS WERE CAVORTING in the late-evening sky, their wings roaring as they dove and swooped. Breeze sat on the glider they'd set on the porch for her mother's recovery. Mostly it now hosted the convalescing Lauren Davis. Breeze had her back propped by the big pillow, one leg up, a bottle of the local Buffalo Brewing beer braced on her hip.

Bats kept darting through the column of insects that swarmed the yard light atop its pole. A lone nighthawk could be heard uttering that eerie *creee* sound down on the other side of the alfalfa field. Sounded like it was calling from the little knoll where Shyla was buried. Somewhere up the canyon, a great horned owl hooted, and if Breeze strained her ears, she thought she could hear coyotes somewhere off to the east.

Boots thumped on flooring inside, followed by the door opening. Breeze glanced up as her father—a glass in hand—closed the door and walked over to pull up one of the chairs; the legs screeched across the porch planks. "Hell of an afternoon," he muttered, dropping himself into the seat.

"Could have been worse," Breeze noted.

"Yep." Frank Tappan was forty-two, just topping six feet. He kept his dark hair close cropped and pretty much fit the bill for a Wyoming rancher and outfitter: broad-shouldered, narrow-waisted, and mostly muscle. His legs had been bowed from a lifetime on horseback, and in cold weather, had a slight limp courtesy of a rodeo injury in his youth. He lifted his drink and Breeze heard ice clatter in the glass. Thought she caught that sweet scent of whiskey.

"How's Sam?" her father asked.

"I got him put to bed. I think he was asleep before I got out the door." She glanced across the yard toward the little guest cabin, the gravel pale in the yard light. "Something tells me he's going to be one sore and hurting puppy come morning. Teach him to go riding off by himself like that."

She could feel her father's eyes on her. "Might do some learning yourself, daughter. Taking off alone while a whole party of pissed-off locals are collecting the bodies you and Sam sent tumbling down the mountain? What if they'd caught you out there?"

Breeze allowed herself a humorless chuckle. "Wouldn't be the first time I shot my way out of an ambush."

She took a swig of her beer. Thought it needed more IBUs, but production of hops in the Basin was a hit-or-miss thing. The little Hot Springs brewery did the best it could with local barley. And an outfit over in Worland was making special sheds to grow more hops.

She added, "Now, when it comes to Sam? I'm not sure how he'd handle it. He's bought into Agar's whole 'We're going to save civilization' idea. Worries me."

The pause was just long enough she knew her father was searching for the right words. "You and Sam? Is there…?"

She chuckled again, amused by her father's awkward approach. "What makes you ask that?"

She could see his feeble shrug. "Just that the two of you…there's a bond there. Like you're…"

Breeze lifted an eyebrow. "Bond, huh? Just friends."

"Friends?" Frank glanced sidelong at her. "That sounds…lame."

Yeah, lame all right.

But she understood her father's unasked question, decided to put him at ease. "No, Dad. We're sleeping on opposite sides of the cabin. We're not having sex—not that it's your business—and he's not interested. He's still grieving for his Shyla."

"Well, be careful, Breeze," her father said softly. "I like the guy, but when stuff comes down like it did today? He doesn't come across as the kind who's headed for a long and healthy life. I know Corwin Cole. He was within a whisker of shooting when Sam walked right up to the muzzle of that rifle."

She could see her father's profile where he stared vacantly across the yard. The great horned owl was closer now, its *hoo hoooo* coming from the slope behind the house.

"Dad, if you're looking to the future, Brandon is the one to bet on." A beat. "Hell, it wouldn't surprise me if he and Shanteel don't start popping out babies. God knows, they spend enough time wrapped around each other making moon eyes."

Again the silence.

Finally, he said, "Breeze, you've paid your dues. Stopped Edgewater, took down Clark Ranch, saved those girls, and freed those people Edge-water took hostage. Not to mention what you did down on The Line. You've earned the right to step back, take some time for yourself. Even Captain Ragnovich said so. And now, with Lauren here, Sam, and these other kids? They could use your leadership."

"Yeah," she whispered. "Nice dream."

"Why do you say it like that?"

"That ceremony Thomas Star made us do? I had a vision up there, Dad. Saw things. Sam and I. There's hard times coming. Thomas said that *puha* and the dead have chosen us. That if we fight for it, we have a chance to save something."

She shook her head. "What I witnessed today? Coles used to be some of our best friends. I had Bradley in my sights. Could have let him ride another couple of steps until he was clear. But all I could think of was that Mom was shot, might be dying. I was reacting like I did on The Line. Shoot first, wonder if it was the right thing to do later, and Brad was leading the enemy." She lifted her beer bottle, staring at the brown glass in the window's light. "As much of it as is my fault, I still don't know that I could walk right up to Corwin's gun like Sam did."

Her father grunted in reply.

She exhaled hard. "On the other hand, maybe I trust to the vision, huh? Figure I can't be the chosen one if I'm dead. So, Thomas's *puha*, Water Ghost Woman, and fate will keep me alive."

"I wouldn't get too trusting of Shoshoni spirits," Frank told her. "That said, I have had some pretty spooky things happen up there on the mountain, and in that very cave. But I've never known God, Jesus, or spirit Power to have an outstanding track record when it came to keeping people alive. Never saw it in Afghanistan, Syria, or, here on the ranch. It always seemed to come out about fifty-fifty. When you think about it, that's like a coin toss."

He sipped his drink. "What's Water Ghost Woman got to do with it? Never knew who she was until I saw that image down inside the cave. Then I find out she's known for seducing men. Drowns them while making love? Not sure I like the notion of her in your dreams."

"She's more than that, Dad." Breeze re-hitched her leg to a more comfortable position. "Thomas says she's a counterbalance to male Power, that she's the embodiment of female strength. That's why she's usually drawn holding a bow and with arrowheads decorating her arms. She's tied to the water world but has a dog as a messenger and scout to do her bidding on land. And, not that I need to worry about it, but she can bestow fertility on barren women."

"That's about the last thing I needed to hear."

Breeze laughed humorlessly. Figured she didn't need to bring up the past. No sense in pulling scabs off old wounds.

Then, her father added, "What the hell do I know? I was up there the day Thomas met those anthropologists in the cave. I heard him tell Evan Holly that the world was ending. His exact words: 'Worlds die, Evan. It's the end of one world and the beginning of another. All things, all people, have their time. Yours is over.' I can hear it as plainly as if he just said it."

"Now who's buying into Native spiritualism?" Breeze tilted her bottle, draining the last of the beer.

"Yeah, I guess," he sounded morose. "It's just that your mother and I lost you once. We don't want to go through that again."

She bit her lip, sighed. "Sorry, Daddy. But that girl who ran off to Colorado in a snit is long gone. I don't know who or what I am now. Lauren, me, Sam? We're just lit fuses going somewhere to explode."

"Breeze, I get it. I wasn't the same when I came back from Afghanistan either. Your mother and me? We had some rough years. But that doesn't mean—"

"Get it through your head, Dad. I'll do my damnedest to save the ranch, save as much of Wyoming as I can. Maybe Governor Agar's right. Maybe we can keep some semblance of civilization alive here. But it's going to take people willing to fight for it. So, Daddy, as much as I love you, don't try to stop me."

"Listen," he said, "I know how someone your age thinks. You have convinced yourself that you're locked into a destiny. But there are other options that don't—"

"No, there are not," she told him, a melancholy building. "Things have to be done. Terrible things. And Sam and I have been chosen to do them."

# INTERLOPER

*Being the "Queen of the Front Porch" is a curious position. I'm an exile, an outsider, surveying a kingdom that isn't mine.*

*Once, I could have been a Tappan. Breeze was dating my big brother, Jim. I was dating her brother, Brandon. Two high school best friends, each burning hot in our first love affairs. Brandon was my first guy. First man I had sex with, knowing it was going to be a "forever thing." It wasn't. Swearing undying love, I went back to school. He went to a rodeo at the Metra in Billings—and fell for a black-haired Montana break-away roper.*

*It seemed so unfair. Breeze and Jim were deeply in love. And I was alone.*

*Then came the night Jim told me he was too drunk to drive, handed me the keys, and told me to drive home. I was fifteen. I drove us into a tree instead. For a long time, Breeze blamed me for destroying her life.*

*I don't think she does anymore.*

*But I blame me. I killed my brother.*

*He was my first victim. How many since then?*

*I don't know…*

— Excerpt from Lauren Davis' *Journal.*

# CHAPTER FIVE

WHERE HE SAT on the Tappan's front step the next morning, Sam wondered if every muscle in his body had been pulled loose from their tuberosities. Tuberosity? That was the spot where the muscles and tendons attached and anchored to bone. Benefit of his undergrad classes in physical anthropology and human osteology. Seemed to be from another lifetime. And, maybe—given his recent traumas—that was the appropriate way to think of it. Knowing the nitty little details of anatomy didn't mean it hurt any less. Just that he knew exactly what hurt.

A cup of yucca-blossom tea balanced on his knee as he gazed out at the alfalfa field where Jon Brimmer and Ashley Tempest were "pushing water" as the Tappans called it. Wyoming colloquial for irrigating the field. The way it worked, they'd hang a plastic sheet across the ditch and stretch it over the bottom. Shovel in dirt to weight the bottom so it didn't wash out, thus making a dam, or what they called a "head." Walking back, they'd pull up a previously set dam that was upstream. The water would rush down, filling the new dam. Jon would cut gaps in the side of the ditch bank so the water spilled out to run down across the alfalfa. Then he and Ashley would go back and replace the sod they'd shoveled out of gaps upstream to plug the leaks and restore the ditch bank. The technical term was flood irrigating, though the amount of water that sheeted over the alfalfa hardly seemed to merit the term.

Sam took a sip of the tea. Wished for coffee—but the last of the beans had been gone for weeks now. It had been Jon Brimmer, Sam's fellow graduate student, who had run the zooarchaeology lab back at university who had begun making teas out of various flowers and leaves. Mint grew wild along the creek. However, the decision had been made early on to limit how many leaves they picked lest they extirpate it. Alfalfa tea had filled in, and various pine needle, phlox, wild rose, and even sagebrush teas had been tried. Had to be careful with sagebrush. Too much of the camphor, terpenoids, and tannins gave a person a roaring headache.

Behind him, Lauren Davis—wearing an oversized pair of jeans and a flannel shirt she'd been given—rested on the glider, her back braced by a big pillow. Sam wasn't sure what to make of Lauren. If he had to describe her in one word, it would have been "spooky." But not in the way Amber Sagan had been with her broken and shattered personality. No, Lauren's brand of spooky wasn't a victim's. Instead it was powered by a too-heavy dose of guilt mixed with more than a little self-loathing.

"How's the tea?" she asked.

"Not bad. Sweet with a hint of…vanilla? No, that's not right. Don't know how to describe it. Guess I was never much for herbal teas. At The Yucateca, we were more into coffee, diet cokes, and Mexican sodas." He winced as he shifted, feeling the agony in his ribs. Prayed he hadn't pulled a muscle or done something stupid.

"Hurts, huh?" she asked as he gasped.

"Might have overdone it yesterday."

"I'm with you, Delgado," she told him. "After that short walk out there to face those riders? Just the weight of the M4 felt like it was popping every rib in my chest. Never been so out of shape in my whole life."

"Hey, a whole truck fell on you. I was crushed by a mere Polaris side-by-side."

He heard the humor in her voice as she said, "Just how the shit came down, Delgado."

Lauren Davis was the kind of woman that made men look twice. A straight nose and full lips dominated by cinnamon-brown eyes were part of an oval face; wavy auburn hair fell down over her shoulders. Like Breeze, she had that supple whipcord body. Athletic. But then, Lauren, too, had been a rodeo barrel racer in her youth.

"Yeah, I know," he told her as he shifted his attention back to the alfalfa field. Wished the thick gray haze that clotted the sky overhead would lift. Damn, he missed the sun. Worse, if the rest of the planet was like this, was it bad enough to pitch them into nuclear winter? Or, had they dodged that bullet?

He added, "I didn't plan ahead either. Breeze and the captives weren't going to make it before Edgewater's goons blew them into bloody bits with those big fifty-caliber guns. All I cared about was making sure they got away."

"Did you ever think you'd have that kind of courage?" Lauren asked softly. "I didn't. Used to try and measure myself against Tyrell. I guess one of the reasons I fell in love with him was that I was always in awe of the things he did. Stuff he'd tell me about his missions. Things I knew down inside I wouldn't have the courage to do."

"So, how'd you end up a hero?" Sam watched as Brandon Tappan and Shanteel Jones led their saddled horses out of the barn. Both where laughing as they checked the cinches. Brandon gave Shanteel a leg up as she stepped into the stirrup and practically vaulted into the saddle.

Brandon was Breeze's twin, born second. She liked to call him "little brother" even though he had a head's height on her. Something about the Tappan men, they all looked alike. Brandon was the spitting image of his father, right down to the signature brown-ringed eyes, strong jaw, and straight nose. As they passed in front of the porch, he rode like a centaur, sitting the saddle as if he'd been glued there.

"He was my first love," Lauren said offhandedly.

"Who? Brandon?"

"I was running with Breeze. She was what you'd call heavily involved with my brother, Jim. It just seemed natural." Lauren smiled wearily. "Brandon threw me over for a Montana rodeo queen with long midnight-black hair." She arched an eyebrow. "So, what's the story behind Shanteel? How'd a fire-breathing black social activist college student from back east end up in Brandon's bed? How does that work?"

Sam tried to ease his sore ribs. "Shanteel came from a tough neighborhood in Philadelphia. A cop shot her mom when a Black Lives Matter protest got out of hand. At the university, Shanteel had been majoring in social work. Signed up for the archaeological field school in a misguided attempt to learn something about her Cherokee and Seminole ancestors. And, it turned out, to avoid having to care for a younger sister who'd run afoul of drugs, gangs, and the kind of trouble that only ended in a coffin. I guess she and her aunt were close, but the area in Philly where she lived was like a war zone."

Lauren shook her head. Probably thought the relationship seemed impossible. A white man and black woman from totally alien backgrounds, histories, and politics, with nothing in common.

Sam said, "Coming out here, I thought Shanteel had made a really big mistake. I mean, the woman had a smoldering chip on her shoulder. Hated the whole world. When she and Brandon met, it was like oil and water, mongoose and cobra. Then the two of them ended up stranded in the high country by a late-season snow storm. People thought it was a recipe for disaster. But the two of them were trapped together, and somehow saw beyond race, culture, and history."

"So, you think they're going to make it?" Lauren wondered.

"How the hell would I know?" Sam sucked down the last of his tea. "I know for a fact that Shanteel is just as blown away by what's happened as the rest of us. Wondering what the hell she's doing with a redneck rancher, and if this isn't just some reaction to culture shock. But you watch them work side by side? It's like two pieces of a puzzle fitting together."

*Like Shyla and me.*

To change the subject, he asked, "Whatever happened to Breeze and Jim?"

"They got engaged." A pause. "Right up to the night I was driving blind-drunk and doing about fifty when I slammed Jim's pickup into a tree. Maybe I blacked out. Don't remember much about that night. Just flashing lights. The Highway Patrol, and ambulance. And Jim's broken body lying there in the grass." A pause. "No seat belt. He went through the window. Nothing was the same after that. Not for Breeze. Not for me."

Sam flinched at the hollow despair haunting her voice. It triggered his own. Never far under the surface, grief now came boiling up. "Yeah," he told her. "I hear you. Sucks, doesn't it?"

"Maybe that's why we blow up trucks, huh?" she asked.

"Breeze ever date anyone after that?"

"Never anything serious. There was Travis LaBeaux and... Well, something happened." A pause while she changed subject. "For a while she hated me. We didn't talk until Cheyenne. I guess time heals even the worst of wounds?"

He knew what the thing with Travis LaBeaux was: The pregnancy Breeze had terminated with an abortion. It had alienated her from her family.

"I wonder...does it?" He closed his eyes, imagining Shyla, seeing her ash-blonde hair shining in the sunlight, her clear green eyes. She was walking across the yard. Coming toward him. That mysterious and taunting smile she reserved just for him on her full lips.

The ache in his soul began to swell. The grief knot tightening under the back of his tongue.

"What about you and Tyrell Ramirez?" The question sounded forced. God, anything to get his mind off the seething sense of loss. He dared not look toward Shyla's grave up on the knoll.

"The last I saw of Ty was Dissolution Day. The morning of the Collapse. He came by the bank. Said he was activated. He and his team were flying off to who knew where? Classified."

From the corner of his eye, he caught her shrug. "Looking back? I'd guess California." A beat. "You know, the Chinese landed those armies from container ships. Can you imagine? They shipped an entire army in specially designed shipping containers. Men, arms, heavy weapons, supplies, and all the logistical support stacked aboard one of those giant ships. And fools that we were, our people unloaded them. Then the shock troops charged out, took over the port, and their people unloaded the rest."

"Or so the story goes." Sam took a deep breath, wiped away the tear that had broken from his eye to trickle down his cheek. *Shyla, Shyla.* God, would the hurt never end?

"Sheer brilliance if you ask me," Lauren told him, her gaze fixed on the alfalfa where Jon and Ashley pulled up another of the plastic sheet dams that diverted water from the ditch. "The ultimate Trojan horse."

"No word from Ramirez since?"

"Not a one." Lauren grunted, resettled herself in the glider. "Not that there would be. I mean, there's no cell service. Ty just said that if he could, he'd meet me here. He knew. Figured that the world was ending." Another beat. "He and his team? They'd have been the first ones in. Right in the thick of it."

"Word is that you were the one who captured that Chinese pilot. Guess that pretty much cinches it. The war isn't just a rumor."

She fingered her chin. "That pilot? He said, 'Don't kill. Free America.' That was all the English he knew. Or all that he'd let us know. We took him back to Cheyenne, and damned if General Kyzer didn't send some of his security people to snatch the guy right out of the hospital. Never heard a word about him after that."

"Think the Chinese got reinforced?" Sam asked.

"I don't think so." She winced as she leaned forward and rearranged the pillow. "I saw four of our nuclear missiles go up from the silos outside of Cheyenne. One of the scariest moments of my life. It was all over town. Word was they went to China. Supposedly the EMP would have stopped their economy cold. Some of the talk I overheard at the hotel was that the banking collapse would have already caused chaos. Speculation was that the EMP would have been the blow that snapped China's spine. Paralyzed it completely."

"Speculation?" Sam asked softly. "God, I've come to hate that word."

"Guess it's the best we've got for the time being." She glanced up. "Car coming."

Sam winced at the pain as he got to his feet, gaze fixed down-valley to where a plume of dust rose behind a white pickup as it came barreling up the dirt road.

He stepped to the door, calling, "Truck's coming!"

"Be right there," Meggan called back.

Sam grabbed up his Marlin from where he had leaned it against the wall.

"You look just like a cowboy," Lauren told him. She grimaced at the pain it caused her to pluck up her M4 and slip it under the blanket on her lap.

Sam considered that as he chamber-checked the Marlin and saw the reassuring gleam of a brass cartridge. ";Hated guns," he told her. "Back in Hempstead, I always thought they were evil."

"The way I hear it, that gun you're holding kept you alive."

"Yep," he told her. "An evil tool for an evil age. But I guess, like Dante's Inferno, we've got to descend to the lowest level of Hell before we can start climbing back to heaven."

Thomas Star emerged from the barn door, a scoped .30-06 in hand. Willy and Danielle stepped out from the tractor shed, Willy wiping his greasy hands on a rag. He stuffed the rag in his back pocket and reached for his .270 where it was propped beside the shed door. Danielle had shaded her eyes with the palm of a hand as she inspected the pickup that rattled over the cattle guard and headed for the house.

Out in the field, Jon and Ashley were cutting across the alfalfa at a jogtrot. Looked like they were headed for the safety of the barn. These days, no one took the arrival of a strange vehicle for granted.

Meggan, Old Bill, and the still-frail Pam emerged onto the porch and fanned out. Each carried a weapon.

Sam thought it could have been the Hatfields and McCoys. A scene right out of the Nineteeth Century, or an old Hollywood Western. But here he was—in the Twenty-first—living it for real. Should have been used to it after all he'd seen, but sometimes the reality of the Collapse still struck him as surreal.

Thomas Star slouched against the barn door, right leg cocked, foot braced against the frame. Breeze came hustling out, her M4 in hand, from where she'd been doing something with one of the pack horses.

Sam stepped down from the porch, walking out to meet her. Together, they stood, shoulder to shoulder, as the white Chevy three-quarter ton pulled to a stop.

"Stand down!" Bill called. "It's Merlin Smith and Fred Willson. They're on our side."

"Makes you wonder what was important enough that they'd waste the gas to drive out here." Breeze relaxed the slightest bit and shifted a booted foot on the gravel.

Both doors opened, Fred Willson dropping down. His weathered black hat was pulled low over his gray hair, a wary look in his faded blue eyes. The large nose didn't do his lined face any favors. He wore a Western-cut shirt and brown duck-fabric pants over work boots. From the driver's door, Merlin Smith stepped out. He had a King Ropes cap clamped on his bald head, its deep-blue color contrasting to the man's bushy white eyebrows.

"What's up?" Bill asked as he hitched his bad leg down the porch steps.

"Thought we'd better drive out." Merlin thrust both hands into his back pockets as he stepped around the Chevy's front. "Seems there's a pile of trouble brewing in town. Mostly the Coles, but Kapitals and Steve Fallow are helping to fan the flames. Seems they found bullet holes in what was left of Bradley Cole's body. They're calling it murder, Bill."

"And they want Breeze, here," Willson chimed in, "to stand trial for it."

"In a pig's eye!" Old Bill growled. "They were coming after my family." He pointed. "You can see the bullet holes in the porch, Goddamn it! Now, Breeze might 'ave shot Bradley up on Slickside, but he was riding with Ed Tubb. And we all know what Tubb raided the ranch for. He wanted women. And we know what he did with the ones he snatched up."

Sam shot a sidelong glance at Breeze, saw the knotting of her jaw, the hardening behind her eyes.

"No one's arresting me," Breeze declared, her voice hoarse. "If Tubb and his so-called posse had run down Brandon, they'd have killed him. For what? Defending his property and people?" She took a step forward. "And Tubb would have taken the women. You damned well know what they did to women they took. A line had to be drawn somewhere. Shyla Adams was dead. Mom was shot."

Fred Willson kicked at the gravel, looking uneasy. "Yeah, Breeze, we know. And the way we heard it, there's a grave out here filled with four-teen bodies. Most of them, well, they came with Edgewater, but a couple of those boys, they were local. Got family wondering what happened to them. And then there was the sheriff and Deputy Crawford. They died up there on the mountain, too."

"Funerals are tomorrow," Merlin added, looking uncomfortable.

"It was war," Breeze muttered.

"War?" Merlin Smith's white eyebrows rose. "That what you call it?"

"Kind of felt that way to me," Pam's weak voice called. "I was the one left with a bullet in my lung."

Sam shifted the Marlin, added, "They killed my wife when she wouldn't let herself be gang raped. Maybe war is too good a term for what they were doing in the Basin. You know what they did to those girls we freed at Clark Ranch."

Sam gestured. "And you two, at that meeting down in Cheyenne, you sided with Governor Agar. If you'd been in Cody, they'd have arrested you. Put you in that wire prison they built up at Clark Ranch. Edgewater brought something ugly here. Breeze, Brandon, me, Amber Sagan, Willy over there, we stopped it." He narrowed an eye. "Just like the governor wanted done. End of story."

Fred Willson nodded, shifted, glanced up at the dull and cloudy sky with an uncertain squint. "You heard the governor that day, Sam. His only requirement was that we didn't turn it into a *Game of Thrones*. Remember?"

"Who says it's going to turn into that?" Bill asked.

"The Coles, Kapitals, and the other folks who lost people here and up on the mountain." Merlin Smith made a face, kicked the gravel angrily. "Listen, you did the right thing. Now we gotta figure out how to keep it from getting out of control."

"What's the governor say?" Sam asked. "He's got a dog in this fight, too."

Willson leveled a stubby finger in Sam's direction. "He's going to say, 'Keep a lid on it.' And he's going to do that 'cause he doesn't want a home-brewed war in the Basin."

Merlin Smith chimed in, saying, "And that ain't all, Sam. Right now, we're sitting on a powder keg here in Hot Springs. But there's another one brewing up in Cody. Park County's got its own problems. A lot of folks up in Cody made their bed with Edgewater. Others up there are calling them collaborators. Not to mention relatives of the guys who got killed or maimed when they joined Edgewater's thugs up at Clark Ranch. And that includes a certain county commissioner whose son had his balls blown off and his pelvis smashed by a .44 slug. Now, I wonder just who was shooting one of those up at Clark Ranch that day?"

"I was aiming at his head," Sam muttered.

Pam had stepped down from the porch. Still frail, she placed a hand on Breeze's shoulder for balance. Cocked her head, and said, "They came here, Merlin. Said they were arresting us all for sedition. Were going to 'interrogate' the girls. That's what they called it. Worst part was that Hank Kapital was in on the whole thing. He knew it was a sham. A way to take girls for sex and confiscate our ranch." A beat. "And we're supposed to let them arrest Breeze?"

"Shit!" Fred Willson slapped an angry hand on the hood of the Chevy. "The country has fallen apart. We're hanging by a thread, and the last thing we need is an old-time feud with people shooting each other from ambush! What the hell are we going to do about this?"

"Call a town meeting," Bill said where he was standing with his thumbs in his hip pockets. "Lay it out. Just like it was laid out here. Event by event. Then ask the town to decide. Ask what any of them would have done in our position. Ask Ginny Duhaven. She was there the day Edgewater confiscated her hides. Hell, let's get testimony from all the merchants Edgewater stole from. Bradley? He wasn't a monster, just took a job with the bad guys. Hank Kapital? Now that's a fish of a different color. He bought into what Edgewater was selling. The deputies killed? I'd say Edgewater and Kapital are responsible."

"Might work," Fred Willson admitted.

"And we could get the governor's testimony," Merlin added. "He'd back us."

Breeze slowly shook her head. "You go right ahead. But don't count on me being there. You don't know Corwin like I do. He's coming for me. Maybe not today, or tomorrow, but someday. And he's going to give me no more chance than I gave Bradley."

Sam could see the certainty reflected in her. And remembering the man's eyes he'd looked into, he figured she was right.

# THE MILQUETOAST

*I had misgivings about Sam Delgado. Maybe it came from growing up as a military brat and sucking up the "Army way" ethos. Granted, the first time I met the guy, I was as fit as a cracked vase. He was barely in a better condition. And, hey, we'd both been blown up, right? But here's this guy, a graduate student from a New York City suburb, whose only life experience was as a bus boy and dishwasher in a Mexican restaurant? Who cares what people said about him? People can say anything. I thought the guy was milquetoast.*

*I couldn't figure why Breeze thought so highly of him. Even harder to understand was why she'd moved into the guest cabin to care for the guy. Breeze had always been into Clint Eastwood, Rip Wheeler, or Casey Dutton types. And to make matters worse, the dude was drowning in grief over his dead wife, Shyla. All the while, didn't matter what Breeze claimed about their relationship, she was falling for Delgado. Rough, tough, made-of-hard-leather-and-barbed-wire Breeze? Doe-eyed over a milquetoast?*

*I've obviously never been a good judge of character.*

— Excerpt from Lauren Davis' *Journal.*

# CHAPTER SIX

THE LIGHT in the cabin she shared with Sam was still on when Breeze trudged her way across the ranch yard. There were three of the little cabins, each built of logs and topped with gabled roofs; they'd been erected back in 1960s to house big game hunters. It had been a lucrative business, and her family had kept Wyoming Game and Fish outfitting licenses for decades.

Given the heavy cloud cover, the darkness came near to being complete. Fortunately, she could almost traverse the yard blindfolded if she had to. Suffice it to say this wasn't the first time she'd been out after dark, though the area around the guest cabins wasn't as familiar as her usual and long-practiced route from the barn to the house.

She knew enough to step wide around the dark shadow of the old hay rake, oriented herself to the bunk house, and crossed the trampled grass to the middle guest cabin.

"You been out late." A voice from the darkness made Breeze jump half out of her skin. With hardwired instinct, she dropped to a crouch, swinging her M4 around. Sucking for breath, heart leaping, she forced herself to relax.

"Thomas?" she cried. "For God's sake, I could have killed you."

She could make out the shadowed form. The old Shoshoni elder was seated on the hay rake's bar—that flat length of rust-dark steel to which the curled tines were attached. He had his head leaned back, and she could barely make out his braids where they hung down his back like streams of silver.

"Find any answers out there?" he asked.

"Excuse me?"

He gestured with a shadowy arm. "You're looking for what to do. You face decisions that will affect many people. Not just your family here. Choose one thing, and you will alter the lives of everyone in the Bighorn Basin. Chose another, and a whole different set of people will see their lives change. In both cases, some for the better...others for the worse."

"Thomas, I don't want to change *anyone's* life. I didn't ask for any of this."

He chuckled softly. "Those who are chosen always say that."

"I mean it."

"Yeah, I know." He shifted on the rake's uncomfortable metal. "But you had your warning that night up there in the *Puha* Cave. You know what is coming. Water Ghost Woman isn't part of my spirit power. She's yours. I don't know what she showed you in your vision, but she wouldn't have chosen you if you weren't a warrior." A beat. "And you are a warrior. You proved that on The Line. And again at Clark Ranch. Breeze, you can't stop being who you are."

"When I shot Bradley Cole, I wasn't thinking about the future. It was all about what I did then, at that moment. I was mad. Scared. And he was riding with people who'd shot Mom." Breeze gestured her frustration. "It felt like a betrayal. Judas and his thirty pieces of silver."

"So, what conclusion did you come to, walking around out in the dark? You gonna back your grandfather, Fred, and Merlin? Stand up in this town meeting? Tell your side of the story?"

She shook her head. "I worked it every way I could. I don't trust myself."

"Want to explain that?" Thomas shifted on the seat.

"Sure." Breeze resettled her M4. "So, I get up in front of everyone. Start telling the whole story. How I hear Mom's shot. The long drive up from Cheyenne, and how that pus-gutted deputy threatened us outside Mom's hospital room. Said he was arresting Dad and Grandpa. The callous way he told Sam that Shyla had been shot by Tubb. How I met Deputy Eddie Lawson at the ranch, what the yard looked like, covered with empty brass, the bullet holes in the house. The blood stains and the shot-up vehicles."

She knotted a fist. "Let's say I'm right in the middle of that, and Corwin shoots his mouth off. Calls me something like a murdering bitch. I'll go for his throat. That's why I don't trust myself."

Thomas was nodding his head. "That's what a warrior does."

"Yeah, well, Grandpa and the rest have talked themselves into this meeting. Now, even if it all works out and everyone agrees that killing Tubb and the posse up on Slickside was in everyone's best interest, it's just going to make it worse for Corwin and the Coles. Not to mention Bradley's wife, Sarah. She's got three boys, one who's dying of diabetes. They're burying their father tomorrow. And then there's the Kapital faction."

"Um," Thomas agreed. "Kapital and that bunch? Hard to make amends when he helped take people's belongings. Confiscate their businesses and property. Maybe he was part of taking girls to be used like they were." He sighed. "Sometimes, it just don't wash to claim, 'I didn't know.' But that's what his people are going to say."

Breeze threw a hand up in despair. "Hey, I've been there. Guess, depending on how you call it, I'm just as guilty. I helped hold The Line. Am I different from Bradley Cole, Kapital, and the rest? I turned people back, Thomas. Killed desperate and innocent women and children. *Children*, for God's sake! Get it? I have flashbacks of families…falling. I can still see my bullets hitting those kids. Know what happens when a 5.56 round blows though a little five-year-old girl at three thousand feet per second? Or a thirty-year-old mother? Or catches a little boy in the stomach? It ain't pretty."

Breeze gave her head and shoulders a shake, as if she could physically rid herself of the memory.

"How many would have died if they had pushed past the I-25 checkpoint that day?"

"How the hell should I know?"

Thomas nodded to himself. "I heard it would have been thousands if they had overrun the roadblock and stormed into Cheyenne. The world no longer works the way it did before the Collapse. Those ways are gone. And though you say that you and Bradley Cole are the same, I note a difference. He took a job, perhaps thinking he was working on the side of law, but he knew he was hunting down an old family friend. After seeing the ranch yard, knowing that Pam was in the hospital, he made the choice to proceed."

"Guess he did." Breeze fingered the fire control on her M4. "So, what happened on Slickside happened. That still leaves me to figure out what I'm going to do next. I guess I could go call Corwin out, tell him we were going to settle it. Not a problem if he puts me down, huh? On the other hand, if I kill him, that just makes matters worse." She frowned. "If I don't kill him, no matter what happens at that town meeting, he'll come for me sooner or later."

"No one ever said being a warrior was easy," Thomas told her in a gentle voice.

Breeze grunted, gave him a wave. "See you in the morning, Thomas. And thanks."

"You got it, almost-a-daughter." He gave her one of those half-dismissive waves the Shoshoni shared.

She made her way to the cabin, opened the door, and stepped in.

Sam was slumped at the table. From the looks of things, he had been waiting. One hand was extended, fingers curled as if they'd slipped off the ornate glass of an empty cognac bottle. His head was laid on his other arm, shoulders rising and falling with each breath.

Breeze took a moment to gaze on the scene. Sam only took the empty bottle out when he was punishing himself with grief. He'd told her the story. How Shyla had produced it the night she and Sam had sided with the Tappans. And, though he'd never elaborated, she suspected it was the night they'd first made love. The hint was in the softness that filled his brown eyes, the tenderness in the curl of his lips.

What would it be like to be loved that much?

Thinking back to Jim Davis, all she could remember was the passion of a teenage girl's first fevered love. How it had burned so hot. Then that rage, fed by the injustice of his sudden death. How she'd hated the world, hated Lauren, hated God. How she'd felt robbed of all that could have been.

"Sure," she whispered under her breath. At the time it was a tragedy for the ages, worthy of a Shakespearean epic. A loss so devastating and final that there would be no recovery.

Fact was—looking back from the perspective of experience—she and Jim, like the majority of first teen loves, hadn't been headed for a happily-ever-after kind of ending.

She laid a hand on Sam's shoulder. "Hey, wake up."

He jerked, cried out, and gasped, one hand dropping to reflexively press his sore ribs. "God, that hurts."

"Come on, amigo. Let's get some sack time."

She helped him up, watched him carefully put the empty cognac bottle in his pack. Then he stowed it in the wardrobe where he kept his few belongings. He waited until she seated herself on her bed and began pulling her boots off before he flicked the lights off.

Undressing, she slipped under her blanket, resetting the pillow.

"Figure out anything?" he asked from across the room.

"Nope. You?"

"We should leave. It's like we're magnets for trouble. I keep getting glimpses of *Nynymbi*. Like he's trying to tell me something." A pause. "Usually, when that happens, it's because someone's going to die."

"That's a happy thought."

"Yeah," he whispered. "I just don't want it to be anyone I care about." Another pause. "Guess that's selfish."

"Nope. That's human." She took a breath. "Whatever happens, I got your back. Now, let's go to sleep. Who knows? Maybe the spirits will come and tell us what to do."

A dry chuckle sounded. Then, voice earnest, he said, "Thanks."

"For what?"

"Being in this with me. Don't think I could do this without you."

A wry smile bent her lips. "Yeah. Me either."

But what the hell did that mean?

# NATIVE VOODOO

*If I had to come up with a metaphor for Thomas Star, it would be that the guy was like an itch between my shoulder blades. The kind you couldn't ever get to so you could scratch. Blame it on my pragmatic roots, but every time he started talking about his spirits and visions, it was all I could do to keep from rolling my eyes. Granted, he and the Tappans went way back. After all, he'd been there to help hold the ranch during the Edgewater days. Yes, the guy had a BS in physics. Talked in terms of photons and quantum wave functions. Somehow that didn't explain what made him so spooky.*

*What irked was the way he'd look at me with those black eyes...and he'd see all the shit I kept hidden inside. Stuff I didn't let anyone see: the fear, the guilt, the self-loathing and fragility. He was the last person on the ranch that I'd want privy to my deepest failings. I'm not sure why, but I always came away with the impression that I scared him. That he knew more about me than I did.*

*Today, he came over and sat next to me. For a long while, he didn't say anything, then he turns to me. "Your face tells a lot."*

*"Like what?"*

*"Like you're killing the whole world inside you. You can stop, you know?"*

*I frown at him. "I'm not killing anything."*

*He gives me a kindly elderly smile. "It won't mean you are weak or a coward. Non-violence is not necessarily the shield of a coward, used aggressively it's the supreme virtue of the brave."*

— Excerpt from Lauren Davis' *Journal.*

# CHAPTER SEVEN

THE COW HUNG UPSIDE DOWN in the barn. Hooks—dangling from loops welded on either end of a three-foot section of pipe—had been pushed through the hollow between the Achilles tendon and calcaneus bone on either back leg. The contraption, called a gambrel, was attached to a chain and hoist. This in turn was suspended from a ring in one of the barn's beams.

Sam used his sleeve to rub at an itch on his forehead. Tried to come to grips with the reality that he and Shanteel were in the process of a skinning a cow. His hands were caked with blood, and his fingers ached where they clutched the knife handle. He stepped forward as Thomas pulled the loose end of the chain, hoisting the cow another foot higher.

"That's good," Shanteel called as she reached out and used a flap of skinned hide to keep the carcass from swinging.

Sam got a grip on his own section of still-warm hide, using the curved skinning knife to sever the pale webbing of tissue that attached the skin to the carcass. Above him, the cow's muscular body was red, exposed muscle streaked with white lines of fat and sinew. The scent, rich in Sam's nostrils, was curiously pleasant as he continued to slip his knife around the resisting tissue. As he did, gravity pulled the hide away from the warm flesh. Like he was peeling it inside out.

Sure, the work hurt his ribs, and his hip ached, but it wasn't all that hard. And he was tired of sitting, not carrying his weight.

"Shorter strokes, Shanteel," Pam Tappan called where she sat on an inverted feed bucket off to the side. "Otherwise you'll buttonhole...uh, put a hole in the hide. Any holes decrease the value, and you won't be able to trade it for as much. Causes Ginny problems in the tanning process, too."

"Got it," Shanteel told her. Then added, "If the folks back in Philadelphia could only see me now."

"Yeah," Sam agreed. "Me, too. Never thought I'd be skinning a cow."

"You worked in a restaurant." Shanteel gave him a skeptical eye. "You oughta be good at this."

"Our beef was delivered, already cut up and frozen. All we did was thaw it and cook it."

Shanteel waved at a pesky fly, glanced uneasily at the cow's previously severed head where it lay on a blue polytarp off to the side. Blood still drained from the neck, the eyes gone gray. "Lot of stuff we didn't know, huh? I mean, being in the city. Growing up, sure, I knew that beef came from cows. Didn't know how it got from cows to those plastic-wrapped packages in the grocery store. That part of life..." She ended with a shrug.

"Just wasn't real?" Sam finished for her.

"Got that straight." Shanteel gave him a sober look before she went back to sliding her blade along the connective tissue around the loins and peeling the skin back.

Sam remembered Shanteel's expression, how she'd jumped when Pam used the .38 to shoot the cow in the head. That look of horror on Shanteel's face as the cow dropped like dead weight, uttered a guttural and deep-throated grunt. As it did, the eyes had rolled up and back.

He and Shanteel both had killed rabbits with a .22, but somehow, the cow's death was different. Hell, it had affected him down to the core. They'd both been leaking tears, on the point of sobbing.

Pam, replacing the pistol—the same one Shyla had once used to kill one of her attackers—had studied them both. Said, "Don't be ashamed of the tears. It means you'll appreciate what you're putting on your plate from here on out."

"But she was such a nice cow," Shanteel had said between sniffs. "Not like she ever hurt anybody. And she had the prettiest eyes."

"It's how the world was made back in the Creation," Thomas Star had told them as he and Shanteel had struggled to pull the cow over on her side. Then he'd carefully cut off the feet just below the carpals and tarsals. Sam had watched in awe as the elder slipped the knife around the joints and then, accompanied by a cracking sound, snapped them off. With Shanteel's help he'd run the hooks through the back legs and begun hoisting the cow up.

"Why this cow?" Sam asked as he ran his knife around the peeling hide. They were working their way down on the ribs.

"She's open," Pam said. "Open means she's not pregnant. Hasn't had a calf for the last two years. Since she's not producing, we'll butcher her and replace her with one of the yearling heifers."

Shanteel's hand began to shake, she closed her eyes, expression pinched. Seemed to be on the verge of losing it.

"You okay?" Sam asked, stepping over, placing a hand on her arm.

She nodded, worked her jaws; a couple tears broke free to roll down her smooth cheeks. "I...yeah. It's just... I mean, damn! Sometimes, it just comes home, you know? That it's all about death. Who lives, who dies. Cows, people. The fact that it's all gone. Back there. The whole East Coast. Philly. The house. Aunt Naome. My best friend, Talicia. Reverend Randall. All of them...gone."

She tried to smile. "Even Elroy. Don't matter what he did. Guess that's a blessing."

"Elroy?" Thomas asked softly.

"My brother." Shanteel looked down at Sam's blood-splotched hand on her brown skin. Met his gaze. "I don't talk about him much. Killed a five-year-old girl in a drive-by shooting over in Kensington. Deal gone bad. Elroy? He got life. Last I heard he was in Waymart. That's the prison up in Wayne County." She paused, rolling the skinning knife in her fingers; its handle looked tacky with blood and fat. "You wonder why I hated guns so much?"

"Yeah, I know," Sam told her. "First time Shyla made me touch Pam's revolver that morning up at the tent? I almost threw up." He glanced over at Pam, who smiled at the memory.

"Oh, yeah," Shanteel said with resignation. "And to think I was handing Brandon bullets the day they raided the ranch. Then, again, when I was spotting for him over at Clark Ranch." She shook her head as she went back to skinning. "Didn't hit me till afterwards. Each time he shot one of those men, I was glad. Since then, I've been asking myself: Was it some deep-seated thing about white men with guns in authority? Coming to take something from my people? Like when that cop shot my mother that day?"

Sam said, "The anthropologist in me will tell you that it's the human condition. It's how humanity lived for most of our species' history. We had a reprieve for a while. Lived in a golden age of safety and comfort. People had some expectation of peace and security. At least for the West and most of Asia. That new world order in the post-World War II era. Sure, there were brush wars, Vietnam, Iraq, Ukraine. But for the most part, people had security."

"Maybe where you were from in New York," Shanteel muttered. "Where I come from in the Tioga-Nicetown part of Philly? Waking up in the morning, you had no clue if you'd live to see bedtime roll around again."

"How'd you make it out?" Thomas asked.

Shanteel frowned. She was back to her normal self again, concentrating on her work as she spoke. "Part of it was Reverend Randall. Each time I went to a funeral for one my friends? He was up there telling us that we had a choice. And my mother, she tried so hard. Wanted all of her kids to have a different life. Elroy? I don't think he ever had a chance. Same with my little sister. But me? I was mad. Filled with rage right down to my bones. Then Mam was shot. And I'd be damned if I was going to stay and continue to live that shit. So, the first university that accepted me, I left." A shadow of a smile. "And here I am, skinning a cow."

"Well"—Thomas pulled on the chain that elevated the cow's carcass another six inches—"you're not going out for latte and a muffin at Starbucks any time soon. That's for certain. So skinning cows is a whole lot better than starving."

"I had a Starbucks coffee one time," Pam noted. "It was up in Billings." She sighed, gaze going distant. "I miss coffee."

"Miss a lot of things," Thomas said. "What I don't miss is commodity food. That crap the USDA gave out on the reservation through the FDPIR program. Most of it was canned or dried. Tasted like cardboard. And then there were those big blocks of yellow cheese. Funny stuff, that cheese. You could fry it, and it would never melt. Sort like a square of plastic." Thomas paused thoughtfully. "I should go back to the Rez one of these days. See how things are doing."

"The cheese wouldn't melt?" Shanteel asked.

"Nope." Thomas locked the hoist chain in place. "They said that commodity food was a balanced diet. It was balanced all right, a balance of chemicals. I read the labels one time. Now me, I got a degree in physics, but I couldn't pronounce all those words. Once I tried to look some of it up. I stopped when I read that they used a hydrophobic fatty acid in the processing. I was too afraid they got it from rabid skunks."

"Maybe you should have been a chemist instead of physicist," Pam said as she shifted and took a deep breath to ease her healing lung.

Thomas indicated the hanging carcass. "I think we're going to be eating a lot better than factory-processed food. More grass-raised beef, elk, deer, and plants. A good friend of mine over on the Rez has started a wild plant harvesting and natural foods drive. The Collapse will be getting a lot of my people off their butts, out of the casino, and back up into the hills."

He pointed at Sam. "Like you said. The benefits of the Industrial Revolution are gone. We're going back to the old ways." Then he twitched his lips Shanteel's way. "And that includes carrying our weapons."

"Watch it around the shoulders," Pam warned as Sam and Shanteel skinned down around the ribs. "That fold of skin around what you'd call the armpit gets tricky. Thomas, pull it up higher so the kids can slit down the front legs to the brisket. Otherwise they're going to make a mess of this."

Sam followed directions, was still half baffled until Shanteel figured out the logic of it and showed him how to cut and free the delicate skin under the front leg.

"Never knew a cow was so big," Sam muttered.

"Wait until we cut it up," Pam warned. "That's when the real work begins. For the time being we're okay when it comes to packaging, um, wrapping the meat. But once the plastic, freezer wrap, and butcher paper are gone? Don't know how we'll get around freezer burning."

"Guess we're back to making jerky like in the old days," Thomas told her. "And pemmican. That and smoking the meat."

"We can trade sugar from the beet harvest here in the Basin for salt coming out the Salt Lake Valley. Salt's a preservative," Sam said. "Court and Dr. Holly were talking about that with Governor Agar. We could—"

"Truck's coming!" Ashley's shout carried down from the hill above the barn.

"Now what?" Pam wondered as she carefully eased her way up from her bucket.

Sam heedlessly rubbed his blood-clotted hands on his pants, stepped over, and picked up his Marlin. Pam had stuffed the .38 she'd used to kill the cow into her waistband.

Thomas plucked up his .30-06, opened the bolt, and glanced down to ensure he had a cartridge in the chamber.

"Hope it's not more white men with badges and guns." Shanteel headed for the barn door, knife clutched in hand. "Every time I hear a car coming anymore? Sends shivers down my spine."

The vehicle was a Wyoming Highway Patrol SUV, one of the Ford Interceptors that once cruised the highways in search of speeders, moving violations, and burned-out tail lights. Not to mention the occasional drunk driver or drug mule.

As it pulled into the yard, Shanteel, standing beside Sam, whispered, "Why do I always have to be right?"

"Don't get too wound up," Sam told her. "The patrol's on Agar's side."

"Haven't heard much from him since he tried Edgewater," Pam noted, her breathing labored as she took a position beside them.

The door opened, Captain Sully Richardson stepping out and putting his hat on with a fluid motion. Slamming the door behind him, he came striding across the gravel, a wry smile bending his lips as he took in the people and weapons.

"Hope I didn't interrupt anything." A pause. "Especially if, given the bloody clothes and hands, you're in the middle of disposing of a body."

"Butchering a beef, Sully," Pam told him. "The kids here have to know how it's done in our brave new world. I can probably send you back with a couple of fresh-cut steaks if you've got time to wait around."

He shook his head, flinty gaze taking in Sam and Shanteel. Resting, for a lingering moment on the Marlin Sam was holding. "That a .44?"

"It is," Sam told him.

Sully's thin smile twisted. "Same one you carried on the Clark Ranch raid?"

"It is," Sam repeated.

"I wouldn't advertise the fact," Sully said dryly. "Seems that one of the county commissioners who got a little too friendly with Director Edgewater has a son. Says the young man in question was innocently shot down while visiting up at Clark Ranch. Seems they took a mush-roomed .44 out of the said victim's..." He glanced uneasily at Pam and Shanteel. "Well, let's just say 'his privates.'"

"I was aiming somewhere else," Sam said woodenly.

Sully's smile tightened. "Like I said, I wouldn't advertise the fact."

"What can we do for you, Sully?" Pam asked, strain now in her voice.

"Frank and Bill around?"

"Yeah, Dad's reading in his study last I saw. Frank and Brandon are out checking fence and trying to get a count on the stuff we've got grazing up in the divide pasture. Larkspur's blooming, and they're worried that some of the beef might have gotten into it."

Stuff. Wyoming rancher speak for the cattle. Sam was still learning.

"Larkspur, huh? That's tough." Sully stuffed thumbs into his duty belt, gaze rising to the slope beyond the barn. "'Bout all you can do with Larkspur poisoning is cut off the ears and tail, hope they bleed out enough to thin the blood."

"Cut off the...?" Shanteel said. "You gotta be kidding."

"Um, it's the only hope for the cow. Bleeding out thins the blood. Tough choices to make." Thomas had shifted his rifle to a less threatening one-handed hold.

"You're not exactly getting to the point, Captain." Pam jutted her hip, crossing her arms.

Sully gave her a knowing squint. "Well, Delgado's here. What about Breeze?"

"She's around." Pam gave a slight shrug.

Sully looked straight at Sam. "The governor's aware that certain tensions are running a little high in the Basin. Festering things. Like that fella whose balls you shot off. And there's this Slickside affair. He's also aware of this town meeting that Bill, Fred, and the rest want to hold."

"That's right," Pam told him.

"Meetings are funny things," Sully said absently. "Never know how they might turn out. The governor's going to be making his position known when it all comes down, but in the meantime, he has an assignment for Mr. Delgado and Ms. Breeze Tappan."

"What kind of assignment?" Sam asked cautiously.

"The kind you and Breeze are perfectly suited for," Sully said. "The kind that will keep you two out of the Basin until tempers cool. And—" he nodded at the Marlin—"you'd better take that along. You might need it next time you're aiming for someone's head."

"And what if Breeze and I decide that we—"

"I said it was an *assignment*, Mr. Delgado. As in, the governor is giving you an order. There's no deciding involved." Sully cocked his head, hard gaze fixing on Sam. "So pack your duffle. Be ready to go by the time this meeting takes place on Friday. Governor wants you and Ms. Tappan out of the Basin."

"But I don't—"

"Mister, I'm a Captain in the Wyoming Highway Patrol. Not the debating team. I'm telling you to be packed. Whatever you'll need for a couple of months. Bedroll, clothes, stuff like that. And now, I don't care who does it, but somebody go find Breeze. I want to look her in the eyes when I give her the message. Make sure there's no misunderstanding."

Sam barely heard the whispered words as Shanteel said, "White men with badges and guns. Never changes."

# CABIN FEVER

*A little over three weeks. That's how long I have been at Tappan Ranch.
Mostly I sit on the porch, my back propped against a pillow, holding
court from the wooden love seat. Not that there is much court to preside
over. I wouldn't say it has been as boring as the fascinating hobby of
watching railroad tracks rust. But for the town guys packing their dead
out of the ranch—that was only one evening of excitement—the biggest
entertainment was watching Jon and Ashley Tempest change the water
on the alfalfa field.*

*Let's just say that after Sully Richardson drove into the yard, my days
of feeling sorry for myself were over.*

— Excerpt from Lauren Davis' *Journal.*

# CHAPTER EIGHT

BREEZE HAD NEVER MET Sully Richardson, but she liked the way the man had given her the governor's order. The guy had been straight up, a no-bullshit cop. And, to tell the truth, the day he told her that Governor Agar and Captain Ragnovich had an assignment for her and Sam, it filled her with a sense of relief. She had waved as his cruiser left a dust plume on its way back to Cody.

Breeze wasn't sure when her feeling of unrest had germinated; somewhere in her unconscious it had been slowly building. As the days had passed since the last of the bodies had been carried down off Slickside, she'd been ever more unsettled, aware that trouble was brewing. That it was only a matter of time.

Unable to share her disquiet—even with Sam—she'd taken to riding off on Joker, seeking the high trails, happy to be by herself in the solitude of the forest and meadows. She found solace just watching the Tappan cattle graze, cognizant that the future rested with the animals. Didn't matter if the clouds remained thick and the temperatures cool, the constant afternoon rains had the pastures as lush as she'd ever seen them. Radiation counts—according to the Hot Springs field extension office—remained only slightly elevated. With each day, it looked like they'd dodged the bullet when it came to fallout.

Those thoughts were in her head as she pulled the cords on her boogie bag tight and gave it a slap. Damn. Felt good. Like she had a purpose again. That she was no longer playing a waiting game. She gave the little guest cabin a final inspection. Sure beat having to live in the house with her folks. Didn't even bother her that she'd been using the outhouse instead of the flush toilet inside. Especially since she'd sprayed the underside of the seat with bug spray to kill the black widow who'd built a web there. The can had to be used sparingly. There wouldn't be any more after it was exhausted.

Breeze turned as the door opened. Lauren Davis hobbled in on her crutches. Lauren took one look at the boogie bag and grinned. "I remember when you got that. Pulled every string, called in every favor in the Guard until you had one just like mine."

"Call it 'boogie bag envy'," Breeze told her. "Didn't come cheap. Cost me a bottle of eighteen-year-old Macallan in trade. I guess it was worth it. Having this bag saved a lot of lives. Couldn't have done the things I did without it."

Lauren's gaze had gone distant. "Wish I was going with you."

"Stay and heal," Breeze told her. "Besides, didn't Ramirez say he was going to meet you here?"

Lauren's flicker of a smile faded; her cinnamon-brown gaze slid off to the side. "I'm pretty sure that Ty's dead. And no, Breeze. Don't bullshit me with trite notions of hope. I've had a lot of time to think about it. Ty knew it was going to be bad. By then he knew the Chinese had landed an invasion force."

"Doesn't mean—"

Lauren lifted a hand. "There you go with the trite bullshit. They'd have put him and his team front and center against the Chinese. That's where he'll stay until they're defeated, he's killed, or what's left of America falls."

"Miracles happen," Breeze told her. "Look at us. We're still alive."

"Yeah." Lauren's fingers fluttered on the crutch handles. "Guess we both know it was an accident, huh?" A faint smile. "Especially with me. Until I came here, I had nothing left. I knew Ty wasn't coming. The things I did on The Line? That *we* did on The Line? All those people we sent back to their deaths? And then that little girl in the tent, holding that stuffed sheep? I went to Marsy Ranch to die, Breeze. Nothing heroic about it."

Lauren sighed, gaze still averted. "Then to wake up, only to learn that Mike Vinich was dead?"

Breeze ran her hand over the rough textile on the boogie bag, feeling the lumps made by the bag's contents. "You got Tiffany out. Saved those kids."

"Sure, Tiff and the kids got out, but she lost Trevor that night. That's going to eat at her for the rest of her life. She loved him. They'd planned the wedding. And he died saving her. That's a lot of guilt."

"Story of our lives, old friend." Breeze stepped over, stared hard into Lauren's eyes. "Maybe that's the lesson in all of this. We've got to live. Especially after everything we've done. The things we regret. The people we've lost. Maybe that's why the Collapse happened. Everyone forgot how precious life was, and what it cost a person to snuff it out. How much it hurts to have someone's blood on your hands. How it corrupts a bit more of your soul every time you watch the life fade out of someone's eyes."

"Becoming a philosopher now, Breeze?"

Still holding Lauren's gaze, she said, "I took the survey class as a freshman. The instructor, a skinny guy with a freshly minted PhD, a bobbing Adam's apple, wearing oversized horn-rim glasses and a rumpled corduroy suit, told us that philosophy was the only discipline that tried to answer the over-arching question: Why? Since this shit started, I've had to ask myself *Why?* over and over. It puts me to sleep every night. Then it fills my mind after I wake up screaming from another nightmare."

Lauren shifted on her crutches. "Tell you what. You find any answers, you call me up a-fricking immediately, okay?"

"Well, girl, at this stage, all I've figured out is that life's a whole lot more elemental."

"Yep," Lauren chimed in. "Like if you're still breathing, with a full stomach, not thirsty, and unhurt when you crawl into bed, call the day a win."

"Assuming you've still got a bed to crawl into," Breeze amended.

Lauren's attempt at a smile failed. "You and I have been through a lot. Most of it pretty shitty. Whatever Agar's got planned for you and Sam, you use your head. There's nothing you need to prove. Not to yourself or anybody else. Not after what you've already been through. You don't owe anyone anything."

"Except the dead," Breeze answered as images of Water Ghost Woman surfaced in her memory. She reached for her boogie bag. Placing the strap over her shoulder, she muscled the heavy bag up. Then she plucked her battered Rand's hat from the antler rack and tugged it over brown hair that she'd pulled back into a ponytail. Finally, she grabbed for the battered old M4, letting it hang in her left hand as her right braced the boogie bag's strap on her shoulder.

Lauren turned. Hobbling out on her crutches, she swung across the threshold and into the haze-tempered morning. Over her shoulder, she called, "I mean it, Breeze. You play it smart, you hear?"

The concern in Lauren's voice brought a humorless smile to Breeze's lips. "I hear. The same to you. When I get back, I expect to see you wrassling grizzly bears and breaking horses."

Lauren flashed her a knowing smile. "Sure thing." A pause. "Hey, you know I love you, right?"

"Back at ya. I'd give you a hug, but I'd hate to rebreak those ribs."

"Hugs are for next time," Lauren promised.

Breeze looked over to where the Highway Patrol unit Sully

Richardson had sent was waiting. Sam had already piled his stuff in the back and was standing by the door, talking with the patrol officer. A brown-haired, uniformed woman who'd been delegated to drive them to town, she might have been in her thirties. Seemed that Agar wasn't taking any chances that either Breeze or Sam might fade away into the hills.

In front of the house, her grandfather, Dad, and Brandon were waiting by old Bill's big Ram 3500 dually. And it was to there that Lauren was making her way with each swinging stride on her crutches.

At the back of the Highway Patrol's Ford Interceptor, Breeze tossed her boogie bag into the cargo space and laid the M4 across it. Walked around to where Sam stood at the open door. He had his eyes on the bunch at Bill's silver Ram crewcab. Asked, "What's that about?"

Breeze followed his gaze to see Lauren, apparently adamant about something as she tossed her crutches into the pickup's bed, and brooking no interference, climbed painfully into the big truck's back seat.

"Guess she thinks she's going," Breeze told him as she slid into the Interceptor's back seat. "But then, that's Lauren for you. When it comes to hardheaded, she ranks 4600 on the Brinell scale."

"The what?" Sam asked as he eased onto the seat beside her.

"Means her head is hard enough to dent a diamond," Breeze told him. "I guess she's decided she's going to this meeting with the rest."

The officer—her badge read Tollston—seated herself behind the wheel, removing her duty hat. "All set?" she asked through the divider.

Sam glanced around. "Cop car, huh? Like the kind you can't get out of?"

"That's right." Tollston glanced at him in the rearview mirror. "Been in one before, I take it."

Sam's shy smile bent his lips; he looked slightly abashed. "First time, actually. But, well, I'm still young so there's a lot of opportunity in my future."

The way he said it tickled Breeze's sense of humor. She liked that about Sam. Especially that aw-shucks smile of his and the half-embarrassed twinkle that flashed in his eyes. That he was self-effacing still intrigued and reassured her. She'd only been a junior at Denver University, and the idea that he'd been a graduate student in a doctoral program back east dazzled her. Especially after the TAs and graduate assistants she'd been exposed to at DU. They'd all had a slightly arrogant superiority. The kind that, unlike Sam, looked down their noses at mere undergraduates.

Funny that. After everything she'd been through—not to mention her and Sam's raid on Clark Ranch—she could still be impressed by such silliness.

As the Interceptor rolled out of the yard, Breeze glanced back, taking one last look at the ranch. A curious flutter stirred down in her chest and grew into a melancholy ache—that feeling that she'd reconnected with herself, healed a wound her in soul, and bathed in a form of redemption despite past transgressions.

Sam, reading her expression, said, "It'll be waiting when we get back. Frank, Pam, Thomas, and Brandon, they're not going to let anything happen to it."

Breeze let the image fix in her brain as Old Bill's Ram dually rolled in pursuit; the gray overcast played on the silver truck as it followed down the lane. In the fields, Jon and Ashley waved as they braced on their shovels.

"Hard to believe," Sam muttered to himself. "Jon lives for that alfalfa field."

She added, "At least Ashley found a way to be useful. What is it with her?"

"Athlete." Sam frowned. "Kind of the ultimate jock. Ashley defined herself through her sports. Especially soccer and softball. She was on a full-ride scholarship. Had articles in the school paper written about her. Thought that coming on the field school would lead to an easy A and get her off academic probation."

"Whatever it did," Breeze said thoughtfully, "it sure as hell kept her alive. What are the odds? Of all those hundreds of millions who died back east, who'd think that a summer field school would be the lone ticket to survival?"

"All I wanted was a dissertation topic." Sam resettled himself in the seat. "Instead, for a brief moment, I found everything I could have dreamed…and lost it all."

From the corner of her eye, she caught the flicker at the corner of his mouth, the sheen of grief in his eyes.

Unthinkingly, she took his hand. Squeezed. "One day at a time, Sam. That's how we get through this."

He nodded, smiled, and gently freed his hand before patting hers in a reassuring manner. "You just keep reminding me of that."

She chuckled, turning her gaze to the familiar sights passing beyond the window. Would she ever see them again? Let alone the ranch? "And it's your job to keep reminding me not to get myself killed. Lauren thinks you're the responsible one."

"Not the most reliable of endorsements," Sam muttered, "seeing as how she's the only other person I know who has been blown up. And with bigger explosives than just a Jeep gas tank."

Breeze grinned at that as the Interceptor rumbled across a section of washboard while passing the old Smith place ranch gate.

"So, what do you think Governor Agar wants with us?" Sam asked.

"You were down in Cheyenne, privy to all the goings on. What's this about?"

She glanced his way and paused to think about it. "My guess is that whatever the job is, he'd rather have Lauren. He knows her the best. She's the one with the real reputation."

"Just as a reminder, Breeze, Lauren didn't kill a bunch of people in the Bighorn Basin. We did. And it makes a heap more sense that Agar wants us out of here and away." He flipped his thumb back and forth, indicating the two of them. "The two of us? We're just as likely to start a war." A beat. "Hell of a legacy, huh?"

"Yeah, hell of a legacy." She turned her attention to the passing hogbacks as the Interceptor went fogging toward town.

# THE INVALID

*Crutches are a great disguise. Hobbling along, you are seen by everyone and taken seriously by none. They're a sort of free pass. They shout: "Hey, I'm hurt. Cut me some slack." No one had a clue.*

*Outside of spying on the relationships that made up the Tappan Ranch soap opera—Ashley, who claimed to be a lesbian, was screwing Jon who had always wondered if he was gay—I got to make objective assessments. One was that the Tappans kept talking about the level of threat posed by the folks who had lost loved ones at Slickside. Added to that, Governor Agar was coming for the Hot Springs meeting.*

*I was looking forward to seeing him. Not that we'd ever been what you'd call the best of friends. In fact, we both considered ourselves to be monsters. How's that for bonding?*

*"...should you ever consider coming back to Cheyenne..." he'd said that day he'd flown me to Cody for Edgewater's trial and execution.*

*On that drive into Hot Springs for the meeting, I wondered if the good governor remembered that conversation.*

— Excerpt from Lauren Davis' *Journal.*

# CHAPTER NINE

DESPITE BEING in the back of a police cruiser, leaving the ranch filled Sam with memories. The day he and Shyla had gone to town had looked like this: gray, dreary. The only difference had been the rain. In Wyoming, he'd learned, rain was life. And on that trip, he'd been holding Shyla's hand. His soul had been light, airy, and euphoric with that exaltation that came of bone-bursting new love. He'd been gone over the rainbow. Rapturous, staring worshipfully into Shyla's green eyes. Still dazzled by the miracle that she'd chosen him, awed that she shared his bed.

Still seemed like a dream. But he'd stared out at these same red sandstone ridges, dotted as they were with juniper and limber pine. Ridden down this same road.

The ache tried to consume him.

The memory of her felt so real, so close. Like, if he closed his eyes, he could will time to flow backwards...change the past.

And then there was the last time he'd traveled down this road. That time, he'd left Shyla behind. He'd been with Dr. Holly and the Tappans on the way to Cheyenne. If only he'd have stayed at the ranch. Never made that fateful drive. Instead, he'd take Shyla, ride up to the field camp up above Slickside, and they'd live there forever. Hunting, collecting plants, spending their days laughing and sharing secret smiles. Their nights would be passed eating roasted meats at the fire before retiring to the tent where they'd wind their bodies together and revel in the joining.

The Patrol Interceptor barely slowed as they made the turn onto

Highway 120, heading south toward Hot Springs; it jolted Sam back to reality.

In contrast to his sensuous, smart, and stunning Shyla, this woman he sat beside was all hardened iron and whipcord tested. Breeze Tappan came from a different world. Western to start with, life had hammer-forged her into something akin to a weapon. The first time he'd seen her had been down in Cheyenne, probably just about that same time that Shyla had been killed back at the ranch. Breeze had walked into the Hilton's dining room in a sort of daze after a tough day on The Line. She'd been on the verge of breaking. Soul-shattered to the point that her commanding officer had dismissed her from duty. Put a guard on her motorcycle to keep her from riding off to The Line.

And despite that, Breeze had pulled herself together on the news of her mother being shot and the raid on the ranch. Had kept Sam from self-destructing in the wake of Shyla's murder. Kept him from getting himself foolishly killed at Slickside. Breeze, along with Brandon, had put together the raid on Clark Ranch. Given him a purpose.

*And now, here we are. Bonded.*

But what did that mean?

Sam gave the woman his full attention where she sat beside him, took in the line of her firm jaw, the angle of her cheekbones and tanned skin. Breeze's straight nose balanced the high forehead and strong chin, all accented by the tangle of brown hair that fell over her shoulders. And then she turned those dark-ringed eyes on his. Wolf-like, predatory in nature.

"What?" she asked, reading his intensity.

"Trying to make sense of it, that's all."

She chuckled, unamused. "Nothing to make sense of. Someone, probably the Chinese, hacked the banks. Credit was frozen. The chaos spread and burned out of control. The country tore itself apart. Distribution of goods and services, failed. Civilization collapsed."

"What the hell were they thinking?"

She shrugged. "Lot of people hate America. There's Russia, pissed off about how we backed Ukraine. North Korea, Iran, and of course the Chinese. Probably figured that toppling American financial institutions would have allowed theirs to fill the vacuum."

"Didn't work out that way."

"Nope."

"That's the thing about wars," Sam whispered softly. "Unintended consequences." A beat. "Lauren told me that all the banks would have gone down. Like, globally. Guess they got more than they bargained for."

"Yeah." Breeze shifted, bracing a leg as they passed Red Canyon

Road. "My bet is that the virus they used to infect the financial system was too adaptive. As hard as the US banking system crashed, it would have taken Mexico and South America with it. That would have brought European Banks to their knees within twenty-four hours. From there, banks around the world would have fallen like dominoes. Might not have taken Russia down given their isolation, but it would have definitely collapsed the Chinese central bank."

"Why's that? If they planned the hack, wouldn't they have taken precautions?"

Breeze was tapping fingers on her worn jeans as she stared out at the passing landscape. "Back when I was a kid, Bernie Munson was going to burn out a patch of spotted knapweed in the field behind his house. It was August in a really hot and droughty year. So Ernie waited until morning when the wind was calm. Used a five-gallon gas can to splash on the knapweed. He had run a hose out across his ditch to keep things from getting out of control. Then he tossed a match onto the gas-soaked knapweed.

"Sure enough, the whole field went up, but in the process it set some of the wood posts in his corral on fire. Bernie dragged his hose over and was watering down his corral poles and trying to keep the dried manure from catching. He was so involved in protecting his corral, that he didn't see the fire burning its way down the ditch."

"Why would he care if the ditch burned?" Sam wondered.

"Because his hose, made of plastic, burned through. In an instant, Bernie's water was gone. So he ran back and pulled what was left of the melted hose from the ditch, but by then a stand of kosha weeds next to his old barn caught fire."

"Oh, shit." Sam guessed, "So, he lost the barn, too?"

Breeze gave him a dismissive shrug. "Hey, it's August. Hot. No humidity for weeks. That wood was like tinder. So Ernie throws his hose down, and runs for the barn, trying to get his tools and anything valuable out. While he's doing that, the fire has burned over to his yard and the propane tank."

"Did he save anything?"

"Well, Martha got out of the house when the fire started up the back porch. She ran screaming to find Bernie, who was piling tools in the drive. He, in turn, ran to get what he could out of the house, which was filling with smoke. Being Bernie, he grabbed up his double-barrel shotgun and his .30-06. He tossed them onto the pile from the barn and was just headed back toward the house when the propane tank went up, which blew out the windows, letting the fire draft like a chimney."

"Lost the whole thing, huh?"

"That's the debatable part." Breeze gave him a knowing look. "He saved his shotgun and the .30-06 he was planning to take to elk camp that fall. Lost the barn, the house, the tractor, the corral...and Martha. See, she divorced him for saving the .30-06 instead of the photo albums, her mother's china, and most of all, the ten thousand in cash that was in the coffee can in the kitchen."

"Wow." As the Interceptor went rolling down Highway 120, Sam realized that the abandoned cars that had been left on the roadside were missing. Someone must have been salvaging them.

"The hackers would have been better off if they'd met Bernie," Breeze told him. "Maybe they thought the US was like Bernie's weed patch. A nuisance. One they could just get rid of with a little fire. They probably figured that, like Bernie's hose, they had a way of keeping it all under control."

Officer Tollston started down the long hill into the town of Hot Springs, patches of juniper, lush grass, and houses passing by. Wyoming's version of urban sprawl. Sam said, "Lauren told me about the day she saw those ballistic missiles. She said at least four of them launched, then curved into the sky." He glanced at Breeze. "Think they went to China?"

Again she gave him that dismissive shrug. "Might have. Or maybe Russia? North Korea?"

Sam noticed that Hot Springs had changed since the last time he'd been here. Laundry hung outside on newly constructed clothes lines. A lot of yards now had firepits out front with a circle of chairs around them. Stacks of firewood could be seen. The cars had a dusty look, which hinted that few had been driven recently. The streets were still empty of traffic. And, sure enough, there were horses here and there in yards, some with carts attached.

"Whole new look to the place," Sam said.

Breeze was nodding as the cruiser slowed for the town's single traffic light. The light was dark. Instead, a yield sign had been erected at the once-busy intersection. Officer Tollston slowed, then took a left, following Highway 20 around toward the State Park. Sam glanced side-long as they passed the fairgrounds where the ill-fated posse had assembled on their way to disaster at Slickside.

At the high school, Tollston pulled the Interceptor into the parking lot, slowed, and eased into one of the reserved spaces before shutting the Ford down.

People stood in knots before the gymnasium door; they turned to watch the Highway Patrol vehicle with sudden interest. To the side, out on the lawn, a couple of horse-drawn flatbeds with straw bales for seating waited; the animals were held by bored kids who let them graze on the un-mowed grass, thick as it was with dandelions.

To the side, in the fire lane, two black Chevy Suburbans with Wyoming state plates waited, drivers standing by the vehicles. Heads topped by wide-brimmed Western hats, they wore tailored jackets that did little to hide the large pistols strapped to their hips. Now they, too, turned their attention to the cruiser.

Up front, Tollston announced, "We're just about on time."

"So, what's next?" Breeze asked.

"As soon as the meeting's over, you get to transfer to the governor's motorcade, and I'm off to wherever Sully sends me. Funny new world. I'm more like a courier and errand girl than law enforcement."

Old Bill's silver Ram pickup pulled in, found a space in the mostly empty lot, and rolled to a stop. The doors opened, Bill, Frank, and the others stepping out to help Lauren as she eased her way to the ground. Brandon retrieved her crutches from the pickup bed. Then they slowly trooped toward the door.

"Hey," Breeze called. "Let us out of here."

"I'm supposed to stay with you until you're delivered to Agar's people," Tollston told her.

"So," Breeze said reasonably, "stay with us. It's not like we're what you'd call flight risks. And everyone's headed inside."

As she spoke the doors opened on the black Suburbans, and Sam saw Governor Pete Agar—dressed in his usual three-piece suit—step out. He was accompanied by a detail of four men, obviously Wyoming National Guard given their ACU uniforms. And, yes, there was Terry Thompson, the ex-Hot Springs County sheriff. Thompson led the governor's entourage to one of the side doors where Merlin Smith opened it.

As they disappeared inside, Sam said, "Officer Tollston, we're on Agar's side. Wouldn't hurt if we could just stand in the back. You know, out of the way? Maybe hear what's being said? Might help us with whatever the governor's got us involved in."

Breeze chimed in, "Uh, like, you didn't get any orders that said we couldn't, right?"

Tollston hesitated as she thought it over, slapped her hands to the steering wheel, and said, "Guess I didn't. I'm just supposed to deliver you to the governor. Guess I can do it in there as well as out here."

So saying, she popped the driver's door, stepped around, and opened Sam's. He paused long enough to give Breeze a hand as she slid out after him. Together they walked toward the red-brick building with its double glass doors.

"Why the high school gym?" Sam asked.

"Only place in town big enough for a town meeting." Breeze gave him a chiding glance. "It's not like we have a concert hall."

As they entered, Sam took in the atrium with its long display case on the back wall. Behind the glass stood the usual high school memorabilia: trophies from years past when Hot Springs had taken state in football, basketball, wrestling, and track. The back was hung with certificates, ribbons, photos of alumni from over the years. On either side were the double doors to the gym and basketball court.

The deputy who stood with hands clasped behind him looked familiar. Sam placed him as Eddie Lawson. The one who'd been guarding the ranch the day he and Breeze had arrived after the raid. Married to Kelly Ann. Two kids: Jennie and Cody.

Lawson, in a crisp and ironed uniform, smiled uneasily as he fixed on Breeze and Sam. Then nodded to Officer Tollston as he said, "Yeah, Breeze. It figures. Don't surprise me that the next time I see you, it's in custody. You under arrest for what happened up at Slickside?"

"Nope." Breeze stopped before him, a lop-sided grin on her face. "We're still on Agar's team. Just here to observe."

"Anyplace we could see and not be seen?" Tollston asked.

"AV and announcer's booth." Lawson pointed to the right. "Behind that door. Up the stairs to the second floor."

"You're a good man, Eddie Lawson," Breeze told him as Tollston headed for the indicated door. "And one of these days, I'll stand you a whiskey. For old time's sake."

Sam saw Lawson grin as he waved them away.

Just another reminder of how, in small towns, history ran deep. As did wounds. Like he'd seen reflected in the faces of Corwin Cole and the Kapital family riders as they packed Bradley and Hank's bodies off the mountain.

Hip hurting, Sam followed Breeze and Tollston up the flight of concrete stairs through a fire door, and into a small room, one side open with a commanding view of the entire gymnasium.

Down in the gym, bleachers had been pulled out, the seats pretty much filled to capacity. Men and women of all ages. Lots of kids. Sam wouldn't have considered it the sort of thing that qualified for a family outing. On the sides, knots of people crowded around where a stage had been set up on the far end. A podium stood there along with a line of chairs against the back wall.

Moving over next to the booth wall—covered as it was with electronic stuff Sam couldn't identify—he slid one of the microphones out of the way and hitched his butt up on the counter. Hip still had a pained twinge, and he figured he could live with the ache in his ribs. Given that the basketball hoops were pulled back the view was unimpeded. The air conditioning was running in the high ceiling; that was a lot of bodies to keep cool.

*Yeah, and in more ways than one.*

A rumble of conversation grew louder as Bill, Frank, and Brandon made their way down the basketball court and climbed the three steps onto the low platform. Terry Thompson emerged from a side door, thumping up the stairs, and taking the podium as the Tappans seated themselves. Lauren Davis, on her crutches, hobbled to one side, and—propped on her crutches—leaned back against the wall, painted as it was in purple and gold—the school colors.

Sam could feel the strain in the room. All those people, the simmering emotion, the ominous sound of the mixed conversations.

"I know we're getting started a little late," Thompson's voice boomed from the PA system. "For you newcomers, I'm Terry Thompson. I was the sheriff here for ten years before Hank Kapital was elected. After the events up at Slickside and what we learned from the trafficked girls brought back from Clark Ranch, I was asked to step into these boots again."

Thompson placed his hands on either side of the podium, looking out at the now-hushed crowd. "We live in challenging times. The country's gone. There has been no communication with the East Coast. I've recently learned that there are, indeed, at least three Chinese armies out in California and Washington. Bad as things are here in Hot Springs, they could be a hell of a lot worse. But we've got our own troubles. Here in the Basin, DHS Director Kevin Edgewater may not have exceeded his legal mandate, but he sure as hell exceeded his moral authority."

A low rumble went up from the crowd, met by whistles and applause.

Thompson raised his hands, calling, "Now, here's the thing. I sat out there with all of you when the Tappans brought those girls in from Clark Ranch. And I heard the testimony given by the freed captives that Edgewater had put in that wire enclosure. And we all know that he was way out of line when it came to confiscating people's property and—"

"Got that right!" Ginny Duhaven, from the tannery, bellowed, all six feet plus of her rising to her feet. "Not to mention the beatings, murder, and outright intimidation he and his thugs dished out."

Another burst of applause, shouts of approbation, and foot stomping accompanied the outburst.

"Yeah, we know," Thompson soothed. "And Edgewater and his enforcers have paid for that. But they did more. They split this county. Forced people to pick sides. And that's why we're here."

Thompson paused, leaning forward as he took in the crowded bleachers as if trying to look each person in the eyes. "Folks in Wyoming consider themselves to be patriots. We cherish and value the flag. The same with concepts of duty and honor. And Edgewater played on that. Asked people to do things, as he said, 'for the good of the country.' Because he was the duly appointed authority, people did. Including Hank

Kapital, the Coles—" Thompson waved to include the room— "and a lot of the rest of us."

Sam watched as the audience shifted, sort of like an undercurrent running through the room.

Thompson continued. "Director Edgewater created the conditions that set neighbor on neighbor. For his own twisted appetites, he allowed Ed Tubb to make that raid on the Tappan Ranch. Why? He wanted to seize women and confiscate the property for his own. And a lot of people died. Some thinking they were on the side of the government, others because they were defending their lives and property." A pause. "And it got worse when Hank Kapital, at Tubb's order, went after the Tappans. And Bradley Cole paid the price."

"Yeah," Corwin stood, a fist knotted. "Shot down from ambush." He turned looking at the crowd. "That's cold-blooded murder."

An uneasy chorus erupted from the crowd. Some approving, others muttering in disagreement.

Sam felt that uneasy squeeze in his guts. Could see Bill and Frank looking anything but happy as they shifted in their chairs. Lauren, propped on her crutches, had pulled her shoulder bag around in front, as if to be more comfortable.

In the booth across from him, Breeze's jaw was clenched. Looked like she could chew fence staples into filings.

"Hey!" Thompson bellowed. "Tone it down. We're here to solve this. We've got to bring an end to the trouble. Work it out between us because we can't allow this to fester." He glanced to the side, adding, "Here to tell us why is Governor Pete Agar. Up from Cheyenne with special news. Ladies and gentlemen, the Governor of Wyoming."

A swell of applause went up as Pete Agar walked through the side door. He looked dapper in his immaculate silk suit, and given his audience's apparel, totally out of place. The four Wyoming National Guard soldiers followed, walking behind in twos before taking positions around the stage.

For the first time, the audience sounded united in applause: a few stood, then, like a wave, the people were rising to their feet, clapping in wild abandon as Agar mounted the stage. He stopped long enough to shake old Bill's hand, then clapped Thompson on the shoulder before taking the podium.

"Ladies and gentlemen," he called, "thank you. Please, be seated. We've got a lot to do here."

Agar waited out the rustling as people resettled on the bleachers.

"We're in trouble. I don't travel around the state on a whim these days, but what happens at this meeting is going to determine the fate of the Bighorn Basin." He paused. "And maybe Wyoming." Another pause. "And maybe America."

He let that sink in before saying, "Yesterday I was in a meeting with General Norman Kyzer, the commanding officer of Francis E. Warren air base outside of Cheyenne. Most of you know it's a ballistic missile base. Because of its importance, General Kyzer has been given updates by what's left of the chain of command. Here's the situation:

"Just prior to the hack over Memorial Day weekend, three giant container ships, the ones that can carry more than twenty-thousand containers, were being unloaded at the ports of Los Angeles, San Francisco, and Seattle. A fourth big ship was supposed to be unloading in San Diego, but was fortunately delayed. The shipping containers, or ISOs as they are called, were specially designed for ventilation and habitation like a giant apartment building, or a small self-contained city. These ISOs were precisely fitted together with ventilation, stairways, kitchens, barracks, hospitals, and latrines. An entire mobile military base to transport a Peoples Liberation Army group. Each boxship carried five thousand troops and another five thousand support personnel, entire weapons systems including tanks, personnel carriers, electronics, complete field kitchens, a hospital, machine shops, ammunition, spare parts, aircraft, and tons of field rations for just about any conditions imaginable."

Agar looked out at the now-silent people as he continued. "Our own longshoremen unloaded the first containers. They concealed the specially trained troops who stormed out, seized the harbor facilities, and began the systematic unloading of the rest."

He shook his head. "Think about it. An entire army with all of its logistics in those thousands of containers. The perfect Trojan Horse. Hitting us at the same time a malware was unleashed on our banking system. Creating chaos. Destroying our financial system."

Sam watched the people squirming on the bleachers, sharing angry looks, shaking their heads.

"So," old Bill called, "what's happened to them?"

Agar paused, as if in thought. "Good question. Here's the best information we've got: Apparently, on news of the bank hack, our two carrier groups in the South China Sea were also attacked. No news on how that operation went. General Kyzer believes one of our ballistic missile submarines might have retaliated on Beijing. Whatever came down, within hours, a nuclear strike on Washington and New York took out the East Coast. Speculation is that to protect Chinese troops on the West Coast, the strikes were localized to the eastern seaboard. EMP still took out everything as far west as Iowa and down to east Texas."

Sam heard the rising anger in the crowd.

Agar held up his hands for calm. "According to General Kyzer, after this was confirmed, six of our ballistic missiles with high-yield nuclear warheads were exploded in the stratosphere over China. The EMP from that altitude would have blacked out the entire country. Fried the electrical grid. Their computers, phones, factories, cars, electrical grid, water, washing machines, trucks, elevators, tractors...anything with a chip or transistor. Like flipping an off switch. Everything is dark. Gone."

Another pause. "Since no additional nuclear strikes have been launched at the United States, it is believed that China has been neutralized. One-point-seven-billion people have no electricity. No food or transportation. No lights but candles."

"What about the Chinese on the coast?" someone called.

"Still fighting," Agar answered. "I think you've all heard about how grim the situation is along the Front Range in Colorado? The burning, looting, murder, and savagery? Word has reached me that it was a hundred times worse in the West Coast cities. Like rats trapped in a bucket they turned on each other. Given that the Chinese had their own stores of food and fuel, they ran right through the rioting masses, bulldozed the freeways clear of derelict cars, and rolled all the way to the Sierras."

"So they've got California?" Thompson asked in disbelief.

"And seem to be digging in if the intelligence can be believed," Agar told him. Then, looking out at the audience, he added, "All we have left of America is the Rocky Mountain states. And that brings us to you. Here. In the Bighorn Basin. I said I didn't want any blood vendettas. The only way we survive is by working together. Now, how do we make peace in the Basin?"

"I'll tell you how," a strident voice called.

Sam craned his head, seeing a thin-boned woman, maybe fiftyish, graying hair pulled back and clipped. She wore a Western-cut shirt, jeans, and stalked forward in high-heeled riding boots. To Sam's eye, she looked tough, had that hard-bitten and unforgiving presence. She walked up to the side of the stage, stopping before one of the Guardsmen. She smiled at the guy, reached into her shirt. Before he could react, she pulled out a short-barreled revolver and shot the man in the stomach. The loud bang echoed around inside the gym.

As he fell, she aimed the stainless steel handgun at the stunned Agar and cried, "I'm Corretta Kapital. Hank was my husband, and you ordered him killed, you son of a bitch. So, here's where it ends!"

Across the distance, despite the hundreds of shocked people, Sam could hear the hammer being cocked.

The *pop!* wasn't as loud, more like a firecracker than the revolver's snapping bang.

Corretta staggered, the revolver wavering, gone rubbery in her grip.

*Pop!*

*Pop!*

Corretta teetered, hunching. The revolver, as if too heavy, dragged her arm ever lower. Then the woman went down like a felled tree,

toppling sideways to smack into the hardwood at the out-of-bounds line
on the basketball court. The steel revolver clattered on the floor just
beyond her outstretched hand.

Sam watched Lauren Davis hitch her way forward on her crutches—
the little black pistol clutched in her hand. Stopping short of the fallen
woman, she braced herself, aiming the automatic. Before anyone could
react, shot the woman in the back of the head.

# WHO KNEW?

*Writing about the incident in the Hot Springs High School after the fact, it's easy to say, "Yeah, well, I had a hunch." The problem is, I don't remember a thing about it.*

*Breeze told me later that Corretta walked up and shot Terrence Smith through the belly, then I just appeared and took her out.*

*Maybe it was because I'd been a Line rider? Or I'd had time to sit and think on the Tappans' porch instead of constantly being tossed from one crisis to the next? Or that I wanted to make a good impression on Agar? See, Governor? I'm right here, next to the stage, available.*

*Didn't matter. I was there, ready. After it all went down, Governor Agar was alive. The assassin was not.*

*In the calculus of the post-Collapse age, that was all that counted.*

*Right? Simply doing a job. Taking care of business.*

*But if it's all so clear, why do I have a blank place in my memory? Like maybe I can't stand to remember it.*

— Excerpt from Lauren Davis' *Journal.*

# CHAPTER TEN

BREEZE WAS HEADED for the stairs even as Sheriff Thompson's voice was booming over the PA, "I want everyone out of here. Now, don't rush. No pushing. Clear the gym in an orderly manner. Then I want you all home! And, for God's sake, anyone who starts anything will spend the next year in the county jail choking down watery oatmeal!"

Breeze was through the AV room door, feet hammering on the concrete steps. At the bottom, she ducked out into the atrium. She could hear Officer Tollston on the steps behind her, bellowing, "Breeze, damn it, get back here!"

People were thronging out of both sets of double doors, parents trying to calm anxious children. The teenagers—boys and girls alike— with gleaming eyes, called "Wow!" and "Did you see that?" "Shot dead!" "Right on the gym floor!"

Their parents didn't seem so amused; they muttered back and forth, shaking their heads. One man calling to a friend, "Well, guess that didn't make much peace."

Breeze ducked to the side, caught a gap in the exiting throng, and zipped into the gym. She was half way across the floor when she ran headlong into Corwin, backed by Bradley's wife, Sandra, and her three kids.

Corwin stopped short. Sandra yanked her oldest boy, Logan—now fourteen—behind her. The other two boys, Gabriel, ten, and Oliver, eight just stared wide-eyed at her. Oliver always looked cadaverous, but then the kid had Type One diabetes. If anything, he looked a world worse than usual, a gray tone to his sunken flesh.

"Your shit doesn't end, does it, Breeze?" Corwin declared, his expression like thunder.

"Hey, you heard the governor." Breeze raised her hands in a gesture of surrender.

"Ought to put you down right here," Corwin continued. "Catch you face to face. But then that would be too good for a back-shooter like you."

He was reaching into his vest. One of those popular heavy-duty canvas cuts with a pocket for a concealed carry pistol.

Breeze, hands still out, backed another step, fully aware of the hate in Corwin's eyes and the loathing in Sandra's. Hell, after Corretta's attempt on Agar, Corwin might just shoot her.

"Don't do it," came the hard order from behind. "Hands where I can see them. Now!"

Breeze snapped a glance to see Officer Tollston, hand on her duty weapon, posed in that slight combat crouch that perched the woman on the balls of her feet.

"Breeze Tappan is under Governor Agar's protection," Tollston continued. "And there's been enough bloodshed here today." She inclined her head. "So, move along."

Corwin jerked a nod in Tollston's direction, removed his hand and laid it on Sandra's back. "Come on. It'll wait."

"I *hate* you for what you did," Sandra practically spat the words at Breeze as she hurried past, still dragging the hot-eyed and scared Logan. The younger brothers—avoiding her gaze—went scurrying ahead. Oliver seemed to have trouble walking and looked as if he were about to fold.

Breeze let them pass, drew a deep breath, and exhaled wearily, her heart bumping against her breastbone.

"I see you really know how to make enemies," Tollston said as she stopped beside Breeze, gaze on the retreating Coles. Sam was coming at a trot, veering wide of the smoldering Cole party as it passed. Beneath the brim of his hat, his face had that pinched look from pain, and he was limping slightly.

"There's no sense in doing things by half measures," Breeze retorted, pushing ahead to where a knot of officers was gathered around the downed Guardsman.

Lauren stood propped on her crutches, her bad leg forward as she waited. Old Bill, Frank, and Brandon were up on the stage standing in a protective ring around an obviously shaken Agar. Sheriff Thompson straightened from where he'd crouched over Corretta's bleeding corpse. He made a *tsking* sound as Breeze passed him.

Surrounded by his three fellows, the wounded Guardsman—Smith was stenciled on his pocket—was being lifted onto a gurney; a guy in an

EMT's jacket yelled, "Come on. Let's go! Emergency's waiting. He's got a chance!"

Breeze could see the blood soaking the uniform shirt; it was spreading despite the compress Deputy Lawson was holding on the man's belly. Then, glancing at the stainless steel .357 revolver that lay where Corretta had dropped it, she thought the EMT might be overly optimistic.

Stepping up to Lauren, she gave her old friend a wary shake of the head. "Didn't know you had a hideout gun."

"Good thing, huh?" Lauren shifted her balance on the crutches. "It's just a little .380. Never shot it that well. Must have been something about being on crutches. Maybe they work like shooting sticks. Didn't miss with a single shot."

"Yeah," Breeze said through a sigh, "well, there's a bunch more Kapitals to go around. Cousins and such. And Corretta was one of the Smyth clan from over around Tensleep. But, maybe, given that she was going to assassinate the governor, that might buy you some forgiveness."

Officer Tollston had taken a position at the edge of the knot of officials and moved to get the door as the gurney was wheeled out. They already had the Guardsman on oxygen.

Sheriff Thompson, looking more than a little pallid himself, reached out a hand, saying, "I'll take that weapon, ma'am." After Lauren reluctantly handed it over, Thompson added, "While I'm aware of the circumstances, you're going to have to come down to the Sheriff's Office for a—"

"She's with me," Agar declared as he descended the steps. "Terry, that's Lauren Davis. *The* Lauren Davis. From The Line. The one who single-handedly took out the raiders at Marsy Ranch."

"Governor," Thompson turned, facing the man. "With all due respect, she really didn't need to put that last shot into Corretta's head. The woman was down, and from the color of the blood leaking all over the floor, she was liver and lung shot."

"But you didn't know that when she went down," Lauren said. "And even then, takes a while to bleed out. That big revolver didn't fall more than foot from her hand. She could have got her wits about her, grabbed it, and still killed the governor. And you, too, sheriff."

Agar, fingering his chin, studied Sheriff Thompson. "I'll trust Lauren Davis any day of the week. Give her gun back. She's with me."

Terry Thompson, glancing uncertainly at the other law enforcement officers in the room, warily handed the little black pistol back to Lauren. She checked the chamber and dropped it into her shoulder bag.

The Sheriff glowered at Agar, adding, "Then take her with you when you leave. I got enough on my plate without having to worry about someone putting a bullet in Davis."

"She's one of us," Old Bill called as he limped his way down the stairs. "We'll see to her safety."

"No, Bill," Agar told him. Then turning to Lauren. "You fit enough to travel?"

Breeze watched the subtle interplay in Lauren's expression as she said, "No. But what have you got in mind?"

Agar glanced around, lowered his voice, and said, "Sheriff, I've already got Delgado and Breeze, here, on assignment. If I take Lauren, can you keep a lid on Hot Springs? Make it known that the trouble-makers are no longer in the county?"

"Troublemakers?" Breeze wondered, only to have Agar, Thompson, and her grandfather simultaneously turn "you-gotta-be-kidding" gazes her direction.

"Yeah," Thompson finally said, slipping thumbs into his duty belt as he stepped wide so that Mick Lansian from the funeral home could attend to Corretta's body. Thompson glanced at Old Bill. "You'll do your best to keep out of Corwin and Sandra's way?"

"You got it." Bill turned to Brandon. "You hear that?"

"Yep." Brandon had pushed his old black hat back, gave a short nod. "Hell, I wouldn't be here now if you hadn't told me to come. Everything I need is back home." A beat. "Unless there's a can of Copenhagen to be had somewhere in town."

"Not so much as a pinch of snoose left in Wyoming as far as my office can determine," Agar told him. "With the exception of alcohol, anyone with an addiction is about as strung out as they can get. If there's any upside to The Collapse, it's that it's played hell with the drug trade."

Brandon just gave him a humorless smile, saying, "Then I guess I'll keep to the hills."

Breeze suspected he was thinking of Shanteel, too.

Agar turned as he stared around the now-empty gym. "How the hell did this get so out of hand?"

"Edgewater," Bill told him. "But before you write this off as a fail-ure, think it through. With the exception of a couple of bitter hard cases, everyone in this room heard what you had to say." He indicated Corretta with a curt nod. "Hell, she put an exclamation point on it in a way you couldn't if you'd got on your knees to plead."

Agar sighed, rubbed a hand over his close-cropped black hair. To the remaining three Guardsmen—all of whom were standing, alert, looking pissed off, sidearms in hand lest some other threat come sneaking out of the woodwork—he said, "Let's go, gentlemen. We can be in Cheyenne by a little after midnight."

"I'll get your stuff moved," Tollston called to Breeze and Sam. Sam had been standing uneasily to one side, his somber gaze spending too much time on Corretta's bleeding body.

Brandon stepped close, hugging Breeze tight. "Hey, Big Sister. Keep your shit together out there, all right? You come home to me."

"You, too, Little Brother," she told him. "Love you."

Then it was her father who hugged her and said, "Love you, girl."

And finally Old Bill stepped close. Looking into her Grandfather's glinting eyes, she said, "You keep them all together. That's in the job description for being a patriarch."

"You got it, girl." And her grandfather gave her a flinty wink. "Do what you gotta do."

She felt her heart sink as they turned, walking steadfastly across the gym floor. Three generations of her family, tough, upright, a legacy she wondered if she could ever live up to.

# PRAETORIAN

This trip to Cheyenne was a totally different experience than my flight up to the Bighorn Basin. The Governor wasn't using the "Wyoming Air Force"—the small fleet of state-owned aircraft—for anything except the worst of emergencies. The planes had only a limited number of flight hours left. After that, there were no more spare parts. Once the planes were declared unsafe, they'd be grounded. Probably forever. So there I was, seated in the back of a black Chevrolet Suburban. One the motor pool could fix with parts scavenged from any of the growing junkyards across the state.

Governor Agar rode in the passenger seat. Me, I had my few belongings which consisted of the cast off clothing from the Tappans I was wearing, my weapons, and a few toiletries.

Word was that my boogie bag would be sent in a couple of days along with my other few possessions. Wasn't sure how I felt about my prize kit being in other people's hands.

We'd just passed out of the head of Wind River Canyon and into the basin north of Shoshoni when Agar turned to give me a sober appraisal over the back of his seat. "Anything I say, like thank you, is just words. That woman had me dead to rights. You saved my life back there."

His dark eyes were fixed on mine as we climbed past the uplifted red and yellow sandstones and into the dry Wind River Basin. He paused for a second. "You were right there when I needed you. How did you know—"

"She caught my attention. Her eyes were too big, her breathing too fast. She scared me."

Don't tell him you don't remember killing the woman.

*"My bodyguards didn't spot her."*

*"Men focus on men."*

*He seemed to mull that over. "Word is going to spread fast. 'Lauren Davis shot an assassin dead.' If you're willing, I want to keep you on my protective detail."*

*Lauren shook her head. "I can barely stand on my crutches for more than a few minutes, Governor. I'm not physically fit to be on any detail."*

*"All I want you to do is watch people. If you spot anyone suspicious, notify my security staff. And maybe stand at my side, when necessary."*

*"Stand at your side?"*

*The governor nodded. "People in Cheyenne, especially on The Line, know you and trust you. You've got a reputation. Just being seen with me sends a message. Think you can do that?"*

*I blinked and looked away while I considered my answer. "Yeah. I can do that."*

*He exhaled hard. "Thanks. From here on out, things are just going to get harder and more dangerous."*

— Excerpt from Lauren Davis' *Journal.*

# CHAPTER ELEVEN

Sᴀᴍ ʙʟɪɴᴋᴇᴅ awake and stared up at the dark ceiling. Took him a moment to figure out where he was: Cheyenne. Back at the Hilton on Central Avenue a block up from Lincoln Way. He was in a very comfortable bed, the thinnest slivers of light leaking past the shade. On the bedside table, the digital clock read 7:38.

He shifted, glanced across the narrow space separating their beds. Breeze was still asleep. Funny thing that. The Guard Corporal who had met them at the curb when their Suburban dropped them off had asked, "You two ok bunking together?"

Breeze, yawning, had said, "Wouldn't be the first time."

And when they'd taken the elevator to the seventh floor and their room, it was to find two queen beds. He'd been suddenly nervous. Glanced sidelong at Breeze, who'd seemed unfazed as she tossed her boogie bag on the floor and headed to the bathroom. At the ranch he hadn't thought twice about Breeze being in the same cabin. She'd been taking care of him in the beginning. And everyone knew there was nothing between them. But here? In Cheyenne? What were people going to think?

Sam swung his legs out, sitting on the edge of his bed. He rubbed his eyes, yawned, and made his way to the bathroom. Closing the door, he stripped off his underwear, turned on the shower, and was surprised to find a little square block of what looked like homemade soap. No miniature bottles of shampoo or conditioner. But the water was hot—and lasted a hell of a lot longer than the little shower in the bunkhouse back at the ranch.

Stepping out, it hit home that there were only two towels. No washcloths or face towels. The once-ubiquitous Kleenex dispenser was missing. In fact, the bathroom had a bare look. That's when he noticed the rags laid over the toilet paper roller. Lifting the toilet lid, he saw the words scribbled in black Sharpie on the underside of the seat.

NOTICE: DO NOT THROW RAGS DOWN TOILET!
AFTER USE, PLACE IN UNDER SINK TRASH BIN FOR
RECYCLING.

Sam blinked. Of course they'd have run out of toilet paper. He made a face as he considered the neatly folded rags. Looked like they'd been made out of fodder picked up at Goodwill given the various colors, patterns, and weights of cloth. But, damn! Could he, like, really use one of the things? Knowing someone before him had…well, wiped his or her butt with it?

He was still staring, trying to come to terms when Breeze opened the door, asking, "You going to be in here all morning?"

Sam was so tormented, it didn't even occur to him that he was buck-assed naked. He just pointed. "Did you see that?"

Breeze followed his point to the rags. "Yeah. When I had to pee last night." She grunted. "There was talk, you know. Last time I was here. They figured they only had a week's worth of toilet paper left in all of Cheyenne. Hotel staff wasn't sure what the hell they were going to do when they used the last of it."

"But…reusing rags?"

"Got a better idea? Or are we all going to be like Bedouins? Use our left hands?"

Sam sighed, making room as Breeze squeezed past him and turned the water on in the shower.

He beat a hasty retreat, snagging up his underwear on the way.

She emerged fifteen minutes later, wearing only a bra and panties. She was rubbing her brown hair vigorously with the damp towel. He was dressed, sitting cross-legged on the bed. "What are we doing, Breeze? I mean, what are we? You and me?"

She stopped short, gave him a knowing look. Crossing to his bed, she seated herself, a pinched expression on her face. "What kicked this off?"

"Um. You walking into the bathroom just now. Didn't that embarrass you?"

"You mean after the sweat lodge? Or living in the same cabin for weeks? Nothing I haven't seen before."

"There was a divider in the cabin."

"There was a sheet," she told him shortly. "A very thread-bare sheet. But, yeah, I hear where you're coming from."

"Most women would be uncomfortable walking around naked in front of a man."

"You're more than 'a man,' you're something else." Her brow lined in thought. "Like, it all changed when Thomas had us do that vision quest. In that cave...Water Ghost Woman...what she told me in my dreams. The things she showed me." A beat. "You were there. Part of it."

He nodded, haunted by his own memories of that night, of the things *Nynymbi* had shown him. "I made a pact with God once. Made the deal that if it came to choosing between sacrificing the entire world or living the rest of my life with Shyla, I'd choose her. Sometimes I think that's why God took her away from me. That it was punishment for being so selfish. For loving her that much."

Breeze reached out, smacked him playfully on the knee. "Or maybe that's why you were chosen, Sam. Because you had the capacity to love that much. Any doubts I might have had about you? They vanished when you stayed behind at Clark Ranch. I'm alive today, along with Shirley Mackeson, the Visanges, Nelson and Baker, not to mention Joelle, Michaela, Mary Lou, and the rest of those poor girls. And don't forget the ones who escaped down the canyon because you blew up that Jeep. The greatest heroes are those who sacrifice themselves to save others."

"Hey, I wasn't thinking about being a hero."

She chuckled humorlessly. "Heroes never do. You think I was thinking at the I-25 checkpoint?" Her expression sobered. "There are no secrets between us, Mr. Delgado. I know exactly who you are. I trust you with my life. That's the kind of intimacy not even lovers can share."

She stood, crossed to her bed, and continued trying to dry her damp hair.

Sam, grousing, said, "Shows what you know. Prancing around half naked. What makes you think I won't jump on you when you least expect it?"

She gave him a sidelong and dismissive glance. "You're too in love with your magical Shyla to give any woman a second thought."

# THE WATCHER

*What did I know about being on a security detail? I weigh one hundred
and eight pounds and still have bones knitting back together. Propped on
my crutches, all I have is attitude.*

*Well, and an M4, which adds a lot to the equation.*

*"Lauren," one of the governor's bodyguards, a tall blond named
Kace Adams, told me, "ninety percent of this job is mental. Thinking
about what can go wrong and making sure that it doesn't. Identify potential threats ahead of time and have a plan. Your job—and your only job
—is keeping the governor safe. You do that by being smart. If you have to
pull your pistol? You've already failed."*

— Excerpt from Lauren Davis' *Journal.*

# CHAPTER TWELVE

THE MEETING with Governor Agar was at 1:00 in the afternoon. That gave Breeze the whole morning to think. Sam had asked the question, one that had been already rolling around, half formed, in her own mind: What was Sam to her?

In the beginning, he'd been something of a nuisance. A witness to her breakdown when Captain Ragnovich had dismissed her from The Line. A kind of non-entity who'd forced himself into her sphere, then compelled her to take command at Slickside. She'd thought him the weak link. The bumbling and clueless Latino kid from the big city turned loose to do dumb things in the back country. Sure, he might have intimidated her by being a graduate student from a big name school back East, but what did that matter when lives were at stake?

That changed at Clark Ranch. First when Sam stood and fought, then took the initiative in freeing Edgewater's captives in that fenced compound. And finally his selfless decision to buy her and the rest time to escape. He'd gone into that knowing he was going to die.

And survived by some miracle.

Breeze slouched in her old booth in the Hilton restaurant just off the lobby. The table where Sam and his friend Court had been sitting that fateful morning was now occupied by two guys in casual dress, though both wore ties. The parts of their desultory conversation that she overheard had to do with water quality. Apparently they'd worked for the Bureau of Land Management in some capacity as resource specialists and now had been coopted into working for the State of Wyoming.

State? What did that mean these days?

"More like nation of Wyoming," Breeze told herself.

What kind of nation was it? Obviously, one without toilet paper, Tampons, or coffee—given that she was drinking a locally made substitute composed of parched wheat, singed corn, and roasted dandelion root. The Tampon thing, however, was going to take some thought. Being a ranch girl, while riding in the high pastures she had made due with handkerchiefs and such on occasion. In the old days, they were called menstrual cloths. How that was going to work now? A couple hundred thousand women in Wyoming were finding out.

With every passing day, people were learning—to their dismay—just how much life was changing. Empty shelves in the pharmacies might have the greatest impact on people's lives, but who knew what condition the state would be in come winter? How did you face a future without Oreo cookies? Staples, light bulbs, envelopes, ball point pens, clothing, seafood, fruits, circuit breakers, windshield wipers, paint, wire, tape, Ziplocs…the list went on. Not to mention that people still carried their smart phones with them, as if doing so was an article of faith that one day the service would magically come on again.

She was pondering the absurdity of that when Sam came striding into the restaurant. He must have assumed she'd be at the booth, because he walked over, laid his .44 Marlin next to her M4, and slid into the seat opposite her. "Coffee?" he asked, indicating her cup.

"They call it Coffree," she told him. Shrugged. "It's not coffee, and at fifty cents a cup, it's not free. But after a couple of years, who's going to remember what coffee really tasted like?" She pointed. "And no pepper shaker. Word is that what's left is being hoarded. People are starting to figure out what the words 'the very last of' actually mean."

He nodded, gestured at the waitress, and pointed at Breeze's cup. She gave him a high sign that she understood.

"You eaten yet?"

"Waiting for you, Delgado. Choices are hot cereal made from oats and wheat, steak, eggs, potatoes, or a slice of toast. They're out of butter until the dairy can deliver on Monday."

"I guess eggs and potatoes sounds the most exotic." He gave her a crooked grin. "At the ranch we had beef, elk, or deer every meal. Where they getting the potatoes?"

"Idaho, I guess. Just like salt from Utah. We're probably able to trade something."

From the next table, one of the BLM guys said, "Coal, oil, gas, things eastern Idaho doesn't have in great supply. There's a whole system of trade being knit together based on who has what. Same with western Nebraska, the Dakotas, and Montana."

"Who's running that?" Sam asked.

"Some sort of cabal headed by a guy named Evan Holly out of the governor's office." The second guy pointed to himself and his companion. "Like us? We're trying to put together a catalog of resources that Wyoming has that other states don't. For the time being, Idaho is sort of the big dog since it has more mining, manufacturing, lumber, and a chemical industry."

The first guy raised a finger. "That's assuming they can keep a lid on their population. If they don't, and rioting breaks out 'cause people are hungry, they won't even be so much as a whipped puppy." He wiggled his finger like it was important. "They've got two million people, with about half living the Boise area. Biggest challenge is keeping them fed. See, the thing is, they don't have a single refinery, and no petroleum reserves to speak of. Doesn't matter that Idaho raises a third of the country's potatoes. If they don't have the diesel to run the trucks to haul food into the cities, people starve and the potatoes rot in warehouses."

"And that's only if the farmers can get the fuel for the harvesting equipment. If they can't run the harvester, the potatoes are going to rot in the ground." The second guy shook his head. "Things over there are looking pretty grim."

"It's all about supply and distribution, isn't it?" Sam said thoughtfully. "On the way down here last night, I noticed that most of the abandoned cars along I-25 are gone."

"Yeah, huge junk yard full of them just north of town off Highway 85. It's like a whole new industry. Pulling tires and storing them out of the sunlight, stripping wire, taking cars apart for the chips, the wire, even the foam in the seats. Couple of guys are turning one of the big warehouses off I-80 into an aluminum foundry. Since Amazon's no longer in need of the space, they figure they can melt down car engines to cast stuff we need."

"Hey, we gotta go," the first said. "Nice talking to you."

Breeze watched them leave a twenty dollar bill and head for the door.

Sam had a thoughtful look on his face. "Whole new industry. Wonder what they can use to make toilet paper?"

# THE LAST PLACE I THOUGHT I'D BE

*When we got back to Cheyenne that first night, I figured they'd drop the governor off, and someone would find me a ride back to The Plains Hotel, or wherever the state was putting people up.*

*When they passed through the high iron gates and pulled up at the governor's residence on Central Avenue just off the interstate, Agar got out, looked at where I was sitting in the back. "My protective detail stays here."*

*I squinted my eyes, then hobbled my way through the governor's official residence.*

*Not what you'd think for a governor's mansion. I mean, nice grounds and all, but for the noise of the traffic. From the outside—with its moss rock and redwood siding—it looked more like a church, or maybe a funeral home. And, yeah, it was nice. Filled with artwork, photos of previous, mostly dead governors and their first ladies. The furniture looked expensive, and décor was swanky. But for my money, if I was governor, I'd spend my time in the office at the Capitol where the ambiance bespoke pomp and circumstance.*

*Agar's chief of staff—a guy named Dudley Gardner—put me in what was obviously a makeshift bedroom in what had been a storeroom in the rear of the sprawling eight-thousand-square-foot structure. The good news was that it was close to one of the bathrooms and the kitchen.*

*As I lay in that uncomfortable cot and pulled a scratchy blanket up to my chin, I had no real clue what I was doing there...let alone what, exactly, the governor expected from me.*

— Excerpt from Lauren Davis' *Journal.*

# CHAPTER THIRTEEN

THE WYOMING CAPITOL building was just as grand as the first time Sam had walked into the rotunda. Maybe it wasn't as spectacular as, say, Grand Central Station had been with its celestial ceiling, but the place still impressed.

Breeze, however, seemed to take it for granted. She hadn't even blinked when they'd been asked to check their weapons with the guard at the door. Just handed over her M4 and boogie bag. Sam, to his surprise, found himself reluctant to surrender the battered Marlin.

"You'll get it back," the uniformed Militia sergeant had insisted after checking a list of names. "Trust me, you're one of the governor's agents. They'd have my ass if anything happened to your equipment."

"So, like, when did the New York liberal get so possessive of a firearm?" Breeze asked as they headed for the stairs to the second story.

"Don't have a clue," Sam told her. As he started up the steps, his hip ached. Glancing down he was suddenly aware of how shoddy his hiking boots looked on the polished steps. Hell, he was dressed in his field clothes. The only garments he had. The first time, he hadn't thought twice about it. Since then, his Levi's, best flannel shirt, boots, and felt hat had taken a lot of hard wear.

Then, as her words sank in, he stiffened, pointing a stiff finger Breeze's way. "Hey! Wait a minute. I was raised a Republican, you know."

She spared him a sidelong smirk. "A New York Republican, huh? Gotta tell you, in Wyoming terms, you'd be considered so liberal even the Democrats would have thrown you out."

"What the hell do you know of my politics?" He waved it away. "And what about you?"

A flicker of smile died on her lips. "It's like this: I went to college. In Denver. Voted for the most progressively liberal candidates that I could. Showing my credentials, don't you see? Proving I'd left the ranch, Wyoming, and all that hick redneck rural ignorance so far behind you couldn't see it through the dust of my passage."

"No shit?"

"No shit." Again she gave him that evaluative Tappan stare. "'Course it was a way to convince myself that I was evolved, smart, part of the intellectual elite who could be outraged over social injustice, inopportunity, and every kind of inequality under the sun. And the whole time— Woke hypocrite that I was—I was studying to be an investment banker. Ultimate goal? A cushy job on Wall Street and an apartment on the Upper West Side."

She stopped on the step, cocked her head, lips curled as she met his eyes. "Guess I was the worst kind when it comes to hypocrisy. The kind who lied to herself."

"We all lie to ourselves," Sam told her, wincing at the pain in his pelvis. Didn't seem as bad this morning. Must have been the Coffree.

They gave their names to the guard at the top of the stairs who pointed them toward Agar's office. Not the meeting room Sam had been to previously. He felt the flutters in his stomach as he gimped his way over the tessellated black-and-white tile floor past the paintings on the wainscoted walls. At the door, an armed guard told them, "Go right on in."

The secretary rose as they entered, and Sam took in the expensive leather chairs and sofa, the plush carpeting, and the paintings.

"Can I get you something?" the man behind the desk asked.

"Coffee?" Breeze asked.

"Sure. One moment." The man lifted the phone on the elaborate desk, asking, "Two cups of coffee, please."

"You're kidding," Sam whispered. "You have coffee?"

"Won't last forever," the secretary told him, replacing the handset. "But while it does, we're sitting on a limited supply." He indicated the arched doorway. "Go on in, the governor is expecting you."

Sam followed Breeze through the arched doorway and into the governor's palatial office that dominated the east end of the Capitol's second floor.

The spacious room was walled on the east by large windows overlooking the Capitol grounds. Beyond them, high government buildings could be seen on the other side of Warren Avenue. In the distance, the irregular green domes of deciduous trees made humps on the horizon. A really big desk made of dark-stained wood, complete with filigree and carvings on the side, plush chairs, another leather sofa, antique-looking walls, and thick red carpet gave the place a sense of splendor. As did the fancy western art hanging from the walls. A large bronze of a magnificent bison stood on a pedestal on the north wall. On the south was a companion piece, a majestic elk, head back, mouth open as it bugled.

Sam recognized Captain Ragnovich, the Guard officer who'd once dismissed Breeze as a Line rider. He stood from the winged-back chair, smiling, benevolent gaze fixed on Breeze.

Breeze, showing no restraint, charged up to the man, wrapping arms around his rumpled uniform in a bear hug.

"Hey, commanding officers are saluted," Ragnovich half-growled.

Breeze gave one last squeeze and surrendered to Ragnovich's efforts to untangle her. "Sorry, Captain, but I'm a civilian. I'm not even in the Wyoming Militia, so military protocol can go to hell."

Sam watched uneasily, stopping short on the thick carpet.

"Still a pain in my ass, aren't you, Ms. Tappan?" But Ragnovich's smile had grown.

"Always have been, always will be, sir."

"That will remain to be seen," Governor Agar said as he rose from the oversized chair behind the great desk. Stepping around the thing, he shook Breeze's hand, saying, "Good to have you here. Everything all right with the accommodations?"

"Just fine, Governor."

"Lauren Davis sends her good wishes. She's at the hospital for a checkup. Took an imperial order to make her do it, but that's the joy of being governor. I said I'd give you her regards."

Then he walked over to Sam, who'd been shifting from foot to foot —and not all of it in an effort to find a posture that didn't hurt. Shaking his hand, Agar said, "Good to see you, too, Mr. Delgado. Harry, come meet this young man. Sam Delgado, this is Captain Harry Ragnovich."

"Glad to meet you, sir."

"My pleasure, Mr. Delgado." The Captain had a firm shake, was giving Sam a piercing appraisal.

Agar told the captain, "But for Breeze Tappan and Mr. Delgado here, things might have turned out a whole lot uglier in the Bighorn Basin than they did, Harry."

"And don't forget Amber Sagan, sir," Sam told him. "She bought us the way in at Clark Ranch. Paid with her life."

"No one is going to be forgotten when this is all over," Agar called over his shoulder as he marched back to his desk. "All of you, sit down. We've got a lot to discuss."

Sam and Breeze, shooting each other "who knows?" glances, settled themselves on the elegantly upholstered leather couch to the side.

Ragnovich dropped back into the big wing-back easy chair where it sat at an angle to the governor's desk.

Agar shuffled some of the papers on his desk, rearranged his pen set, and shoved a stainless steel revolver off to one side. Looked like the .357 Corretta Kapital had used in her attempt to kill him. Seeing Sam's startled look, Agar added, "It's an uncertain world these days, Mr. Delgado. As we have observed so recently." A flicker of smile. "Since its previous owner has no further use of it, I'll keep it for sentimental reasons."

"Sam, please, sir. Mr. Delgado was my father."

Both Agar and Ragnovich gave curt nods. "Sure. Sam it is."

At that moment, a young man Sam's age, wearing a three-piece suit, entered with a silver tray. Offering it to Sam and Breeze, it held two cups of steaming black coffee. As Sam took his, he thought the smell was heavenly.

"Thank you, Ryan," Agar called as the guy left.

A frown marred the governor's brow as he leaned forward, braced his elbows. "We have no shortage of daunting challenges. At the same time, we have a huge number of opportunities. We're three months into this thing. We've contained the threat of being overrun from the Front Range, and our scouting flights in that direction, quite honestly, are grim. Lots of burned-out downtown areas, what appear to be roving gangs. Entire neighborhoods with no signs of life. A wealth of vehicles abandoned on the roads. And the bodies left lie...well, call it medieval."

"Raiding is down," Ragnovich said. "They don't test The Line like they used to, but when they do, it's with a massed assault. Generally, we know about the raid in advance from our drone reconnaissance. If we can't break them up south of The Line, we're able to reinforce before they hit." He glanced around. "But that ability is short term. We can only recharge the drone batteries so many times before they're worn out."

Agar added. "Yes, well, batteries are whole different problem. From hearing aids, to night vision goggles, to lawn tractors, to automobiles. You name it. The lifetime for anything electrical is limited to its battery. Now, we can make lead-acid batteries for things like tractors and cars, but they're crude. When it comes to silicone and lithium? We're screwed. Same thing if something fries a chip. Maybe we can do like the Russians did in Ukraine? Cannibalize chips from washing machines and repurpose them? But that's way out of my expertise."

"That's all well and good," Breeze said cautiously, "but neither Sam nor I can rewire chips. So, why are we here?"

Ragnovich gave them both a penetrating look. "We need you for a mission."

Breeze gave the governor a wary lift of her eyebrow. "What sort of mission?"

"What do you know about insulin?" Agar asked, steepling his fingers and staring at the ornate ceiling above his desk.

"Not much," Breeze told him. "It keeps diabetics alive. Allows glucose to enter cells and regulates blood sugars. Made by the pancreas, right?"

"Or in a lab from bioengineered bacteria or yeasts," Sam added. "I had an aunt with severe diabetes. I assume that we don't have a lab in Wyoming that can produce the stuff?"

"Nope." Agar told him. "Here's our problem, we've got people dying all over the state. Granted, the disease can be partially managed by diet, but right at forty thousand people in Wyoming have diabetes. Another thirty thousand are diagnosed with what's called prediabetes. Now, I'm told that with the elimination of tobacco, candy bars, and fast food restaurants, and with diets going back to basics, it will be helpful. But insulin supplies, though rationed, are exhausted. A big chunk of Wyoming's population is dying. For the most severe, there's nothing we can do. For the rest of the population, there's a chance."

"You have a lab hidden away somewhere that can make insulin?" Breeze asked. "And if you do, what do you need Sam or me for?"

"I do have a lab. And the people who can run it. My problem is that it's just north of Boulder, Colorado, on the road to Lyons. I can save the lives of maybe thirty to forty thousand people in Wyoming. To do that, I need the equipment and those technicians extracted to Laramie." Agar gave her a tight smile. "And that's where you and Sam, here, come into play."

"Um," Sam told him, aware of Ragnovich's now-grim expression. "How do you expect the two of us to get into Colorado, load up a lab, and get back? Sounds like you'd need an armored column."

"Correct," Agar told him. "The vehicles are easy. I can cut an order for whatever we need. I want volunteers to drive them."

"And that's where the two of you come in," Ragnovich added. "Especially you, Breeze. You're a local hero. Everyone on The Line knows you. Knows what you and Sam, here, did up in Bighorn Basin. How you freed those girls. If you two lead this raid and recovery, you'll have the best of the Wyoming National Guard volunteering to go with you."

Sam watched Breeze swallow down the last of her coffee. She stood, pacing uneasily over to stare at a painting of the Tetons at sunrise. "I barely got out of Colorado last time. I saw what it was like."

"How do you know this lab even exists?" Sam asked. "It's probably stripped clean like everything else down there. And if it made insulin? It would have been number one on someone's list for looting."

"Same with the people who ran it," Breeze added. "You know what it was like south of The Line? What it's still like? Doesn't matter who you are, the mobs will kill a physician just as soon as they'll kill a ditch digger…assuming they can get anything from him."

Agar nodded sagaciously. "I agree. But they contacted us. Seven people, holed up in the lab. They saw one of the Guard C-130s fly over on a reconnaissance and remembered the planes were based in Cheyenne. They assumed that if we were still flying, maybe we'd avoided the chaos. The story is that they built a radio, took them a while to find our Militia frequency. Then it took a while longer to work up the chain of command to get to Colonel Steadman."

"I've talked to them," Ragnovich said. "There's seven of them. PhDs out of the University of Colorado who started their own genetics and bio research lab. The place is called Boulder Mountain Biotek. They claim they can make insulin from bovine and pig pancreas glands until they can genetically create the bacteria to do the same thing. All we have to do is go down, load up their equipment, and get them safely to Wyoming."

"It's not like we don't have a supply of beef, even if we're a little short on pigs," Agar added. "And right now, all those pancreas glands are being ground up and made into sausage. Better if we could be turning them into insulin."

Ragnovich gave Breeze a knowing squint. "We can save a lot of lives."

"And we don't already have this kind of equipment in Wyoming?" Sam asked, reading the tension that built in Breeze's body.

"Nope," Agar told him. "Granted, the labs at the University of Wyoming, like in the chemistry department, can process just about anything, but only in limited quantities. Dr. Avery assures us that if we can get him the pancreas glands, he can make all the insulin we need." A beat. "And that's just for starters. He says they can produce thyroid pills, adrenaline, heparin, estrogens, and the like."

"Wait a minute," Breeze interjected. "If the entire electrical grid is down on the Front Range, how are they talking to us?"

"They have a backup generator. Runs on a propane tank. They say they use it sparingly to keep the refrigeration running, and only when they know it can't be heard from a distance." Ragnovich gestured with his hands. "They tell us that they're in a fenced compound. That they made it look like it already had been looted. Defaced their sign. Broke out some windows. Done everything they can to discourage interest in what might be inside. Just kept waiting for things to blow over."

Agar broke in, saying, "Which, of course, we all know never did. Good thing they contacted us. But according to their broadcast last night, the looters have taken on a new interest. Tore down their gate." He smiled tightly. "They're almost out of propane for the generator and refrigeration. We may not have much time."

"And all we have to do is drive down to Boulder, load all of this equipment into trucks, and drive it back across the border?" Breeze asked. "Why does that sound way too simple?"

"Because it is," Ragnovich told her. "Look, talking to Dr. Avery, it's going to take a twenty-six-foot box truck to haul all of their equipment and supplies. Chemicals and the like. That means we have to get your team down to their lab between Lyons and Boulder, hold the place while we load the truck, and get it back across The Line. And between here and there, who knows what we'll encounter? Armed bands? Definitely. Road blocks? Stalled and looted vehicles? Ambushes? Who knows?"

"What about fuel?" Sam asked.

"Got to carry it," Ragnovich said. "Enough to get down and back. Same thing with rations."

"You thinking of running right down I-25 to the exit that leads over to Lyons?" Breeze asked. "Then heading west?"

Ragnovich shook his head in a sad negative. "From our overflights and reconnaissance, it would turn into a debacle. Too many vehicles to move out of the way. Not to mention the roadblocks that locals set up back in the early days. I mean, we could do it. Put a couple of D 9 Cats out front and bulldoze our way, but it would take a couple of weeks. And the one thing we don't have is time. I want to roll this thing as soon as we can assemble the convoy."

"So, how are you thinking of getting there?" Sam asked. "Flying on the backs of eagles?"

"Through the mountains," Ragnovich said as he rose and retrieved a map from the corner of Agar's desk. "From the checkpoint at The Forks on US 287, you travel to Colorado Highway 14, then up Poudre Canyon, over Stove Prairie Road to Masonville, then to the Big Thompson. Around Carter Lake then down the hogbacks to the Lyons junction. From there it's only a couple of miles south on Highway 36 to the lab." He paused. "Avoids Fort Collins, Loveland, and skirts the northern edge of Longmont."

Breeze leaned over Sam's shoulder as Ragnovich ran his finger along the route.

"What if we hit trouble?" Breeze asked. "I mean, all it takes is a jackknifed semi and we're stopped."

"We're leading with two snowplows," Agar told her. "They can push most of the stalled cars out of the way as well as your standard every-day barricade of tires and junk. For something like a semi-truck?" He shrugged, looking hopefully at Ragnovich.

"Wyoming National Guard has a M1089 wrecker. I can have it down from Guernsey by morning." Ragnovich squinted an eye. "Given that we can't just requisition another, it's kind of a valuable piece of equipment."

"So's a lab full of biochemists with all of their equipment," Governor

Agar replied. "And I dare say, your wrecker is more survivable than my two snowplows."

Sam watched Breeze counting on her fingers. "So we've got two snowplows, a big wrecker, and a twenty-six-foot freight truck. What else?"

"I'd say a JLTV with a turret-mount chain gun." Ragnovich glanced at Agar. "I think this mission is important enough to warrant the firepower."

"Thought we were running out of ammunition for the chain guns." Agar lifted a questioning eyebrow.

"We are," Ragnovich told him. "At the rate diabetics are suffering and dying off in this state, just how do you define the cost/benefit scale? Ever watched a person die from diabetes, Pete? Watch them go sallow, eyes hollow, as their organs shut down?"

Agar gave him the eye. "Yeah. I keep track of what's happening in the hospitals. You'd be surprised what you can learn about your people by taking the occasional walk through." A pause. "All right, you can have the chain gun and a couple hundred rounds."

"Thirty-five rounds," Ragnovich told him. "I won't risk more."

"What's a chain gun?" Sam asked from the corner of his mouth. He knew what a JLTV was: Joint Light Tactical Vehicle. Lauren had blown two of them up. They were the armored trucks the military used. But he was having trouble picturing a gun that shot chains.

Breeze gave him that knowing look. Like this was serious business. "It's an M242 twenty-five millimeter autocannon. They call it a Bushmaster."

"And a couple of Humvees for scouting," Ragnovich added.

"Better throw in an MTV to carry all the supplies." Agar sounded firm.

"MTV?" Sam asked, starting to become bewildered.

"Five-ton all-terrain truck," Breeze told him. "Medium Tactical Vehicle. One of those ugly cab-over jobs."

"Why don't they throw in some tanks?" Sam whispered under his breath.

To his chagrin, Agar heard him. "Because we don't *have* tanks. And I'm not taking a chance on losing one of our three Bradleys."

Sam figured he didn't need to ask what a Bradley was. He'd never been much on Army stuff. As if The Yucateca's busy kitchen would have ever allowed him the opportunity.

Agar continued to grouse, "It's bad enough we're putting a chain gun at risk, but if one of the gangs somehow manages to take it, they'll play hell finding ammo once they shoot up the few rounds we're sending."

"Pete," Ragnovich gave him a hard look. "Stop worrying. Given the strength we're sending south, it would take a couple of companies to stop it, let alone capture any of its assets. And our people will be fully contained."

Agar just grunted. "Harry, if this wasn't so important..."

"We do this," Ragnovich reminded, "and we're going to save the lives of tens of thousands of people. And for God's sake, think of the trade value it gives us. Especially with the Dakotas and Montana."

"Yeah, I know." Agar exhaled wearily. "Ms. Tappan, Mr. Delgado? Got anything to add?"

Breeze was looking thoughtful, her arms crossed as she stared down at Ragnovich's map. "Who's in charge?"

Ragnovich gave Breeze a slight smile. "You remember Susan Daniels?"

"Yeah," Breeze told him. "She was in charge of a line of OPs in the Bravo section. Was there the day we fought off the raiders trying to disrupt the cattle drive at Bravo Alpha. Called in one of the Guard helicopters to finish the job Lauren and I started."

Ragnovich sounded firm when he said, "I'm putting her in charge."

Breeze couldn't hide her distaste as she asked, "What about Caiden Howard?"

Sam didn't miss Ragnovich's hardening gaze. "He's moved up the chain to my second in command. He's running The Line these days. You got a problem with Susan?"

"Tough lady," Breeze said. Then: "We don't always see eye-to-eye, but she'll get the job done. No matter what it costs."

"A tough mission deserves a tough commander," Agar told her. "So I back the Captain's decision. He knows who his best people are." And with that politician's smile, Agar added, "Which is why you and Mr. Delgado are being assigned to this mission."

Sam didn't miss the emphasis on "Mr. Delgado." Like, this wasn't a *suggestion*.

Ragnovich turned back to the governor. "I'll go cut the orders. Should have everything ready by tonight. If you can have your people get in contact, tell Dr. Avery we're on our way. With any luck, we should have him, his people, and that lab back and on this side of the border before the end of the week."

Agar made a dismissive gesture with his hand. "So, there it is. No eagles, Mr. Delgado, just a rescue column."

Sam nodded. "Guess the eagles wouldn't have had a chance."

Harry Ragnovich was staring at the map. "The way I see it, the American eagle fell on Dissolution Day."

Agar summarily said, "You all have things to do. Have a good day."

Sam could see the worry in Breeze's eyes. He stood and winced at the pain in his ribs as he caught just the wrong angle. To his chagrin, he realized he had been so distracted, he hadn't even tasted the coffee.

# FITTED OUT

*That first day in Cheyenne, Agar insisted I be checked from stem to stern at the hospital. I got two-thumbs up for progress and was told I was ahead of the curve when it came to healing. Even the place where they'd taken a big chunk of shrapnel out of my lung and wired my ribs back together was knitting. Best news came from the orthopedic surgeon who said my hip was knit well enough with something he called callus that as long as I didn't overdo it, I could ditch the crutches. I was supposed to pay attention to the "not overdoing it" part.*

*I figured I'd be given an ACU like the rest of the security detail wore, but Spencer Stenholm, the detail leader, told me, "Like in the Hot Springs auditorium, the governor wants you unobtrusive. You got any decent casual clothes?"*

*I gave him my you-gotta-be-kidding look, and said, "I take it you mean what I'm wearing isn't decent?"*

*His gaze went over my best faded blue jeans and grease-stained tee-shirt. "We'll find you something more presentable."*

*When I hobbled my way into Governor Agar's office that afternoon, it was a whole different Lauren Davis. White turtleneck, black Levi's, and a denim jacket to cover my holstered .45. Agar had looked up from his desk. Seemed to do a double take and gave me a nod. "Perfect," he said.*

*"So, what do you want me to do?"*

*He stood, walked over, and met my flinty gaze.*

*"For now, just watch and learn."*

— Excerpt from Lauren Davis' *Journal.*

# CHAPTER FOURTEEN

IN THE BACK corner of the Hilton Bar, Breeze toyed with her glass of stout. She sat in her familiar booth; the location was as private as the place offered. Which wasn't much. She was aware of people looking sidelong at her, of the whispered conversations. "That's her! Breeze Tappan!"

Sam, seated across from her, was doing a pretty good job of ignoring it all; though occasionally someone would really give him the eye, as if they'd ID'd him, too.

The waitress, Jen, set his glass of Wyo Gold Ale in front of him and hurried off.

"So, what's the word on Susan Daniels?" Sam asked as he raised the glass and drank.

Breeze pursed her lips as she considered her words. "You know the old saying, 'Bull in a China shop?' I guess that sums up Susan Daniels. I mean, there's no stop in the woman. She just charges headlong through whatever lies in her path."

Sam shrugged acceptance. "Well, I guess if we're riding through Colorado to the rescue of a bunch of scientists who can save tens of thousands of people, that might not be such a bad thing."

Breeze ran fingers along the sides of her glass. "Maybe not. Could just be me. Well, and Lauren. And the rest of the Line riders. It was always like Daniels dissed us. Sort of like we weren't good enough to be real soldiers. Just menials. Like bus boys in a fancy restaurant. Sort of ignored nonentities who ran errands."

"I *was* a bus boy." Sam's voice carried his irritation.

"Sorry. Wrong choice of...no. Right choice of words. Like you just now. That's how we all felt. Didn't matter that we were risking our lives with every ride. And sometimes worse. Like that day at OP Bravo Alpha. A bunch of Colorado ranchers were trying to get their cattle to safety north of The Line. Lauren and I stumbled onto the raiders, shot 'em up before they could stampede the cattle. Daniels was almost impossible to deal with after that. Like she resented that we broke up their attack." She paused. "Maybe that's it. Resentment. For the fact that it added to our reputations as"—she made air quotes with her fingers—"'Heroes of The Line.'"

Sam glanced uneasily around the bar, aware of the curious gazes. "Yeah, well, just now I overheard a couple of WNG guys in the men's room. Ragnovich is pushing his recruitment campaign for what they're calling Operation Fallen Eagle. You get top billing." He grinned. "I'm hardly mentioned. Just the casual note that I was the guy who killed Edgewater."

She smiled at that. "Yeah, some reputation, huh?"

His lips quivered as he looked down at his beer. "That day in the courthouse when I shot him? I was empty, Breeze. Pulling the trigger had the same emotional impact as cleaning the toilets back at The Yucateca. Just an unpleasant job that had to be done."

"The guy was a monster."

Sam nodded in slow agreement. "It was the weirdest feeling. Like I wasn't me. I was some kind of zombie. Moving on autopilot, you know? Not even thinking."

"What about now?" She sipped her stout. Still weak on the IBUs, but that was supposed to be changing. She crossed her fingers, wishing the hop farm in Worland all the best. "You're not going to, like, do something stupid are you? Maybe take the first opportunity to get yourself killed?"

"Not planning on it."

"You did walk right up to Corwin Cole's rifle and told him to shoot you. And, Sam, he was more than ready to do it."

"I was trying to stop a war. We can't afford to be the Hatfields and McCoys."

"Maybe, with us out of the Basin, Old Bill can conjure up some magical fix." She frowned at her stout. "We've got enough on our plates with Fallen Eagle. Tomorrow morning a car picks us up and drives us to the assembly point at The Forks. From there? Who knows?"

Sam gave her an evaluative squint. "You know more about this than I do. What's going to happen? I mean, we've got everything we need, right? It's not like there's an enemy army down there. Just what's left of a bunch of traumatized people. And we're taking the back roads. Not going through the cities."

She took a deep breath. "Shouldn't be a problem. Sounds like Agar and Ragnovich have all the bases covered. And no, a bunch of disorganized survivors shouldn't be too much of a threat. And even if they have something like one of these welded up dump trucks, the chain gun should take it down."

"As long as we don't run out of ammunition," Sam told her.

She nodded. Wondered why the uneasy feeling was growing inside her. She turned, looking over her shoulder. Had that eerie feeling that Water Ghost Woman was there, could feel her dark and glassy eyes, hear the Spirit woman's sibilant whisper.

"What?" Sam asked, cuing on her disquiet.

"You been seeing *Nynymbi*?"

Sam shook his head. "Not since leaving the ranch. And, if you ask me, that's just as well."

Breeze lifted her beer, chugged it down. Slamming the glass to the table with a thunk, she said, "Well, at least there's that."

"Maybe I'm not seeing him because I'm smart enough to know that on this trip down south it doesn't matter that we've got guns, trucks, and armor. We're going to see things, Breeze. Do things. And anything we find down there? It's going to be the stuff of nightmares."

# WHO'S SHE?

The trona delegation was ushered into Agar's office at three that afternoon. What's trona? It's a salt called sodium carbonate; it forms in lake bottoms. Southwestern Wyoming was a huge lake for millions of years and has the largest trona deposits in the world. Trona is used in making glass, fertilizer, baking soda, cosmetics, paper, textiles, tooth-paste, you name it. If you have ever eaten a slice of bread in the US, you've eaten Wyoming trona.

So, for an hour, I sat perched in the background, essentially ignored while Governor Agar and the mining association talked about how to build trade relations with the Dakotas, Montana, and Idaho. With national markets gone, how long could they maintain production, keep their mining equipment running, keep their people fed, and transport their product?

Speculative glances were cast my way while Agar put together a plan to cement relations with the surrounding states that would promote Wyoming trona exports.

After the meeting, as they were all shaking hands, one of the men leaned close to Agar, inclined his head in my direction. "Who's she?"

"That's Lauren Davis. Yeah, that Lauren Davis." Agar gave him a grim smile. "I know that when it comes time to shoot someone, she won't hesitate."

A queasy feeling slipped around my stomach. So, that's why I'm really here.

Not to watch. To kill.

— Excerpt from Lauren Davis' Journal.

# CHAPTER FIFTEEN

SAM AND BREEZE were the sole passengers that morning. They were riding in the row seat behind the driver of a Ram van provided courtesy of the State of Wyoming. The fact that Governor Agar had authorized a van demonstrated how important their mission was. It didn't matter that Cheyenne had its own refinery, gasoline was still carefully rationed. Not to mention that what had once been acceptable wear and tear on vehicles was now a major concern. Fuel filters? Air cleaner elements? Transmission fluid? Radiator hoses? Spark plugs? After the Collapse, replacements weren't as close as the nearest NAPA auto parts store. Tires had to be sourced from abandoned vehicles. As did brake pads and other standard parts that were once delivered by UPS.

It made travel a great deal more precious.

Sam was dwelling on that as the van pulled away from the Hilton Hotel's covered entrance.

Breeze's boogie bag and Sam's backpack were in the rear, but for this trip, both had their rifles at hand. The driver, Martha Jean, a woman in her mid-twenties, sported a Wyoming Militia patch on her right shoulder and had a black semiautomatic pistol strapped to her hip. She'd introduced herself, apparently awed just at being in the presence of the legendary Breeze Tappan. She'd barely given Sam a second look.

Martha Jean had driven them out Lincoln Way to I-80, and then west, past the checkpoints along the interstate. These days they were monitored by Wyoming Militia.

Along the way, Breeze had pointed out spots, saying, "Yeah, I was shot at just off that exit." Or, "Big firefight there. A bunch of refugees snuck across the border, strung a chain across the highway. When the first of the three Militia trucks slowed, the raiders charged out. Didn't expect a crew-cab pickup full of armed fighters."

"My brother was in on that," Martha Jean called over her shoulder. "He was in the second truck. By the time the gunplay was over, two of our guys were dead, four were wounded, and all eighteen of the raiders were shot to maggot meat."

The way she said it set Sam's teeth on edge. Like the woman didn't get it that these had been fellow Americans. And what did it mean that the term "fellow Americans" had lost all value? Refugees had become raiders. Raiders had become targets. Targets would become corpses.

To get his mind off it, Sam turned his attention to the country as they climbed; grasslands gave way to rolling ridges, not thickly forested, but sporting patches of pines. Occasional groves of fir grew on the northern slopes; outcrops of weathered gray and tan rock left bare patches where the soil had weathered away. Looked like exfoliated granite covered with thin soils, brush, and bunch grasses.

Then came the drop down to the Laramie Basin and more checkpoints that the van—with its state markings—was waved through. He didn't get a good look at Laramie; the highway looped around the southern outskirts. Was only able to see the rooftops where clumps of trees didn't obscure them. Martha Jean turned them south on US 287. Past the old fort and the cement plants. As they crossed the red Triassic soils and passed the checkpoint at Tie Siding, they began to encounter the occasional burned-out vehicle. The few ranches he caught glimpses of were either charred skeletons or appeared dismal and looted with their broken windows and gaping doors.

"Looks pretty violent down here." Sam fingered the Marlin's stock where it was propped beside him.

"Not so bad now," Martha Jean told him. "I mean, no one takes travel lightly, and there are still the occasional raiders who get through. But between the Guard manning the OPs and the roving Militia patrols we've got things settled down."

Cresting the heights, the highway crossed a wind-blown ridge sprinkled with stunted limber pines. Breeze pointed to the burned buildings beside the road. "That used to be the Stateline Bar."

He wouldn't have known when they crossed the border had Breeze not indicated a splintered brown sign, bullet-riddled and charred: "Welcome to Colorado."

So, this was Colorado? He took in the low scrubby hills rising to the cloud-topped high slopes off to the west. From the time he'd been a boy, Sam had always wanted to come here. He'd seen the pictures of the Colorado Rockies—high, snow-capped above dark evergreen-timbered slopes. Thinking of it had been to conjure fantasies of ski areas, people on horseback, driving Jeeps on precipitous and rocky roads that clung to sheer slopes. He'd even thought of trying to get into the University of Colorado's PhD program, but he would never have managed the out-of-state tuition and fees. Besides, his folks would have gone ballistic.

*"What? Colorado? You got obligations here, boy! We got a restaurant to run!"* His father's voice echoed in his memory.

And what if he'd managed to find the loans, grants, and scholarships? The people he loved would be just as dead, and he'd have been trapped in the horror that had become the Front Range when the Collapse came.

At the next collection of charred and tumbled remains, Breeze told him, "That's Virginia Dale. Used to be a stage stop way back when."

The ribbon of asphalt wound down into a valley bounded by granite outcrops topped with ponderosa pines; the understory consisted of grass with currant bushes and slopes of dark green brush called mountain mahogany. Off to the west rose the mountains, the peaks and high country hidden in the ever-present gray haze that seemed to suck life out of the very air. Beneath the glowering haze, the slopes looked like a patchwork, sometimes thickly forested, almost a dark green mat. In other places the mountains had bald patches of gray that looked furry in the distance.

"Old forest fires," Breeze told him. "If there's any benefit from all this, it's that global warming is finished. Maybe the forests will have a chance."

Sam studied the far off high country through brooding eyes. "Carbon dioxide will spike with all the burning. This constant cloud cover is cutting solar radiation to the surface. The particulate is increasing rainfall, which will clear the air and fertilize the soil. Most mammals and birds will be dead in the irradiated areas. When I took Dr. Chang's course in cultural economics, eighty-six percent of the US population lived in cities. Urban, right? All of those areas depended on trucking and trains to supply them with food and consumables. As soon as the trucks stopped running, hunger would have set in in a matter of days. Maybe a week at most."

Breeze turned her attention to a burned-out school bus that lay on its side in the borrow ditch. "I was there. In Denver that was happening as early as Saturday night. I mean, not only couldn't the delivery trucks buy fuel, but the roads were clogged by people running out of gas and abandoning their cars. That led to riots and looting, and who'd risk sending a truck in after that?"

Sam winced as they passed a pile of corpses that lay just across the right-of-way fence. Crows, a couple of eagles, and a flock of squawking magpies fluttered over the gruesome mound. Might have been eight or nine people, their bodies swollen and ravaged, their clothes, once colorful, now stained and disheveled by the carrion eaters.

The shallow valley they'd entered was bounded by steep hogback formations capped by resistant tan sandstones that loomed to either side. From his geology class, he recognized the feature as an east-dipping anticline. A cluster of high-dollar houses had been built on the gentler western slope, the higher ones perched on exposed bedrock. Each looked desolate. Doors gaping, occasional windows broken, the yards gone to weeds. Items of clothing, pieces of furniture, dishes, and storage boxes could be seen where looters had thrown them out as worthless.

This had been pretty country once. He looked up at the sheer sandstone that topped the ridge to the east. Looked like a wall. Blocks of it had broken off to tumble down the steep slope and come to rest in the grass and mountain mahogany below.

"Glad you got out of Colorado when you did."

"Barely," she reminded.

"We're all statistical long shots, Breeze." He cracked a macabre smile. "Enough so that we can revel in the misery of survivor's guilt for the rest of our lives."

The checkpoint at The Forks had the appearance of an armed camp. The buildings on the northwestern side of the junction had a rustic quality: the lodge, restaurant, bar, and convenience store looking suitably Western, rural, and quaint. The central two-story building—supposedly once a stage stop—had a historic aura with its broad veranda and upper deck.

To Sam's surprise, a tanker truck was pumping fuel into the tanks that serviced the gas pumps. A string of RVs and camp trailers lined the south side of the Livermore Road. Across from them were four Humvees. A mismatched collection of late-model four-wheel drive pickups with Wyoming Militia signage looked dusty and in need of a wash where they were parked in the lot. Another line of cargo trailers stretched out to the west; some, with their tailgates laid down, were watched by a collection of armed sentries.

Behind the lodge, amid a cluster of dwellings, a series of olive-drab tents had been erected, the whole of it surrounded by a tall fence. Only a handful of people could be seen walking around in the enclosure. At sight of it, Sam's stomach soured. It reminded him of the detention compound Edgewater had set up at Clark Ranch.

Ahead of them, on 287—taking up the right lane—was what had to be the Fallen Eagle convoy. The MTV with a tarped load, the turret-mounted JLTV, the two Humvees, a big cargo truck with the letters NPT on the sides of the box, and an ugly cab-over military wrecker waited. The snowplows, painted Highway Department Yellow, looked out of place where they were parked in the line. Soldiers in National Guard ACUs, as the uniforms were called, lounged by the sides of the vehicles. Seeing the van, they began trickling out as if in anticipation.

Martha Jean pulled up behind the wrecker, shifted to park, and killed the ignition. "End of the line," she called.

Breeze slid the side door open, stepping out. Sam followed, heading around back to open the cargo door. Breeze, her M4 slung, reached for her boogie bag. Sam, his Marlin dangling from one hand, collected his backpack and slung one of the straps over his shoulder.

"Good luck!" Martha Jean called hopefully as Sam and Breeze headed for the convoy.

Emerging from the knot of WNG soldiers came a woman, maybe thirty, wearing a pressed ACU. Her brunette hair was collected in a tight bun behind her cover. She walked in a sure stride, dark eyes fixing first on Breeze and then Sam. From the set of her lips and cocked jaw, she looked full of purpose. Stopping as they approached, she adopted a parade stance, left eyebrow lifted.

"Lieutenant Daniels," Breeze greeted. "Good to see you again."

"You, too, Ms. Tappan." Daniels' tone didn't match her words. She reached a hand out to Sam. "And you must be Mr. Delgado. Lieutenant Susan Daniels, your commanding officer."

Daniels had what Sam would call an aggressive handshake. "My pleasure, uh, Lieutenant. But you can call me Sam."

"And you can call me Lieutenant Daniels, Mr. Delgado. This isn't a social club." She was giving him a hard look, as if in anticipation of some challenge.

"Yes, ma'am," Sam told her, unsure if he should salute since he was just a civilian conscript. From her tone, he wondered if she chewed up roofing nails just to prove she was tough.

"Stow your gear in the MTV," Daniels ordered. "We're gassed and good to go."

As Breeze led the way past, Daniels added softly, "No heroics this time, Ms. Tappan. We're just headed down to get some scientists. A rapid insertion followed by a more rapid exfiltration."

Breeze hesitated, shot Daniels a cocked glance. "Governor Agar said Sam and I are here to be symbols, so we're just along for the ride. Outside of that, it's your show, Lieutenant."

"As long as that's the case, we'll have no issues," Daniels told her. "Dismissed."

*Dismissed?* Sam wondered.

He was hot on Breeze's heels, feeling really uncomfortable as they passed the first soldiers. The weight of the backpack had his ribs in agony, enough so that the stitch of pain in his hip could be partially ignored.

"Hey, Breeze!" one of the privates called. "Good to see you again!"

"Back at ya, Tully," Breeze called back. "Caught any bullets lately?"

"Nope. Just the one." He worked his arm. "See? They fixed me up real good."

"Breeze Tappan," a round-faced and slightly overweight blonde called. "So, they didn't lie!"

"How you been, Shanna?" Breeze responded. "They still using you to draw fire out in Bravo section?"

"Naw." The woman gave Breeze a sly grin. "Turns out that as desperate as the raiders were getting for beautiful women, they were all flocking to whichever OP I was stationed at. Soon as the head shed figured that out, I got transferred to Alpha." A beat. "Tough work being a sex symbol."

Another private, tall, black-haired, reached out to slap palms with Breeze. "Hey, Tappan."

"How you been, Krandal?"

"Haven't been shot at for at least a week, now. When I heard you were leading this, I just knew it would get hairy."

"You never were smart, Kran. Governor Agar just sent me along to be eye candy. And don't let the LT hear you say I'm leading anything but the way to the chow line, or she'll have you tied to the bumper of the first Humvee as a bullet sponge."

Most of them just stared at Sam with curious reserve as he passed. The feeling he got was that they figured he was some sort of aide or assistant to Breeze. Maybe like a messenger boy? It was in the way they were looking him up and down so dismissively.

"Hey, Brylan," Breeze called to another private.

"Back at, ya, Breeze. You brought any chocolate with you?"

"Haven't seen any since that last run out to OP Alpha Lambda. Never should have wasted what I did on the likes of you back then."

And on it went, Breeze calling, "By God, Tortilla Gomez! Good to see you!" And "Shane Goggles! Why are you still here? They won't let you back on the Rez?"

Seemed to Sam that she knew them all. Right up to the whipcord-thin woman wearing a sergeant's chevrons who waited at the rear of the MTV. The name stenciled on the ACU pocket read White Eagle. A knowing smile bent the woman's lips as she greeted, "Been too long, Tappan."

"They made you a sergeant, huh?" Breeze tossed her boogie bag into the high back of the MTV.

When Sam lifted his pack, the pain in his ribs stabbed clear through his chest. He gasped, bit his lip, and struggled to get his backpack over the tailgate. Fortunately, Breeze and the rest missed it. She was too busy giving White Eagle a quick hug.

Sergeant White Eagle turned Breeze loose. "They always give Native people stuff no one else wants. Shitty land. Crummy commodity food. Bad health care. That's why they made me a sergeant."

"Ragnovich is no one's fool, Sally." Breeze slapped the woman on the shoulder. "You held the hardest part of The Line when times were toughest. Finding you here? Makes me think our chances for success just went up by a factor of about five hundred."

"The LT's all right," White Eagle told her. "I heard the rumors about you and her. Don't count her out." And then she turned to Sam, offering a hand. "So, you're the notorious Sam Delgado?"

"Don't know about the notorious part, ma'am." Sam took her hand, finding the grip firm, a gleaming curiosity in the woman's dark eyes.

"Don't call me 'ma'am', Mr. Delgado. Save that shit for the lieutenant. I'm just a non-com. My only job in the army is to actually get things done."

"And I'm just Sam." He gave her a wry smile. "Save Mr. Delgado for my father." Too late. The pinch in his breast reminded him that no one would ever call his dad Mr. Delgado again.

White Eagle seemed to sense it, just gave him a slight nod before turning back to Breeze. "Pick your ride. Got seats in the lead Humvee but you'll have to endure Shane and his sheep jokes. In the JLTV you can squeeze in the back but Packo hasn't had a bath in two weeks. If it were me, I'd go for one of the snowplows or the wrecker."

"Where's the lieutenant?" Breeze asked.

"Second Humvee with Tortilla. Snowplows are best riding, and you can see better. Not to mention hang out the windows if one of you has to fart."

"Then I guess we'll take the snowplow," Breeze told her. "Come on, Sam. Looks like everyone's saddling up."

As Sam made his way along the line of vehicles, he asked, "How long is this supposed to take?"

Breeze looked up at the dull sky. "If we'd don't hit some obstacle and everything goes like clockwork, we could be there by nightfall."

"Yeah, right," Sam told her. "So, how often has that ever happened?"

# THE BUSIEST MAN ALIVE

Governor Agar said goodnight to the Platte County commissioners a little after 10:30 that night. They'd been reporting on the predicted harvest across the agricultural lands in their county. Trying to project how many tons of wheat, barley, corn, beans, and sugar beets would be forthcoming. Of particular concern had been fuel and trucking. Not to mention that Nebraska Panhandle communities were offering storage in the silos in Scott's Bluff, and asking for fuel in return.

Agar had agreed, saying, "I've always felt the panhandle was more Wyoming than Nebraska, anyway. Get me a proposal on paper, and we'll see what we can do."

That's when I shuffled over to the couch. Agar was busy making notes at his desk. Kace Adams stood slightly behind him with one hand on his belted pistol and his hard blue eyes on the door, watching the commissioners file out. My knees were shaking. I figured maybe I could just sit down for a while...

"Sorry to interrupt your beauty rest, but it's late." The voice was accompanied by gentle prodding of my foot.

I blinked, sat up, and yipped at the pain that lanced through me.

Kace stood over me, his blond hair shining in the subdued light. "No more meetings tonight. Get some rest, Lauren. Tomorrow's going to be busy."

Agar headed for the door. I got stiffly to my feet and followed. Kace trailed behind me, closing the door softly behind him.

Out in the front office, Spencer Stenholm was waiting, standing at ease as Agar passed.

*I asked, "You always work this late?"*

*He smiled wearily. "Yeah, for the most part. You still up for the job?"*

*"Not sure," I growled. "The hours were better when raiders were using me for target practice on The Line."*

— Excerpt from Lauren Davis' *Journal.*

# CHAPTER SIXTEEN

"IT'S ONLY a little more than eighty miles by road," Private Tully Harmon told them as he sat behind the wheel of the Wyoming Department of Transportation snowplow. Tall as the Mack GU713 truck's cab was, Sam could see over the two Humvees and the JLTV with its formidable turret-mounted chain gun. The thing looked more like a small tank than a truck. The whole trip felt leisurely; the fifty-mile-an-hour speed was dictated by the big M1089 wrecker at the back of the column.

Each jolt the big truck made sent a spear of it through Sam's chest. He sat, right arm on the window sill, the breeze blowing by. The notion that the snowplow—on its big thirty-two-ton truck chassis—was the smoothest riding? Tully explained that the heavy blade hanging off the front contributed to the rocking-horse motion every time the truck hit a bump. Had to mean that riding in the other trucks must have been like being hammered with bats.

"Not necessarily," Tully told him. "Most of the guys figure they're Guard. Real soldiers drive real army vehicles. They'd be crowding the JLTV, but with the chain gun, it's a whole lot of cramped in the back."

"So why are you driving a snowplow?" Breeze asked where she was propped in the middle of the cab. She was staring out at the piles of stuff people had abandoned on the side of the road. When they weren't allowed past the checkpoint most had just dumped a lot of their more ponderous belongings before heading back south. Looked kind of like what you'd see in a dump, but all strung out, and not as much moldy paper.

Tully had a luminous smile as the Allison shifted gears for the section of curves the Humvees were rounding. "I'm from over at

Torrington. Drove a beet truck. This Mack is just a little bigger, and I get
the fun of pushing a really cool blade. Makes me, like, invincible, you
know? Get in my way, I can just lock the differentials in the twin-screw
axels and shove you out of it."

Sam pulled his hat brim down against the wind and turned his attention to the abandoned houses they were passing. Before the Collapse,
this must have been a lovely area with its scenic sandstone hogbacks, the
patches of the timber, and rich grassy slopes. The houses out here—set
back from the highway and scattered around on five and ten-acre lots—
had the look of money with their log and stone siding, the high prow
roofs and glass-fronted great rooms. Some had been burned, others with
smashed glass, but most had been left with doors gaping; they looked as
if the occupants had just walked away. Weeds were growing in the gravel
drives; the ones that had been paved looked lonely as they snaked up
from grand wrought-iron gates.

The farther south they went, the more derelict vehicles had been
pushed off the road. The occasional human body—or bodies—grew
more numerous. They exhibited various states of decay, the fresher ones
usually accompanied by crows or magpies. Mostly they were recognizable by the clothing—colorful patches of fabric that stood out in the tall
grass. But here and there, someone with a morbid sense of humor had
propped some poor corpse in a pose. The first he saw was seated on a
tractor seat, body and head held upright by wires to the safety roll bar.
Another was wound into the barbed wire right-of-way fence as if
crawling spider-like along the wires. And some held impromptu signs,
most with faded lettering, but a few still legible. One—the corpse
propped beneath a roadside tree, an empty whiskey bottle suspended
upside down over the tilted-back head—read, I'M JUST DYING 4 A
DRINK.

And there were a lot of discarded belongings: colorful coolers;
bundles of clothing; suitcases; ripped sections of blue poly tarp that had
caught in the fence; a crib; broken furniture; tossed out appliances; the
occasional camp trailer; and even an entire motorhome—one of the big
ones built on a bus chassis. It had been driven into the ditch and tilted on
its side, the windows broken out.

"What is all this?" Sam wondered.

"People headed for the border," Breeze told him. "They got stopped
cold at the road block where Agar set up the checkpoint at The Forks.
For a long time they waited, hoping the travel ban would be rescinded.
When it wasn't, a lot of them tried to make it back south, figuring there'd
be another way across the border."

Tully smacked his palm against the steering wheel as the big truck
rolled along, engine humming, tires whining on the pavement. "Lots of
them just left their cars at the checkpoint 'cause they didn't have the fuel.

Headed south on foot. Since that happened, most of the cars they left have been what we call salvaged. Towed up to a field north of Laramie where they'll be stripped for parts. Down here?" He pointed to where a line of cars had been pushed off into the ditch, Subarus, Toyotas, and a Chevy pickup. All looked unharmed. "No one's been this far south yet to pick them up."

"Road's open at least," Sam noted, his nose wrinkling as the snow-plow rolled past a tour bus that had run off the road. The thing was riddled with bullet holes and stank of decomposing humans. Something about that sour-grease smell. Dead human couldn't be mistaken for anything else.

"Thank a Guard recon team," Tully told him. "Used plows to clear away anything blocking easy passage clear down to the Bellview Road on the north side of Fort Collins. The idea was to see what could be salvaged from Colorado State University. Especially like from the veterinary medicine school. You know, drugs and stuff. But it got too hairy."

Tully shrugged. "Might be different now. Maybe enough of them have died off or shot up their ammo so that a team could get in. Or maybe it's too late, and all the good stuff's gone. Same with the hospitals and pharmacies."

Sam caught movement as a human, looking scared, abandoned a derelict Kia he'd been searching. He slipped getting across the barbed wire fence, kicked loose, and limped his way toward the distant trees. All the while, he kept looking back. Bearded, hair matted, his whole manner that of a frightened animal.

"Scavenger," Tully muttered. "We'll see more as we get closer to Fort Collins."

"What about the route we're taking?" Breeze asked. "Up Poudre Canyon into the mountains, then across Stove Prairie? Anyone been up there?"

"Nope." Tully squinted as the lead Humvees veered far left onto the shoulder to avoid the scorched wreck of a Peterbilt that blocked most of the south-bound lane and—given the way it was angled—part of the north as well. The tractor was a hulk. The fire had burned so hot it had melted the front of the fifty-three-foot aluminum cargo trailer. Not only had the tires burned, leaving the rig sitting on the rims, but it had melted into the asphalt; the whole thing looking like it was sunk into a slick-looking puddle.

Rounding the obstacle, it was to discover that the doors were flung wide on the trailer. Boxes, all broken open, lay strewn about. Packages of what looked like white PVC pipe fittings, new electrical boxes, spools of wire, and blue-plastic barrels had been spilled.

"Guess they had no use for that stuff," Breeze muttered. "It's the waste that really sucks. You wonder how many trucks like this are just sitting? Full of parts that we could use. Things that will never be made again."

Sam grunted, fixing on a woman's body. She lay face down at the edge of the highway, spread eagle, the back of her head gaping where something had eaten out her brain. The raw edges of her skull could be seen amidst the dirty spill of her once-blonde hair. She looked so out of place amidst a cascade of white-plastic elbows used in drain pipe gas traps; they flowed out of a ruptured cardboard crate.

Sam rubbed his eyes as they hit a relatively open stretch of road. On the slope above, a fire had left a black patch where it had burned up the side of the hogback.

At the junction with Colorado 14, the Ted's Place convenience store and service station had been gutted. The cluster of abandoned cars, campers, and trucks along with make-do tarped lash-ups in the parking lot hinted that this had been a camp of sorts.

At the sound of the convoy, people appeared: five, then six, all gaping as they emerged from vehicles and RVs. Then they started forward. Scarecrow figures, waving, shouting, almost stumbling in their run. When it was apparent the convoy wasn't stopping, they cursed, waved for the Guard vehicles to stop, to come back. One—a woman— dropped to her knees, head bent.

Sam watched them fade into the distance as the convey turned west, headed for the mouth of the Cache la Poudre Canyon. This was riparian bottom land, thickly forested with cottonwood trees surrounding small grassy meadows. Here, too, had been farms and residences. The few that hadn't been burned looked fortified. Windows boarded from the outsides, heavy vehicles blocking drives and doorways. Coils of barbed wire were strung through yards.

"Out in the country like this, you'd think more of these places would have made it," Sam said as they passed a weed-filled driveway leading back to a small farm among the cottonwoods.

Breeze's expression had a grim set. "There were what? Almost four hundred thousand people in Larimer County? All of them hungry, looking for food. And when the ones trying to get out couldn't get past the checkpoint, they came back this way."

"And then there were the gangs," Tully added. "After the first wave of refugees, they were the ones who banded together. Understood that staying alive was a matter of taking what they wanted from others. Like, law of the jungle, right?"

Breeze nodded. "Oh, yeah, big time. Saw what they became on The Line. You know, like those *Mad Max* and *Road Warrior* movies? And it's not like killing a family for their food was going to bring the law down. It only meant the killers went to sleep that night with full bellies."

"And there's more," Tully said. "Since you went back to the Basin, stories have made their way up from the south. About how when the food had been eaten, all the dogs, horses, and cattle killed and cooked, there was only one meat source left."

"No shit?" Breeze turned knowing eyes on Tully. "Heard that was just down in Denver."

"Well, word is that it's pretty common everywhere south of The Line."

"We talking cannibalism?" Sam asked.

Tully squinted as the convoy slowed for a pile up of cars blocking the road. "Pretty spooky, huh? Like, *The Walking Dead*, but with real people instead of zombies."

"Probably where they got the idea," Breeze said absently, her attention on the Humvee in the lead. A late-model Ford pickup had been left at an angle that took up most of the middle of the road. Behind it another couple of cars blocked the way.

The Humvee turned wide, then nosed into the Ford pickup's left rear. The Humvee used it's bumper to push the F 150 sideways. The lighter truck slid stubbornly off to the side before the Humvee backed, got another angle on the cab, and crushed the bodywork as it shoved the vehicle off into the ditch.

"Aw, man," Tully whined. "Spoil all of my fun."

Sam smiled crookedly as the Humvee, in a similar fashion, disposed of the Cadillac Escalade, the Subaru Outback, and two minivans before leading the way down the now-open road. Sam barely noticed the scavenger-ravaged bodies lying in the grass as they passed. Caught the now-common scent of rotting human flesh. Some of the corpses had been crushed by the cleared vehicles as they had been skidded off the road.

*Funny,* he thought, *a month ago, I would have been horrified.*

When had death become so ordinary? Murdered human beings so meaningless?

"A single death is a tragedy," he whispered under his breath. "A million dead is merely a statistic."

"What was that?" Breeze shot him a sidelong glance with her pensive Tappan eyes.

"A quote from Joseph Stalin to one of his sycophants." Sam pursed his lips as they crossed a bridge, the Poudre River running clear and fast beneath. "Joseph Stalin might have been a monster, but you can't argue with the logic."

"Nope," Breeze agreed. "I guess that beyond a certain point, the human brain just can't comprehend the immensity of it all."

Travel slowed as the Humvees encountered more obstacles, shoving the occasional car from the road, or winding around discarded tubs, piles of clothing, suitcases, and the occasional piece of furniture.

They entered the mouth of the canyon, the walls of stone—brush covered, sporting pines and juniper—rose to either side. Sam, a hand on his hat to keep it from blowing off, leaned out to stare up at the heights rising to either side. Mountains, canyons, and the roaring rivers that ran through them were still a novelty. He could smell the musk of the cotton-woods, the sweetness of the willows, and the scent of the river beyond.

Made him wonder what it must have been like to drive up the Poudre before the Collapse.

They didn't make it more than a couple of miles when, rounding a corner, the road ahead was blocked. Totally. A line of cars, trucks, vans, and motorhomes clogged both lanes. The canyon wall rose close on left side, the river edging the embankment to the right. Chokepoint. There was no going around.

"Son of a bitch," Tully muttered from the side of his mouth as the convoy rolled to a halt a hundred meters back from the last of the stalled vehicles.

*"Get frosty, people,"* Lieutenant Daniels' voice came through the battle com. *"Whatever this is, it's not good."*

# MAKING LYE

*If anything opened my eyes during those first days working with Agar's security detail, it was how much of nothing we had. Think everyday stuff. Like bleach. Sure, we had the raw ingredients to make bleach. All it takes is sodium chloride. Salt, right? Plenty of that available in trade with Utah. From the hydro and coal plants we had more than enough electricity for electrolysis. All anyone could want. But it would take time to build a plant to make chlorine.*

*So what do you do in the meantime to sterilize surfaces, clean clothes, and wash your hands?*

*Make soap. The animal fat part was easy. Wyoming was full of cows. What about the lye? Overnight, hardwood ash became a coveted and hot commodity.*

*Stuff like fabric softener? Paper towels? Ziplocs? Tin foil? Vacuum bags? Paper cups? Plastic trash bags? Maybe they hadn't been necessary in the first place.*

— Excerpt from Lauren Davis' *Journal.*

# CHAPTER SEVENTEEN

"WHAT NOW?" Tully asked as he hunched over the steering wheel.

Breeze wondered the same thing. How far ahead did the log-jam of abandoned vehicles stretch? "Guess we should have brought a bike. I could do a quick scout up along the shoulders, see what's up ahead."

Even as she said it, she could hear the buzzing; a drone rose from the open roof hatch in the lead Humvee.

"Well, that was smart," Tully told her.

"What's happening?" Sam asked, his arm braced out the window. He had been craning his neck, peering past his hat brim at the canyon walls that rose to either side with their patches of gray and weathered bedrock, the scatters of talus, and clinging pines. Currant bushes were flowering, and wildflowers intermingled with the sparse grasses on the steep slopes. Over the idling diesel, the roar of the river could be heard where it spilled over rapids just below the embankment.

"Daniels has sent a drone up the canyon to see how far this goes." Breeze leaned forward, flexing her back muscles in an attempt to ease a growing ache. Snowplow seats in Mack trucks weren't designed by La-Z Boy.

"*What do you see, Brylan?*" Daniels' voice came through the dash speaker. Each of the vehicles was tied into the what they called "the battle com."

"*LT, but for the motorhomes, I think we can push the cars blocking the right lane off the side. Looks like maybe two hundred yards, then there's a barricade where somebody has dropped a couple of trees across the highway. Got some boulders tumbled down from the mountain to keep them in place. Might be an hour's work.*"

A pause. *"Um, LT? Got a fancy motorhome set up on a pullout just back from the barricade. Smoke from a fire. Looks like five guys and three women. Got coolers, piles of canned food, and a shit load of camping stuff and other plunder. And there's some kind of racks over the fires. Wait. Yeah, they've got a whole stack of rifles. Looks like a flanking position on the slope above the barricade. Uh, LT, there's a guy up there on the slope with a scoped rifle giving me the evil eye."*

"What's the road look like on the other side?" Daniels asked.

*"Clear as Christmas, LT."* A beat. *"Wait. They're looking up. They've made the drone. Running for the guns. I'm pulling our bird back."*

Breeze could hear the distant popping of gunfire, like fading staccato as the sound echoed up and down the high canyon walls.

Sam flinched in the seat beside her, instinctively grabbing for his Marlin where it was propped, muzzle-down beside him.

"Never goes away, does it?" she asked him.

"Huh?"

"That gut reaction that makes you duck and grab for your rifle."

"Nope."

The periodic rifle reports continued to reverberate, sending a quiver of unease through her and giving her stomach the flutters.

The battle com announced, *"LT, drone's safely back and up. Be a lucky hit if they tag it now."*

"You still got eyes on them?" Daniels asked.

*"Roger that."*

"Let me know if they head our way." A pause. "Meanwhile, pull the Humvees off to the left. Tully? You and Krandal, bring the plows forward. Chain up to anything too big to push. You can drag it back far enough that you can double-team to shove it off the road. I want this highway cleared."

"Roger that," Tully said into his mic. Shifting the plow into low gear, he started forward as the Humvees and JLTV pulled into the left lane to make room.

"Okay," Tully told Breeze and Sam, "let's see how this works."

With hand on the hydraulics, he angled and lowered the big plow blade, keeping momentum.

Breeze raised herself in the seat, bracing hands on the dash as Tully aimed his blade. Just as it hit the rear of the white Tesla, he punched the throttle, steering into the resistance. The impact jolted the truck. The crunching and screech of buckling metal made her spine crawl.

Sam whooped where he'd stuck his head out the window, watching as the Tesla rolled off the apron and ended up in the weeds on the shoulder.

Then came the Nissan Pathfinder as it slid down the angled blade and rolled off to the side. The big snowplow jerked and banged on impact with each vehicle. Tully steering, used the throttle to keep momentum as the plow clawed its way forward. Encountering the Chevy three-quarter-ton, the plow had a tougher time, engine roaring as the heavier pickup resisted and the plow crabbed sideways. Nevertheless, the Chevy gave, its body work crumpling and screeching as the blade shook and danced down the truck's mangled side.

Breeze braced herself as Tully powered forward; she figured the impact with the Fun Rambler travel trailer would shake her to the bones, but it just crumpled and flipped to the side, the sheet-metal wall snapping and popping as it went. Sam ducked back as the travel trailer's windows exploded, spraying out a diamond rain of glass.

"Whooo!" Tully cried. "Mama! Yes! Haven't had this much fun since…like, ever!"

When the plow hit the diminutive Kia Soul, Breeze watched the little red car careen off like a batted ball, tossed far enough that it rolled down the embankment before lodging in the cottonwood trees at the river's edge.

Sam had stiffened, gaped, then called, "Uh, guys? That little car? It's got people in it."

"You're kidding." Tully shot him a look as he slammed the truck to a stop. The Mack rocked like a cradle as the big blade pulled it forward.

On the battle com, Daniels asked, *"Got a problem, Tully?"*

"Checking on something, LT," Tully replied. Then to Sam. "Go check."

As Sam opened the door, Breeze added, "I'll go, too. Slip ahead, make sure we're not tossing people over the side."

She was hot on Sam's heels, grabbing her M4 from the floor. Her feet had barely hit the asphalt before she heard, *"What the hell are Delgado and Tappan up to?"*

"Might have people in some of these cars, LT," was the last thing she heard Tully say as she headed forward, rounding the now-scarred plow blade.

"They're dead," Sam called from where he was staring down at the wrecked Kia. "Bullet holes in the windows."

"I'm headed for the van up ahead," she called, approaching the white Ram next in line. "Sam, you come up on the other side."

But it wasn't just the van that concerned her. She had the cars and pickups in the left lane to worry about. Be just like her luck to have some raider unexpectedly leap out and knife her in the back. But, glancing through the window of the Corolla on her left, it was to find the seats empty.

"Got it," Sam called back, hurrying forward, a thumb on the Marlin's hammer.

Breeze felt that old quickening, the rush of adrenaline. She was breathing deeply, blood pumping, pulse accelerating.

The Ram ProMaster's driver's door was open, the smell coming from inside unmistakable. Breeze, M4 up, glanced in. Saw the swollen corpse. Still, she used a toe, pulled the door open wider, and called, "Anyone in there?"

She let a couple of heartbeats pass before glancing at where Sam— now staring in the passenger-side window—gave a negative shake of his head. Turning, she raised a hand and made a clearing gesture to Tully. Checked the Range Rover in the left lane, saw blankets and kids' toys as well as a car seat in the back, then started for the Ram 2500 up ahead. At the same time, she kept track of the Ford Expedition in the left lane. Bullet holes had spiderwebbed the glass, the black stuff sprayed around the inside, she assumed was long-dried blood.

The snowplow's roar was mixed with the crunching of metal and plastic as Tully attacked the white Ram van.

Stepping up to the pickup's driver-side window, she could see Sam looking in from the passenger's side. Empty. But the glove boxes had been left gaping, the console between the seats open and papers, pens, and a cup left after the pilfering.

Behind her, Tully shoved the ProMaster off the road to tumble down the embankment. Then he threw the plow into reverse and backed up to reposition the blade. Second in line, Krandal had his blade shifted to the right to ensure the wreckage was completely cleared from the lane.

"Shit!" Sam shouted over the rending and screeching of metal coming from behind.

"Whatcha got?" Breeze called, stopping, her M4 up, eyes roving the line of vehicles.

"Bodies!" Sam called. "Down off the side of the road. Looks like they've all been... I mean, there's legs missing. Like...they've been cut off, Breeze. You know, like we do when we're butchering a cow."

She glanced back, seeing that Tully was waiting for her signal, and gave him a "hold" gesture. At his nod, she darted between the Ram's bumper and the open back of the baby-blue Jeep Wrangler up ahead. From just a glance, she could see that all the packs, cases, and gear in the Jeep's back had been rifled.

Stepping to Sam's side where he stood on the shoulder, she looked over the edge. Made a face at the stench. But, yeah, piled in the chokecherry bushes as they were, swarming with flies, the bodies looked almost comic. The two men, three women, and two kids still wore shirts, but the legs were missing. Neatly, almost surgically, they'd been removed so as to leave the concave curve of the hip bones, the sockets empty of the femoral heads. The genitals on both sexes had been left untouched, protruding from the pubis in a most vulgar fashion like beaks.

"I can see that woman's head," Breeze pointed. "Little round hole in her forehead? See it?"

"Yeah," Sam said, his voice gone husky.

"I'd chalk that up to a .22 round," she told him. Then she caught the black stain in the gravel on the roadside. "Dried blood. And over there. All wadded up. That's what? Five pairs of pants? And tossed over there? Shoes, Sam."

"I don't get it."

"I think you're right. They were killed here, butchered for the legs, and the torsos tossed over the edge."

Sam's face worked, his fingers flexing nervously on the Marlin's wrist. "What do you want to do about it?"

Over the snowplow's idling diesel, she could hear the approaching drone as it came buzzing back from the front of the line of vehicles.

"Breeze!" Tully was standing in the plow's door and called over the idling diesel. "We got hostiles inbound. LT says to get your asses back in the truck. Now!"

Breeze covered her nose as the wind shifted, bringing the stench her direction.

"Come on," Sam said, pulling her back. "No need to piss Daniels off. We're probably in for an ass chewing as it is."

Breeze jerked a nod and followed Sam at a trot, rounding the Ram pickup. She was climbing up, reaching to open the snowplow's door. A bullet cracked past her head.

"Get out of here!" she screamed at Tully, who was looking all-fired nervous and licking his lips behind the plow's windshield.

Breeze leaped off the step, almost knocking Sam off his feet in the process. The impact left him grunting in pain and wrapping his left arm around his ribs.

"Get down!" she cried as the plow rumbled into reverse, backing away. With a hollow *pock,* a star-shaped hole appeared in the plow's windshield. Tully'd ducked to the left, away from it as he stomped the accelerator. Behind him, Krandal had already thrown the second plow into reverse, racing back for the Humvees.

"Now what?" Sam asked through a pained breath as they hunched behind the Ram pickup's tailgate.

Overhead, the drone was still buzzing. Keeping an eye on them for Daniels, no doubt.

Sam had eased to the side, pulled off his hat, and was peering around the Ram's bumper. "Got two guys coming down the shoulder. Both of them in a crouch, what looks like AR15s at the ready."

Breeze looked up at the drone again, held up two fingers, then pointed in the direction of the approaching men.

To her delight, the drone made two darting motions in the same direction, then three darting motions at an angle to the left.

Breeze held up three fingers, pointing that way.

The drone made a dipping maneuver, like a curt nod.

"Sam, we've got three more incoming. They're working their way in from the left."

"Got it." He shot her a worried look. "Butchered people? A road block? No way these are friendlies, is there?"

"Nope," she said, feeling the familiar flutter under her heart. "Shoot to kill. You with me?"

"Yeah." Sam took a breath, winced, and blew it out, saying, "Whew! Okay. Got this."

He eased onto his belly, wiggling forward so the pickup's tire protected him. A pair of the discarded pants that had been left wadded up against the wheel, helped to break up his outline.

Breeze glanced up at the drone that was still darting at the same angle in patterns of three. She gave it a thumbs up, eased her head past the bumper, and glimpsed down between the line of vehicles. Could see nothing, but based on the direction the drone was darting, figured they were coming down the outside of the vehicles blocking the left lane.

She waddled forward in a duck walk. Keeping low. Glancing up as she did to keep an eye on the drone. It was still darting.

The close sound of a shot made her drop flat. She could hear the drone buzzing rapidly away. Didn't matter. The message had been delivered. They were close.

She tucked up next to an older model Yukon's back tire. The vehicle's rear hatch had been left open, the contents, including empty coolers, camping gear, and discarded clothing were scattered in confusion on the asphalt behind it. Ducking down, she peered beneath the vehicle's undercarriage. Didn't take long. Maybe six...seven seconds? Feet appeared. Clad in fancy hiking shoes, they were placed carefully, as if stalking. Then a pair of expensive-looking ostrich-skin western boots came into her view.

Breeze scuttled to the Yukon's front as they two passed down the other side. She hunched by the bumper, heart hammering, that familiar rush in her blood. With a careful thumb, she eased the M4's fire control to burst. Then she swallowed hard.

*Where is the third guy?*

Damn, she wished the drone was still overhead.

*Bang!* The gunshot made her jump. Partially muffled by the vehicles, it came from Sam's...

*Crack! Crack!* The snap of high velocity reports were unmistakable. Had to be the AR15s with their .223 rounds.

Then, *Bang!*

Silence.

So, what happened?

Should she go? Slip between the back of the Chevy Silverado and the Prowler camp trailer it pulled? See if Sam needed help?

She rotated on her heels—still in a crouch—as someone kicked an empty bottle where it lay on the asphalt behind the Yukon. Breeze pulled her M4 up, got a knee down, and had the weapon shouldered when the guy in hiking boots eased into view. He wore a Rockies baseball cap, a nice fawn-colored leather jacket, new jeans, and carried an AR15. His attention was on the white Ram pickup where Sam had been.

As if in sudden awareness, the guy's head swiveled her way. The instant his eyes met Breeze's she triggered the M4. The three-round burst made his leather jacket dance as the sixty-two grain bullets tore through. The guy hit the pavement hard enough that his hat bounced off, did a cartwheel.

"Holy hell!" the gritted words could be heard from the other side of the Yukon.

Breeze threw herself down on her shoulder, extended the M4 under the Yukon. She could only see the left ostrich boot; the tire obscured the right.

Figuring what the hell? Breeze triggered the M4. It wasn't more than six feet. She could see the boot leather jumping, scraps of ostrich hide, pink blood, and bits of bone blown out the other side. But the guy didn't fall, just staggered sideways. The shriek was bloodcurdling.

Breeze flinched, rolled, and scrambled behind the Yukon's right front tire as ear-cracking reports echoed around the canyon walls. Bullets snapped into metal, and glass exploded from the Yukon's windows as the guy worked his trigger.

Glancing around the tire and under the engine, Breeze watched the guy hobble off to the side, doing all he could to favor his now shattered and bloody foot. The string of curse words was epic.

*Shoot and scoot!* The old Guard adage popped into her head. She took a deep breath, did a crab-scuttle to the safety of the next vehicle in line. A gray Toyota Tundra. Snugging up to the right rear tire, she again peered under the truck. Nothing. Duckwalking to the front, she sneaked a peek around the right fender and past the bumper. Saw no one and crept around the Toyota's front, hemmed in as it was by the Toyota Sienna up ahead. The Sienna, too, had an open cargo hatch. Breeze lifted her head high enough to still be screened by the Tundra's hood, but through the Sienna's windows, had a view up the canyon.

Guy number three was still missing.

"Son of a bitch!" Ostrich Boot was yelling. "I'm gonna kill you! Come on out, damn you!"

In the distance, she could hear the sound of the Humvees coming closer.

Taking a chance, Breeze threw herself prone, braced the M4 on its magazine, and could see the ostrich boot guy as far up as the waist. He was still hobbling, trying to keep his bleeding foot up.

Using his fly as an aiming point, Breeze triggered another burst.

As the brass went tinkling across the pavement, and her ears rang from the M4's deafening muzzle blast, the guy went down. Hard. His black rifle falling from limp fingers. Then he screamed. A tortured sound. As if it were tearing out his throat. He was a blond. Maybe thirty, heavily muscled, bearded jaw, with the most remarkably crystalline-blue eyes.

God, he just kept screaming and screaming, as if to burst the lungs right out of his chest.

*Where is the third guy?*

Breeze scrambled back, raised her head to peer through the Sienna's windows, searching. Could see nothing but mountain side on the left; one of the pop-up tow-behind trailers blocked her view on the right. The Honda Odyssey it was hooked to had been rifled, the doors and rear hatch left gaping. Personal items lay scattered around where they'd been tossed. Most poignant was the family photo album. One of the old ones with plastic leaves, the color snapshots age-faded. Record of a now-dead family heritage.

Was number three still coming? Or had he or she fled at the sight of friends being shot down?

And what about Sam? What did the shots on his side of the column mean?

She was just raising her head when a voice from the side, called, "Got you!"

Breeze whirled, saw nothing, then looked higher on the slope. There, perched twenty yards up between two currant bushes, boots dug into the scree, a woman in a Levi jacket, wearing blue jeans, and a holding a scoped Mini 14 had Breeze in her sights.

"Kill me, and you're dead!" Breeze cried.

"Sorry, bitch," the woman told her. "But, I'm going to enjoy cooking your meat."

Breeze tensed, expecting the impact. Her entire body tingled at the anticipation. That cold sweat—

Accompanied by the cracking chatter of high-velocity rounds, the woman, the dirt behind her, and bits of currant bush, exploded into a mixed haze of dust, blood, and blasted rock. Even the Mini 14 burst, the stock splintering, bits of splattered metal shining as the barrel and receiver flew away.

The woman dropped like a stone, tumbling in a limp-doll kind of a roll, legs and arms flopping.

Breeze took a lungful, blew it out in weary relief.

As the racket echoed off the canyon walls and died away, Breeze raised herself on unsteady legs to see the Humvee easing its way along the left shoulder, off-side wheels climbing over stones and brush in the bottom of the ditch. Standing in the hatch, Private Goggles was braced behind the roof-mounted M249 SAW.

Across the distance, she thought she could see that little curl of blue smoke rising from the barrel. Or it could have been her imagination.

"Sam?" she muttered, leaping out, darting around, and vaulting the pop-up camper's hitch. Breeze took a moment, readied her weapon, and glanced around the camper's square corner. Two bodies were sprawled out on the roadside. Not three feet between them, they lay by the white Ram pickup's passenger door. The one in front was dressed in snazzy slacks and wearing what might have been a cashmere sweater. No need to worry about the guy in back, his head was a blood-matted mess. He was in a tan leather dress jacket, some kind of fancy designer jeans, and had been wearing brand new Nikes. As Breeze stepped out, she could see the pool of red spreading across the gravel. Call it cosmic irony, it was blending with the blackened blood left by the butcher victims.

"Breeze?" Sam called. "What's happening?"

She watched as Sam tossed the rumpled pants to one side and emerged gingerly from behind the pickup's right rear tire, his Marlin at the ready.

"The bad guys are down." She pointed. "What's this? These guys, like, they're not ten feet from you."

"Yeah," Sam told her, looking ashen. "Thought the only chance I had was to let them get close. Then, just when it seemed they never would, they finally lined up so I could shoot through the first and get the second. First guy fell like a log. Second one sort of hunched, backed into the front of the truck, and started shooting. Like right into the dirt at his feet. Weirdest thing I ever saw, so I took him out with a head shot."

The sound of feet was accompanied by Privates Deana Capriolli and Paco Vermijo, each trotting up in a combat crouch, weapons ready, eyes roving for threats.

"You guys all right?" Capriolli asked.

"Yeah," Breeze told her, flipping the fire control on her M4 to safe. "What's the drone see?"

"Got more of them waiting up at the barricade." Paco gave her a wry grin. Kicked the first dead guy. "What's with these guys? I mean, the clothes? You'd think they were movie stars or some such shit."

"Looters," Breeze muttered. "Probably started early, smashing into stores. Killing anyone who got in their way as they took the very best."

"Lot of good it did them," Capriolli said. "We're supposed to take it from here. The LT wants you to hump your sorry butts back to the command Humvee so she can ream new assholes in both of you."

Breeze noticed that Sam was fighting the shakes when he said, "Figures."

# THE PAPER

*I'd just finished eating a breakfast of two eggs, side pork, and delicious yucca blossom muffins that Edna, the governor's cook had whipped up. I'd barely finished my cup of tea when Kace Adams, dressed in a leather jacket and blue jeans, leaned in the kitchen door and called, "You coming? We're rolling in five."*

*I would learn to always be on call. Might not have put that together if I hadn't lived with Tyrell for those few months.*

*The first stop that morning was at the* Cheyenne Tribune Eagle. *It was a big day. Along with internet and digital distribution, newsprint was a thing of the past. And what good is a newspaper without paper? News, as we knew it, had died with the Collapse. Right along with cell phones. Granted, computers still worked. But they only ran programs that didn't need any kind of internet access. So, what was this about?*

*I got to follow behind Kace's right elbow—trying to figure out which of the editors or reporters might be a threat—as he led the way into the lobby. There, surrounded by the entire newspaper's staff, the governor signed the top sheet from a ragged stack of waist-high paper. The first sheet the* Tribune Eagle *had recycled from trash in the city dump.*

*Turned out that the dump was full of paper. All it needed was dug up, sorted for quality, ripped and pulped in blenders, and run through a screen, press, and dryer. For now, the newspaper would be a single sheet. And kind of grainy. But Agar and the press were back in business.*

— Excerpt from Lauren Davis' *Journal.*

# CHAPTER EIGHTEEN

SAM WATCHED the last of the logs—a big fir tree with splintered branches that had been dropped across the road—as the M1089 wrecker lifted it, swung it to the side, and released it over the edge to crash down into the willows that lined the Poudre River's bank. The thing fell with a hollow thump, the cracking of branches like gunshots. Then the upper third of the trunk snapped in two as it high-centered on a car-sized boulder; it parted with a loud bang. The pieces flopped and finally came to rest, the tree's butt extending out into the current.

Sam turned, fingers inserted in his back pockets as he walked back to the fancy Venetian motor home parked in the pullout. It was one of the exclusive units with tip-out rooms in the side, luxury interior, and a sleek metallic-brown finish. Dennis Conchlen, the guy driving the NPT truck, said that models like this started at a half million. Sam could believe it. No telling what had happened to the original owners. Didn't matter that it had no fuel left to run the generators. For the post-Collapse world, it had been a pretty awesome home for the guys who'd built the barricade.

All those looted cars, trucks, and campers, the ones now pushed off to the side, or over into the river, had provided the ambushers with fuel, food, and plunder...until the food had run out. After that, they turned the next best source for meat. Evidence of that was in plain view, thin-sliced, draped over the willow-pole drying racks above a six-foot long and smoldering fire pit. The collection of stripped human leg and arm bones tossed down the slope was proof of where the meat had come from.

Most chilling of all, a gambrel hung from a nearby fir tree, the hooks on either end of the bar gruesome. After skinning the cow that day in the

Tappan's barn, Sam needed but to close his eyes and imagine a human hanging there by the heels. Upside down. Dangling meat.

Sam gave the closest of the dead cannibals—a young woman, maybe in her late teens, long flowing blonde hair and a slim-but-endowed body —a somber look. Despite the bloody holes blown through her chest, it was easy to tell she'd been gorgeous. Deana Capriolli had shot the girl down during the storming of the barricade. A cannibal shouldn't look like a *Sports Illustrated* swimsuit model. Left him wondering about what kind of person she'd been.

"What do think?" Breeze asked as she stepped up behind him, her M4 slung.

"I was wondering what went on inside that girl's head while she was eating one of those pieces of meat." He shook his head. "God, the stereotypes we're still stuck with. Pure cultural baggage. Look at her. Like, she should be the head of the high school cheerleading team. Modeling for *Vogue*. Maybe headed to Hollywood. I'm an anthropologist for God's sake. I should know better, but I'm shocked. She's a fricking *cannibal*, Breeze!"

"Yeah." Breeze slugged him playfully on the shoulder. "Bet she had all the breaks." A pause as she studied the young woman's body. "Young as she is? Bet she was trading on her looks. That she came from down in that line of cars. I mean, she's so much younger than these guys she was with."

"You think she offered herself?" Sam asked, thinking back to a woman he'd met on his first visit to Cheyenne. She'd had a WFFF sign. Will fuck for food. He'd given her twenty bucks. Told her to go have a meal. Had it been any different for the blonde girl?

"What price will a person pay for survival?" Sam asked. "Maybe they forced her to eat people. Put a gun to her head. Told her to do it or die."

"Or maybe she was all for it." Breeze gave him a censoring look. "You still trying to accommodate your stereotypes? Just because she was beautiful doesn't mean she wasn't willing to do anything it took to keep breathing."

The sound of revving diesels from the snowplows carried up the canyon. Sam could hear the crashing and rending of metal as the last of the highway was shoved clear of abandoned vehicles. The M1089 had pulled in its outriggers and re-hitched and secured its boom. Black smoke shot from its stack as it growled its way forward, pulling off to the left just past where the barricade had been. Making room to allow the first of the plows through.

"That's our ride," Breeze said as Tully slowed, waving a "come on" in the graying light. Night was falling sooner than it should, but then this was the bottom of a sheer-walled canyon. And the thick layer of haze hung low on the rocky and forested slopes above.

Tightening his grip on the Marlin, Sam gave the flashy motor home, the drying racks with their still-smoking meat, and the pretty blonde girl's corpse one last look.

*There but for the grace of God go I?*

As if reading his thoughts, Breeze asked, "Think you could ever do this? I mean, block the road, ambush travelers? Shoot them down in cold blood and butcher them?"

"Hell no!" He gave her a sidelong look. "You?"

With a slight shrug of the shoulders, she said, "I don't know."

"God, Breeze!"

"If you'd asked me last May? Back in Denver? Before the Collapse? I'd have told you I could never kill another human being. But now?" She sniffed, probably to scent the cleaner air now blowing down the canyon, thick with the scent of conifers as it was. "Given some of the things I've seen...done? Given the right situation?" She gave him a *who knows?* shrug.

They'd reached Tully's snowplow, and Breeze, reaching up with her left hand, took the step and swung up, opening the door.

As she crawled into the cab, Sam followed. The climb sent a stitch through his ribs; then he slid onto the seat, stowed his Marlin, and closed the door.

"Heard you got cussed up one side and down the other by the LT," Tully greeted as the Humvees and JLTV took the lead. He shifted into gear, sending the big Mack truck rumbling and rocking its way forward.

Sam—still feeling the butterflies in his stomach—said, "She started on Breeze. Looked her right in the eye, and said, 'You just can't help yourself, can you?' And then I made the mistake of blurting out, 'It's my fault.' I only got as far as saying, 'We needed to know if anyone...' And, wow! She tied into me like I've never—"

"She wasn't really mad." Breeze had pulled a leg up, booted foot braced on the seat, fingers laced around her ankle.

"Huh?" Sam asked. "With that squinty-eyed look? The way she was glaring with those hot eyes? And the tone in her voice wasn't exactly warm and fuzzy, if you'll recall."

Breeze was chewing her lips, eyes on the winding strip of asphalt as they followed the lead vehicles into the canyon's growing gloom. "Granted, she's never really liked me. Or, worse, Lauren. Now, those two could really butt heads. But here's the thing: We're back in the snowplow with Tully. I know Daniels. If we'd actually pissed her off? We'd be riding in the back of the NPT cargo box, in the dark, on the bare floor, so we could reflect and then dwell on our sins."

Sam shot her a questioning look. "She's that much of a badass?"

"It's not that," Tully said as he braked for a corner and the Mack downshifted. "Word is that she's freaked about everything that's happened since the Collapse. Like, she knows the stakes. The things that have to be done. What happens if we fail. She thinks we're hanging by a thread. If that thread breaks, and Wyoming gets overrun, or implodes, or falls apart, she's determined that it won't be because of her or her people."

"She doesn't like people doing stuff on their own." Breeze gave Sam a sober look. "I mean, she got what happened today. Was watching it on the drone camera. But if we hadn't tried to get back to the snowplow before the shooting started? Well…"

"We'd be riding in the cargo box of the NPT truck, meditating on our sins," Sam finished.

"See? Told you she wasn't mad." Breeze gave him a friendly slap on the knee.

"And that's good news?"

Breeze grasped her ankle again. "If you ask me, the only good news is that we lost no more than three hours clearing that roadblock." She glanced at the truck's glowing digital clock. "We should be across Stove Prairie, past Masonville, and rounding Carter Lake by now."

Tully reached up, tried to fit his little finger into the bullet hole in his windshield. "Yeah, well, I don't mind being late. I just hope that's the last time we get shot at on this trip."

*Yeah,* Sam thought. *Me, too.*

# THE DUMP

*Who would have thought? Outside of petroleum, electricity, and agriculture, our most valued resource turned out to be the county land-fill. Same for the rest of the state. Within a month of the Collapse, the dump was being mined, and not just for old paper. Glass bottles could be sterilized and reused. All those electronic devices people had thrown away were suddenly a source for copper—a biggie—silver, and rare earth elements. And then there were the recyclable plastics, aluminum found in everything from cans to old racks and shelving, electric motors, iron, steel, all kinds of stuff.*

*Springs! I'd never given them any thought. You'd never guess how many things worked on springs: guns, refrigerators, cars, printers, sewing machines, tools. Or that manufacturing them took sophisticated metals and the machinery to extrude and temper them.*

*Rubber, however, was going to take time. When I asked about it, Agar told me, "We've got the hydrocarbons, coal, and natural gas to make naphtha, and then produce the monomers. After that it's just a matter of catalysts to form the polymers." I could see his gaze go distant as he added, "That's for next year. Got enough on my plate for now."*

— Excerpt from Lauren Davis' *Journal.*

# CHAPTER NINETEEN

THE PLACE WAS CALLED MISHAWAKA. There, a line of trucks, a school bus, and stock trailers had been pulled across the highway to block the road just down from the fortified buildings. Breeze watched as the lead Humvee pulled up short of the roadblock; headlights and spotlights illuminated the obstructing vehicles, shining off glass and chrome, reflecting dull colors of paint. And right in the middle was the big yellow school bus, it's sides glowing with reflective tape.

To either side of the right-of-way, pines and firs made a black thicket. On the south, the canyon wall rose to merge with the inky night sky. On the north, the trees screened the river. No telling what they hid.

*"I don't like this,"* Daniels' voice came through the com. *"On your toes, people. We could be flanked from the timber on both sides."*

A string of *"Roger that*s" could be heard.

Breeze told Sam, "Guns up, Delgado. You're in the passenger seat. Anybody comes fogging out of those trees, you shoot to kill. Got that?"

Sam shifted, winced as he stretched the muscles in his chest, and awkwardly poked the Marlin out the snowplow's window. "Better if we were in the back," Sam said. "Not as awkward for shooting. And the steel walls would protect us."

"Too late now," Tully whispered, one hand on the gearshift, as he concentrated on the line of vehicles blocking the way. "Someone's there."

And sure enough, Breeze could see people, flashes of their movement in the glare of the convoy lights as individuals slipped between the gaps. Looked to her like they were taking defensive positions in the barricade.

"What the hell?" Sam wondered. "I mean, do they really think they can stop us?"

Even as he said it, Daniels' voice could be heard through a loud speaker. "Attention! We're Wyoming National Guard. We mean you no harm. All we request is free passage through your barricade. Repeat: We mean you no harm!"

"Think they're going to believe that?" Tully asked.

Breeze shrugged, keeping one hand on her M4 where it rested against the seat. "How do I know? All they can see in the dark is the glare of the headlights."

"Go away!" A voice could barely be heard over the idling engines. "We'll shoot! I swear it!"

Daniels' voice through the loud speaker responded, "We're Wyoming National Guard. We mean you no harm! All we want is free passage. Don't make us use force."

"This isn't going to end happily," Sam prophesied.

"It didn't work out so well the last time you pieces of shit tried it!" the strident voice called.

"I repeat," Daniels' voice blared. "We're Wyoming National Guard. We're on a peaceful mission. We will not fire unless fired upon."

"Bring it on!" the voice called back.

"Shit!" Breeze muttered, that sense of rising panic building. "Let me out, Sam."

"Huh?" Sam shot her a questioning look.

"Tappan," Tully warned, "whatever you're thinking, you don't—"

"Out, Sam! Now," Breeze gave him a shove; to his credit, Sam opened the door, grunted and favored his chest as he stepped down to the pavement. Breeze landed right behind him, slinging her M4, and starting forward.

As she passed the JLTV where Daniels was poked up through the hatch, Breeze called, "Hey, LT, let me try!"

"Tappan?" Daniels asked. "What the hell are you doing? Get your ass back in the snowplow!"

Breeze ignored her, slapping a hand to the Humvees as she passed. Paco Jimenez was on the top-mount M249 as she passed. "So, Paco. Don't take me out by mistake."

"You got it, Breeze."

While from behind, Daniels was snapping, "Tappan, get back here. That's an order!"

Breeze raised her hands as she stepped into the halo cast by the Humvee's lights, calling, "Hold your fire! I'm coming in! I'm Breeze Tappan. Don't shoot!"

That unsettling tickle formed in her gut—the one she got when bullets could be blasting through her in the next instant. So, like, how many hostile weapons had her in their sights? Ten? A hundred?

Step by step, she advanced, bellowing, "Hold your damn fire! I just want to talk! I'm Breeze Tappan. I'm with the Wyoming National Guard. Don't shoot!"

"All right," a voice called from the rear of the school bus. "Stop right there!"

"Who are you?" Breeze called. This close to the school bus, she could see bullet holes in the metal and the characteristic shattered circles in the windows. The side read: Larimer County School District No. 1.

"Mark Leskowski. What's it to you, you walking piece of abomination?"

"Abomination? Wow. I've been called a bitch, a cunt, a...well, there's some other things a whole lot more offensive but we won't go there. So, listen, here's the thing: We're from Wyoming. All we want is to get to the Stove Prairie road. We're trying to get to Lyons. That's a town north of Boulder."

"That's bullshit. No one gets up the canyon. You cannibals have it blocked. Now turn your murdering, sick ass around, and beat it back to your motorhome before we blow your disgusting—"

"Canyon's open," Breeze interrupted. "We just cleared it. The cannibals are dead. I killed two myself." She pointed over her shoulder. "These lights? If you look closely, you can make out the blocky outline of the first vehicle. See it? You can kind of see Paco Jimenez. He's on the pintle-mounted machine gun up top. Then comes the JLTV with the chain gun, two snowplows, a cargo truck, an MTV, and a wrecker. Not the sort of shit your cannibals would be driving."

For the first time, Leskowski stepped out where she could see him. Older man, maybe sixty, steely white hair hanging down from beneath his wide-brimmed leather hat, a Savage bolt-action rifle in his hands. He was squinting in the light. "You're serious?"

"Yeah," Breeze told him as she gave him a big smile. "We just want to get through to the Stove Prairie Road. And then pass through on the way back."

"And all those cars and trucks? Those trees they felled? The cannibals?"

"We took them out. Road's clear all the way to Ted's Place and back to The Forks checkpoint."

The man leaned wearily against the school bus's back bumper. "So there might be an end to this nightmare after all?"

"Don't know about that," Breeze said, aware of Daniels' wavering silhouette as she approached.

The lieutenant called, "Coming in! Don't shoot!"

As Daniels stopped short, her expression sour in the lights, she was giving Breeze the "You're dog meat" squint-eye that promised mayhem.

"Lieutenant Daniels," Breeze said. "This is Mark Leskowski. Seems they were having some trouble with that bunch of man eaters we disposed of this afternoon."

To her surprise, Leskowski stepped forward, offering his hand. "Lieutenant? Good to meet you. Sorry. We didn't know. Just saw the lights. Thought they were going to hit us again. Said they'd be back."

"My pleasure, sir," Daniels told him. "If you'd be so kind as to move these vehicles, we'd really like to be on our way."

He seemed to catch on something, his smile fading. "Thought you people in Wyoming were killing anyone from Colorado that you could find?"

"No, sir," Daniels told him. "Only people in violation of the travel ban seeking to cross The Line. My only purpose down here is to proceed to my destination, and then get my command back to Cheyenne."

Leskowski turned when a woman walked out from behind the school bus. Her first words were, "What can they trade, Mark? We've got our own problems."

Leskowski quickly asked, "You got medicines? Food? Ammo?"

"Excuse me?" Daniels asked.

*Oh, shit!* Aloud Breeze said, "Might be worth it, LT." To Leskowski, she added, "Maybe we can make a start here. You're not that far from The Forks. You've survived the worst of the Collapse. You are obviously not raiders. Maybe it's time we started establishing relations. Maybe trade?"

Daniels was giving Breeze the eye again. "Medicines, we don't have. Food we do. We can drop you a couple of our ration packs."

"And fuel," the woman said sharply. "Especially if you want us to move this damn school bus out of the way. You see, it's empty. Like everything else we've got. So, you trade us food and fuel, we'll open the road."

"And a doctor," Leskowski said. "You got one of them?"

"I've got a combat medic. Good enough?" Daniels asked.

"Trained in gunshot wounds?" the woman asked, squinting.

"One of our best," Daniels said, turning. "Corporal Fields, front and center! And bring the med kit."

"Roger that, LT," came Fields' call from the rear.

Leskowski blew out a weary exhale, smiling as he turned to the woman. "Well, Margaret, as terrified as I was when we saw those head-lights coming, I guess miracles really do exist."

Margaret was grinning, dropping her AR to dangle from her right hand. "Amen to that." And to Daniels, "And about that ammo? If you've got anything that will fit our guns, after that last fight with the man eaters, we've only got twenty-six rounds between the lot of us."

"Twenty-six rounds?" Breeze asked. "And you were going to fight?"

Leskowski's expression went wan. "We'd made up our minds. But each of us—" he reached into his pocket, pulled out a cartridge "—we all saved the last one for ourselves."

# THE SPOTLIGHT

*It was one thing when I was a Line Rider. Another after the Buffalo Camp fight. And after Marsy Ranch, I never doubted my confidence. Just throw me into the shit, and I'd handle it. It was an entirely different matter the first time I followed Governor Agar up onto a raised platform surrounded by a crowd. Kace and I stood behind the governor, while Stenholm had the bottom of the stairs, with Donovan Knuckles and Jayson Hasen along with some WNG guys he'd recruited to keep anyone from climbing up, and any assassins at bay. I think I was supposed to be the last line of defense.*

*Agar was giving a speech at the Union Pacific railyard in Cheyenne. Maybe five hundred people were crowded around. As I looked out at all of those faces, I couldn't help thinking of the hundreds who might want Pete Agar dead. And the thousands south of the border that his order had condemned. How many were out there in that crowd? How did I kill them before they killed Agar?*

*Every fricking eye was fixed on me. People pointing. I could hear "That's Lauren Davis!" "She's his new body guard!" "Would you mess with her?" "She's a real killer!"*

*Then Agar's voice boomed out, "At this very moment, the governors of Nebraska, Utah, and Idaho, like me, are welcoming the return of service to the Union Pacific Railroad between Grand Island, Nebraska and Boise, Idaho!"*

*I didn't hear the rest, about what it all meant for the West, for Wyoming. I was suddenly overwhelmed by the fact that, no matter how vigilant I was, no matter how I scanned faces, postures, hands, any lunatic out there with a rifle could kill Pete Agar, and there wasn't a thing I could do to stop it.*

*Until that moment, it had never occurred to me that each time Agar stepped before an audience, it was an act of bravery.*

— Excerpt from Lauren Davis' *Journal.*

# CHAPTER TWENTY

SAM SAT by the blaze that crackled in the fire ring. As another piece of burning wood popped and shot sparks up in to the night, he held his hands out to the heat. Turned out that firewood was the only thing Mishawaka Inn had in abundance, and the fire ring was perfect, a stone circle about three feet across in an open space surrounded by towering fir and pine trees. Flickering yellow light illuminated the branches and the side of the log lodge behind him. Perfect rustic charm with the shushing roar of the river in the background.

The Mishawaka Inn was the sort of place where he would have loved to have spent time before the Collapse. As the Guard soldiers had gone to work moving the blocking vehicles, he'd taken a stroll through the lodge and restaurant. Stood on the deck overlooking the river and wondered at the century-old cabins along with their modern counterparts. Not to mention the amphitheater where music had been played. Must have been a wonderful place before everything fell apart.

An engine coughed, sputtered, and roared to life out on the highway. When it came to clearing the barricade, there was more than just the school bus to be pulled off to the side. The gasoline had been siphoned out of each of the blockade vehicles to prevent theft. Then, as time passed, it had been used to run the generator which kept the freezers and water well running. At least until it had become achingly clear that no help was coming. After that, the survivors at Mishawaka had only run the generator in times of emergency. Even so, by the time the convoy arrived, they were down to less than three gallons.

Sam looked up as Breeze walked over, pulled up one of the wooden chairs, and seated herself beside him. She, too, extended her hands, eyes thoughtfully on the flames.

"What's happening?" Sam asked as another of the vehicles was re-parked out on the road. That was accompanied by sound of the Humvees pulling through and making room for the following vehicles.

"Well, Corporal Fields is up to her elbows in gunshot wounds. One's critical. Another two…let's just say 'not good.' Nothing that couldn't have been taken care of in a clinic, but up here? What did they have? Just cloth bandages torn from sheets and soaked in whiskey."

"Got that taken care of," Lieutenant Daniels announced as she appeared out of the night, stepped around the fire, and seated herself across from them. Her hard gaze fixed on Breeze. "Going to send the wounded back to The Forks, then on to Laramie."

The frown lines in Daniels' face deepened. "What the hell were you thinking, Tappan?"

Breeze rubbed her hands together, expression pinching. "I was thinking they didn't have the foggiest notion who we were. Just head-lights on bright beam and blinding spotlights coming in out of the night. And we didn't have any idea who they were. We'd just shot it out with the scum of humanity. And for the last three months, we've been in a constant state of siege. Our first instincts are to shoot. Eliminate the threat. But what if it's not a threat?"

"You bet your life on that, Tappan. You know that, don't you?"

Breeze shifted uncomfortably. "Didn't feel right, Lieutenant. That voice that called out? Leskowski was scared. Terrified."

"And, without orders, you walked right out into a terrified man's field of fire?" A beat. "You get where I'm coming from here?"

Breeze spread her hands, as if in surrender. "Yeah, my gut was crawling the entire time. But looking back, it was the difference between here and the cannibals. What we hit down-canyon? All those cars stopped, looted, and abandoned? The bodies? This wasn't a trap, it was a fort. Defensive."

"You thought all that out? Ever think it might have saved some fric-tion between the two of us if you'd explained it to me *before* you took it on yourself to get shot into hamburger?"

Sam watched Breeze's brow knot as she considered. "I couldn't have put it into words, Lieutenant. It was hanging by a thread as it was."

Daniels leaned back, blew a hard exhale. "What the hell do I do with you? Half of me wants to put you in irons, and half of me wants to let you charge out and get shot like you damned well deserve. And yeah, I know I'll eventually have to explain your grisly death to the governor. Not to mention Ragnovich, who fucking adores you. Which will be nothing nice to endure. At this point, I just don't know if it wouldn't be worth it."

Sam couldn't stop his amused grin.

Daniels—unfortunately—saw it. "You think it's funny, Mr. Delgado?"

He took a breath, shifted. "Lieutenant, I don't know what to do with Breeze either. Ever since I first met her, she's either intimidated the hell out of me, or been the inspiration that allowed me to do things I never thought I was capable of. But here's the thing: So far, her instincts have always been right."

"Until they're wrong, mister." Daniels pointed a finger his way. "And you only get one mistake. One incorrect decision. One bad call."

Sam told her softly, "Breeze and I know we're long past our expiration dates. We've accepted that we're not getting out of this alive, and—"

"Not on my watch, you don't," Daniels snapped.

"Hey, Lieutenant," Breeze told her. "Ease up. We're not looking for ways to commit suicide. Promise. But from here on out, we're all going to have to think differently. Know when to take out the monsters, know when to talk. Like here, tonight."

Daniels sighed. "You *might* have a point." She rubbed her hands together, glared at the crackling flames. "Like what do we do about these people? I'm keeping Corporal Fields with us, but sending Private Morse back with the three wounded. He'll carry my orders to the check point, ensure that they get medical treatment in Laramie. The rest here? They are trying to figure out a way to stay. Hold their ground now that the cannibals are dead."

Sam watched sparks fly as another piece of firewood popped. "Might be worth moving the check point south from The Forks to Ted's Place. That would protect the canyon from raiders out of Fort Collins."

"It would shorten The Line," Breeze agreed. "Bring it straight across from the Rawhide Power plant. Create a wider buffer area."

"This is Colorado," Daniels reminded.

Sam arched a challenging eyebrow. "Colorado doesn't exist anymore. I'd ask the people here what they want. Might be they are willing to become part of The Line in exchange for a regular supply of gasoline for their generator. Bullets for their guns. What are they doing for food?"

"Made nets," Daniels told him. "They're seining the river. Caught rabbits and are breeding them. Said that most of the deer were shot out in the early days. Closed the road after Mishawaka was raided by folks from Fort Collins. I guess it was pretty hairy for a while."

Breeze said, "Self-reliant fighters sound like they'd be an asset."

Daniels nodded as if to herself. "I'll see if they're interested."

Sergeant White Eagle appeared out of the dark, stepping into the fire's light and saluting. She was followed by Leskowski and Margaret.

White Eagle said, "Lieutenant? We've got the road cleared."

"I've got a request," Leskowski said. "Margaret and I have been talking. I mean, we're so grateful that you're sending our people back for medical, care, but what if another raiding party comes rolling up the canyon tomorrow?"

White Eagle added, "LT? We've got those rifles and that ammo we took from the cannibals. It's a small damned arsenal, but nothing we can use."

Daniels nodded. "I'm with you, Sergeant. Can't think of a better use than leaving them here." To Leskowski she said, "Sam, here, thinks we should move a checkpoint down to Ted's Place to control the canyon mouth. If we do that, are you and your people willing to work with us? Hold this part of the canyon? Become part of The Line? Maybe in return for fuel supplies to keep your generator running?"

"You'd do this?" Margaret asked skeptically.

"It's not like it comes free," Daniels told her. "Controlling the canyon means you'd be patrolling for raiders. Your job will be to take them out, get it? It's shitty work that boils down to us or them."

Leskowski had pursed his lips. "We're already doing shitty work, Lieutenant. The folks that owned Mishawaka? They're dead. But they gave some of us a chance, who gave others a chance. The things we've done? God will damn us. We've been threatened from all sides since we blocked the road, and we're slowly starving. A couple of fish and the occasional netted bird or squirrel added to our rabbits won't keep us fed. Figured it was just a matter of time until we were overrun."

Margaret had crossed her arms, a grim set to her lips. "You come with us in the morning, we'll clean out the canyon all the way to the Cameron Pass summit. There's some mean folks who took over up at Rustic and Idlewild. With your armored trucks and fire power, they'd never stand a chance."

Daniels stood, meeting the woman's gaze. "Tempting as that is, I've got a mission to complete. But how about this? I'll radio up to Captain Ragnovich. Have him send a Guard detail down. Once they secure Ted's Place, they can tackle your bad guys and secure the canyon."

"Sure make us sleep a lot better." Leskowski hesitated. "But what do you people get out of it?"

"Control of the back roads to Cherokee Park and Wood's Landing. But, most of all, allies, Mister Leskowski." Daniels smiled. "And as you people have just discovered, allies are few and far between these days. And very, very precious."

# PEP TALK

Somehow, I toughed out the meetings with the highway department, the Bureau of Land Management integration team, the Wyoming State Health Commission, and the Shoshoni/Arapaho Wind River Indian Reservation Economic Development and Relief Committee. Try saying that fast ten times.

After the public appearance that morning, how was I supposed to keep alert while the governor listened to hours of road repair priorities, rising rates of respiratory infection among five to ten-year-olds, and emergency plans to shore up a ten-million-dollar factory project on the Wind River Res when all the funding went up in a mushroom cloud back east?

Just after midnight, Agar slapped the report he'd been reading on the table. Told Randolph Meyer, his secretary, to call it a night.

I followed him out with Kace on my heels, and met up with Spencer and the rest of the team to walk him down to the Suburban where Bill waited behind the wheel. Agar climbed in back, Spencer in the passenger seat. The rest of the team and I followed in the second Suburban.

After passing through the gates at the governor's mansion, and seeing Agar inside, Kace grasped my elbow and said, "Got a minute?"

"Sure."

"How'd you do today. You seemed a little stronger."

I shrugged. "Frankly, I was stunned the entire day. I mean, anyone out there could have had a rifle. And with all of those depot windows to shoot from? Easy kill."

"That's my department," he told me. "Your job is in case anyone gets close. The story is out about how you killed Corretta Kapital, and we're

*capitalizing on it. Making sure that everyone knows why you're standing
next to Agar. That if they try, they'll die."*

*"Makes me sound pretty bloodthirsty."*

*He smiled. "In security work, any time a threat is deterred from
acting, it's a victory. If they do act, your next responsibility is to get the
principal away from the threat. Keep him alive by whatever means."*

*He frowned. "Learn this. Concentrate. You're not just to be seen.
You're there to see them. Watch them. Study them for any possible
threats. Identify the assassin before he makes his move."*

*"I'm better when no one expects anything from me."*

*Kace gave me a smile, a twinkle in his eyes. "If you're that good
when no one expects anything from you, think how fantastic you'll be
when you expect everything from yourself."*

— Excerpt from Lauren Davis' *Journal.*

# CHAPTER TWENTY-ONE

AT THE STOVE Prairie road turn off, the Humvees had to pull aside to let the snowplows clear a makeshift barricade of logs, branches, and small boulders that had been piled up around a burned-out Forest Service truck. Someone had torched it in the middle of the road.

Breeze, from her elevated perspective in the cab, caught the wink of a muzzle flash from up on the slope. A bullet made a *pang!* sound as it struck metal.

She caught a glimpse of three figures running and stumbling between the tree trunks as a spotlight on the lead Humvee splashed light on the slope. It illuminated a makeshift camp of tarps and piled breastworks on a commanding flat a hundred yards above the junction. From the side, Krandal fired a burst from the M249; 5.56 bullets kicked up dust and ricocheted on the heels of the fleeing offenders.

"Bet that just ruined their whole night," Tully noted as he pushed the blackened remains of the Forest Service truck into the ditch on the west side of the road.

The Humvees again took the lead, headlights illuminating the roadway, the asphalt potted from lack of maintenance. The highbeams gave the passing trees a somber look, casting shadows that seemed to swing and dart into the night.

As the climb began, the big Mack's diesel strained, headlights fogging in the pale dust stirred up by the lead vehicles when they crossed sections where rivulets of flood water had washed dirt across the pavement. The road here was hemmed by a treed slope on the left, the right dropping off into a willow, cottonwood, and chokecherry-bordered creek. Like a snake, the county road wound its way up the canyon bottom. Both ditches and the gravel shoulder were littered with bottles, bits of trash, and the occasional abandoned truck or car. The vehicles had been pulled off to the side; taillight lenses glowed an eerie crimson in the headlights.

Tully yawned; the Allison transmission was whining as it found a lower ratio.

As the Humvees and JLTV pulled ahead, Tully had to go for yet another gear. "Steep damn climb," he muttered. "Narrow as this is? Hope we don't run into an ambush. They could sit up there in the dark and roll rocks down. Middle of the night? I'd hate to have to fight our way out of it."

That sent a shiver up Breeze's spine. Caused her to stare up at the looming brush, timber, and rocky outcrops they passed beneath. That feeling of eyes, of being watched, made her swallow hard. Didn't take any stretch of the imagination. To her mind, each of the wavering shadows up there hid some half-starved and crazed attacker.

They ground their way past another abandoned car that was nose down in the drainage ditch to the right. One of the doors was open, a partially skeletonized body laying across the sill.

"Guess we're back in no man's land," Sam muttered.

A pile of logs had been laid across a two-track branching off into the trees, and a shot-up F 150 was pulled to the side, hood buried up to the cab in a pine tree's lower branches.

Here and there, piles of belongings, abandoned clothing, and personal effects like paintings, trophies, photo albums, and books marked the location of a looted vehicle.

The first time they drove over a flattened human body, Breeze felt a quiver run through her. Clothing, crushed bones, and dried flesh had been ground into the pale pavement. No more than a mile beyond, they ran over another. A child this time, identifiable as human only by the compacted and filthy pants and shirt.

"Just when you thought it couldn't get more bizarre," Sam whispered, and pointed where a tall gate—like the entry to a ranch—was chained closed. On the high pole frame above, two skeletons hung. Mostly desiccated meat and sinew, the macabre sight was no more than glimpsed before disappearing into the darkness behind as the heavy snowplow passed.

"Think they're trying to make a statement?" Breeze ran a nervous hand over the gooseflesh that had broken out on her arm.

"You know as well as I do that people fleeing the cities would have turned first to the mountains." Sam sniffed, rubbing his nose. "At the height of the Collapse, I'll bet this country had nothing on the Donner Party."

*Oh, sure, Sam. You just had to say that, didn't you?*

Rounding a switchback, they came on the lead vehicles. Jimenez's Humvee was finishing the job of pushing a wrecked Mercedes Benz G 550 out of the way. The expensive vehicle lay on its side, could be heard grinding across the asphalt as the Humvee clawed for traction, tires breaking and throwing gravel.

"Hope they have a sympathetic insurance agent when they make the claim," Tully said, leaning over the steering wheel.

"Don't think they're making a claim," Breeze told him as the Humvee backed away, turned, and made its way past the gouged pavement where the luxury four-by-four had been. She pointed to where desiccating bodies lay side by side, face down in the thick grass at the roadside. Looked like they'd been laid there. Or perhaps ordered down before being shot in the back. She couldn't tell, given the brief glimpse.

Breeze clamped her eyes shut, recalling visions of a little girl: She's dead. Clutching a filthy stuffed animal. A sheep. Her body alone in a bright yellow tent. Flies are crawling all over. The memory is crystal clear. The stench is in her nose. Slipping up like a miasma from her memory.

She fought the shivers.

"You all right?" Sam asked, staring her way in the glow of the dash lights.

"I'll be okay. Just get me the hell out of this canyon."

"Too much time on The Line," Tully told her. "And the farther south we get, the more likely we're going to see some horrible shit."

She nodded, biting her lip.

On the dash clock, it was just after midnight. They should have been in Lyons by now.

# KYZER

The following morning, when General Norman Kyzer and Major James Reynold strolled into the governor's office, each with his cover under his arm, I was prepared to step out on Kace's heels. To my surprise, Agar gave us his "stay" hand sign, telling General Kyzer, "Mr. Adams and Ms. Davis have my confidence."

To me, he added, "Lauren, you've met the general. You should know that Major Reynolds serves as liaison between F.E. Warren Air Base and my office."

When I shook the guy's hand and looked into his eyes, it was a no-bullshit kind of situation.

"Hear that you were on the ball when that woman would have taken out the governor," Reynolds told me. "Anything I can do to help, let me know."

"Thank you, sir." Not knowing what to do with myself, I took a position off to the side by the window, and spent my time watching Kyzer and Reynolds. Did they pose a threat? Doubted it, but the truth is, you never know.

Reynolds started out, saying, "We're still monitoring shortwave transmissions. Most are in the Rocky Mountain west, down through Mexico and into South America. All report tough times, civil collapse, and shortages."

"And from back east?" Agar asked, perching on the corner of his desk.

"At first," Kyzer said, "we heard some chatter from preppers who built fallout shelters, but that's decreased over the last weeks. Maybe *they were hunted down. Maybe they lost the will to live when they figured out just how bad it was out there."*

*"And the Chinese?" Agar asked. "Any news there?"*

*Kyzer told him, "Not much. We've gotten snippets of information, mostly rumors. Apparently, they were counting on more container ships full of resupply and reinforcement. They landed three armies and came within a whisker of a fourth before the Navy took out every container ship in the Pacific."*

*"And what does that mean for the three Chinese armies here?" Agar asked.*

*Kyzer cocked his head. "They're in trouble. That there's no resupply for either side. For example, at Miramar, they're down to less than a thousand gallons of jet fuel. And all the while, the Chinese are sitting on the central California oil fields, and refining their own fuel."*

— Excerpt from Lauren Davis' *Journal.*

# CHAPTER TWENTY-TWO

SAM BLINKED awake as Tully pulled the snowplow to a stop behind the JLTV and lead Humvees. He didn't remember drifting off. Just the road, the brush passing in the headlights' beam, and the rocking sway of the plow. Sometime, Breeze had settled against him, her head on his shoulder. As he shifted, she started and jerked awake. Gave him a weary smile as she straightened in the seat.

The dash clock read 3:33. What should have been a twenty-minute drive had taken three hours as the convoy had to stop, push, or winch abandoned vehicles out of the road, and in several cases, pluck fallen trees from where they'd either been cut down or fallen.

At the Rist Canyon junction, they had been forced to push their way through a tangle of abandoned cars, trucks, and RVs. The way they were run together didn't make sense. Looked like they'd all stopped in lines that converged at a cargo truck that had been parked in the middle of the intersection. One line of vehicles had come from Rist Canyon, the others headed in opposite directions on Stove Prairie Road. All bumper to bumper. Then, from the looks of things, a major gunfight broke out. Given the bullet holes, shattered windshields, and the way the corpses had fallen down between the vehicles, they might have all gone mad in an orgy of mass murder.

The afterimages had filled Sam's dreams, replaying over and over as the snowplow rocked and bounced its way down the Buckhorn Valley.

Breeze untangled herself, and Sam stretched, staring out over the JLTV and Humvees. The usual chaos of deserted vehicles blocked the road. He resettled, prepared to wait it out as the obstructing vehicles had to be pulled back and shoved to the side. Only then did the reason for the jam become apparent: Someone with a backhoe had pulled up the pavement and dug a trench across the highway, then down to either side of the right of way, across the barrow ditches, and into the trees on the right. On the left, the trench ran down through the barbed-wire fence to Buckhorn Creek. Backdirt had been piled behind the excavation to create a berm, and then a log barrier had been erected, the trunks carefully laid into a breastwork.

"*Think we can bridge it?*" Lieutenant Daniels asked on the com.

"*Negative,*" Paco Jimenez called back from the lead Humvee. "*From where I'm sitting, the trench looks about as wide as our wheels. We fall in, we're going to have to be pulled out.*"

"*Ideas, people?*" Daniels asked.

"*Got a spare Caterpillar in the emergency gear?*" William Krandal asked.

"*Cute.*" Daniels didn't sound amused.

"*Whoever built it wasn't fooling around. We could probably attack that backdirt with shovels. As long as no one shoots at us, we could backfill that trench in a couple of hours, then we could use chains to pull the log barrier apart.*" Jimenez sounded thoughtful.

Breeze reached for the mic. "I got a better idea. Pull the M1089 around. We can cherry pick the logs, drop them into the trench to fill it. Then one of the plows can drive across, drop its blade, and pull the backdirt over the logs to make a crossing."

"*Love it,*" Daniels answered. "*How the hell did you come up with that?*"

"I guess none of you guys grew up on a ranch where you had to backfill over a culvert?" Breeze smiled smugly, replacing the mic.

"*You heard the lady,*" Daniels ordered. "*Get the wrecker up here. It was a narrow enough road before we started shoving these cars off to the side, so we're going to have to do some fancy maneuvering. Don't get anything stuck in the meantime. Let's do this smart, people. Corporal Nonan, I want flankers out with night vision. Someone's going to be upset about us taking their fort apart. I want us to see them first.*"

"*Roger that, LT,*" came the calls in reply.

It took the convoy a great deal of backing, shuffling, and repositioning amidst the grinding of gears and shining of lights, to get the convoy resorted and the M1089 up front. Then spooling out its cable, the logs had to be chained up. Where enough gap could be found to allow them to wrap the chain was never anywhere close to the balance point. That meant the logs had to be pulled apart, then re-chained at the balance point so the top log could be lifted high enough to be swung up and lowered painstakingly into the trench. Call it anything but a precise operation.

Sam gave up trying to sleep as the wrecker's diesel roared and the bright lights cast white shadows across the wrecked cars, trucks, and camper trailers they'd shoved off the narrow road. All had the new trademark of abandonment: Doors had been left open, cargo hatches gaping, the fuel hatches stuck out, caps missing where thieves had siphoned any remaining gas that might have been in the tanks.

"I'm going out for air," Sam told Tully who was sleeping with his head against the window.

Breeze stirred, blinked, and tried to stretch in the truck's confined cab. "What are you doing?"

"I need out," Sam told her as he popped the door, grabbed his Marlin, and, favoring his sore chest, climbed down to the ground. He wasn't all that surprised when she followed him, slinging her M4.

"Gotta pee," she told him. "Watch my back."

Breeze ducked into the dark behind an abandoned Prius. The night air was cool, the scent of conifers, water, and damp grass mixed with the tang of diesel exhaust drifting up from where the M1089 growled and banged as it moved logs.

Breeze emerged, buckling her belt. She resettled her hat, pulling the brim low. "Let's go take a look."

Sam followed in her footsteps, walking in the glare of the headlights.

Rounding the wrecker, Sam heard Sergeant White Eagle call, "That's good!"

The latest log stuck up from the trench, sort of humped in the middle, broken branches sticking out in a sharp abatis. White Eagle stepped down, unfastening the chain. She straightened, climbed out of the trench, and gave the operator a thumbs up as the hook was withdrawn.

"What about the rest of the logs?" the operator called down from the boom controls. Sam could see maybe five were left in the barricade.

"Lay them off to the side," Lieutenant Daniels called.

With a belch of diesel, the boom swung around. Private Krandal grabbed the hook and tugged it over to where the remains of the breastwork still blocked the road.

Breeze took the opportunity to dash across, stepping on the highest log in the trench, then scrambling up the earthen berm. Clambering over the last of the barricade, she called over her shoulder to Sam, "Wouldn't it have been nice to have had a wrecker at Clark Ranch?"

"Yeah." He found a spot out of the way to watch as Krandal wrapped the cable around a couple of logs, gave the thumbs up to the operator, and stepped back as the cable went tight. The M1089's exhaust blatted loud in the night, the heavy logs lifted, spreading apart as they did. As the operator swung the boom around, the logs cracked and banged as they were dragged to the side.

Sam laid an arm over Breeze's shoulder, thinking back to that day. "Amber would still be with us. Lot of things would have been different."

Breeze leaned against him, warm, firm. "Looking back twenty years from now, that can be our motto, huh?"

He nodded as the boom swung back for another log, the hook and cable swinging in the bright lights.

"LT!" Shane Goggles came trotting up the road. His night vision gear was tipped up onto his helmet. "Got an ATV coming up the road. Private Gomez says he's got people on horseback, too. Three coming up the creek bottom, weaving through the brush. Another two riding through the edge of the timber where it skirts a big alfalfa field. Tortilla and Brylan are keeping an eye on them from a flank position. If they're hostiles, we'll have them."

Lieutenant Daniels stepped across the last log as Kran found a gap beneath it that he could slip the hook through. She was staring down to the south where the road faded into the night. "They have night vision?"

"Not that we could see, LT." Goggles turned to point. "There and there, but they're armed. My guess, they're carrying ARs. Seems to be the weapon of choice down here."

The M1089's barking exhaust accompanied the last log as it was dragged summarily to the side and unhooked.

"Want to bet that whoever's coming built this barricade?" Sam asked.

"No takers," Breeze told him, pulled away, and slipped the M4's sling from her shoulder.

As the big wrecker backed away, the puttering sound of an ATV could be heard. Sam thought it sounded like an oversized lawnmower. Cousin Reuben, in Brooklyn, had had a lawn. Reuben. Hard to believe. He and his wife Amy, the three kids...all dead. His beloved lawn to be forever untended.

Krandal had taken to guiding the plow as Tully eased it forward, the big blade up.

Sam watched the front wheels as they rolled up against the protruding log. Tully gave the truck throttle, the tires rising onto the rounded surface. With a mighty crack, the logs collapsed, dropping the truck six inches. Despite the banging and clanking of the rocking plow, Tully drove forward, blade taking down part of the backdirt berm.

In the headlights, Kran turned his thumb down.

Tully dropped the blade on the far side of the dirt berm, threw the big Mack truck into reverse, and backed. As he did soil bunched behind the blade, scooped back and across the trench as the tandem rear duals spun and grabbed for traction.

"Works like a charm," Sam noted.

"It'll take Tully a few passes, but it will be smooth as a baby's butt," Breeze promised. Then she turned her eyes on the approaching ATV.

"Flankers out," Daniels said into her battle com. "Be ready for anything, people."

As the ATV barreled forward into the glare, Sam used his forefinger to press the Marlin's safety off.

The machine was a Honda side-by-side. Through the windscreen, Sam could see two people. Stopping maybe fifty feet short of where he, Breeze, and Daniels stood, the driver killed the ignition. A man wearing a ball cap emerged, while from the passenger seat, a woman stepped out. Both carried cut-down ARs. Their dress consisted of jeans, work boots, and button-down work shirts under Carhartt jackets. What Sam would have called ranch wear.

"Who are you?" the man called, squinting against the light.

"Wyoming National Guard. I'm Lieutenant Susan Daniels. We mean you and your people no harm. We're just passing through. Headed down to Lyons to extract some personnel and valuable equipment. Then we'll be back through on our return trip."

"What the hell? You took down our barricade?" the woman asked. "Do you know what you've done?"

"It's a county road," Daniels snapped in no uncertain terms. "Like I said, we're just passing through."

The man stormed up, eyes slitted against the glare. "God damn it! Do you know what we've been through? That barrier keeps the looters and thieves out. It's a goddamned war! These bastards just shoot anything that moves. Human, critter, it don't matter. As it is, we've only got six of our cattle—"

"Damn it, Jason!" the woman cried. "Keep your mouth shut! They'll take it all."

Breeze stepped forward. "We're not interested in your cattle. We've got plenty north of The Line. Like the Lieutenant said, we're just passing through." She extended a hand. "Hi. I'm Breeze Tappan. This guy is Sam Delgado. Who are you?"

"Marge Gallagher. This is my husband, Jason."

Jason was squinting from under the bill of his cap. Looked to be in his sixties, smooth-shaven face lined by the years, a bitter tension in the set of his mouth. "Those Humvees I see behind the plows?"

"They are." Daniels pointed at the dark. "We've got your riders under surveillance. Please don't try anything."

Jason swallowed hard, resistance seeming to drain from him. The woman, Marge, still skeptical, shifted uneasily. "Just safe passage?"

"Down and back," Daniels added. "Fast as we can."

"And meanwhile, we're laid wide open to who knows what kind of horror coming down the valley." The woman paused. "Assuming you're who you say you are."

"Marge," Jason said. "We're outgunned. Don't push this thing. Against military, we don't stand a chance."

"Hey," Daniels cried. "Like I said, we're not going to hurt you."

Sam asked, "Where are all the people from the cars we just cleared away?"

Marge's expression pinched as she tried to meet Sam's eyes. Hard to do in the glare of the lights. "People who can't take no for an answer... well, it's our property. Our cattle. Our home. Been tough enough making a living in this damn state. Cattle prices...the idiotic rules and regulations. And then there were the damn taxes. It's a ranch, not a money machine for county social programs. Got sued by the lawyer from Denver who bought the forty acres south of us. Can you believe? Said our cows were a nuisance that polluted *his* creek! And then this?"

"Marge," Jason told her. "That's enough." He'd adopted a defensive hunch, grip tightening on his weapon.

Sam shifted so he could pull the Marlin up fast, loose a snap shot. Not that he'd ever tried it before.

Daniels, looking weary, said, "I could give a flying fig. Jason, Marge, listen. You're flanked. Outnumbered and outgunned. We're not here to cause you any harm. Just let us pass and you can go back to your war with your looters."

"What about our barricade?" Marge cried. "And the one on the south?"

"How about we drag a couple of logs back across the road?" Breeze asked, glancing sidelong at Daniels. "It's little enough."

"That suit you?" Daniels asked.

"Guess it will have to be," Marge agreed. Turning she called, "Guys! Come on in. No shooting tonight."

Sam exhaled, swung his Marlin up and propped it on his shoulder. "Not that there's that much threat left behind us. But for a few starving stragglers, most everyone we've seen coming across from the Poudre has been dead."

"Yeah, well," Jason told him, "from what we hear, there's plenty of two-footed animals as you get closer to town. Think like all Hell busted loose. Like demons, they're doing anything and everything for a meal. I tell you, I'd have never thought it could have come to this."

"Given what we've seen" Marge added, "there's no limit to abomination. And, Lord knows, we've come close a time or two ourselves."

Jason's lips twitched as he turned guilty eyes to the side.

# WORLD WAR III

*It's one thing when you've heard all the rumors. Another when you're standing in the same room as the people who are fighting World War III. Me, I'd seen the missiles go up. Been there when that Chinese pilot was shot down over OP Charlie X-Ray.*

*As night fell over Cheyenne, Agar stepped over to the window. "What are the long term expectations for California?"*

*"Static," General Kyzer told him. "The army is holding the Sierras as well as the Coastal ranges from Ukiah in the north and south to Monterey. The San Joaquin Valley squeezes out like a Chinese bulge in the San Francisco salient. The Los Angeles salient is limited mostly to the city with a salient north to Bakersfield. Most of the Chinese army is swarming over the LA Basin. Marines at Camp Pendleton still hold the south, the Army is dug in in the mountains around San Bernardino. Seattle is pretty much the same. The Chinese control the city from Tacoma in the south to Marysville in the north. The army holds the high ground on all sides. Logistics is the key to ending this."*

*"What the hell were they thinking?" Agar asked quietly, as though talking to himself.*

*Kyzer gave him a weary smile. "The US was supposed to collapse so far that the Chinese could arrive as saviors. Restoring order. Taking control and bringing security to a nation tearing itself apart."*

*"Worked, if you ask me," Agar said as he leaned forward. "I've got a reconnaissance column in Colorado called Fallen Eagle. They're headed down to hopefully bring back an insulin lab. They're reporting cannibals and just about every horror you can imagine."*

*"Yeah," Kyzer leaned back in his chair. "Well, China didn't figure on*

*two things: They didn't expect their computer virus to keep mutating until it took down the entire world banking system, including their own. And they didn't figure that we'd be in a position to blanket their skies with EMPs. Now their position is just as precarious as ours." A pause. "And if our intelligence is right, they've got almost two billion people starving."*

*Agar shook his head lightly. "That means they're even more desperate than we are. I suspect they'll do anything necessary to get to the agricultural heart of America."*

— Excerpt from Lauren Davis' *Journal.*

# CHAPTER TWENTY-THREE

DAWN HAD TURNED the gray skies pale; the morning glow seemed sickly off to the east beyond the low peaks rimming the Buckhorn Valley. Many of the slopes had burned off in the series of fires that had ravaged the northern part of the Front Range in the 2020s. The ranks of dead trees gave the slopes, outcrops, and darker and deeply shadowed drainages a furred appearance.

Sam sat on one of the logs the big M1089 wrecker had pulled from the southern barricade and laid to the side. It was now wrestling with a Ponderosa where it was intertwined in the remaining logs that blocked the lower Buckhorn Road. To the west, the long-burned ramparts of Storm Mountain vanished into the low overcast. A light rain was falling, more of a mist actually.

"Yes, sir. I understand, sir," Lieutenant Daniels spoke into the radio. She stood in the door of the JLTV, the handset to her ear. She had called Ragnovich. Was reporting their achingly slow progress.

From inside, the radio could be heard. *"Susan, I've been on the radio to Dr. Avery at Boulder Mountain Biotek. Says he's not sure how much longer they can hold out. Said the last of their water ran out yesterday. They're under attack and on the last fumes of fuel to keep the freezers running. You know what's at stake. I have every confidence in your ability."*

"Thank you, Sir." A pause as Daniels gave the barricade a hard squint. "Fallen Eagle One, out."

*"Best of luck, Susan. Cheyenne actual, out."*

Daniels reached in to clip the handset to its holder, straightened, and gave Sam a worried shake of the head. Then she strode off to where the wrecker was wrestling the heavy Ponderosa to the side.

Breeze had taken a seat on the ground beside him, back to the log, legs drawn up. Her head was down, the misty rain beading on her old Rand's hat. She'd had it custom made back in her rodeo days by a hat maker in Billings. Nice hat. Sam reached up to feel his own. A second-hand gray Resistol that Old Bill had scrounged up for him down in Hot Springs. What mattered was that it fit tight and did what cowboy hats were supposed to: it kept the rain off his head and shaded it from the sun. Or would. Assuming the sun ever came out again.

The guy walking up from the remains of the barricade was in his thirties, wearing a green North Face windbreaker, a John Deere tractor cap, brown-duck pants, and those ugly square-toed western boots that had been in vogue before the Collapse. He had a lean dark face, long thin nose, and sharp black eyes. He'd introduced himself as Phil Collins and rode one of the buckskin horses.

Now he walked over, settled himself on the log to Sam's right. Leaning forward he braced his elbows on his knees, rubbed his hands together, and watched as the wrecker pulled another log loose before swinging it to the side. Said, "A lot of work went into building that. Scaling them down from the slope. The digging of the trenches. And then stacking the logs. All of it done with loaded rifles, not to mention a couple of firefights. Hard to see it come down."

"I don't think the threat's as great," Sam told him. "You heard that we cleared the man eaters out of Poudre Canyon. Mishawaka's going to patrol it with Wyoming Guard and militia help. Don't know that anyone can get up Rist Canyon, and if they do, they'll have to clear the logjam of derelict vehicles on that side of the Stove Prairie junction. It's been over three months since the Collapse. Gas and potable water are gone. Food's pretty scarce, and the few people we saw getting here last night were looking half-wild and starved."

"There are others," Phil told him. "Sure, the weak ones, the suburban family types, the soft ones, they're all dead or fled. Now, as to what's left in Fort Collins, Loveland, and along the foothills? They're the tough ones. Mean." He looked down at his wet hands, water dripping from his hat bill. "The ones who will do anything to stay alive."

Sam glanced at the line of cars, trucks, vans, and SUVs waiting to be pushed out of the way on the other side of the barricade. "Something tells me that folks like that aren't just down in the towns. Something Marge said last night. About coming close to abomination."

Phil shot him a "fuck you" look from under his hat. "Don't get high and mighty on me, Wyoming."

"Wouldn't think it." Sam gestured around at the green alfalfa field beyond the ditch. All the barbed wire had been stripped from the right-of-way fence leaving lonely t-posts in a row, and, from what he knew of fences, another six strands had been added to the boundary fence that ran from the barricade, east-west along the base of the field. It continued across the valley, and up into the trees. That wasn't for the containment of any cattle.

Pointing back over his shoulder, Sam indicated the burned-out wreck of the once-spectacular log house that dominated a flat on the side of the mountain. Said, "That's not what the Tappans would call a two-by-twice broken-down ranch house. I'd say this forty acres once belonged the lawyer guy from Denver who sued Jason and Marge over their 'polluting' cattle."

Phil rocked his jaw, stare narrowing. Then he made a snuffing sound. "Yeah? Hell, what do I know?" He rubbed a wet finger under his razor-like nose. "The story is that Brandeis, that's the Denver lawyer guy, about a week into this mess, well, he shot one of the Gallagher cows that got through a hole in the fence. Or he cut it. Nobody knows."

Phil stretched out a leg, shifted, his pants soaking in the rain. "Jason walked up on him while he was cutting up the cow. The place was crawling with people trying to get out of Fort Collins. Coming from everywhere, on foot, in cars. Looking to get away from the mess in town. You know, find a place to lay low in the mountains until order was reestablished?"

"Yeah." Sam's mind went back to field camp. How Kirstin and Dylan couldn't wait to make a break for Denver. Never to be heard from again.

"Anyhow, things got heated. If you can believe the stories, Brandeis never did know when to keep his mouth shut. Fancy high-rolling lawyer, you know. And Jason had already had too many cattle killed. Been harassed and threatened too many times." A beat. "Paybacks are a bitch."

"So Marge and Jason took his forty acres?" Breeze asked, apparently no longer asleep.

"Used to be theirs in the beginning," Phil told her. "Wouldn't have sold it in the first place if they hadn't needed the money." Phil gestured. "Sold it for a million six. Used the money to pay off a huge amount of debt. They'd had to borrow against the value of the ranch to pay the property taxes. Didn't matter that it was ag land. Prices around here? They'd gone sky high. Anyhow, Jason got his forty acres back for the cost of a measly .223 cartridge."

"And Brandeis? Where's he now?" Sam asked.

With a tip of the head, Phil told him, "With a lot of others. Up on that bench yonder, beneath six feet of cobbles and dirt. Guess it don't hurt to tell you. Not like any law is left in this country. And most of the bodies up there, except for the ones who died defending the ranch, were killing cattle, shooting people here. When it became apparent that Jason and Marge couldn't patrol the whole three thousand acres, some, like me, volunteered. Said we'd help guard the place from looters and scum in exchange for a meal." He made a huffing sound. "Just five of us left. There were seventeen once upon a time."

Phil glanced again at the terrace above Buckhorn Creek. "Having a backhoe sure made the grave digging easier. Only about six gallons of fuel left for it now."

"One for each cow," Breeze declared.

"Yeah." Phil went back to rubbing his rain-wet hands. "Two heifers, a steer, and three old cows. No future in that if we can't find a bull somewhere."

"Wyoming has bulls," Breeze told him.

Phil gave a dismissive snort. "Right. As if we could get there in the first place." A pause. "And assuming none of the scum and looters sneak in and kill what's left just to cut a steak off and run."

# WYOMING BEEF

*I will always remember that feeling of shock: The world died as a result of unintended consequences. China completely misread the American reaction to the bank hack. Instead of a country in social and political turmoil, they landed in a full-fledged Armageddon. The total chaos they marched into had broken down to the point there was nothing left to "Free." No government to offer a surrender. And worse, no functioning distribution system to commandeer to feed the desperate urban masses who were burning, looting, and murdering each other. No power grid. Nothing a modern army could use to restore order.*

*The use of the cargo container ships had been brilliant. The perfect covert mass military infiltration to complement their Trojan malware that was corrupting the banks. But the latter worked too well, and the former not well enough.*

*I was mulling that, wondering where Tyrell was, and if he might even still be alive, when Kyzer asked, "So, the trains are running again?"*

*"From Grand Island, Nebraska, to Boise," Agar told him. "We're working on from Salt Lake to Reno."*

*"What's the problem?" Kyzer leaned forward, barely concealing his interest.*

*"Security along the line. A lot—and I mean a lot—of refugees came spilling out of California. Reno's a mess. There's no telling what condition the tracks are in." Agar pointed a finger. "And, General, even if we knew we could run a train that far, there's no guarantee that it wouldn't be swarmed by starving refugees. Eastern Nevada is a no-man's-land as it is, and the Salt Lake Valley would have gone down every bit as hard as*

Colorado if the Mormon Battalion hadn't stepped in. Even then, restoring order left a lot of bodies on the streets."

Kyzer now pointed his own finger. "You understand, don't you? The Chinese aren't the only ones starving. So are our soldiers. Wyoming has beef. Our soldiers, the ones who are dying fighting the Chinese, have empty bellies."

"All we have to do," Agar mused, "is get that beef through a famished mob of starving refugees."

The meeting might have lasted another ten or fifteen minutes. Kace and I escorted the officers out, handed them over to Randy in the outer office. When I turned back, I stopped short. At his desk, the expression on Agar's face reminded me of a dying martyr's. I could read pain and futility in every line and angle. Then, as if stifling a cry, he leaned his head forward onto the blotter. A figure of total defeat.

I quietly closed the door.

— Excerpt from Lauren Davis' *Journal.*

# CHAPTER TWENTY-FOUR

WHAT ONCE HAD BEEN Masonville lay in ruins. As Breeze saw it, the only thing memorable about the community these days was the formation of police cars. Three of them with the words Larimer County Sheriff's Office—along with the silver star emblazing the door—stenciled on the side. They'd been parked, front to rear in a triangle at the three-way junction of Stove Prairie Road, the road to Fort Collins, and the Buckhorn Road that lead south to the Big Thompson Canyon and Loveland. Definitely defensive. Sort of like a sort of three-sided fort. One had been burned, the other two had their windows smashed out, bullet holes here and there on the body, doors left agape. No sign remained of the deputies.

The small community must have been quite something, charming, quaint, with its store at the crossroads, the trendy cafes, quilt shops, and local ceramic shop in a barn. All shaded by ancient cottonwood trees. Someone determined had boarded up the store's windows and doors in an attempt to keep looters out. Someone even more determined had smashed their way in. The ground around was strewn with empty bottles, plastic packaging, beer cans, and broken liquor bottles.

Colorful frame houses dotted the older part of town down along the creek. Fancier places on two and three-acre lots with trees gave way to million dollar spreads on ten and twenty acres. All of them hinting at an exclusive Fort Collins bedroom community, located as it was, a mere twenty minutes from the city limits.

As the convoy rolled in, it was to pass through a ghost town. Stuff had been scattered about, doors gaped, windows were broken. Some, as per the norm, remained only as incinerated shells, the fires having blackened and scorched the overhanging cottonwoods and willows.

But the road was mostly open; the few vehicles generally were pushed to the side. From the looks of it, people had worked to keep the road clear right up to the last. Perhaps it had been the work of roving gangs—the kind the Gallagher bunch said they'd built the barricade to deter.

Whoever had done it, the convoy made good time in the pale morning light as it rolled down the Buckhorn Valley on Larimer County Road 27, past quarries where the sandstone slope rose immediately to the west. Orchards, pastures, and abandoned farms lay to the left as the valley widened between the hogbacks. Most of the farmhouses, occasional acreages, and roadside businesses gaped empty, though a few—looking like forts with their barricades, boarded windows, and coils of barbed wire stripped from fences—appeared to be occupied. Many even had rifle loopholes cut in the walls.

"At least somebody made it," Breeze noted.

Another tangle of vehicles clogged the road at the intersection with Highway 34. The bottom land here was thick with old cottonwoods, orchards, roadside businesses, and small acreages set back in the trees. Must have been a nice place to live with the Big Thompson River running behind the small fields and just beyond the screen of trees.

Evidence of another of the Larimer County Sheriff's road blocks could be seen where a couple of pickups and two cruisers had been shoved into a road-side tavern's parking lot. The bodies here had been laid at the edge of the parking lot, all placed in a neat row. The only jarring part was how their clothes had been disheveled by the ravens, crows, and the five buzzards that took to the air.

"You'd think we' d see rats and cats and things going at the corpses," Sam noted.

"Nope. They were all eaten at the start of the Collapse," Tully told him.

Heading west up Highway 34, past all the lodges, restaurants, and small farms, the oddity was that the road allowed unfettered travel without as many derelict vehicles or trash.

"Makes sense when you think about it," Breeze told him. "This close to Loveland, people fleeing still had full tanks of gas. It was only when they got into the back country, got held up and robbed, or turned back, that they ran out."

"Might be, but there's little sign of anyone alive down here. These businesses, the shops and farms, all of them look abandoned."

They made the turn south onto Carter Lake Road, still making good time as they wound past housing developments, rural acreages, and up the hogback under the dam. The route passed along a hillside dotted with pines amidst patches of wild plums and the darker greens of mountain mahogany.

Sam could finally get a handle on the geology, on the extent of development, and a feel for the scale of the post-Collapse depopulation. All those houses and subdivisions on the surrounding hillsides and down in the valley. All were dark, nothing moved. No vehicles, no horses or cattle, no people out and about. Only the birds. Some sorts of wrens or finches. Magpies, and the constant crows with occasional raptors.

Approaching a gap at the top of the ridge, a large sign that had once proclaimed the Carter Lake Recreational Area had been slapped over with white paint. Crude black letters warned: BLACK ZONE! CLAIMED LAND! WE WILL KILL YOU! STAY OUT!

In the flat parking area around the sign with all of its interpretive plaques and the usual posted rules and regulations, a pile of rotting bodies added to the effect. The column of flies buzzing above it made a black fog that wavered as a flock of magpies and crows exploded from the intertwined limbs and fluid-stained clothing.

Tully muttered, "Guess the LT isn't too worried about the Black Zone, huh?"

In reply, Breeze said, "Must be something about having a chain gun on the JLTV."

Sam gave a sad shake of the head as they drove past. "Hard to believe. Must have been thirty people in that pile. Three months ago, sight of it would have stopped the entire world in its tracks. But now? It's just another pile of dead people."

Breeze gave him a flat stare from under her hat brim. "What's hard to believe is that it only took what? Three days? Just that quick, one world died and another was born."

"I'd have never believed it," Tully told them as he braked for the slowing Humvees up front. A barricade had been set up at the end of the gap where the highway passed through a cut in the sandstone. It consisted of a Ford F 250 and a Chevy Silverado pulled across the road. Atop the sandstone on either side, stood guys with rifles positioned to shoot down at whatever vehicle was stopped below. Sam figured that the sight of armored vehicles must have had a sobering effect, because they were backpedaling out of sight.

"*Attention,*" Daniels' voice blared out through the PA. "*We're Wyoming National Guard. You can clear the way, or we will clear it.*"

A bearded man had been seated in the Ford's driver seat. The guy had a ball cap on his shaggy brown hair. Looked to be a burly sort in filthy jeans. He stood on the Ford's doorsill, bracing himself on the open driver's door, and shouted back, "What do you want here? We're Black Zone. Carter Lake is claimed ground. Uh, like, our property!"

*"We only want to pass through,"* Daniels answered. *"This is a county road."*

"Hey!" the guy yelled back. "We don't want no trouble. Not with army. Give me a minute to move these trucks. Don't shoot!"

The guy scrambled to get back into the cab, slammed the door, and started the Ford. Took him a couple of tries to get it clear of the Silverado. Then he backed it out of sight behind the gap. Moments later he came trotting back, jumped into the Silverado, and wheeled it around and out of the way.

From his high vantage in the snowplow, Sam could just see the guy atop the sandstone to his right. He was peeking over the side, the muzzle of his rifle barely visible.

The Humvees started forward, the rest of the convoy following. The pickups had been parked in a pullout past the hump of sandstone. As they passed, Sam could see cars, pickups, SUVs, and vans where they'd been pushed off the embankment where a road teed before crossing the Carter Lake dam. A lot of cars. Maybe twenty-five to thirty.

The highway turned south, following the slope on the east side of the reservoir. Most of the lake bed was empty, ringed like a drained bathtub. Muddy flats could be seen where the bottom shallowed out. Looked like someone had pulled the plug. Along the receding shore, the occasional camp had been made. The vehicles, camp trailers, and tents having been left high and dry. Possessions and the occasional body lay scattered about. But most startling were the boats. Canted on their sides, looking like some perverted driftwood that had washed up on the beach, only to have the water drain away and leave them stranded, looking desolate.

"What do you think happened to the people?" Tully asked. "I mean, they came here. Maybe expecting to fish? Figuring they'd be able to live off the lake until things got back to normal?"

"There, in the water down by the dam." Breeze pointed. "Two small boats. Looks like they're dragging a net. And see? There, on the shore? That lash-up of tarps. Like a shanty? What's that? Fifteen, sixteen people?"

Sam craned his head. Even across the distance, he could see that they all carried rifles, were watching warily as the convoy passed. A couple of four-wheel drive trucks with oversized tires had been driven down. The backs were filled with coolers. The way the watchers stood, how they handled their weapons, the group gave off an ominous air.

"I'd call that a bunch of tough customers," Sam said softly.

"Filling those coolers with fish?" Breeze asked. "Black Zone? Claimed land? I think I get it."

"Yeah," Sam told her as he watched the people below scrambling around, taking defensive positions around the trucks. "The lake is a food resource. They control access. That roadblock back there? It was trap.

Stop any vehicle driving into the gap. Shoot the people. Pile their bodies out by the sign, loot the vehicles for fuel or food, and dispose of it over the edge of the dam."

"And meanwhile, they're fishing," Tully added, making a face as he warily glanced up at the pine-dotted and brush-covered slope leading up to the rimrock. "Tough bastards right up until they're face to face with a chain gun, huh?"

Breeze's lips had pinched, her glare fixed on the abandoned camps and pathetic boats where they'd lodged as the water receded. "Fucking bunch of predators. Should have just shot our way through."

"Start killing predators," Sam cautioned, "you'll be at war with everyone south of The Line, and maybe half the people north of it. Edgewater and his band weren't exactly the kind with the milk of human kindness by the quart in every vein."

"You ask me," Tully said from where he was scanning the mountainside, "the only so-called good people in this country are the corpses."

Sam shook his head. "The folks at Mishawaka were all right."

"Maybe." Breeze, too, was keeping an eye on the slope above. "But the Gallaghers? I've been thinking about them. About all those cars we pushed off to the side at the barricades. Want to make any bets as to our reception if we'd just showed up driving a Toyota Camry?"

Sam shot her a sidelong glance. "You think we'd be resting peacefully under... What did Phil say? Six feet of gravel and rock?"

Breeze barely shrugged. "There may be some good people holed up somewhere. If they had a basement full of groceries. And no one knew about it. And looters didn't show up, bash their door in, and take it all. Those people might have bought some time. But eventually they're going to come out of their cellars. Guess what kind of people they're going to find?"

"Black Zone," Sam answered as the road climbed up over a gap in the hogback. As it did, the Humvees slowed. If the junkyard of cars tumbled down the slope to lodge in the mountain mahogany wasn't a good enough clue, they'd found the back door to the Black Zone. The roadblock was laid out in the same configuration: Two pickups blocking a chokepoint. Shooters positioned off to either side. Unlike on the north side, the guards here didn't even bother with a hail.

The guy who'd been lounging in the fancy Ford F 350 dually, just took one glance. Seeing the line of military Humvees, he slammed the door, hit the ignition, and throwing the truck in gear, backed enough to clear the F 250 across from him. Shifting the truck into drive, he hammered the throttle, threw gravel, and went racing off down the hill.

The guys on the sides, figuring they, too, were screwed, fired a couple of shots over their shoulders as they ran for all they were worth.

Bounding from sandstone slab to sandstone slab, they vanished into the scrubby pines.

The com crackled to life. *"Tully,"* Daniels' voice came through, *"I'm not feeling generous. Drop your blade on the way through. Knock that Ford pickup out of the way."*

"Roger that, LT," Tully said with a grin.

Sam figured that Tully had been getting enough practice. Using the hydraulic controls, he set the blade. Had the angle just right. He barely slowed as he slid the big Ford with its chrome custom wheels onto the shoulder, and lifting the blade at just the right moment, rolled it onto its side.

As the convoy started its way down the winding switchbacks, Sam got his first look at the Colorado piedmont. Where the city of Loveland lay spread out some six or seven miles to the east, it didn't matter that they were three months into the Collapse. A smoky haze still rose over the distant buildings.

# DEMONS

*Marsy ranch...*
   *That's where I am.*
   *Exhausted and afraid.*
   *Shivering in the cold dark barn. The air is thick with the smell of blood, urine, horses, mold, and the scent of fresh hay. I lean against a tractor tire; it's gone flat from a bullet strike. I have just put my hand down on a dead man's face. Tyrell's trusty old M4 lays heavy on my lap. Through bullet holes and gaps from shrapnel in the thin steel walls, beams of light turn motes of dust into dancing lances.*
   *The looters are out there, illuminating the barn where I hide with trapped Militia, their horses, and a couple of terrified kids. The looters have two Browning machine guns mounted on JLTVs. They can kill us whenever they want. Shred the barn like it's tin foil.*
   *But they want us alive.*
   *My hands shake, and the urge to throw up never leaves my churning stomach. It's worse when one of the horses in the back screams. Horses do that when they're gut-shot and dying. They kick, defecate, and grunt at the pain.*
   *I swallow down a fear-tight throat. Force myself to crawl over the dead man and place my eye to a shrapnel-torn hole in the bottom of the overhead door. I can see the JLTVs, the silhouettes of the machine gunners behind the roof-mounted M2s.*
   *From the darkness behind me, a voice whispers, "Davis? What did you see out there?"*
   *"Most of the wreckage from the ranch house explosion has burned out. Means we can't see them coming anymore."*

*Time shifts...*

*The view through the hole blurs, smears into contorted images as the
fifty-caliber guns flash in the night. I can feel the passage of each bullet
as it blows through the barn like a seismic wave. Bits of metal are
blasted out of the big tractor. Screams. Flying body parts. The meaty
slap as big bullets rip holes through the panicked horses.*

*I am lifted in a blinding flash...*

*And jerk full awake in bed.*

*It's dark. Quiet. No glaring lights through tortured steel walls.*

*I pant for breath, feel the sweat running cold down my skin and
soaking my sleep shirt.*

*I've strained my healing ribs and the surgical incision. My hip hurts.*

*But there are no wounds. I am not shot. Or bleeding.*

*Sucking air, I pull on my pants. Slowly my heartrate drops, leaving
me empty, drained.*

*I pad out of my little ad-hoc bedroom, and pace through the gover-
nor's residence, the paintings and sculptures, the photos, all dark.*

*I see a light on in Agar's office. The door is open just a crack, and I
peek in. Agar is leaned back in his fancy chair, bare feet on his desk,
listening to the faintly audible chatter of a shortwave radio. The man
I've always seen in a three-piece suit is wearing a white robe. He holds a
glass of some brown liquor, but his tortured gaze is fixed on infinity. I see
him lift his free hand and rub it over his face, as if to scrub away whatever words are coming across the air waves.*

*Maybe I'm not the only one suffering flashbacks and cold-sweat
nightmares.*

— Excerpt from Lauren Davis' *Journal.*

# CHAPTER TWENTY-FIVE

THE ROUTE WAS MARKED County Road 27E. It took the Fallen Eagle convoy to CR 23E, and then south. This was mostly ranch country, rolling, open, and grassy interspersed with widely spaced homes on small acreages, a couple of wineries, orchards, and horse properties. The ranches, of course, had been cleaned out of stock in the first weeks of the Collapse. Breeze could see the skeletons of cattle and horses—now nothing more than bleached-white bones in the waving grasses. Adding to the landowners' plight, whole sections of barbed wire fence were down. The ends neatly snipped by cutters to allow raiders access to the animals and an easy escape after their raid.

The houses—set back from the road among tight clusters of cotton-woods and elms, often with a conifer windbreak—had been uniformly burned. As if in a final "up-yours" from the raiders. To her surprise, the grain bins, too, had been torched. Some still smoldered. Made her wonder if the looters and pillagers just didn't know the value of the feed, or if the ranchers had set it afire to deny the looters that one last score.

Might be the latter.

Signs now became common. Fixed on fences, gate posts, or to t-posts hammered into the ground, they read "Trespassers will be shot!" "Claimed Land" "Don't Even Think It" "Armed Homeowner, Will Shoot" and any number of other threats. Many of the places sporting those were burned. Some, however—looking particularly well-fortified —might have still been occupied. It was hard to tell. The only people she saw were few and far between. Mere glimpses as they fled from view. More like wild animals than the humans she'd known.

From the number of vineyards, orchards, horse properties, "pet resorts," and small family farms, it had been a pleasant place to live. This was Boulder County. Prosperous. Filled with the once-renowned Colorado vibe that had lured millions of up-and-coming young professionals seeking quality of life.

Gone now.

At the junction with Colorado 66, they turned west. For Breeze, the notion that an entire thriving community of upscale properties, businesses, and "country living" could now be so devoid of life seemed impossible. While there were the occasional corpses in yards or sprawled in the ditches, the paucity of bodies flew in the face of the number of houses, the hundreds of vehicles and fancy horse trailers parked in yards, or the shuttered businesses they rolled past. So, where had all the people gone? The immensity of it began to hit home.

Maybe it was reflected in the trash, the stuff that had been strewn about outside vandalized and ransacked dwellings and commercial buildings. Folks had tried to hold out, waited, and in the end either had the choice of starvation in their boarded-up houses, or setting out on the road.

Following St Vrain Creek—a thickly wooded bottom filled with pastures, groves, and orchards—they passed the cement plant. The gate, closed, sported giant TRESPASSERS WILL BE PROSECUTED signs on the high chain link.

"As if there was anyone left to prosecute anything," Sam declared beside her. He was yawning again, eyelids drooping. The guy looked exhausted.

But they all were. What had it been? Twenty-four hours since they'd stepped out of the van back at The Forks Checkpoint?

"I'll be damned." Tully pointed over the steering wheel to a knot of people—Breeze counted seven—plodding down the center of the road. Like quail, they scattered, running for cover, scrambling off the highway to tumble over the fence and take cover in the irrigation ditch. They left their packs behind them in their haste.

As the convoy passed, Breeze got a glance, seeing that each had a rifle up, aimed, ready to shoot.

"Whew," Tully said through an exhale. "You know, this cab ain't bulletproof." To remind himself, he stuck his pinky in the bullet hole in the windshield.

Breeze told him, "Bet no one shoots down here if they don't have to." She gestured around. "See any place to pick up another box of ammo?"

"Nope." Tully squinted, worked his jaw. "Wanna bet Cabela's was one of the first places looted."

At Sam's puzzled look she said, "Big box store. Sporting goods. Probably not the sort of going concern you'd find on Long Island."

"Okay," Tully said, taking his foot off the accelerator, the diesel cackling as he hit the jake brake. "Now what kind of shit show is this going to turn into?"

The green highway sign said they were approaching the Highway 36 junction. Up ahead, another of the way-too-familiar collections of abandoned cars had been shoved off to the side of the road. Others had been parked in such a fashion as to create a restriction that funneled traffic down a single middle lane.

A slight mist began to fall from the leaden overcast as the lead Humvees passed between the lines of cars. The signature sign of open fuel hatches and missing or dangling gas caps indicated more than anything that this was a trap. The Humvees slowed as the vee narrowed. Breeze could see that Noonan had taken a position behind the chain gun, while up ahead, Paco Vermijo was manning the second Humvee's M249.

Sure enough, up ahead, a big sign had been slapped together with the phrase, GAS, GRASS, FOOD, OR ASS. NO FREE PASSAGE!

This time, the blocking vehicles were a pair of dump trucks situated at an angle to control the east, west, and southern approaches to the three-way intersection. The boxes in the back appeared to have plate welded to the sides, and both had steel shielding with loop holes. Given the way the looted vehicles had been placed, there was no going around. People could be seen as they ran to man the trucks.

"*We're Wyoming National Guard,*" Daniels' voice announced through the PA. "*We're on official business. All we want is free passage.*"

To Breeze's surprise, another bullhorn blared back. "*We don't care who you are. But, hey, we're a business. What have you got to trade? Any ammo, food, or fuel will be acceptable. Or, like, maybe you surrender one of those Humvees, and we'll throw in a pile of rifles and handguns. Some are damn nice. Got Weatherbys, some really trick hunting rifles, even a British double.*"

"Why would they give up guns?" Sam wondered.

"Got me," Breeze replied.

"Shit, of course," Tully said, slapping the steering wheel. "It's all stuff they don't have ammo for. I mean, a British double? You got any .470 Nitro Express laying around in your glovebox? Or maybe some .25 Winchester Short Magnum? 8mm Remington Magnum?"

Daniels replied, "*Sorry. No trade. We mean you no harm. All we ask is passage to Highway 36. And then return passage on our way back.*"

"*Think it through,*" the voice replied in a reasonable tone. "*Say we don't trade for a Humvee. You leaving us with a thousand rounds of 5.56 and maybe a couple of your automatic rifles? Beats the chance of this getting out of hand. No need for shots fired.*"

"*I agree. Let us pass.*"

*"You got some thin-skinned trucks back there, Colonel. Your 5.56s won't dent our plate. But let's not get into measuring cocks here."*

Through the battle com, Daniels asked, *"Sergeant? What do you make that armor to be?"*

White Eagle's voice returned, *"Maybe quarter inch sheet. I think the guy's right. It's going to take some horsepower to get through it."*

*"Roger that."*

Through the PA Daniels said, *"Last chance, people. We only want passage to Highway 36."*

*"You can read the sign, Colonel. We can't start making exceptions. Bad for business."*

Tully said, "He should never have called her colonel."

"Bet he's about to figure that out." Breeze shifted her M4 from where it had slipped down.

Through the com, Daniels said, *"On your toes, people. This guy's pissing me off."*

Breeze made a face. "I know that tone. Sam, be ready to bail. Tully, when the shit hits the fan, duck low in the cab."

*"Corporal Noonan? You on the chain gun?"*

*"Roger that, LT."*

*"Now, conserve your rounds, but take out the firing positions on those dump trucks."*

"Go!" Breeze cried, poking Sam's side as she clawed for her M4.

As the chain gun let loose from the JLTV's turret, Sam popped the door, dropped to the step, and hit the pavement. Made that familiar grunt of pain. Breeze was right behind him. Wished she could have seen the 25 millimeter rounds taking out the plate. It sure made a hell of a racket. Figured that anyone behind it, if they weren't torn apart by the slugs, was having a miserable day as thousands of hot metal fragments sliced through their bodies.

As quickly, silence fell, the thunder from the chain gun fading.

Sam's instincts were good. He squirted straight to the rear of the Jeep Liberty, ducked low, and was headed for the right rear when a semi-auto began cracking from somewhere behind the blocking line of cars. With each supersonic crack, Breeze could hear the bullets impact on Tully's plow with a *tink, tink, tink* sound.

Firing broke out along the line.

Breeze leaped from the front of the Liberty to a position behind the left rear wheel of BMW 6 Series. Nice car. Funny how the world worked. Here, left behind and abandoned, the fuel hatch pried open, gas cap gone, it wasn't worth any more than the Liberty Sam was peeking around. Both were relegated to bullet sponges.

Breeze dropped low, duckwalked to the front fender. Could hear the drone going up, its buzz obliterated when Paco's turret-mounted M249 let loose with a burst.

"Bet you got more than you bargained for," she told the unknown idiot on the bullhorn.

At the front wheel, she peered around the BMW's fender, could see what had been a roadside fruit stand with faded signage that advertised local cherries, peaches, and apples. As she did, she triangulated on the rhythmic banging of a high-velocity rifle. There. Top of the stand. Behind the grape sign.

Breeze hunched forward, scurried to the protection of the adjacent Chevy van, and braced herself on the bumper. Getting her sight picture over the BMW's hood, she placed the red dot on the shooter's head. Triggered a three-round burst.

Checking her shot, it was to see an arm flopped out beyond the sign. The handguard and barrel—probably from an AR—protruded beside it.

Sam's .44 banged, bullet whizzing loud as it passed just on the other side of the van. The slapping of lead into flesh made Breeze flinch, so close did it sound. Then the Marlin banged again.

She ducked down. Peered under the van, surprised to see a guy laying on the gravel, gasping. His eyes were blinking, right leg kicking out as blood began to bubble bright red and frothy in his mouth. What looked like an AK lay just beyond his outstretched hand.

Shit! He'd been on the other side of the fricking van. All he need to do was step around, and Breeze would have been crouched there like a deer in the headlights.

"Thank you, Sam."

The sharp detonation of a grenade came from the other side of the road. Over the crack of rifle fire, Breeze heard someone shout, "Get the fuck out of here! They'll kill us all!"

Breeze scrambled to the van's front, peered around, and carefully eased along the bumper until she could see the parking lot and fruit stand. Keeping low, she spotted two men, guys in jeans, hiking boots, and hoodies. They had abandoned the dump trucks, running, turning, shooting as they ran. Probably in a poor attempt to cover themselves as they sprinted for the trees on the other side of the parking lot. Breeze lifted her M4, put the dot high on the lead guy, and triggered a burst. Saw him stagger, drop his rifle.

The guy behind, to Breeze's astonishment, tossed his own rifle to the side. Grabbing his buddy's arm, he took the man's weight; both of them went stumbling in the direction of the junction convenience store beyond the blocking dump trucks. In that instant, Breeze let her finger caress the trigger. Could have killed them both. Let them go.

The cracking reports from the guns went sporadic, then stopped. The only sound left that of the drone circling overhead.

Sam stepped out, looking pale. Swallowed hard. One hand to his sore chest, he walked warily to the shooter with the AK. Then he shot a glance at Breeze. "He was going to kill you. I mean, like, when you shot, he knew. Another second, Breeze. That's how close it was."

She blew out her tension, stood, and walked up to him. Pulling him close, she felt his arms tighten around her. Laid her head on his shoulder. "Naw," she whispered. "Never gave it a second thought. Not with Sam Delgado covering my back."

He stroked her hair with trembling fingers. "You know, Breeze, there's times when you just really worry me."

# DREAMS

*After I'd gone back to bed, that same damn flashback to Marsy Ranch woke me twice. Brought me bolt upright, twisted in sweat-soaked sheets. After the third one, I said fuck it, took a shower, and got dressed for the day—blue jeans and a charcoal-gray shirt. Then I belted on my HK before donning the denim jacket. As I walked to the kitchen, I found Edna, Agar's cook, bustling around, getting the meals ready for the house staff, the security team, and governor.*

*Aware of the disapproving look, I poured a cup of tea and wandered out, taking my time, looking at the artwork. It wasn't like I'd ever had the chance to really look at paintings, and this stuff was some of the best Western art ever produced by Wyoming artists. I stopped to admire one by a Dubois artist that showed the Ramshorn at sunrise.*

*I had the damned jitters, the ones you get on The Line when you know it's going to be a rough day. Aftereffects of the nightmares. I don't like to call them PTSD. I tell myself that normal people have nightmares all the time. Only traumatized and wounded people have PTSD. Yeah, I know I'm lying to myself. Given the amount of reality I have to live with —not to mention face every day—I figure it's all right to indulge in a little self-deception.*

*But I jumped hard enough to drop the tea cup when a voice behind me said, "I've always liked his work."*

*I heard the cup shatter on the floor as I clawed for my pistol, heart thundering—and found myself face-to-face with Kace Adams. I mean, I was in combat mode, ready to kill. At his startled look, I snapped, "I could have killed you, damn it!"*

*He glanced down at the broken teacup, then to where I clutched the*

*black Heckler & Koch in a fist. The barrel was inches from his vest. Had
to see the fear and panic in my eyes.*

*Cool as a November breeze, he lifted his hands over his head.
"Could we talk?"*

*Shaking, I slipped the H&K back in its holster, took a deep breath,
and said, "What do you want?"*

*He slowly lowered his hands and gestured to the two chairs sitting
down the hallway. "Come and sit with me?"*

*"Yeah. Okay. Sure."*

*I walked down the hall and slumped into one of the chairs. Kace
cautiously eased down into the other. For several moments, he just
stared at me. "You don't remember me talking to you last night, do you?"*

*Confused, I say, "What? When?"*

*His eyes tighten. "Around two in the morning, I was standing guard
at the front gate. You trotted down the driveway and hunkered down
behind a tree trunk with your pistol drawn and aimed out at the road
beyond the fence. I called out to you, but you didn't answer. I kept calling
as I walked closer to you."*

*I frown at him. "Are you sure it was me? I don't remember any of
this."*

*He gives me a level stare. "It was you. You were mumbling to your-
self and sweating like it was August."*

*I blink and look away, trying to fathom what...*

*"You could have been sleepwalking, but it looked like a flashback.
That ever happened before?"*

*"Not that I know of."*

*He leans forward in the chair and props his elbows on his knees as
he glares down the empty hallway. "Listen, I don't know how to say this,
but given the strain we're all under, I don't think you should carry a
firearm."*

*A wave of panic shudders through me before I manage to stop it.
"You're not taking my gun. Ever."*

*He hasn't blinked in too long, as though he's afraid to take his eyes
off me. He begins softly: "When I was in the war, I shot an old man. He
came out of the dark with an antique knife in his hand and lunged at me.
It was pure instinct. I just dodged aside and killed him." Kace takes a
breath, lets it out. "Before he bled out, he told me, 'Death has only one
eye, and it never looks back.'"*

*"What does that mean?"*

*He points to my HK. "It means you need to give me that gun before
you do something you can never take back."*

— Excerpt from Lauren Davis' *Journal.*

# CHAPTER TWENTY-SIX

SAM CLIMBED UP GINGERLY, careful of his smarting chest, to peer into the back of the dump truck. Amazed, awed, and horrified. Three guys had been in the back, manning the shooting positions behind the plating. Noonan's chain gun had used eight rounds on this particular truck. The guys in the back never stood a chance. Not only had the heavy bullets and flying metal blown them apart, but the ripped and torn pieces were still seeping red. So were the splattered ropes of entrails where they lay strewn over the dump bed's dented and rusted floor. The armor welded to the dump truck's box had just added to the carnage.

Sam had never seen the like.

This once would last him a lifetime. Right up there with Amber Sagan's body after she'd taken out the Clark Ranch barricade.

Still trembling from the shooting, the sight did nothing to soothe his nerves. Wondered if he'd ever get over the queasy shakes. Seemed he got them every time he was in a gun fight. Well, but for Clark Ranch. That time he'd been way too unconscious to know what he was doing.

He slapped the mist-wet metal, stepped down, and took in the junction they now controlled. To the west, US 36 headed up between steep grassy slopes and into the overcast gray mountains. From here, any view of the lower valley was blocked by trees. Lyons, Colorado, was a few miles up the road. Not that there'd be anything to see. Just more of the same old depressing shit. Burned and abandoned buildings. Looted businesses. Bodies left to rot.

Glancing back, he could see where the two wounded—Shanna Clugg and Devon Makelroy—were being cared for. From the glance Sam had had, it didn't look good for Makelroy who had been shot through the chest. And maybe not for Private Clugg, either. She'd taken one through her hips. Corporal Fields had the "blow out" kit open. Was doing her best to staunch the blood, ease the pain. Despite the reassuring tone Jennifer Fields used, Sam had seen the panic behind her eyes.

He snugged his Marlin .44 under his arm and walked over to the convenience store. There he found Corporal Noonan and Sergeant White Eagle cataloging the booty: a literal stack of rifles, buckets filled with various types of ammunition, handguns, canned food, bottles of whiskey, gin, vodka, tequila, and other spirits, medical supplies, bottles of water, a plastic bin full of jewelry and watches, another brimming with defunct phones. There were binoculars, fishing rods, piles of tools, all laid out on the empty store shelves. Even a cardboard box full of cash. He'd barely begun to take it in when Breeze leaned in the door, a look like bottled thunder on her face.

"Sarge?" she asked. "Where's the LT?"

"On the radio with Ragnovich." White Eagle looked up from where she was inspecting a really fancy looking rifle. "Holy shit! This is a Gunwerks 300 PCR—"

"I don't give a shit," Breeze told her. "We got a problem. Now."

White Eagle, with seeming reluctance, laid the rifle down, rising to follow Breeze.

Sam had that way-too-familiar tension building in his stomach as he kept pace a step behind. Was watching Breeze's stiff back and the way she strode forward; her knuckles had gone white where she clutched her M4. Thought about how scared he'd been when the guy with the AK was so close. How the looter had jumped when Breeze fired her burst. Like, within mere feet.

*I didn't think. I just stepped out and shot him.*

What if he'd hesitated? How would he live with the knowledge that he'd let her down?

And then she'd walked up, hugged him so close. Damn it, she shouldn't be so trusting of him. Shouldn't be so... What?

The destination was the house behind the convenience store. It was a white-frame thing. Looked like it was fifty years old, with a small yard surrounded by lilac bushes and shaded by giant cottonwoods and a rather gnarly old elm. Had a chain link fence around it. A garage off to the side.

Breeze led the way to where Shane Goggles, looking grim, stood by the door. He gave Sergeant White Eagle a curt nod, chewing on his lips as he did so.

Sam instinctively placed his thumb on the Marlin's hammer, his nerves beginning to tingle as he stepped inside. The living room was maybe twelve by fifteen, the furniture missing. In the dim light, Sam had to blink. Realized that the things on the floor were mattresses. That the naked bodies, all of them female...

He swallowed hard. Eyes adjusting enough to recognize the chains, how the ends were secured with bolts to the old hardwood floor. Seven of them. Young women who stared up at him with terrified and wounded eyes. Cringing back, some were whimpering, another sobbing silently. The little girl, over in the corner, kept staring at nothing with oddly blank eyes, face expressionless. A plastic container, various buckets, and tubs had been placed beside each of the makeshift beds. From the stink of urine, Sam could guess their purpose.

"What the fuck?" White Eagle asked, stunned.

"Bad choice of words, Sarge." Breeze sounded on the verge of mayhem. "And I thought what we found at Clark Ranch was enough for one lifetime."

Sam turned, said over his shoulder, "Last thing those girls need is me in there. I'll go get the LT."

And damn it, Breeze was right. Once was enough for a lifetime. Maybe it was time for humanity to be wiped clean from the face of the earth. The last time, God had tried it with a flood. This time, he only needed to leave it up to humanity itself.

# MORNING AFTER

*Every morning our detail loaded up in the black Suburbans. The first, or blocking vehicle, was driven by Donovan Knuckles while Kace Adams rode in the passenger seat. Bill Dunlap was driving the second, Spencer Stenholm in the front passenger seat, and me in the back next to Agar. Each day we'd pull out through the fancy gates of the governor's residence and onto Central Avenue to follow it east and then south around Frontier Park. Once the park had been home to Cheyenne Frontier Days. Now the sprawling grounds was host to a vagabond camp of refugees who'd been stranded by the Collapse, as well as for the couple thousand who'd somehow made it past The Line and managed to claim a bit of sanctuary.*

*Tents, RVs, camp trailers and vans, and even automobiles served as shelter for the nearly seven thousand refugees. Wyoming provided enough beef, corn, and wheat to keep them from starvation, if not epicurean culinary delight. Some, with skills, had trickled into the community, others out into the state. But for so many, each day was a struggle. Most had arrived with the clothes on their backs. Period. As we passed that morning, the usual signs lettered on cardboard, claiming, WILL WORK FOR FOOD. HELP PLEASE!! NEED WORK! HUNGRY CHILDREN, PLEASE HELP!! Though fewer in number than in the past, the WFFF signs were still raised by forlorn-looking women along the sidewalk.*

*"We really ought to have the Cheyenne Police run those folks off," Spencer said as he turned in the passenger seat to glance back at Agar.*

*The governor looked right at me. "What's your take on that, Lauren?"*

*I blinked, still rattled at having pointed a pistol at a friend's vitals that morning. "Run them off to where?" was my instant response. At Agar's raised eyebrow, I thought it a little farther through. "I mean, you can't stop it, right? Arrest them? Put them in jail? What have we got for them, Governor? Keep in mind that the churches all got together in the weeks after the Collapse to offer desperate women a choice."*

*He nodded. "So why are these women—"*

*"And some men," I interjected.*

*"—still here, still waving signs?"*

*I looked him dead in the eye. "Because when it comes to people, you just can't save everyone."*

*Hell, I wasn't even sure I could save myself.*

— Excerpt from Lauren Davis' *Journal.*

# CHAPTER TWENTY-SEVEN

BREEZE HAD DONE IT. Used bolt cutters. The ones from the Humvee. They'd become a necessity on The Line. Didn't matter that she had needed every ounce of her strength. She wouldn't quit until the last of the women were free. Seven in the living room, another three in the first bedroom, two more in the smaller bedroom in back.

Breeze had braced herself, strained, and the final chain gave with a snap and a clink.

That sound would remain—sort of burned into her soul. But each of the girls and young women had been freed. She chewed her lips as she stared at her hands. The ones that had broken the chains.

She now sat outside on the little white frame house's front porch. Every ounce of her being was wrung out, exhausted, and enraged. She leaned back, head against the clapboard wooden siding. Closed her eyes, the sound of the drone buzzing above as it kept an eye peeled lest any of the pieces of shit they'd ran off decided to sneak back.

She could hear Deana Capriolli and Lieutenant Daniels saying something soothing inside. Deana had brought clothing. Stuff she'd found in abandoned vehicles. Anything to clothe the naked women and girls. Capriolli began singing softly. Maybe to the little girl. She might have been nine? Maybe ten? Golden hair, big blue eyes. More like a doll than a girl. No telling how the sick sons of bitches had used her. The kid still hadn't said a word. Barely responded, her gaze distant, face expressionless. Catatonic?

Corporal Fields, having done what she could for Clugg and Makelroy, had bustled her way in maybe ten minutes past to see what she could do for the traumatized women.

Breeze knotted a fist. Wished she could hunt down the survivors. Wished she'd taken that last shot. Killed the two she'd allowed to hobble away.

She glanced up as Lieutenant Daniels stepped out, walked to the edge of the porch, and took deep breaths as if in need of fresh air, her hands on the small of her back.

"What are we going to do with them?" Breeze asked. "Can't leave them."

"Nope." Daniels kept knotting her jaws, the cheek muscles jumping. "Got Tortilla, Paco, and Goggles refueling the vehicles. As they empty a Jerry can, they're siphoning what's in the dump trucks to refill our supply. When I called in our sit rep, Ragnovich says the Biotek bunch is practically screaming for help. Said they're about to be breached. They could be overrun any second. And our people are staggering on their feet from fatigue."

"Maybe give our people an hour to catch some sleep?"

Breeze heard one of the women inside pleading. Couldn't make out the words. Begging for what? A bullet to the brain? Fields was saying something reassuring.

"It's six miles." Daniels pointed south. "Down there. We're the best of The Line. We'll take a break when we're in that compound. After we've got the techs and the equipment under protection."

"Yes, ma'am." Breeze cleared her throat. Stood wearily. "There's that Jayco motorhome back in the line of abandoned cars. It'll hold twelve. Maybe detail Private Capriolli to drive it? I'll go see if it has keys in it. If it does, I'll figure out how to get it started and get it fueled up"

She turned her fatigued feet in the direction of the vehicles. Sam stepped out from where the privates were siphoning diesel out of the dump trucks. Since taking down the blockade, the shot-up trucks been pulled to the side and disabled. The Humvees now controlled all approaches to the intersection.

"Hey," Sam greeted, the Marlin balanced over his shoulder as he matched step. "What's up?"

"Gotta rustle up transportation for the women." She gave him a narrow-eyed glare. "What the hell, Sam? What is it with you men? Huh? Chained naked on those mattresses, to be fucked whenever and however? Left with a fricking plastic bowl to pee in? You're a man, you tell me. What twisted kind of shit goes on in the male brain? I mean, you don't see women chaining naked guys down to service them. Do you? Tell me what makes men think that way? Think that it's okay to use a woman that way?"

Sam winced at the loathing tone, raised a hand in surrender. "I guess, down deep, it's in the amygdala. Something about testosterone. That lizard brain that Lauren always talks about. And maybe it's because humans are the third species of chimpanzee. That down under—"

"That's *bullshit*! What did those women do to deserve what those guys did to them? Men don't fucking deserve to live."

Sam had sucked his lips in, eyes narrowed in a pained squint.

"From now on," Breeze told him, thumping a hard index finger into his arm, "I'm shooting every stray male I see."

Exhaling, Sam nodded. "Yeah, guess I can't blame you. Not after Clark Ranch. Not after what I saw back in that house."

She gave him a suspicious squint, part of her disappointed that he sounded so contrite when all she wanted to do was to rage, to vent, and blame him for every male sin in the book. Fuming, she stomped up to the motorhome. Saw the bullet hole in the driver's side windshield.

The Jayco looked new. Had *Alante* emblazoned in big scrawly letters on the side. Opening the door, she climbed in. Saw the blood on the driver's seat. Looked like someone had done a half-assed job of wiping it up. Probably the same asshole man who'd been detailed to drive it here to its place it in the line.

To her surprise, the keys were in the ignition. Turning them, the instrument panel lit up. The engine turned over, and the thing came to life. The fuel gauge read empty, but Breeze shifted it into reverse and backed it into the Audi SQ5 tucked close behind. Heard the grillwork crunch as she shoved the car back into the Toyota behind it. Shifting into drive, she managed to crunch the rear left corner and taillight on the VW van ahead of her.

Didn't care. Pissed off as she was, it felt good to break something.

Sam was braced on the back of the passenger seat. Probably not wanting to get too close lest she rip his head off.

"Don't say a fucking word, Sam."

"Wouldn't think of it," he told her.

Pulling up behind the M1089, she killed the ignition and leaned over the big steering wheel. After grinding her jaws, she said, "This thing runs on gasoline. Think you can find their stash? Don't know how much it takes to fill it, or how far it goes on a tank, but we're going to get those women back to Wyoming." A beat. "If I have to kill every slimy man between here and the border to do it."

"Yeah, the bastards have a whole line of gas cans in the fruit stand. I'll get Tully and Paco on it." He sounded whipped as he turned, opened the door, and stepped out.

She just sat there in the long-dried bloody seat, staring past the bullet hole in the windshield at the back of the wrecker. In her head, she kept reliving how she had gone from bed to bed, telling each terrified and tortured woman she was safe. Meeting those wounded and half-crazed eyes. Seeing their filth-matted hair. Hearing their pleas. Appalled by the stains on the mattresses, the way those women huddled, like shattered creatures.

Maybe God was tired of humans. Maybe it was time they all died. Let the planet heal.

She dropped her head on the steering wheel.

# THEM

*That noon we headed to the TV station. This was a big deal. When the internet, satellite, and national providers went down, they took Wyoming's TV with them. Part of the ever-increasing corporate stranglehold on the entire nation, the West, and Wyoming depended exclusively on big providers and their advanced tech. The upshot was that it had taken three months for the local Wyoming TV stations to re-create the past and cobble together a system that would be able to broadcast to the state. And then interfaces had to be built between the various cable companies. Rebuilding the old analog broadcast system, the kind that used rabbit ears, wasn't an option. Turns out nineteen fifties technology wouldn't work with any of the modern digital systems.*

*And people who had depended on satellite providers were just SOL.*

*Our security detail arrived a half hour early after Stenholm and Adams had conducted an advance, ensuring the governor's safety. Bill would drive the governor's Suburban up to the back door, Stenholm would open it, and Agar would step out, and then immediately inside as I followed behind. It came off without a hitch.*

*I was at the governor's elbow when we entered, wearing my jacket over the H&K—of course, I still had it—and with my shoulder bag slung, the .380 in its zippered compartment. To my surprise, as Agar walked into the studio Dudley Gardner caught me by the arm, and said, "The governor wants you on air. Says you'll be good for the visuals."*

*"He wants to paint a target on my back?" I blurted.*

*His lips twitched. "All you have to do is stand where they tell you to and look mean."*

*Worst part was that Dudley insisted that I be made up before the* noon launch. *Never gone through the process before. Didn't like it. Lemissa, the make-up lady, took to it like I was a real challenge. When she was finished, I had no fricking clue who that person was looking back at me from the mirror.*

*And then we marched out onto the set. I stood where I was told, just behind and to the right of Agar's chair, squinted into the lights, and watched as one of the camera ladies counted down to on-air.*

*"Welcome!" Jerry Finger, the station manager, was seated to the side. "We're delighted to welcome our viewers back to KCHY 9 TV. It's been a difficult process interfacing with, and often creating, the technology necessary to return to the air. Yes, the world has changed, but once again we are serving the great state of Wyoming.*

*"And now, to join us, let's welcome Wyoming Governor Pete Agar. Welcome, Governor. You, more than anyone, fast tracked the process to return us to the air..."*

*I shifted slightly, took a deep breath, and gave the camera an evil stare.*

— Excerpt from Lauren Davis' *Journal.*

# CHAPTER TWENTY-EIGHT

US 36 FOLLOWED its sinuous path south through the rolling uplands at the foot of the Lyons hogbacks; to either side were grassy meadows, many with drives that led to houses or barns set back from the road. A lot of trash had been left behind. Sometimes next to forlorn vehicles that had been pulled off the road. Much of the stuff scattered around and in piles looked like beloved heirlooms. Scrapbooks, family photos, and the like. Each begged the story: Why were they left by the side of the road? The people decided they didn't need them? That they were a burden? Or did each mark a place where someone was stopped? Ambushed? Maybe had their cars searched and looted by raiders? To what? Be left standing there to watch the thieves drive off? And what had happened to the people?

Sam, cradling his hat in his lap, head against the window, watched as they passed a Toyota pickup down in the ditch, the doors open, two rotting bodies piled together on the far side by the right-of-way fence. Coolers, ripped open black-plastic bags, an antique-looking grandfather clock, bicycles, and open storage tubs remained in the truck's bed. What looked like white china had been tossed out to shatter on the road in a thousand white shards. They crunched under the plow's thick tires.

Sam fought a yawn, blinked at the fatigue behind his eyes. Glanced at Breeze. Could see the haunted rage in her expression—a smoldering thousand-yard stare. Had seen it the first time he'd ever laid eyes on her in the Cheyenne Hilton. Just before Captain Ragnovich dismissed her from being a Line rider. Ragnovich's words from that long-ago day came back to haunt him: *"You've lit the slow-burning fuse, and it's just a matter of time before you detonate."*

He took a breath, shifted, attention turning to the JLTV and the

Humvees leading the way down that narrow ribbon of blacktop. Wondered if what he'd seen in that little white house wasn't a condemnation of everything male. Being an anthropologist, he might intellectually understand that males were hard-wired to violence. That was their role. The experimental half of the species. One of the reasons human society had survived the Pleistocene. Males were expendable. A hunting, gathering, harvesting band could send them out to explore, to fight off rival groups, attack large beasts with pointed sticks, to take chances and risks. If they died in the process? No big gig as long as enough genetically differentiated males were left to mate with the fertile females. And yes, to commit rape if that meant they could perpetuate their DNA.

Evolution didn't care.

There was nothing romantic about it. Just simple Darwinian fitness. Morality played no role. Suffering? Injustice? Individual feelings? Or even love? Inconsequential. The equation boiled down to the survival and perpetuation of breeding-age individuals, no matter what the male-to-female ratio. Success was only measured in the production of viable offspring.

Evolution was amoral and emotionless.

*But I am not.*

He closed his eyes, knotted a fist around the barrel of his Marlin. Wished he could have shot them all. Realized he'd become a stone-cold killer. Talk about a hell of a journey from the kitchen in The Yucateca to here; it had started with the look that Edgewater and his goons had given Shyla that day in the tannery. Predatory. Glinting and rapacious.

Until that moment, Sam had never really understood *true* hate.

He did now.

"It's because when you boil it all down, sex and death are everything," he told Breeze. "That fundamental reconciliation of opposites lies at the heart of what's happening to us. Without sex, there is no life. Life ends in death. And these days there's death everywhere. The two are tied. Way down deep in the brain. Down in the limbic system. Especially the male brain. That's what makes men monsters. Why I had to kill Tubb. Why I didn't feel a thing when I shot Edgewater."

"Edgewater didn't chain those women and girls to the floor to be raped," Breeze snapped.

He watched her jaw muscles knotting as she glared down the road. Tully was smart enough to keep his mouth shut and concentrate on driving.

"They are all Edgewater." Sam watched as they passed another body —partially skeletonized—where it lay half hidden in the grass. "If my Shyla had been stopped at that roadblock, they'd have chained her to that floor. From here on out, Breeze, it's us and them. No more hesitation. No

second chances. No tears and no regrets. Just the unemotional mathe-
matics of survival."

She gave him that piercing Tappan glare that threatened violence and
pain. "Good, because I'm not feeling very forgiving at the moment."

"In an ethics class I took as an undergraduate, I heard a statement
that went something to the effect that every time we look in the mirror,
the image staring back at us is a partial reflection of both Adolf Hitler
and Mother Theresa. At the time, I thought it was ridiculous. Back then
when I looked in a mirror, all I saw was Sam Delgado." He yawned. "I
don't know who is looking back at me these days."

She took his hand in hers and gave it a forgiving squeeze. "Guess
that makes two of us. How about I keep you from becoming Mother
Theresa, and you keep me from becoming Hitler."

"Shouldn't be too hard. You don't have the genetics to grow the
stupid little mustache."

"Heads up, people!" Tully called as the lead Humvee slowed, took a
right on a paved road turning off to the west.

Sam's gaze followed the sloping lane up to a fenced enclosure
around a large blue-steel building. Looked like two stories with high
windows in the front. Most had been broken. Some of the panes,
cracked, still remained in the frames. Maybe rocks had been thrown
through them. Cars could be seen parked in the lot out front. Someone
had smashed the heavy chain link gate; it was crumpled and piled off to
the side.

As Tully slowed and wheeled the plow around the corner, Sam saw
that the Boulder Mountain Biotek sign had been spray-painted in black
paint. Looked like a rattle-can job that was done in a hurry because up
close, some of the letters could still be made out.

As the Humvees approached the enclosure, a man and woman ran
out into the parking lot. They turned, calling back to others who
appeared from the south side of the building. Then both bolted, running
full out for the gate. They made it through and pelted headlong, heading
south for who knew where?

*"On your toes, people!"* Daniels' voice came through the com. *"Last
we heard, Biotek was under siege. No telling what we're going to find."*

A series of *"Roger that"* replies followed.

The lead Humvee drove through the gate and turned wide to the right
to block the parked cars along the front of the building. The second
curved off to the left, Paco on the M249. The JLTV headed straight to the
front door where it gaped open; a tangle of corpses had been laid around
it in a half-circle. Might have been seven of them, given what Sam could
see of the intertwined bodies.

Tully pulled the plow around and stopped inside the fence as Paco's
Humvee headed down the south side of the building to where a group of

people were fleeing. One guy, in a red ball cap and wearing a green sweatshirt, stopped long enough to pull a revolver from his belt and pop a couple of shots. Then he lit out on the heels of the others. Not that they were going far given the high fence with its coils of concertina wire that surrounded the property. Reaching the rear, the small mob took cover behind the building.

"Bet they're unhappy," Breeze noted as she pulled her M4 from the floor.

"*All right, people. Anyone takes a shot, we put them down,*" Daniels ordered. And through the PA, her voice boomed: "*We are Wyoming National Guard. Any resistance will be met with force. You will place your weapons on the ground. Proceed in single file to the gate for search. Keep your hands clasped on the tops of your heads at all times. Then you will be allowed to leave the compound. Anyone failing to obey will be shot.*"

Sam took a deep breath. Held it.

Took about fifteen seconds. The first of the women emerged from around the back of the building, marching humbly with hands atop her head along the line of tall shop doors. Then another. Then came a man. One by one, until, at the last, red cap with his green sweatshirt plodded uncertainly forward. The whole time they were under the muzzle of Paco's M249.

Shane Goggles, backed by Sergeant White Eagle, emerged by the gate. Ready to provide covering fire, Brylan Jones and Tortilla Gomez brought their weapons up.

The rest of the convoy, including the NPT truck, the MTV, wrecker, and Jayco motorhome waited on the access road while the property was cleared.

"Let's go," Breeze told Sam. "See if there are any more hiding back there."

He opened the door, climbed carefully down to the pavement, and got a good look at the big steel building. Attackers had tried to hack through the tall overhead doors, leaving the steel scarred. One hole was almost man-sized. The edges looked singed. Several bullet holes surrounded it where someone had shot into the door.

Sam kept his Marlin ready, walking forward, thumb on the hammer. Every ounce of his attention was fixed on the corner of the building.

"Stay close to the wall, Sam," Breeze told him. "That way anyone hiding around the corner will have to lean out to shoot. You so much as see a head peek around, you take a snap shot. They've been warned. Had their chance. Anyone who didn't take it is a hostile."

"Got it." His heart beat fast, that slippery feel going liquid down in his guts.

*Easy. Breathe.*

Passing the last of the abused doors, Sam realized that wet foam was leaking down from a hole someone had battered with an axe in the steel cladding. Foam?

Then he was at the corner, heart out of control in his chest. Shit. It was his turn to peek around, and being right-handed, the Marlin wasn't as easy to deploy.

Before he could lose his nerve, he shot a fast glance around the angle, saw nothing, and took a step, Marlin up. The distance between the back of the building and the fence was no more than six feet. Bedrolls, coolers, plastic bottles and empty food boxes, a blue poly tarp, and wrappers lay around. So, too, did a revolver—Red Cap's no doubt—a couple of ARs, and three .22s of various designs, including a little Marlin lever action.

"Clear," Breeze called from behind him.

That's when the closest shop door began to rattle up.

Sam, hot on Breeze's heels, rounded the corner in time to see the foam-dripping door rising slowly. As Sam ducked close against the wall and craned his neck for a better view, loafer-clad feet appeared at the bottom. Brown duck-twill pants. And to one side, peering from beneath the rising door, a face with relieved brown eyes behind glasses.

The woman cried, "Don't shoot! We're unarmed!"

Breeze stood to the side, her M4 shouldered.

"You're National Guard?" came the man's call as he yanked the door high enough to expose himself. In his other hand, he held a red fire extinguisher, foam leaking from the nozzle. "I'm Rymart Avery, PhD. This is Dr. Margo Simone. Damn, you got here just in time."

"Good to meet you," Sam told him. "Governor Agar sent us. I'm Sam Delgado. She's Breeze Tappan."

"Thank God," the woman in glasses, Simone, uttered through a strained whisper as she sank to her knees and slumped. "They were almost through."

"What's with the fire extinguisher?" Breeze asked.

"We'd tried everything else. Poison gas, fire, electrifying the doors, make-do spears. Jim constructed a crude crossbow, but they got wise." Avery wiped his eyes where tears had started to streak down his cheeks. "Never heard a better sound in all my life than that voice. 'We're the Wyoming National Guard.' Another five minutes? Or as soon as they figured out the foam wasn't deadly? They'd have been in."

Sam looked past the packed boxes. Two other women stood back, out of the way. Now they hurried forward, as if anxious to see for themselves.

"Sorry to be late." Breeze grounded her M4 by its butt. "Took us a while longer to get here than we planned. Call it a tough trip."

Lieutenant Daniels was striding up, that fatigued wariness in her dark eyes. "What's with the plastic wrap around the front door and the corpses?" she called.

"Stay away!" Simone called. "It's coated with a deadly toxin. Keep your people clear of that!"

Daniels lifted her com, calling, "No one goes close to the front door. Stay the fuck away from the bodies. It's toxic."

The brown-haired woman with a nametag that read Blix said, "It was the only way we could think of. We knew the office door wouldn't hold. So we lined it with plastic, and, well, turned the foyer into a gas chamber."

"Let 'em get inside," Simone added. "Packed together as they attacked the lab door. Then we released the gas. It's a simple $C_4H_8Cl_2S$... Um, a mustard gas we whipped up. I wanted to make Zyklon B, but Blix and Jim had ethical concerns."

"Hydrogen cyanide is a lot more dangerous to manufacture," Blix added.

"Tough country you've got down here," Daniels said, stepping forward to shake Avery's hand. "My people are about dead on their feet. Let us get some rest. Then we'll get you loaded and make tracks back north. Your little lab here? If you can really make insulin? You're in the position to save tens of thousands of lives."

Avery told her, "About damn time."

Simone added, "We've got wounded. Jim has been shot through the arm. He's in a cot up by the office. It's bad."

Daniels turned to her com, "Corporal Fields! Front and center. Bring your med kit."

"I see four of you, and you said one's wounded?" Breeze asked. "We heard there were seven."

"There were," Avery said bitterly. "Drs. Matheman and Bates-Ferrell were killed when the looters shot through holes in the doors."

Blix leveled her smoldering gaze on Avery. Sam wondered what that was all about.

"Sorry," Daniels told her softly.

Simone narrowed an eye. "That really true? That up in Wyoming, this whole mess didn't come down? It's not..."—she gestured around—"well, like this?"

"We're doing all we can to keep it together," Daniels told her. To Breeze she said, "Let's get the NPT truck in here." To Avery she asked, "You need anything?"

"It's two days since we've had anything to drink." In a sharp voice, he said, "Obviously, water would be a start."

"You've got it, and you don't even have to do anything toxic to get it."

Sam stepped outside of the big garage door to get out of the way, placed his back to the steel wall and allowed himself to slide down until his butt hit the pavement. He removed his hat and laid it crown down, as he'd been taught, on the asphalt.

As Breeze settled beside him and braced her M4 on her lap, Sam studied the pool of foam where it had puddled on the pavement. "Holding looters back with a fire extinguisher? Who'd believe that?"

"Anyone who'd seen his friends gassed," Breeze told him through a yawn. "There's a lesson there, somewhere."

He glanced off to the south. Most of the people they'd chased out of the fenced compound were out there, maybe three hundred yards off. Standing in little knots, they dotted the grassy knoll that overlooked the lab. Like a knob, it stuck up on the ridgeline that ascended to become the rocky Lyons anticline off to the west. Fine, let them wait. When the convoy pulled out, the goddamned looters could have whatever was left.

"Yeah, well, we made it. Got our lab." Sam shifted to put his arm around Breeze's shoulders. He didn't even mind the stitch in his much-too-sore ribs.

She pulled her hat off and, to his surprise, settled it, crown-down inside his own so that the two of them were cocooned. Then she laid her head against his shoulder, exhaling wearily. "Now, all we have to do is get back."

Nice feeling, Breeze pressing against him. Soothing. He blinked, trying to orient his thoughts. Replaying the roads they'd travelled in his memory.

Breeze, however, had fallen asleep.

Wasn't bad. Her body against his, her head heavy in the hollow of his shoulder.

Felt...reassuring.

And then he, too, nodded off.

He didn't see the four-wheel drive truck that eased down from the grassy knoll to the south. How it bounced through a hole in the right-of-way fence and accelerated off toward Boulder.

# EYE CANDY

Leaving the TV station, I heard Jerry Finger talking to Dudley Gardner. As I was following Governor Agar down the hall, Finger asked, "So... that's Lauren Davis, the Line Rider? The hero of Buffalo Camp and that ranch fight outside of Laramie?"

"That's her."

"Holly shit! She's drop-dead gorgeous. I mean the image we have of her... You know, tough, squinty, machine gun in one hand, grenade in the other? Dressed in oversized fatigues. I want to run a one-on-one piece on her, maybe talk about how she foiled the assassination attempt, or what really happened at Marsy Ranch. When can we schedule it?"

An icy-sick sensation invaded my stomach...

Kace caught my elbow in a hard grip, saying softly, "Let it go, Lauren."

"I'm not doing any dog-and-pony bullshit."

"I'll have to check her schedule," Gardner said smoothly. "Right now, we're slammed."

When we walked outside, a gentle rain was falling from the perpetually gray sky.

I ducked into the Suburban, took my seat in the back across from Agar.

"That went well," Pete told Dudley as the chief of staff slipped into the passenger seat up front. Kace slipped into the third-row seat behind us.

"Yeah," Dudley said, turning in the seat. "Finger wants to interview Lauren."

*"Not going to happen," I replied.*

*I caught shadow of a smile that played at Gardner's lips before he glanced away. "We'll see."*

— Excerpt from Lauren Davis' *Journal.*

# CHAPTER TWENTY-NINE

BREEZE CAME TO, blinked at the sound of a forklift. The NPT truck was backed into the dock two doors down. A thump and a bang were accompanied by muffled voices from inside the van. Down the lot, next to the fence, the Jayco motorhome door was open. She could see the women in their hastily assembled wardrobes of cast-off clothes, wandering around, heads back, faces lifted toward the perpetually cloudy skies. Some had arms around each other's shoulders. Sisters in misery sharing support.

To the south, the exiled raiders continued to linger up on the knoll. Seated, they watched from the distance. Waiting? For what? What chance did they have against WNG weaponry?

Breeze still lay tucked under Sam's arm. Warm in the cool air, drowsy and happy to be held. Damn it, it just felt safe, comfortable.

How long had it been since she'd been held by a man this way? One she craved to have hold her. Maybe all the way back to Jim Davis? That fateful summer before he was so tragically killed? It sure hadn't been during the wild times that followed. She'd attempted to punish herself with alcohol and a couple of passionate flings. Had tried to kill the sense of loss. Usually by dragging some cowboy with a hard-on into the nearest horse trailer.

Her punishment for that was the abortion. The rupture with her parents. The flight to Denver and college. Where, to her dismay, she hadn't been able to stand the men.

Oh, yeah. Good old University of Denver's famed Daniels College of Business, where the women were strong, and the men preened in mirrors. The same with the males she worked with that summer at Seakliff Investments. Didn't matter that they worked out in the gym and could name every player in the Broncos offensive line, or that one drove a Maserati. They just hadn't measured up.

*Too many Tappan ancestors in my blood.*

So what did she do about Sam? Just use him as a snuggling rest? Everything that had happened since that cleansing ceremony up at the Spirit Cave had linked them together. And, if she let herself think about it, it went right back to that morning in the Cheyenne Hilton. As if—as Thomas said—the Spirits had thrown them together the moment Shyla was killed. Then came the ride back to Hot Springs, to Slickside, to the Clark Ranch raid, to the healing ceremony.

Her gaze fixed on the hats. Hers, smaller, fit into his so nicely. Like they were molded for each other. Just as perfectly as she fit against his body. With it came the realization that she could snuggle thus for the rest of her life. She and Delgado, yin and yang, male and female, and all that implied.

"And here I am," she whispered under her breath. Closed her eyes to enjoy the moment. Feel his easy breathing, chest rising and falling. He shifted slightly, his cheek coming to rest against the top of her head. It felt so natural.

The forklift whined inside the building. Dr. Avery's angry voice rose as the forks clanged metallically across the concrete and banged into a pallet. Then the strain of the engine as it lifted whatever piece of equipment, supplies, or whatever.

Avery snapped, "That's delicate, you idiot! If you've broken it, I'll have your ass!"

*God, lighten up!* Breeze thought. *We came down here to save your ass.*

Not to mention that it had already cost Clugg and Makelroy their lives.

A low rumble of thunder sounded over the haze-covered mountain to the west. It would be dark soon. They were nowhere near ready to go.

She turned her attention back to the raiders out on the ridge. They'd stirred at the sound of the thunder. Sensing, no doubt from experience, that this time of year thunderheads had a habit of rolling out from the peaks to pelt the flatlands with rain and hail.

Where the Jayco was parked down by the gate, Breeze could hear laughter. Hope lay in that given what the captives had been through. She'd seen it among the women they'd freed at Clark Ranch. Granted, they'd never be whole. Would always carry the scars, the loathing and distrust. But then that was the same no matter what the cause of the trauma might be. She'd never suffered gang rape, but she'd carry her own scars from Willow Creek Pass, the I-25 checkpoint, and The Line.

Thinking that, she slapped Sam playfully. "Hey, lover boy. You're crinking my neck."

He shifted, raised his head. "Lover boy?"

"Okay, maybe I forgive you for being male, poisoned with testosterone, and subject to all the other faults of your gender."

She shifted as he pulled his arm back. "We're not all like that, you know." He yawned. Straightened and made a face. "God, what I'd give for a bed and twelve hours of sleep."

"Later." She found her M4, pulled it up, and glanced at the darkening sky. The people beyond the fence had moved closer. What the hell were they waiting for?

Breeze yawned and stretched. Her butt had fallen asleep. "It's just that we're seeing the worst in humanity. I think men just fall faster and farther than women do."

"My cousin, Ronaldo? He'd argue that with you. He coached a women's softball team. After they hit a losing streak, he said they turned into piranhas." Sam plucked up his .44 Marlin and climbed stiffly to his feet. "How long did we sleep?"

"No clue. But it's getting dark and sounding like rain."

"What's this?" He pointed with the Marlin.

Breeze turned, seeing the four vehicles approaching on the highway from the south, slowing as they came in sight of the lab. Four-wheel-drive pickups, each packed with people riding in the back. One even used turn signals as the pickups turned off the highway, climbed through a hole in the fence, and followed what looked like tire tracks up the hill, finally vanishing behind the knoll. The sound of the engines died. At their arrival, the waiting raiders were headed up the hill, disappearing behind the knoll. Faint voices could be heard.

Someone had alerted Lieutenant Daniels. Now she and Sergeant White Eagle emerged from behind the NPT truck. Tortilla stepped out from the closest Humvee and handed Daniels binoculars.

Breeze led the way over, peering south in the gloom. Taking a position beside Daniels, she said, "You see anything?"

"Nope." The lieutenant lowered the binoculars. "Just a couple of people perched on that knoll. They keep looking back over their shoulders." She turned to Private Gomez. "Pete? Did you see anything threatening?"

She always called Tortilla by this first name, probably thinking somehow it was more culturally sensitive, which amused the hell out of Tortilla.

"No, ma'am," Tortilla told her. "Just four pickups. Maybe ten guys per truck. Each one had a rifle. Looked like scoped bolt-actions. As soon as they drove in, those raiders up there all hustled back over and out of sight. That gives them about sixty-some folks."

Sergeant White Eagle, eyes slitted, said, "That's about four hundred yards to the crest of that knoll, maybe a twenty-yard elevation from here. Definitely what I'd call a commanding position."

Daniels lifted the binoculars. "Yeah, here comes. A bunch of them are topping the rise to get a look. All of them with scoped rifles. Some of them look like long-range rigs. Big-assed scopes, long barrels, fancy chassis. PRC stuff."

Sam leaned close to Breeze to ask, "What's PRC?"

"Precision Rifle Cartridge. Think long-range ballistics." She kept her wary gaze on the knoll, not liking it one bit.

"Think we ought to clean them out?" White Eagle asked. "Pull around with the JLTV and Paco's Humvee? Drive them off that hill?"

Breeze felt Sam stiffen.

"What?" she asked him.

"Nothing." He was staring out at the dark grass just beyond the high chain link, jaws clamped.

Daniels used the binoculars to scan the hill. "The new guys are definitely getting the lay of the land. The guy with a red cap and green sweatshirt is pointing, doing all the talking."

White Eagle fingered her chin. "Why bring in the extra guys now?"

"Because we're here," Breeze said. "See it from their side. Up until our arrival, this was just another place to be looted. Sure, they could tell it had been a lab of some sort. Wouldn't have been important if it didn't have this big frigging fence with the concertina wire. After they pushed the gate down, it was only going to be a matter of time before they broke in. Eventually Avery's people would run out of food or water, right?"

"And then we show up." Daniels jerked a nod. "What could be so important it would lure the Wyoming National Guard down here to get it?" She hooked a thumb at the NPT truck. "That we came with that? Means whatever's in the Biotek lab, it's damn valuable."

"Not to mention the rest of the convoy," White Eagle added. "Any takers on what a JLTV and a couple of Humvees might be worth to these people?"

Daniels—still staring through the binocs—said, "It's getting pretty dark, but I think I see a couple of them dropping down—"

"Run!" Sam cried. At the same time, he grabbed Breeze by the arm and gave her a hard jerk to the side.

"What the...?" Breeze fought for balance as the crack-*slap* of a high velocity bullet hitting flesh split the air.

Sam was half dragging her as he pulled her behind the safety of Tortilla's Humvee.

Breeze got her balance, hunched down behind the Humvee's reassuring bulk. Tortilla was yelling, "We're taking fire!" into his battle com.

Sam, from his hunched position, screamed, "Sarge! Get the hell out of there!"

Breeze looked back, saw where White Eagle was bent, had her fists knotted in Lieutenant Daniels' ACU and was tugging the woman across the paved lot. Saw when White Eagle looked up, realizing her peril. Her determination as she tugged harder, dragging the LT's limp body across the...

*Crack-pock!*

The distant report of the rifle followed the sound of the bullet's impact as Sergeant Sally White Eagle jerked and flopped loose-limbed atop the lieutenant.

Sam sank down against the Humvee's thick tire with a tortured expression.

"How did you know?" Breeze asked, whipping her M4 around. Figuring the elevation and distance in the gloom, she braced over the Humvee's hood and fired a burst. She doubted she'd hit any of them, but those hot rounds should have sent the bastards running.

As if in answer, a scatter of popping rifles could be heard, bullets pinging on the Humvee, smacking and buzzing as they hit pavement and ricocheted into the lab's steel walls.

From Paco's Humvee, the M249 fired a burst, tracer fire lacing the knoll top.

"*Nynymbi.*" Sam wiped a hand under his nose as he stared at where Sally White Eagle lay lifeless stop Lieutenant Daniels' bleeding body. "He was out there, dancing just beyond the fence."

Breeze fixed the red dot above where a distant muzzle flash marked a shooter and triggered another burst. "Yeah? Well, tell your Shoshoni Spirit Helper I said thanks."

Another distant muzzle flash was fading as a supersonic round snap-cracked in the air beside her ear. Breeze dropped down, scared half out of her wits. Damn that was close.

*Okay, so the LT and the Sarge are dead. What the hell are we going to do now?*

# IDENTITY PLEASE?

*I've had more than my share of trauma, both physical and mental. I was pretty much functioning on full psychotic during those last days on The Line. But this felt different...*

*Call it PTSD, shell shock, combat fatigue, whatever.*

*I was in need of some serious medication. Given the night sweats and the fact that I came within a whisker of shooting Kace Adams, maybe I needed to head back to the porch at Tappan Ranch.*

*Instead, I spent the afternoon in the governor's office, enduring meeting after meeting. People shuffling through the office included: the stockmen's association; the US Forest Service Director and staff; Ragnovich giving his daily report with the welcome news that Breeze and Daniels had made it to the lab; then Harry Salem with the Wyoming Highway Patrol report. And every time, they stared at me.*

*Wondered.*

*I had no clue what they wanted.*

*But all day long, I've been having these mini flashbacks. One flash, I'm tossing ration packets out the back of the MTV as bullets whack around my head at Buffalo Camp. Shooting women and children as they try to swarm the truck. Emptying magazine after magazine to break up the raiders attack on the cattle drive. The time I dropped the KTM on the gravel in a running gunfight with two refugees. How that woman's breasts flopped from the impact when I shot her through the sternum.*

*A little girl, dead of thirst, abandoned in a yellow tent, clutching a stuffed sheep as flies crawl...*

*After the last meeting, I gave Randolph a glance and said, "Could I have a moment alone with the governor?"*

*"Sure thing," he called, leaving his desk and locking the door behind him.*

*The governor looked up from his paperwork. "What's up?"*

*I crossed to his desk. Picked that really uncomfortable corner and hitched my butt onto it. Sheath skirts—no matter how good the material —are not meant to be worn when you perch on a desk corner. "You remember* Game of Thrones? *That character who changed with every face she put on? I'm starting to feel like her."*

*"You're doing great." He pushed back in his chair.*

*"No. I'm not. I'm on the verge of a psychotic break. I mean a real, honest to God, grippy socks vacation. You get it?"*

*"Lauren, you're tougher than that."*

*"Hey, Governor, three months ago, I was a college student with a summer job as a bank teller. Today I'm sitting at the Governor of Wyoming's right hand, having killed more people than I can count. I keep having one flashback after another. It's not safe to be around me."*

*"Let me be the judge of that."*

*I raised my hands in despair. "Don't you get it? My presence here puts everyone in danger."*

*He rubbed his face the way I'd seen him do in his study. "We're all strung out and on the edge. All of us are making decisions that will change, and even end, peoples' lives. Judge, jury, and executioner."*

*"That's not what I mean, Governor. I—"*

*"Listen. Since you've been at my side, crowds have been more subdued, easier for me and my team to control. Don't abandon us now, Davis. Just keep it together for another month, okay?"*

— Excerpt from Lauren Davis' *Journal.*

# CHAPTER THIRTY

THAT SOUND of a high-velocity bullet cracking through the air beside Breeze's head set every nerve in Sam's body on fire. Made his stomach feel like it wanted to turn inside out. And it wasn't like that runny feeling was getting any better no matter how often he felt it these days.

Now here he was, hidden behind the Humvee's bulk in the gathering dark. Breeze hunkered beside him, barely having been spared by that damnable last bullet.

Turning his glance to the side, he could see *Nynymbi*; the big-eyed Shoshoni spirit seemed to dance as it waved its stick-thin three-fingered hands.

"Could have warned us five minutes sooner," Sam told him. "Assuming we don't die here."

"It's a long distance rifle," Breeze was saying, her voice half drowned as Paco's M249 chattered and sent a stream of 5.56 rounds toward the knoll. "It'll be topped with a scope. Expensive...high-magnification glass. And it's getting dark."

"Yeah," Sam agreed. "Like, we're never going to see the guys that kill us."

"Glass," she repeated as she glanced his way in the growing dark. "An optic. Get it?"

"Nope."

She gave him that disgusted scowl. "So, did you ever use your binoculars to see anything at night? A rifle scope works the same way. Probably why he missed with that last shot."

"Binoculars weren't considered essential equipment for bussing tables or washing dishes in The Yucateca's kitchen."

She sighed, and Sam heard Paco talking on the battle com.

"Sam," she told him. "They're out of shooting light. Those high-powered scopes? They're useless after dark. And let's say they've got a rifle up there with a night scope or a thermal imager. It's four hundred yards. That's a damn long shot for anyone but a trained sniper with a hell of a good imaging device."

"LT?" someone cried. "Where are you?"

"She's dead!" Breeze called back. "So's the Sarge! Keep your head down. They're shooting anyone who moves."

"Breeze? That you?"

"Yeah."

"It's Noonan. What's the sit rep?"

"Maybe sixty looters up on the knoll. Mostly carrying scoped hunting rifles. One, maybe more, really good long-range marksman. Think F Class. A top shooter capable of putting rounds into a three-inch group at four hundred yards. They took out the LT first, Sally second. We're staying low behind…"

The long blast from Paco's M249 drown anything else she might have said.

As the report faded, Sam could hear distant screaming, cursing from out beyond the fence.

From the Humvee, Paco called, "Breeze? I know you're not on battle com. I had 'em on NV. They were filtering down from the knoll. Coming down in a nice line, can you believe? Bunch of them are down. Others wounded."

The screams from up on the knoll got louder. Above it all: "*I'm shot! I'm shot!*" and "For God's sake! *Help me!*"

Another voice yelled, "We'll get you for this, mother fuckers!"

Paco answered with a short burst.

"I guess that's a mistake they won't make again." Sam resettled himself against the tire.

"Hey, Noon," Breeze called. "We're coming in."

"Do it fast, Breeze," Noonan replied.

She turned, took Sam's hand. "You ready?"

"Hell no! I'm in love with this tire. It's big and thick, and it's got a whole Humvee between me and the bad guys."

"Aw, you're just a sappy sentimentalist. Come on."

Sam had barely gotten to his feet when Breeze sprinted for all she was worth for the partially open garage door next to the NPT truck. His ribs were on fire as he passed the sprawled forms of Lieutenant Daniels and Sergeant White Eagle; the sight sent a hollow sensation through his gut. And all the while, his back crawled with the anticipation of a bullet. But no shots came. At the garage, Breeze scooted into the black interior, ducking to the side and grabbing Sam along behind her.

"Whew!" He followed it with slight whistle.

"Noon?" Breeze called.

"Here!" A flashlight beam marked his location.

Sam let Breeze lead the way as they made their way past boxes, around the forklift, and equipment-stacked pallets to where Corporal Noonan, Tully, Brylan Jones, and Shane Goggles were standing behind the partially loaded truck. Dennis Conchlen, the truck driver could be seen inside, illuminated by the lights inside the cargo van. He was strapping a big blue plastic barrel atop it's mate. Looked like some kind of chemicals. From the number of boxes, crates, pallets, and barrels still to be loaded, not to mention the freezers and their generators, Sam wondered how it was ever going to fit.

Avery, arms crossed, was scowling where he waited by a large crate marked "Centrifuges." He didn't look happy as he tapped his loafer-clad toe on the concrete.

Tortilla Gomez appeared with a lantern and set it for low illumination. As he did, Sam could see the man's hands shaking. He'd been standing right at Daniels' side when she was killed.

To his com, Noonan said, "Okay. Everyone's accounted for. Paco, keep eyes on the slope. Kran? Now that you've got your NV gear, you and Deana keep an eye out on the flanks and rear." A pause as he listened. "Roger that. Stay frosty, people."

Looking up, Noonan had an owly look. Swallowed hard. "No chance the LT or Sarge are alive?"

"Nope," Tortilla told him. "Did the eye test just now on the way back. It's probably dark enough we can bring the bodies in. Tarp them. Put them with Mack and Clugg for the return trip."

"I say we go waste their fucking asses." Brylan was shifting from foot to foot and acting jumpy.

"Yeah." Noonan licked his lips, glanced over to where Avery and his people were watching by the office wall. "What the hell where they thinking? Shooting at us that way?"

"Nobody kills our people. Especially not the LT and Sarge!" Tortilla cried, looked like he was on the verge of tears.

"Tactical mistake," Breeze said.

"What are you onto, Breeze?" Sam could see her thinking. Knew that slight squint as she put the pieces together.

"Something you were saying earlier," she said. "About evolution. That survival doesn't have morals. They're looters, right? The reason they're still alive is because they've always done the killing. They've always had the weapons and the will to use them. That's their tactic. Shoot down the living, take what they want from the dead. Ergo, shoot us down, one by one, and they walk in and take the lab, the JLTV, the Humvees...all of it."

Noonan frowned. "Not to rain on your parade, Breeze, but we've got another ten hours getting this lab packed into the truck. We've had cat naps, but everyone's running on nerves. There ain't so much as a cup of coffee to buck us up, and bennies went away that first month on The Line. Even if we could work all night, by the time we're packed and wrapped, we'll be sitting ducks out there. All they have to do is shoot the drivers and we're out the NPT truck, the snowplows, the Jayco, and whoever else they can tag."

Sam always dreaded when the corners of Breeze's lips quivered like they now did. She said, "So, why the hell should we wait around?"

"You can't leave now!" Avery declared, stalking forward. "That's not even half of the lab! And the freezers are packed with bio—"

"Rymart!" Simone snapped, darting forward to snag the man's arm. "Stop it! We could all die here!"

"They were supposed to save us." Avery shook her arm off. "And you, Simone, don't you *ever* lay a hand on me again, or you can go beg in the street." And with that he stalked off toward the office, a knotted fist raised.

Breeze stepped forward, saying, "Simone, we're not leaving any of this behind. That's not what I meant."

"You think we should go out after them?" Goggles asked.

"Fuckin' A," Brylan said, his jaw working. A glitter lay behind his eyes. "We owe 'em. For the LT, for Sarge."

Breeze lifted a suggestive eyebrow. "How long do you think it's been since anyone has attacked them?" She glanced from face to face. "They're used to being in charge. On the offense. They know our officers are dead. They expect us to adopt the defensive. To hold them off."

"So"— Tully fingered his chin— "if we move on them, it'll be a wash if they've got night vision gear. Just like when Paco shot up that bunch coming down the hill. They'll see us coming."

"If they've got NV." The grin Breeze gave them was sending the willies up Sam's spine. He kept glancing at the dark corners, expecting to see *Nynymbi* dancing in the shadows.

"If?" Noonan was giving her a skeptical look. So were the others.

"Hey, you guys spent the last months *holding* The Line. Stop thinking in defensive terms. That's what those mother fuckers out there are counting on." She slapped a hand on Sam's shoulder. "Delgado and me? We learned a different tactic when we raided Clark Ranch."

"Uh, yeah," Sam told her. "We used a fricking D9 Cat."

"So?" She gave him that oh-so-innocent why-didn't-you-think-of-it-before look. "This time we've got two Humvees and a JLTV. And unlike Clark Ranch, we've got the people to drive them."

"Go out there and run them down?" Noonan asked.

"Fuckin' A," Brylan repeated with a vengeance.

"Why not?" Breeze asked. "Corporal, we owe them for the LT and Sarge. We can't evacuate until morning, and unless we do something about it, we'll take more casualties. We've got the NV capability, and they sure as hell can't stop us. It's your call, but I say we take it to them."

Brylan made a fist-pump of approval.

Sam was chewing on his lips, seeing the logic to it. Not that driving around out in the dark didn't come without risks. And not like he'd known Lieutenant Daniels all that well, let alone the beloved Sergeant White Eagle. But, damn it...

"Yeah." Noonan lifted his collar com. "Paco? What's happening out there?" For Sam and Breeze's benefit, he said, "They're camped up on the other side of that hillside to the south. Paco says there's a slight glow. Like they've got a fire behind the knoll."

"Any sign of active NV?" Noonan asked his com.

Breeze told Sam, "If they're using an IR system for night vision, our gear will see it."

"That's a negative." Noonan said. "All right, people. We're tired. We're pissed. They killed the LT and Sarge. Time to take scalps. Here's what we're going to do..."

Sam glanced over at the dark corner. *Nynymbi* was weaving from foot to foot, hands waving in mockery.

# SAY...WHAT?

*Thoughts were whizzing around like bees inside my skull as Gardner ushered in the next appointment. This was with Dr. Evan Holly and a kind of pudgy oversized kid named Court Hamilton.*

*I'd heard all about them. Dr. Holly had been part of the field school that stayed at Tappan Ranch. Court, a computer gaming nerd, had been one of the students. Now they were part of some arcane cabal, plotting with Agar on how to organize and manage redistribution of resources in Wyoming. Among the projects was a plan to build a refinery in the Bighorn Basin, reopen the South Pass iron mine, increase mineral production, mine gold outside Cooke City, and process coal for all kinds of things.*

*They were half way through their reports on which county commissioners were going to be a problem when Captain Ragnovich opened the door, knocked authoritatively on the frame, and stepped in to say, "Governor? Sorry for the interruption. Something's come up."*

*Agar raised a hand to stop Court, who, once he started on a subject, seemed to gush like a firehose. "Yeah?"*

*Ragnovich looked uneasy. "Lieutenant Daniels is overdue on her report. Granted, she's not on what you'd call a fixed schedule. Still, we expected a progress report. When we try to contact her, we don't get any answer. Just thought you'd want a heads up."*

*"Thanks, Harry." Agar gave him a nod. "Keep me informed."*

*"Yes, sir." Then Ragnovich bowed out, closing the door behind him.*

*It took another half hour before Holly and Hamilton picked up their maps, graphs, and charts and beat a retreat.*

*Agar dismissed Randolph for the night, watching as the Kace closed the door behind him, then he leaned forward, elbow braced on his blotter, chin resting on his thumb. In an instant his "governor" face dropped, replaced by the harried and haunted man I'd seen through the crack in the door. "Kace? You think there's a problem with Daniels?"*

*"Those people all came off The Line. They're the best we've got, sir." He straightened his shoulders. "If anyone can get that lab home, they will."*

*Agar exhaled wearily. "You know what's at stake? Insulin, for God's sake. Without it...?"*

*I watched the governor shake his head, gaze gone a thousand yards distant with hopelessness.*

— Excerpt from Lauren Davis' *Journal.*

# CHAPTER THIRTY-ONE

BREEZE LED the way through the darkness as they started up the long grassy slope toward the knoll. She wore the fancy ENVG-B night vision goggles retrieved from her boogie bag in the back of the MTV. The downside to tonight's little foray was that she only had a sixty-percent charge in the NV batteries and no spares. When they died, that was it. Maybe forever.

The goggles had been part of what Lauren had called her "boogie bag envy" while Breeze had been on The Line. Breeze's solution had been to swap a bottle of eighteen-year-old Macallan with Corporal Sondergrass out at OP Bravo Sierra. The way she'd presented the argument to him, it wasn't like he was selling government property on the black market. She was a Line rider. And the advanced NV goggles would allow her to make her runs in safety on pitch-black back roads when the use of her lights would alert raiders to her passage.

Fact was, she'd never had the opportunity on The Line. Only used them on the Clark Ranch raid. She heard Sam trip in the darkness behind her. Whispered over her shoulder, "Sorry. Should have told you about that rock."

"Yeah, well," Sam rasped back, "it's blacker than the pits of hell out here."

"Got a little hump of grass here. Take my hand."

She led him over the clump of needle-and-thread. There were occasional rocks hidden in the grass and forbs. Not to mention foot-turning holes and depressions down under the ground cover. Behind her, the lab seemed to glow from its thermal radiation. The sound of the forklift, the thumps and bangs as Dr. Avery stomped around berating, and

Corporal Fields soothed. But the loading of the truck carried on the still night. Meanwhile, they'd talked Jenna Blix, Simone, and Kathy Goodrich into slipping around the parking lot. They would flick a flashlight on for a second, then hurry to a different location and flash it again. Made it seem like the whole command was seeing to the lab's defense.

In the glow of her night vision, Breeze could see where the lookout was positioned on the knoll top. The good news was that it was just a single woman. And, better yet, her head wasn't bulky with NV gear. Just plain old human eyes. Call it the perfect audience for the flashlight show being staged around the lab.

Not that someone with NV goggles wouldn't eventually show up to check for themselves, but so far, the raiders were behaving according to plan. The question was, where were the other lookouts?

Glancing back through the goggles she could see the JLTV as it was pushed slowly and silently past the crushed lab gate. The access road was all downhill. Once the Guard had the heavy vehicles out the gate, gravity would see to the rest. That had been Noonan's idea. No sound of engines to tip off the looters. After the corporal laid out the operation, the rest had jumped on it with both feet, figuring this angle and that twist. The vehicles would coast downhill to the highway and then momentum would carry them in velvet silence to the gap in the right-of-way fence.

Meanwhile, two teams on foot would advance using night vision to scout for lookouts and take flanking positions. Breeze had volunteered to climb the slope under the knoll, circle, and find a position above the looters' camp.

For men and women who'd been shot at in foxholes for so long, they'd all taken to the notion of being the attackers for once.

A patch of clothing was Breeze's only warning; it lay in the thick grass. Her heart leaped, fear like lightning in her nerves. She clamped hard on Sam's hand. Her signal that something was wrong. Damn it, she'd almost walked right up to the guy. Wasn't more than ten feet below him. The barrel of his rifle was up, and through the waving heads of grass, she was staring right into his half-lidded eyes.

*Damn it!* Another step and...

Breeze fastened teeth in her lower lip, studied the guy's face. Almost gray-green in the goggles. Should have been shining from IR. And now that she got a better look? He might have been laid down to sleep. Those eyes didn't move, didn't blink.

What the...?

It hit her. Paco's long burst just after dark as he'd hosed the infiltrating looters. This had to be his work. She eased forward, her M4 raised in one hand, guiding Sam with the other. Could see the guy's body now. And there, just beyond, another. She caught a whiff of drying blood, and then the sour scent from punctured intestines.

Carefully, she picked her way around the guy, then the next, and a woman after that.

*Guess the looters just leave their dead lay.*

Why wouldn't they? It wasn't like friends and family meant much to a pack of beasts.

"What's that smell?" Sam leaned close to whisper.

Of course he couldn't see. Not with the overcast sky, the midnight-like dark.

"Bodies," she barely mouthed the words. "The looters Paco killed. We're right in the middle of them."

Sam squeezed her hand in understanding. Let her lead him to the uphill side of the slope. They had to veer wide, circle around the lookout. For this to work, she and Sam needed to have elevation. A position to shoot from that commanded the looters' camp.

But where were the other lookouts? Surely the scum buckets had other eyes out here. Scan as she might, she caught no trace of a thermal glow. Only the slight signature of stones still warm from the day.

She'd been given Lieutenant Daniels' com. Now the earbud asked, *"Breeze? We're in position at the break in the fence. Brylan and Goggles are working up the south flank. Sit rep?"*

She placed her mouth beside the mic, speaking low, "Skirting below the lookout now."

*"Time to action?"* Noonan asked.

"Fifteen?" she guessed.

*"RT."* Shorthand for "roger that."

She picked her way past another woman face down in the grass, this one having dragged herself partway up the slope. To Breeze's surprise, the woman was still breathing; each gasp rasped softly. Looked like her back was black with blood. Shot through the chest?

From here, the brow of the hill hid the lookout. Breeze led Sam wide of the dying woman. Squeezed his hand hard for silence when woman let out a whimpering moan. Coughed wetly.

Only when they were past did she ease up on Sam's hand, take a deep breath of her own.

"What was that?" Sam whispered.

"Dying woman."

"And you just left her?"

She could see the worry in his eyes as he glanced back in the darkness. "Got a better idea? Maybe call out, 'Hey, you got a dying woman down here?'"

"It's just…"

She tugged him along. "A looter. Like the one who killed Daniels and Sally. Now, let's make tracks. Brylan and Goggles will be in position any time now."

He jerked a nod, let her lead the way up the hill. But, glancing his way, even in the deeper shadow beneath his hat brim she glimpsed the worry and fear in his eyes. The sense of revulsion.

"If it had been a dying man?" she barely whispered. "Would that have bothered you this much?"

"Nope."

"God, you're a sexist."

He felt his way along behind her, letting her lead him around the stony outcrops. As they crested the ridge, she could look down. See the lookout on the knoll below. The woman still had her eyes fixed on the lab, seemed totally unaware the Breeze and Sam were thirty yards uphill. The sounds of laughter, an occasional outburst of profanity, the barely audible murmur of voices could be heard from behind the brow of the hill.

*"In position,"* came Goggles' muffled voice through her com. *"Make it forty-two guys, thirteen women. Got a big bonfire. Assholes are having a party. Got a couple of bottles of what looks like hard stuff. Whiskey maybe? Tequila? Rifles stacked or leaned against the pickup sides."*

*"RT,"* Noonan's voice replied. *"Breeze?"*

"Need five, Corporal."

*"Roger that. On your command."*

"Roger that," she answered.

"Can you believe these guys?" Sam hissed, his eyes on where the glow of the big fire was coming visible around the curve of the hill. The leaping flames gleamed on the fancy four-wheel-drive pickups. Two Fords, a Chevy, and a Ram. Raucous sounds of laughter broke out. Breeze ducked lower, her advanced goggles compensating for the tongues of flame. She scanned the slope ahead, seeing no one posted on guard. Were they idiots? Or so damn cocksure of themselves, they thought themselves invincible?

Ducking low, she led the way to an outcrop of resistant sandstone. Flipped up her goggles as Sam crawled up next to her and peered over.

The camp consisted of the four pickups all pulled into a line, headed uphill. The fire had been built out of what looked like old wooden pallets. Most of the men were seated in a ring around the fire, eyes on the leaping flames and dancing sparks. Other knots of people were clustered in groups or had shaken out bedrolls beyond the trucks. What looked like wounded were laid out on the downhill side, several swathed in bandages.

"Hey, you assholes going to talk all night?" a woman yelled from a bedroll on the other side of the trucks.

"Fuck you," came the answer from a big bearded man at the fire. "We're planning how to pick them soldiers off in the morning."

"If I let you come fuck me, will you shut the hell up so I can get some sleep?"

Another called, "Hell, Becky, the way Robin fucks, you'll be asleep way before he comes."

"And that'll be in mere seconds." The guy in a baseball cap lifted a bottle of what looked like whiskey into the firelight.

Laughter followed, a couple of the guys slapping at the glowering Robin.

"Be a pleasure shooting each and every one," Sam said curtly as he pulled up his Marlin and reached around for the box of .44s he had stuffed in his back pocket.

Lifting the com to her lips, Breeze said, "We're in position. About fifty yards uphill. Behind a rock outcrop, so don't shoot us by mistake when you come charging in."

"*Roger that.*" Noonan's voice sounded terse. "*For Daniels and Sally. Let's roll people.*"

Over the rude sexual banter being shouted back and forth down at the fire, Breeze barely heard the sound of the WNG engines coming to life down on the highway.

She told Sam, "Don't make the same mistake they are. Don't look directly at the fire. Keep your gaze off to the side. Like, where the lookout is. Look directly at the fire, and you'll be night-blind. Understand?"

"Yeah. You and Brandon taught me that. Thanks for the reminder. I'm still new at this wilderness warrior thing."

"You do all right, Sam Delgado." She settled her M4, resting the magazine on the stone, sighting through the red dot. One by one, she fixed on the ring of men illuminated by the firelight. Imagined triggering the gun. The sound of engines was getting louder.

"Hey!" Someone from the dark side of the pickups called. "You hear that?"

Another yelled, "Quiet! All of you! Listen. We got incoming."

Breeze could see movement around the trucks, men and women rising, peering down the dark slope.

"What do you see?" a voice asked into the growing silence.

"Not a goddamned thing. It's blacker 'n the hubs of hell down there."

One of the guys from the fire, Tobin, the bearded one, bellowed, "Arm up, people. Time to fight."

"Like you fuck, huh?" another asked. "I say they're running. That's headed down the road."

"Those engines are getting closer." A blue-sweat-shirted fellow stepped over and pulled a long-barreled rifle from where it had been leaned against a bumper. "They've got night vision. I say we run while the running is good."

"You always were a yellow piece of shit, Rolland," the guy in the cap said as he pulled out a large revolver. "You'll stay. And if it's the army, you'll fight."

Rolland braced the fancy rifle over his shoulder. Must have been one of the long-distance shooters, given the chassis and oversized scope. "Sure, I'll fight. I killed those two officers, didn't I? But I'll fight from out there. In the darkness."

*I killed those two officers...* Breeze clamped her jaws, laid the red dot right on the man's back and flipped the fire control to burst.

Cap Guy cocked the big revolver. "You'll fight from here. With the rest of us. Where we can concentrate our fire."

To Breeze's amazement, everyone had stopped to watch the interplay between Rolland and Cap Guy. Didn't matter that the growl of approaching engines was growing louder. What the hell was wrong with these people?

The one called Robin stalked out into the firelight after pulling a scoped hunting rifle from the stack near the Ram three-quarter ton. "Stop being idiots. Rolland, you go up the hill. That Creedmoor of yours will be of more use covering us."

"Forget it." A young blond guy hurried to the Ram's driver's door. "I'm out of here. Who's with me? Bail into the back."

Cap Guy didn't hesitate. He wheeled, and as the blond pulled the Ram's door open, Cap Guy shot him. One loud pop, and the blond fell.

In the silence, Cap Guy ordered, "Take positions. Jelly Roll! Get the Bamba out of the truck and get up the hill with Rolland and Smith. When the army guys get in the light, you take them out."

Breeze watched them scramble. Aware that on the dark side of the trucks where Cap Guy couldn't see, looters were melting away into the darkness, heading off across the slope as fast as they could stumble their way in the near black.

"What the hell kind of gun is that?" Sam pointed to where a muscular guy in an Australian-style bush hat was lifting some kind of oversized rifle with an equally long scope from the bed of the outlying Ford. Even in the firelight, Breeze could see the guy's biceps swelling at the weight. If that was Jelly Roll, he was poorly named. With ease, he carried the big gun past the fire, climbing the slope after Rolland and his 6.5 Creedmoor.

*"We're made, Corporal!"* came over the battle com as Goggles and Brylan Jones opened fire from the flank. Breeze could see the winking of their muzzle flashes off to the south.

"Guess the runaways ran right into them, huh?" Sam asked.

Cap Guy now ran to the edge of the camp, shouting, "Stop firing! Get back here. They're coming up from below. I said, *stop firing!*"

If anything, the popping of guns increased. To Breeze it sounded like panic fire. Muzzle flashes here and there in the darkness. Someone screamed.

And then the M249 opened up, streaming tracers from below to spatter and flash among the people behind the pickups. Screams, curses, could be heard. The ones who could, retreated to the safety of the trucks, crouching down in the firelight behind fenders, bumpers, and the reassuring bulk of big engines.

"You ready?" Breeze asked.

Sam took a deep breath. "Yeah." He cocked the Marlin, focused on the sights, and braced on the stone. Then the .44 banged.

Breeze had lost sight of Rolland. She found her red dot. Put it on the bunch hiding in front of the Ford. Cap Guy was there, shouting orders.

"For Daniels and Sally," she whispered as she triggered the M4.

# DANGEROUS WATERS

*I remember the first time I ever saw Pete Agar. That was in Frontier Park. He executed four people convicted of murder and rape. Shot each of them in the back of the head. I had an interest in that, having allowed two of them to escape when they tried to waylay me on a run to one of the OPs. I hadn't known at the time that they'd murdered a family. After they shot the men and boys, they raped the women for a couple of days, and then set fire to the ranch house to burn their surviving victims alive.*

*From that moment on I had built an image of Governor Agar as a pillar of strength who took over and ran the state like some kind of superhero.*

*Now I see a terrified man who's filled with the knowledge that if he fails, or makes a major mistake, our world here will die. The entire state teeters on the verge of collapse. Because of the constant cloud cover and low temps, the harvest was going to be about a third of what everyone had expected. But, pending a hard frost, it might be enough to keep bellies from gaunting up to the point that people would turn on each other come spring.*

*But then, everything is hanging by a thread. Just as an example, take our electrical grid. All those coal-fired power plants, the hydro-electric from the dams, and the countless windmills? Should have made Wyoming an energy paradise, right? Except that all that raw electrical power was run through substations, transformers, capacitors, buss bars, switches, and breakers. Power companies kept replacement parts in stock when something failed. That's how they fixed outages within hours. But as soon as they did, they ordered another capacitor or whatever. It would be shipped the next day from New Jersey, or Texas, or even Europe or China.*

*Suddenly we were in a scramble to come up with replacements. Stuff that we could make in local shops that worked on coils of wire, springs, and contacts.*

*And if a bearing broke in one of the vaunted windmills, thousands of which dotted Wyoming? Think you could just run down to Walmart to pick one up? Even before the Collapse?*

*Being on the inside, I could see what Agar was up against. How every night, he prayed that nothing would break, that he could keep current in the power lines, natural gas flowing in the pipelines, and food moving from ranches and elevators to peoples' plates.*

*Then the first signs popped up along Central Avenue and Lincoln Way asking:* WHAT ABOUT ELECTIONS?

*According to Wyoming law, the governor was limited to two terms, and Agar was in his second. Elections were supposed to be in November. It was September twentieth.*

— Excerpt from Lauren Davis' *Journal.*

# CHAPTER THIRTY-TWO

SAM LEVERED THE MARLIN, braced it over the rock, and settled the shadowed front sight on a guy just back of the Ford's tailgate; muzzle flash winked each time he triggered his AR at the approaching Humvees. Sam lost the shot in the recoil, felt the stab through his healing ribs, but when he looked, couldn't see anyone standing where the guy had been.

*Did I kill him?*

Or had it been a clean miss?

And then he stopped, stared as the JLTV emerged like magic out of the darkness below the parked trucks. The roar of the engine could be heard through the rattle, pop, and crack of high-velocity gunfire. Corporal Noonan, barely visible in the turret, was crouched behind the chain gun. Used it to shoot through the F 350 Ford that offered cover for a bunch of looters. The blast and *pang*! split the night.

The JLTV swung wide, seemed oblivious as bullet strikes spattered on its armored sides. In the firelight's glow, the armored truck's over-hanging nose, slanted headlights, and squat windshields gave it a shark-like appearance.

In its wake, the Humvees clawed their way out of the darkness, swinging around to the south. Paco—firing away with the M249—kept raking and mauling the fleeing raiders. Sort of like two land crabs, the Humvees churned their way around the sloping hillside below the knoll.

Which was when a horrendous blast split the night just below Sam and Breeze's position; he jumped half out of his skin. Sam blinked at the muzzle flash, like spears of light that shot out from the gun's compensator. It was accompanied by the simultaneous *clang* as something hit Tortilla's Humvee.

"Holy shit!" Breeze rose to peer down.

Sam reached up, grabbed her by the shoulder, and yanked her down an instant before a bullet cracked through the air where her head had been.

"What the hell was that?" she demanded.

Sam heard the snick of a rifle bolt, ducked to the side, and wormed his way around the edge of the sandstone outcrop. He could make out Jelly Roll on the firelit slope below him. The big muscular guy stuck some really big bullet into the oversized rifle and slammed the bolt home. Then the guy snugged down on the skeletonized stock as he put an eye to the scope.

Whatever the thing was, it's effect was clear. Steam was boiling out of Tortilla's stricken Humvee. That's when Tully, Kran, and Tortilla bailed out of the vehicle, crouching low, firing with their M4s in controlled bursts.

Sam watched Jelly Roll line the ugly rifle on Paco's Humvee. Resettle himself…

Taking a knee, Sam winced at the stitch of pain, and braced. Shot. Levered another round. Figured where Jelly Roll's mass was in the darkness behind the big gun. Shot. Worked the lever.

He heard the snap of a bullet as it whacked past. Felt his shirt jump on his upper arm.

Saw Jelly Roll rise up into the sights. Shot. Worked the lever.

Breeze's hand came out of nowhere. Tugged him off balance and dragged him behind the sandstone as bits of rock and bullet jacket peppered the side of his face.

Then Breeze was up, fired a burst from her M4. Sam saw the guy— Rolland, with the long-barreled rifle—topple over backwards as he worked the bolt for another shot. Hell, Sam hadn't even seen him. Hadn't known he was being shot at.

Half hidden in shadow Jelly Roll squirmed to one side of the big gun, looking over his shoulder in an attempt to locate Sam's position. From his hip, he pulled a large pistol. In the flickering firelight the thing appeared as a mere silhouette of something big. It made a hell of a noise, and the muzzle flash was like a strobe. Sam felt the sandstone jump as a big bullet exploded fist-sized chunks of rock from their hide.

Teeth gritted, Sam rolled out, swung the Marlin around, and tried to get a sight picture. The strobe of muzzle flash gave him a burning after-image. He shot. Levered. Shot again.

From the other side of the outcrop, Breeze's M4 split the night with flashes of 5.56.

Sam blinked at the afterimages, clamped his eyes shut. Squinted.

Jelly Roll struggled to rise. Seemed to curl up from the dirt like a tormented worm, twisted sideways, and flopped onto his side. Tried to brace an arm, push himself up. And collapsed.

"Son of a bitch," Sam told himself.

The firing was sporadic now. Just the occasional blinking of either Goggles' or Brylan's flanking fire from the south. In the JLTV, Noonan had vanished from the turret. The truck had stopped on the steep slope.

"Reload," Breeze ordered. She'd just slapped another magazine into her M4.

Sam—heart beating so hard it might break through his smarting chest —struggled for breath. Not sure when he'd gotten so starved for oxygen. His hands were shaking as he fumbled for his box of cartridges. Dropped the first ones in the dirt.

*Easy. Easy. Breathe.*

That was it. He swallowed down a dry throat. Got the first stubby cartridge into the loading gate. Then the next and the next.

Damn. How many times had he shot?

The spotlights on the Humvees flashed on, illuminating the camp as Sam fished around in the dirt for the .44s he'd dropped. He stopped short, gaped.

"Fuck me," Breeze whispered. "It's the I-25 checkpoint all over again."

Sam closed his eyes, what he'd seen like a vision from hell. All those people. What? Thirty? Thirty-five at least. All laying around. As if they'd been tossed out of a giant can to land in a scatter like broken dolls. And worse, too many were still writhing, crying, some trying to rise, only to flop back to the bloody ground. Others groaned; some screamed as pain and terror wracked their bleeding bodies.

Then, on the slope below, to Sam's complete horror, Jelly Roll somehow struggled to his feet. Right arm nothing more than swinging meat where the upper arm had been shot through. He made a step, and then another. Jelly Roll's right knee gave. The big man twisted as he fell. Head back, he landed with a thud across his oversized and ugly rifle.

Gasped.

Kicked.

And lay still.

# TORMENTS

*Buffalo Camp...*

*I'm staring at Mike Vinich as we bounce down the old ranch road through the refugee camp. Then people come at a run to crowd around the growling MTV as it heads for the big barn that houses the working facility with its pens, buffalo chute, and alleyways. Mike and I are in the back, packed in among all of those boxes of FEMA emergency rations. Rain falls from a low, tortured-looking sky. One of the gray days, wet, the kind that dampen anyone's spirits.*

*But the MTV keeps running slower and slower, its engine struggling, like the spring that powered it is running down. And then we come to a dead stop.*

*Silent.*

*Surrounded by tens of thousands of people. A sea of them, endless, just standing in the rain, staring at me. The sort of thing you'd see in a zombie movie. All of their eyes are empty, like hollows in their bloodless faces. They say nothing, just start shuffling closer, pressing up against the truck. Pushing it, making the MTV rock as they shove it.*

*"Mike? We gotta do something!" But when I glance down, my friend sprawls on the ration boxes, blood running from his shattered chest.*

*Human bodies swarm into the back of the truck. They're oddly clumsy, slow, reaching for me with dirt-crusted fingers as they scale the cargo racks.*

*In a terrified instant, my heart tries to beat its way through my chest, I suck for breath. Can't find the air, and the terror just gets worse.*

*The M4 feels cold, wet, and slippery as I lift it, flip the fire control to auto, and shoot, and shoot. Screaming, fear running bright in my veins, I twist back and forth, the gun hammering, brass flying out in an endless stream.*

*Scared out of my wits, I reach for Mike. Think maybe I can pull him back. But when I glance down, it's Pete Agar.*

*He looks up at me with tear-filled eyes, crying, "Can you stop them?"*

*The dead climb over the racks. I feel the first one grab my coat. I'm still shooting and screaming, the M4 vibrating in my hands, bucking, spitting brass. Try to wrench away...*

*Fall.*

*Hit the floor...and blink around in the darkness. I'm sprawled on a carpet, drenched in sweat, the sheet tangled around my legs.*

*My heart beats like a machinegun.*

*The dream must be a warning. Deep in my subconscious, I'm worried I'll get Pete Agar killed.*

— Excerpt from Lauren Davis' *Journal.*

# CHAPTER THIRTY-THREE

THE DODGE RAM 2500 still ran, but the two Fords and the Chevy had taken disabling hits during the firefight and were now junk. In the gray morning light, Breeze watched the Ram pickup back slowly around, the cab and bed loaded with bleeding and dying people. Three had surrendered; now, supposedly saddled with care for the wounded, they were driving away. Corporal Fields had told them they could evacuate back to Boulder, to whatever situation they had there.

Shifting the three-quarter ton into drive, the lady at the wheel—last night's lookout from the knoll—started her slow descent down the ridge, following the tire tracks to the hole in the fence and US 36. With each lurch and bump, the wretches in the truck bed moaned or cursed.

Breeze wondered how many of the gasping and crying wounded would make it. And how many would be dropped at the side of the road as soon as the truck was out of sight.

She sighed, walked over past the smoking remains of the bonfire—now burned down to gray ash. Around her, most of the Guard soldiers were laid out, sound asleep on the ground. Unaware even of the Ram's departure.

The Guard hadn't gotten off scot-free. Private William Krandal lay to the side, his head wrapped in a blood-soaked towel so the shattered skull and leaking brains couldn't be seen. Corporal Noonan had taken a bullet through the shoulder. He'd been evacuated to the Jayco after Fields had shot him up with a morphine syrette and bandaged his mangled shoulder.

Breeze glanced up at Sam who perched on the blasted sandstone outcrop overlooking the camp. The side of his face was covered with dried blood, and he had a bullet groove through the skin above his right deltoid muscle. Looking numb, he kept staring at Jelly Roll's corpse where it lay in a tangled heap. Paco had rolled the guy off of the big Hummer-killing .50 caliber rifle.

Breeze had never seen one before. The thing was a thirty-five pound ArmaLite AR-50. A big bolt-action single shot. The kicker—no pun intended—was that Jelly Roll only had two cartridges left when Sam shot him. Which would have been enough, since Tortilla's Humvee was toast. The ArmaLite had blasted a 700 grain bullet through Tortilla's grill, radiator, and engine block. That second round could have taken out Paco's Humvee, and a third—if placed right—the JLTV.

As Breeze watched, Tortilla and Goggles were stripping the dead Humvee's carcass of tires, tactical gear, and critical parts. Those were being loaded onto the MTV where it had been driven up the hill to assist in the salvage.

According to the survivors, the plan had been that come dawn, they'd position Jelly Roll below the gate. With the Bamba—as he'd called the big ArmaLite—he'd disable anything trying to leave the compound. Doing so would block the gate, trapping the other vehicles inside. Meanwhile the snipers would shoot anyone exiting the lab building.

Corporal Fields stepped her way across the scattered dead, a look of total exhaustion on her face. The woman was almost stumbling. But then, it had been way too long since any of them had slept. Funny how a gunfight could stimulate adrenaline.

Right up until the shooting stopped.

Most of them had caught naps in the hours before dawn. Breeze had. Hadn't cared when she threw herself down on an abandoned bedroll, heedless that she slept within inches of Cap Guy and Robin's still-bleeding corpses.

"Hey, Corporal. You look wasted." Breeze gave Fields a wry smile. She sniffed, aware that she could smell herself. Too long since sleep. Too long since a bath.

"You don't look so hot yourself," Fields returned. Glanced up the hill at Sam. "He going to be all right?"

"Nope."

"I tried. He wouldn't let me pick the bits of bullet and rock out of his face and side. The graze on his arm's going to hurt like hot shit for a while…and leave a cool scar." She shook her head. "What was he doing? Exposed like that?"

"Saving our shit, Corporal. I didn't get it. Not in time. That big guy over there with the fifty? Without Sam, he might have taken out all of our strength." She indicated Jelly Roll's bloody corpse.

"You get a close look at him?" Fields asked, shifting on weaving feet. "Sam shot the shit out of the guy. Then someone peppered him with small stuff. And I heard Tully claim the guy still got to his feet."

"He did. I saw it. Really freaked Sam out." She shifted her gaze to Sam, felt the worry.

"Got a call. Avery says they've got everything they need in the cargo truck. Generators are hooked up so we can keep the refrigeration units working every time we stop. Dennis says he's got that cargo space packed to the rafters. Says we can go any time."

"Jennifer, we're like the walking dead. You're stumbling on your feet. Half our people will be asleep at the wheel in minutes."

Fields yawned, swayed, blinked. "You want to take a chance on staying here?" She indicated the Ram 2500 as it turned onto the road and accelerated south. "No telling what the hell's in Boulder. Maybe this bunch? Your pal Cap Guy, as you call him? What if he's a lieutenant for some gang lord? What if that bunch we just let go sends another bigger bunch back, and they're better armed?"

Breeze didn't have the energy to shrug. "With Noonan out, it's your command now, Corporal. All right. Let's beat feet. Maybe make the Lyons Junction?"

"Assuming we don't all pass out and drive off the road," Fields told herself in a distant-sounding voice. The woman's eyes were unfocused as she said, "Carter Lake. The road up. At that choke point. It's defensible." A pause. "Or do you have a better idea?"

"Me?"

Jennifer Fields tried to smile. Failed. "Breeze, I'm a glorified EMT. Ragnovich made me a corporal because it let me boss cantankerous soldiers around while I was slapping bandages on wounds. I've never even fired a gun. Now I'm in charge?"

"It's not like we've got another lieutenant hidden away in the MTV."

"They'll listen to you," Fields said softly. "Most of them came because of you. If you tell them to make it back to Carter Lake, they'll figure out how to do it."

Breeze took a deep breath. "I'm not Guard, Jennifer."

"No, you're more." Fields blinked, used hands flecked with dried blood to scrub her eyes. Yawned. "We can't stay here…not sure we're capable of leaving…"

"The girls," Breeze said.

"Huh?"

"The girls from the Jayco. They can drive."

"Breeze, you wouldn't. Not after what they've been through."

"Jennifer, you weren't there on that trail back from Clark Ranch. Sometimes, when people have been brutalized…well, the best thing is to thrust 'em into something that makes them find themselves. Right now, the last thing we need are victims, and that's how they see themselves."

Breeze turned, calling, "Let's go, people. Conchlen says the truck's packed. We're moving. Now."

To her surprise, Fields was right. The few who were awake kicked those asleep onto their feet. Breeze waved to Sam, was relieved when he stood and started down the slope. Fields was standing at the JLTV, opened the passenger door, and gestured for Breeze to get in.

She hesitated. Saw the almost pleading look on Field's face. Daniels had always ridden in Tortilla's Humvee. By taking that seat...

Breeze bit her lip, stepped over, and racked her M4. She saw the questioning look on Sam's face as he climbed into the back, took the seat under the turret; it was still damp with Noonan's blood. Then she slipped into the passenger seat and slammed the heavy door. Studied the sparse dash, the utilitarian gauges, and the big touchscreen. The com gear was in the console between the seats.

"Doesn't have nearly the view, does it?" she asked.

"Nope," Goggles told her. "We going home now?"

"That's the plan. We need a rotation. I want everyone to at least grab a slab of jerky, drink all they can hold, top up fuel in the vehicles, and draw ammo from the MTV. Then they can rest up while I talk to the girls in the Jayco. I need volunteers to teach them how to drive for the first leg. Everybody else is sacking out in the Jayco. As soon as we're clear of any kind of retaliation from Boulder, we'll stop, cook some real food, and reassess the situation."

Goggles gave her weary grin. "Yes, ma'am." Then he saluted and started the engine.

Breeze didn't look back, didn't flinch as the JLTV crunched over a couple of bodies as it wheeled around and left the campsite behind. She stared numbly at the tracks beaten in the grass as they descended toward the hole in the highway fence.

# MESSENGER

*I'm wounded, deep down, but it isn't the kind of wound that shows up on an MRI or CAT scan. Somewhere down in the subconscious, the neural paths kept digging around for memories of horrible events and sending them up into my dreams. As if whatever's broken down there needs to torture me over and over. For what purpose?*

*Just out of pure selfish survival, you'd think a brain would want to keep churning out hope. Evolution should have selected for that. Pure Darwinian fitness: Yep, a sabretooth cat just ate my husband while I climbed a tree and watched. So, now that I'm back on the ground, let's go find a new mate and have more babies!*

*Right? Doesn't that make more sense?*

*Then what the hell was the selective advantage of leaving me shattered and so afraid to sleep that I lay here and wonder if it wouldn't be better to end it all? If I wasn't such a coward, I would.*

*Especially since I'm terrified that Kace Adams is right...*

*And, dear God, I don't want to hurt anyone else.*

— Excerpt from Lauren Davis' *Journal*.

# CHAPTER THIRTY-FOUR

DRIVING a snowplow might have been the most daunting thing Sam had ever attempted. The only advantage he had was that he'd watched Tully's actions behind the wheel of the big Mack truck. So at least he had a grasp of the controls. Of course, he'd flicked on the rotating and flashing warning lights, getting off on their strobe patterns. Mounted on high stalks, the brilliant lights were meant to be seen through even a thick haze of blowing snow.

At the stern and reproving look Tully gave him, not to mention the rolling of his eyes, Sam had reluctantly switched them off.

In light of the things he'd been part of since the Collapse, the raid at Clark Ranch, Slickside, the fights he'd been in, nothing should have intimidated him. Sitting in the driver's seat, punching the button that started that big diesel and shifting it into gear, however, had turned him into a quivering bundle of frayed nerves. Then he'd eased off the brake, barely pressed on the accelerator, and lurched forward.

"Easy there," Tully kept telling him as Sam steered his way toward the gate, taking position behind the JLTV where Breeze now rode. "It's a diesel. You have to be smoother on the accelerator than when you drive a gas engine."

In the seat beside, him, Jackie Feeley was watching, keeping track of Sam's every move. She was a svelte blonde, endowed with big blue eyes, a petite nose, and exotically angular face. Prior to leaving the Lyons junction, someone had found her an oversized hoody with too-long sleeves and designer jeans with the stringy white threads exposed above the knees.

Tully, meanwhile, had collapsed against the passenger door, head braced by the window. Just that fast, the guy dropped off into a deep sleep, each breath rasping in his throat.

"Wow," Sam whispered as he steered through the gate. "I'm really doing this."

Jackie leaned back, arms straight as she gripped the cuffs of the over-sized sweatshirt. In a self-conscious voice, she asked, "So, you and Breeze? You do this a lot?"

Sam shot her a sidelong glance. "Nope. First snowplow I've ever driven."

"I mean, stuff like this?" She gave a slight nod toward the JLTV up ahead. "Army stuff?"

Sam rubbed at the bandages on the side of his face. Winced at his sore ribs, the way his right upper arm ached from the graze. He'd finally let Corporal Fields pick out the little bits of bullets and sandstone before sterilizing the worst of the lacerations. Because Breeze had been there, he'd gritted his teeth to keep from howling like a wounded puppy when she'd applied the alcohol. Shit. The hurts just kept piling up.

"Yeah, I guess." He yawned. Hadn't been tired when he volunteered to drive the snowplow. Figured he'd had enough sleep on the way down. He gave Tully an envious sidelong glance. The guy's breath was purling in his throat, mouth open, totally dead to the world.

"Tough lady." Jackie stared absently down at the designer jeans she wore.

"She is that," Sam replied. He rocked the truck forward as he over-braked and slowed at the bottom of the hill. Damn thing reminded him of a hobby horse, over-weighted as it was by the heavy blade sticking out front.

Looking into the mirror, he could see the second plow. Behind it, came the NPT truck and the Ford Excursion carrying the five Biotek people. The Ford was packed full of computers, files, and stacks of documents along with the staff. They were followed by the big wrecker and the MTV. In the last spot came Paco's Humvee.

Jackie reached up to tuck back a lock of blonde hair. "What happened to her?"

"To Breeze? I don't understand."

Jackie took a deep breath. "After the gunfight. When she came down the hill and got us together in the motorhome. The way she talked to us. That tone of voice. The way she looked us in the eye and explained the situation. Um, I mean... how we were needed. Had to pull our weight." She shook her head as she looked away. "Nothing will ever be the same, will it?"

"Nope." After turning onto the highway, Sam laid his hand on the

steering wheel the way he'd seen Tully do. In the mirrors—and the big
Mack had a lot of mirrors facing every direction—he could monitor the
rest of the convoy making the turn onto northbound 36. Sam slowly
accelerated to fifty-five, the speed that they maintained given the big
M1089's top end.

"You're like her," Jackie said. "Tough, hard. Like life can throw
anything at you, and you'll survive."

"Really?" He felt an amused smile die on his lips. "I sure as hell
don't feel that way."

"You're from New York? That's what they said."

"Yeah. Hempstead. On Long Island outside of the city. But that's all
gone now. Family. Friends. Memories. All of it."

"Breeze's, too?"

"No. They're all alive." Sam squinted at the rear of the JLTV where
Breeze rode. Figured that they'd put her in charge. "You want to know
what happened to her? She got out of Colorado. Back after the shit really
started to come down. It cost her. And then she did things on The Line.
Terrible things. And later, she and I led a raid on a really bad man up in
the South Fork. People died. Other people lived because of it."

He grimaced as the image of Jelly Roll—golden in firelight, staggering to his feet—replayed in his memory. The sheer horror of that
wobbling rise, the broken arm swinging loose. The man had to have been
in agony, like some avatar from hell.

Sam had looked at the body. Seen that it had been one of his shots
that broke the guy's arm. Punched all those holes in his guts and leg.

"In the motorhome, Breeze told us there are no victims. Only
survivors." Jackie was fidgeting with her hands. "I mean, after what they
did to me... Well? Is she right? That someday, the memories...what they
did..." She glanced away, wiped at a tear that trickled down her cheek.

"That's not what she meant," Sam told her gently, images of Shyla
flashing behind his tired eyes. "The things that have happened to us, the
people we've lost, the atrocities we've seen and survived..." Memory
replayed the moment Jelly Roll's leg gave out and he toppled backward
onto his rifle. "You just shove it back, push it down, and do what you
have to do next."

"You and Breeze make it sound easy."

"Nothing easy about it. Never think it will be." From the corner of
his eye he could see the way her lips trembled. "I was an anthropologist.
A good, sensitive kind of guy. We had a shooting at my high school
once. Happened behind the bleachers. Everybody went in to counselling.
It was required. School was shut down for two weeks. We had sessions
on how to deal with trauma. Grief. Training on how to talk about our
feelings. They taught us strategies that would allow us to cope in a way
that would keep us from being scarred for the rest of our lives.

"I mean, looking back, what kind of chickenshit was that?" Sam slapped his hand on the steering wheel. "My wife was shot dead by would-be abductors and rapists. I killed people and horses. Watched a friend blow herself up. Executed a human being. Saved some like you. Lost others. And last night I killed more people so that we can save a laboratory that will give life to tens of thousands." A beat. "Where the hell is my grief counselor now?"

He shook his head, resettled his hat to raise the brim. "I gut it out, Jackie. Because I God damn well have to." He paused. "Make the decision, and you can, too."

She was watching him through wary blue eyes.

"Makes you wonder, doesn't it?" Sam shifted in the seat. "Who were those weeping high school students? The ones who broke down in the halls and couldn't sleep because of the nightmares? The ones who said their lives were forever traumatized and bruised because Tony Lopez was shot over a bad drug deal? Those ever-so-sensitive grief and trauma counselors with their pious words and solicitous advice? Wonder what they'd tell the refugees in Frontier Park?" A beat. "How they'd deal with the shit we've been living?"

"Guess it seems pretty silly, doesn't it?" Jackie pulled her knee up, wrapping her long sleeves around her ankle the way Breeze always did.

God, he missed Breeze. Wished it was her sitting next to him.

Sam glanced out the side mirror, checking on the convoy. He was starting to get the feel for the big plow. Wasn't all that tough. Not like he'd have to deal with traffic. The bullet hole in the windshield was only a minor annoyance.

"Delusional is a better word," Sam told her. "America, the western world, urban post-World War Two culture. We lived in a bubble. A fantasy construction built on a surreal understanding of reality. Never knew how incredibly fragile civilization was. That it could die so fast. Like, what? A week? That was how long it took to switch from refinement and law to barbarism?"

"What do you mean by a bubble?"

He glanced at her. "You're what? Twenty-two?"

"Twenty-one."

"So, did you ever worry where the next meal would come from? Ever see a dead person before the Collapse? Ever? Because surely someone in your family had to have passed away. Grandparent? Some great aunt or uncle? Or some friend's family member?"

"No." A frown lined her high forehead. "I mean, that's what mortuaries are for."

"Ever kill anything except maybe a fly or a spider? Ever have blood on your hands? Or did you always get your food in a grocery store or restaurant?"

"Get real," she told him, the first bit of personality leaking into her voice.

"An illusory bubble," Sam repeated. "But, hey, I didn't get it either. And I was the guy who'd studied hunting and gathering cultures, read the paleopathological reports documenting violence and conflict. I was supposed to have a handle on what it meant to be human."

He blinked, yawned. "Silly damned fool."

Jackie was studying him from the side. "I keep reliving it. How they just shot David down. Pulled me out of the car. The way they laughed as they ripped my clothes off. Threw me down on that mattress... and...and..."

She swallowed hard, looking away. "And you tell me that's always going to..."

Sam sighed when she couldn't finish, Shyla smiling from his memory. "If you're going to survive, you make it part of you. That's the piece of the puzzle those moron counselors back in high school didn't get. Yeah, it happened. They did what they did. Nothing can change that. So, pay attention: Here's the important part. Just because it's part of you doesn't mean it has to own you. You own it. Use it to make yourself stronger."

"You make it sound so simple." She shook her head, eyes downcast.

He turned his attention to slowing the big plow as they approached the abandoned cars south of Lyons Junction. "Never, ever, confuse simple with easy. Keeping myself together? Going on? Day after day? It fucking sucks, lady. But I can't quit. I've got to keep on doing, keep on living because I swore to my Shyla."

"And that makes you a survivor?"

"It does. Now, reach down. Grab the barrel of my rifle and pull it up. That's it."

"What's happening?" She sounded tenuous, holding the Marlin's barrel like it was a venomous snake.

"Probably nothing," he told her, easing on the brake as they entered the funnel of cars. "Huh, look. They're running."

He pointed to where three guys at the roadblock hopped into a van they'd pulled across the intersection. The white Ford started, lurched back to crash into a blocking pickup. Then it wheeled around, tires smoking as it rocketed away up 36 headed for Lyons.

"Guess it's a good thing we disabled the dump trucks." Sam smiled as the lead Humvee threaded the tight alley created by the lines of cars and campers and turned east on Colorado 66.

As they rounded the corner, Sam steered the plow wide. Judged it wrong as he heard the blade scrape the closest car. Well, could have been worse.

He heard Jackie whispering, "Make it part of you."

She had a steely glint behind her narrowed blue eyes as she fixed them on the little white house behind the fruit stand. She leaned out, watching it for as long as she could as the convoy drove past. When she looked back at Sam, a strange and calculating light flickered behind those blue orbs.

# RAGNOVICH

On the ride down Central Avenue to the Capitol, Kace Adams was driving. I spent most of it pondering what was going on inside Agar's head. Like, how he was supposed to distribute food and fuel around the state when we weren't sure Wyoming could make through the winter.

But that didn't turn out to be the biggest worry.

Colonel Joseph Steadman was camped outside the governor's office when we climbed the steps to the second floor. So was Captain Ragnovich. They'd been waiting, looking impatient in their dress uniforms. Their expressions were grim as the governor led the way from the stairs and across the tessellated tile floor.

"What's up?" Agar asked as he led the way into his east-wing office.

"Daniels still hasn't checked in," Steadman declared as he followed Agar through Randy's office and into the governor's lair. "There's no word from Fallen Eagle."

I took my usual position off to the side, trying to find a way to stand so my healing hip and ribs didn't hurt. I'd really taken a wallop when I fell out of bed. Somehow, I just couldn't stomach the thought of taking my seat while Ragnovich and the colonel were standing. Must have spent too much time on The Line. Kace took up his position at the door, one hand propped on his belted pistol.

Daniels hadn't checked in?

I felt a cold tickle slip its way around my gut. Breeze? Where the hell are you?

I couldn't help but glance off toward Colorado, as if I could see beyond the Capitol's walls. I'd been south of The Line. Not as far as

Breeze and Daniels had gone, but nothing I'd seen down there had been anywhere close to warm and fuzzy.

"They should have had the firepower to tackle anything the gangs down there could have thrown at them," Steadman declared. "With the chain gun, they could have taken down anything short of an Abrams."

"If they had enough ammunition," Ragnovich said so softly I barely heard it.

"Maybe it's a radio malfunction?" Agar asked.

"Battle coms don't malfunction," Steadman insisted, hands clasped behind his back as he paced before Pete's desk.

The governor shot a glance my way, asking, "What do you think, Lauren? Breeze is in the middle of it. Think we should risk a reconnaissance flight?"

Steadman gave me an irritated "who the hell are you?" look, as if I might have been an annoyance, and cut me off by saying, "No, Governor. The weather's closing in. We won't have the ceiling. I won't risk losing an air asset."

"We could send a small recon force," Ragnovich countered. "We know—"

"I volunteer," I said.

Ragnovich pointedly ignored me as he continued. "We know that Fallen Eagle cleared the way past Mishawaka to Stove Prairie. Have the recon team probe as far as the road is open with orders to disengage and retreat at the first sign of opposition or resistance."

"I'll go," I said, stepping forward. "I'll do it on a bike. Something fast and mobile. I know that country down there. I could—"

"No!" Ragnovich turned, glaring at me. "Good Lord, Davis, do you have a death wish? Hell, you were gritting your teeth just getting up the stairs. You don't fool me, Lauren. You hurt standing there."

The comment about having a death wish goes straight to my heart. I stiffen my spine, and across the room by the door, I see Kace Adams narrow his eyes. He watches me like a hawk, as though he already knows the answer to that question.

"I agree," Agar said softly. "Lauren, I know that you and Breeze are like sisters. And you damned well know how important that lab is, but you are not physically able to tackle this mission."

Turning back to Steadman and Ragnovich, he said, "Provide me with options, people. I need them—now."

— Excerpt from Lauren Davis' *Journal.*

# CHAPTER THIRTY-FIVE

BREEZE LIFTED THE HANDSET, having been assured that the radio was set to Ragnovich's WNG frequency. She sat in the passenger seat in the JLTV, staring out at Carter Lake with its descending bands that reminded her of oversized bathtub rings. The abandoned camp trailers, fifth-wheels, and tent-campers remained as they'd been the last time she'd seen them. Well, maybe some of the trash around them had spread a bit with the wind. She couldn't see the mountains, hidden as they were by the low clouds and curtains of rain.

Misty drizzle fell from the leaden sky to speckle the windshield. Corporal Fields, wearing a dripping hood and slicker, stood in the JLTV's open door. Waited with a pensive expression on her damp face.

The convoy filled the parking area overlooking the lake. Paco's Humvee guarded the road to the north, Breeze's LTV with its turret-mounted chain gun faced south. If pursuit appeared out of the storm, all she had to do was pull the cover off the Bushmaster's barrel, access the fire control, aim, and trigger the big gun.

Between them—parked in tight formation—were the plows, the big wrecker, and the Jayco. The NPT truck with its valuable cargo and Avery's Excursion were safely sandwiched in the middle. So far, no one had given the convoy a second look from the fishing camp down in the bottom of the lake.

Breeze took a deep breath. Thumbed the transmit button. "Hey, Captain Ragnovich, you there?"

"That's not exactly Guard protocol for radio communications," Fields said dryly.

"So, they can sue me." Breeze gave Fields a crooked smile. "Means they'll have to come down here to serve me with the papers, but then I can turn command over to whomever, and I can crawl in the back of the Jayco on one of those plush beds and sleep for a couple of centuries."

*"This is Cheyenne actual. To whoever's transmitting, you are on a restricted military bandwidth for authorized Wyoming National Guard communications only. Please—"*

"Tell Captain Ragnovich that Breeze Tappan needs to talk to him. I've got a report to make. That's Breeze Tappan, get it? I'm with the Fallen Eagle convoy Governor Agar sent to get the lab."

A pause. Then, *"Roger that. Captain will be with you in a moment."*

Fields lifted an eyebrow. "You really get a kick out of doing that, don't you?"

"Doing what?"

"Being the one-and-only Breeze Tappan."

"Yeah, well, I could try being the one-and-only Lauren Davis, but I don't want to put on airs." Breeze frowned. "And something about being Lauren? Who wants to be that gloomy all the time? Who does she think she is, Hamlet?"

*"This is Cheyenne actual. Captain Ragnovich speaking. Breeze? What's happening? Where's Lieutenant Daniels?"*

"Hey, Captain. Got some bad news. We ran into a little trouble at the lab. Seems a bunch from down in Boulder wanted it. Turned into a hell of a fight. Lieutenant Daniels, Sergeant White Eagle, and Private William Krandal are KIA. I repeat: They're dead. Corporal Matt Noonan is badly wounded. The looters took out one of the Humvees with a fifty-caliber rifle."

*"Okay. Roger that. What's your status?"*

"We've got the lab, Captain. It's packed up in the NPT truck. Portable generators are keeping the freezers running. Dr. Avery's people are all safe. We've made it back as far as Carter Lake west of Loveland. We're pulled up in a parking area on the west side overlooking the lake. Had to call a stop, Skipper. Our guys are exhausted. Running on fumes. I've got some of the women we rescued from Lyons Junction cooking in the motorhome. Figured our guys could use a hot meal when they wake up."

*"Rescued women? Motorhome? Breeze? What the hell's going on down there?"*

"Lieutenant Daniels didn't tell you about the women we rescued?"

*"No, she did not."*

"Think Clark Ranch, Captain. Same shit. Chained to the floor on mattresses. Couldn't leave them, and they're pulling their weight. Doing some of the driving. Got a couple walking the perimeter on guard duty while our guys sleep."

*"I see. Who is the senior officer?"*

"That would be Corporal Jennifer Fields, sir. Want to speak to her?"
*"I would."*

Breeze offered the handset to Fields. "Corporal Fields, sir."

*"What's your situation, Corporal?"*

"We're good on fuel, having replenished supplies as we've encountered looted stocks. We've expended about half of our ammo. Got two cases for the 5.56s. I think there are still thirteen rounds for the chain gun. Like Breeze said, we're down one Humvee. The one we have left is a little shot up but running fine. I've used up half of the blow-out kits for the wounded. I only have two ampules of morphine. We've hardly touched the food. Been too busy."

*"And your relationship with Breeze Tappan?"*

Fields gave Breeze a thoughtful look as she said, "Captain, I'm a combat medic. Not a field commander. My wife is diabetic. To date, I have never taken advantage of my position in the medical corps to sneak her insulin. More than once I have been sorely tempted, but what little Ginny is rationed has kept her alive. That ration is running out. More than anyone, I know the value of this lab. I want Dr. Avery's people making insulin north of The Line. If that means turning command over to Breeze, I'm doing it."

*"I'm not sure I follow."*

"Yes, sir, you do. Every beating heart on this trip came because Breeze did. That's why they volunteered. Breeze will get the lab home. No matter what it takes." Fields fixed her gaze on Breeze, adding, "I'm betting my Ginny's life on it."

Breeze could hear Ragnovich muttering in the background. *"What do you need from us?"*

Breeze took the handset. "Captain, I think we've got the road open back through Masonville to the Poudre. The corporal and I are giving our people a good six hours of sleep. Then we'll pull out after they've had a hot meal. If we're not back at The Forks by dawn, send the cavalry."

*"Roger that."* A pause. *"Cheyenne actual, out."*

Breeze studied the handset as she clipped it to the radio. Glanced at Fields. "Betting your wife's life? On me?"

"Yeah, no pressure, huh?" Fields gave her a grin, rain pattering on her hood.

# VOICES IN THE NIGHT

*Beyond my door, I hear a hushed conversation shared between worried people.*

*Rising, I pull on my pants, slip out of my room, and pad down the hall in bare feet, where I see Dudley, Margaret Bates, and a guy in grungy denim wearing a worn Levi jacket and holding a Bailey's hat in his hands.*

*As they enter the governor's office. I ghost my way to the door, listening.*

*Dudley Gardner says, "Sorry for the late hour, Pete. Margaret and I thought you'd better hear Dusty's report."*

*Agar's chair squeaks. "Good to see you again, Dusty. When did you get in?"*

*"Not an hour ago, sir." Had to be the guy in Levi's. "Hell of a trip. Governor Brainard sends his regards. He was a real help getting me through Utah. His representative is here. Wanted to meet with you tomorrow."*

*"And Nevada?" Agar asks.*

*"Nevada's a whole different kettle of fish, sir. They've got most of the government moved to Ely, and Governor Halifax is hanging on by the fingernails. Down in Clark County, one of the gangs claims they're the new government. Maybe they are, at least as far as the Las Vegas city limits. But Halifax and his people only have control of eastern Nevada. That's Wendover, Elko, Wells, and some of the mines in the central part. Reno, Carson City, that whole part, well, it's a dog eat dog no man's land."*

*"What did Governor Halifax say about the military situation?" Agar asks.*

*"Says that he doesn't know much. Just rumors. He's been so busy trying to keep any kind of state authority together, it's all he can do." A pause. "But sir, he begged me, almost with tears in his eyes. Said, 'Tell Governor Agar, if he can, whatever he can spare, send us food and fuel.' And I'm supposed to tell you, sir, he said if you can't, what's left of Nevada will be reduced to eating dirt and sagebrush."*

— Excerpt from Lauren Davis' *Journal.*

# CHAPTER THIRTY-SIX

LIGHTNING FLASHED on the backs of Breeze's eyes, and an instant later, the crack of thunder brought her bolt upright in the JLTV's passenger seat. Heart gone crazy, fear bright in her blood, she clawed for her M4. Reflexes in the middle of a firefight. Flashes of tracers, the deafening report of gunfire...fading...

Panting for breath. The battle vanished.

Breeze struggled to understand. The adrenaline haze kept pumping like wildfire in her veins. The gunfire...the fear... She blinked in confusion.

She was in a truck. The day gray. Rain pattered rhythmically on the windshield. Instead of in the midst of a fight, she sat on an uncomfortable seat, cold and alone, in an empty vehicle.

Shit.

Breeze drew a deep breath, watched another lightning bolt pulse and wiggle through the clouds. The aftereffects left a black shadow-snake across her vision. Seconds later, the crashing boom rolled across the angry sky.

Breeze cursed, stretched, and yawned. Massaged the cramp that now ached where she'd slept wrong. Then she pulled her Rand's hat down tight, grabbed up the carbine, and opened the door. Stepping out into the rain, she adjusted her poncho over the M4 to keep it dry. As raindrops rattled on her hat, she looked around. Saw nothing but wet vehicles gleaming in the dull light. She arched against the twinge in her back. The way she saw it, JLTV seats were never meant to be slept in.

Rain beat down harder as she considered the wet roadway that had been carved out of the hogback. Above the road cut, patches of mountain mahogany came across as dark blots on the grassy slope; chunks of fallen sandstone looked morose.

She walked over to where Tabitha Jenkins—one of the freed women—hunched in the protection offered by the MTV's elevated cargo box. Water pattered and ran down the tarps covering the fuel, rations, and ammunition in the truck's bed. Glancing at the way the tarps were tied, it was unnerving to think of the bodies of Lieutenant Daniels, Sergeant White Eagle, and the rest of the KIA's in their rolled and bungee-corded ground sheets.

Tabitha looked up with red and swollen eyes. The young woman cried a lot. Would break into trembling fits, and go blank, whispering, "No, no, no" as she relived episodes from her captivity and endless rape.

"See anything?" Breeze asked.

"Motorcycle." Tabitha's voice could barely be heard over the rain. "Not too long ago." She pointed to the spot a quarter mile away where the road crossed the hogback. "Just appeared. Stopped. The rider took a look, spun around, and rode back over the hill."

"A guy on a bike, huh?" *In rain like this?*

"Didn't seem like a threat." Tabitha kept her eyes averted, staring down to where water drained from the MTV's bed into a spattering puddle. "Didn't think I should bother you."

"Yeah, well, it's probably all right." Breeze gave her a reassuring smile. "Keep an eye peeled, though, okay?"

"I will."

"We're counting on you," Breeze told her, gave the woman a thumb's up, and detoured long enough to climb up and glance in the MTV's cab. Through the rain-streaked glass, she could see Private Tim "Torpedo" Hayes scrunched up under a blanket. The guy had wadded up a pack so he could brace against the door.

Breeze set off, splashing through puddles. Her worn hiking boots with their red laces hadn't been waterproofed in years. Now they went dark as the leather soaked. She thought she ought to take better care of them; it wasn't like she'd ever find another pair.

Guy on a bike, huh? Refugee? Or a scout? And if a scout, for whom?

She rounded the bulky M1089, water dripping from the cab and bed. From the edge of the parking lot, she could look down on the lake bottom. Saw no movement among the abandoned campers below. At the far end, by the water, the fishing camp with its tarps and nets looked miserable. They had a smoky fire burning under a ramada.

Breeze climbed up to glance through the wrecker's water-spotted passenger window, saw Goggles and Private Matisse both sleeping uncomfortably.

She dropped to the ground, checked the first snowplow; a blanket-wrapped form was sacked out in the driver's seat. Same with the MTV.

Lightning continued to strobe in the sky followed by hollow rumbles of thunder. And, damn it, it was getting colder. She puffed out a breath, watching it fog.

At the Excursion, she tapped on the driver's window, and Avery rolled it down partway.

"How's it going?" she asked.

"Wish we were moving," Avery told her. "All these breaks are doing is wasting precious time. I mean, you do understand that, don't you...*lady*."

Lady? Asshole called her lady? And in that tone of voice? Breeze could see that the seats were fully reclined, and now Simone, Blix, and Goodrich were leaning forward.

"Yeah, well, we're planning on rolling out a little before dark. Had to let my people get a little shuteye or we'd all be asleep at the wheel."

Avery gave Breeze an irritated look. "You're not even army. Hope you know what you're doing."

Breeze stopped herself before she told the guy to fuck off and take his chances back in Boulder. Said instead, "This is the WNG we're talking about. We'll get you across that border."

"You'd better," he said stiffly, rolling the window up to forestall any further discussion.

Breeze figured it might be impolitic to use the butt of her M4 to smash his window in so she could drag him out by the throat. Ground her teeth and moved on to Tully's snowplow where it was parked on the north side of the lot. She climbed up and glanced in the passenger side. The woman, Jackie, was peering back through the rain-streaked glass.

Jackie eased the door open and carefully climbed down. Breeze got a glimpse of Sam where he was half-tucked in the driver's seat. His Resistol hat was pulled low, his arms crossed tight on his chest to keep warm. That he didn't awaken was proof of how exhausted he was.

"You all right?" Breeze asked as Jackie pulled her sweatshirt's hood up against the rain.

"Sure. I guess." Jackie was giving her a wary look.

"What?" Breeze asked.

"I guess...uh...I was wondering."

"Yeah?"

"You and Sam?"

"What about us?"

"You got a thing?"

"A thing?" Breeze shifted, water slicking down her poncho. "That covers a lot of territory."

"Sorry. I mean... I was just..." Jackie glanced away, stared vacantly at the puddle that patterned in rings where the stream of water ran off the cab.

"Bit early to be interested in a man, don't you think?" Breeze asked softly, aware that a slow anger was brewing inside.

Jackie's now-clever eyes belied the silly smile she adopted. "Sam's different. I mean, stuff he told me. Like it didn't matter what happened... back there..." She sniffed. "Like Sam didn't hold it against me. Didn't treat me like...like..."

"Spoiled goods?" Breeze supplied.

"I guess." Jackie didn't meet Breeze's eyes as she shrugged in her raindrop-stained sweatshirt with its oversized sleeves.

"He's not that kind of man." Breeze knotted her jaw muscles at the way Jackie was looking thoughtfully up at the cab. Figured she knew what that sudden hope behind Jackie's eyes meant. "He tell you about Shyla?"

"A little."

"Well, she's too freshly dead. And what about you? After what you went through back at the junction? Seems to me I'd take a while. You got a lot to deal with."

Jackie's eyes flashed. "What's it to you?"

In a lower voice, Breeze said, "Latching onto the first man to come along isn't going to solve your problems. Isn't going to ensure that you—"

"You jealous?" The flash of anger deepened the blue in Jackie's eyes. "That it? He turned you down. Well I think he can make his own choices when it comes to who he wants to spend time with."

Breeze gaped. Felt her heart leap. "God, woman. You need help, you know that?" Didn't add, *You sick bitch!*

Sure enough, that gleam of righteousness brightened behind Jackie's fierce gaze. Reflected in the woman's stance, feet braced despite the rain.

Breeze raised her hands, stepping back. "Hey, Sam's his own man. He sure as hell doesn't need me to keep his ass out of a wringer."

Jackie's lips pursed. "That's just it. I didn't get it with David. I mean, what good was a hospital administrator when it comes to the end of the world? That million-dollar house and his Audi RS7 didn't keep him alive. Wasn't worth shit when those asshole bastards shot him dead and dragged me off."

"Hey, get a grip," Breeze told the woman as a tear broke loose to streak down Jackie's cheek.

Jackie sniffed, the crazed look taking possession. "Sam's a man. With a rifle. You said yourself. He's not like that." Then she shivered, seemed unaware as she clamped her arms around her pulling the sweat-shirt tight under her breasts.

"Your funeral," Breeze muttered, turning away.

She tossed a glance over her shoulder as she went to check the

Humvee guarding the northern approach. Jackie was climbing back into the snowplow's cab. Breeze hesitated.

Go warn Sam? That warning tingle was in her spine.

"He'll figure it out himself," she said, breath fogging before her.

At the back of the NPT truck, the rear doors were part way open, the sound of the generators rhythmically puttering away. The woman, Simone, appeared from within, pushed the door wide, and leaped down. She landed with a grunt, legs almost buckling. Then caught sight of Breeze.

"You okay?" Breeze asked.

Simone, reached up to the deck, recovered a denim jacket, and used it to cover her head and shoulders like a shawl. "Just wanted to check the refrigeration units. The temps back to ten below. That's centigrade. The reagents and cultures are doing fine. So are the tissue samples, ova, and other biologicals."

Breeze glanced back in the direction of the Expedition. "I would have figured Avery would have been the worried one."

From beneath the folds of her jacket, Simone sniffed derisively. "Rymart? Concerned? Yeah, if he was going to be late for an interview with the press. And God forbid if he wasn't wearing a William Westmancott jacket, Zegna shirt, and Loro Piana slacks."

"What are those?"

Simone's lips twitched. "Yeah, exactly. Rymart's budget for clothes, his ambition for advancement, and need for fawning supplicants knows no bounds."

Breeze tilted her head so water trickled from the brim of her hat. "I guess there are quirks that go along with being brilliant."

Simone started to say something. Bit her lip.

"What?"

"Nothing."

"Come on, Simone. As much as we've all got riding on this, it's no time for secrets."

Simone's gaze slipped off to the side. "Forget I said anything." Then she pushed the cargo door back to shield the inside from the rain.

Breeze watched the woman start for the Expedition. Hesitate.

She turned back, the jacket over her head shadowing her face. "Whatever happens? If it comes down to it, you want to be sure that Jim Perry, Kathy Goodrich, and Jenna Blix make it across that border. You understand what I'm saying, right?"

Breeze frowned. "What about you?"

"Those three, Ms. Tappan. They make it all work." And then she wheeled, hurrying for the Expedition as the rain fell with a greater fury.

Breeze was about to follow, demand an explanation, when she heard the motorcycles. Hurrying back to the MTV, she pulled up next to

Tabitha who'd emerged from the truck's shelter to stare south. The woman lifted a poncho-covered arm to point. "There."

The four motorcycles—engines popping and buzzing—had to be dirt bikes. They took the road that led down to the south-end camping area. Seemed to be wobbling and bobbing as they left the pavement and started down into the lake bottom.

Breeze circled around the MTV, keeping an eye on the bikes. Each rider carried a passenger on back who wore a bulky pack. Not to mention the packed saddlebags by the rear wheels. The rifles—barrels sticking up like antennae above their bobbing heads—added to the feeling of menace.

The riders weren't what you'd call top notch, fighting the bikes down the slippery slope, weaving as they fought for traction. Seemed like each time one of the bikes was about to fall over, a fast dab by a frantic foot averted disaster. Even though the drivers were fixed on keeping their machines moving and upright, the passengers, wearing helmets, kept their attention focused on her and the Guard vehicles. That fixed way they stared sent a fluttery sensation of premonition up Breeze's back.

Somehow, all four bikes, throwing rooster tails, made it across the lake bottom without falling or getting stuck in the mud. They passed wide around the fish camp, where the occupants had taken refuge behind cover, their own rifles bristling from behind coolers, barrels, and vehicles.

The riders ignored them, making instead for the old boat ramp on the north end; hitting the concrete, they accelerated like buzzing bees for the campground, and then the snaking road that took them past the deserted marina and up to the highway. The last sight Breeze had, the bikes shot off behind the dam and through the notch where the Black Zone gang had once blocked traffic.

"What do you think that was about?" Taliya Zollinger, the twenty-year-old with short-cropped brown hair asked as she emerged from where she'd been keeping watch on the road to the north.

"Four bikes, eight guys with rifles," Breeze said thoughtfully. "What the hell kind of threat would that be?" She shot a glance at the Humvee with its tarped M249 SAW, the armored sides slick in the rain.

Taliya fought a shiver, looking cold. "Maybe they're just trying to get away, huh? Like all of us were doing back before..." She blinked hard. "Before..."

"Yeah," Breeze told her, feeling totally drained. She damned well ought to head back to the JLTV. Catch another nap. Four guys on bikes weren't...

"Breeze?" the call came from behind.

She turned to see Tabitha as the woman rounded the side of the Jayco.

"Yeah, what?" Breeze gave Zollinger a thumbs up, and tried to force her weary muscles into a trot.

"Better see this," Tabitha told her, voice filled with nerves.

The young woman led the way. She was shaking, half soaked and miserably cold.

Breeze kept shooting the woman skeptical glances, figured she was on the point of falling apart as they rounded the Jayco and Tabitha pointed.

Even from where she stood, Breeze could see down the road. There, where the highway crossed the hogback and started down the switch-backs, she could see a truck. It was stopped, right there at the curve. Waiting.

A white Ram with big fancy wheels, and behind it, another truck. This one a Chevrolet Silverado. Behind the cabs, the beds were filled with men, and even from the distance, Breeze could make out the rifles. These guys were armed to the teeth.

Sure enough, she knew that white Ram with the fancy wheels. Had last seen it headed south on Highway 36, loaded to the gills with wounded and dying looters from the Biotek lab fight.

# FALSE HOPES

*I'd been looking at the map of northern Colorado. Tracing the route Fallen Eagle had travelled south. I understood full well why they'd taken the back roads through the mountains. Any time you got close to a population center—be it Fort Collins, Loveland, or Longmont—the amount of debris, traffic-jammed roads, barricades, and other obstacles increased. Not to mention the gangs of survivors who'd staked out territories in neighborhoods and subdivisions. By this time, there was no telling what they were eating. Probably stockpiles of food they'd killed to collect. And then there were the other rumors—the kind that Daniels had confirmed at the Poudre Canyon roadblock.*

*In the mountains, people would have been more spread out. Didn't matter that millions had run for the high country, figuring they'd live on deer, rabbits, and elk. Chew on pine trees and harvest the wealth of the land. In the early days, there would have been enough deer being spooked out of hiding by bumbling city folks to partially pay off. But after the first night spent out in the cold rain trying to make a fire from wood too wet to burn? Suffice it to say the luster would have faded. The most desperate would have realized hunting other humans was more productive than trying to be Jeremiah Johnson.*

*After three months, I suspect the attrition would have thinned the ranks to mere hundreds. Daniels had proved that on the way south.*

*So, all I had to do was take a fast motorcycle, an adventure bike like a KTM, BMW, or a Honda Africa Twin, and...*

*Harry Ragnovich burst into the office, calling, "They're alive! Fallen Eagle has made it to Carter Lake. Lieutenant Daniels and Sergeant White Eagle are dead. Tappan is in charge."*

*"Dead?" Governor Agar cried, rounding his desk to where I was staring at the map on the conference table. "What happened?"*

*"Looters from Boulder. Guess it was a hell of a fight. Our people lost a Humvee. Breeze said they're forted up. Had to rest."*

*"Where's Carter Lake?" Agar bent over the map next to me. I caught his scent. The guy smelled like lilacs.*

*I pointed. "Here. From where they're at, it's a short hop across the Big Thompson, then back over the pass to the Poudre."*

*Agar followed my finger as I traced the route.*

*"And they've already cleared that," Ragnovich noted, leaning close.*

*"What could possibly go wrong?" Agar asked in a voice laced with cynicism.*

— Excerpt from Lauren Davis' *Journal.*

# CHAPTER THIRTY-SEVEN

WHEN TULLY RUDELY YANKED THE snowplow door open, Sam came within a whisker of tumbling out and down. Barely caught himself in time. Doing so sent a stitch of pain through his way-too-tender ribs. Would have been a long fall, glancing off the step, before hitting the ground. And...

"What the hell?" he glanced past Tully at the falling flakes of snow.

"Hey!" Jackie snapped from where she jolted awake in the passenger seat. "Careful, you big lout! You could have hurt Sam!"

Tully, wrapped in his too-light coat, gave her a silly-assed grin. "Naw. Sam's young yet. He would have bounced." Then he added, "Wake up. Breeze wants everyone ready to go in fifteen minutes. You've got ten to hustle your butt over to the Jayco, choke down all you can eat, and get back."

Sam stretched, flinched at the sore spots, and felt every muscle in his body cramping. "What's happening?"

"While we were sacked out, four bikes, packing double, slipped around through the lake bottom and headed north. At the same time two pickups of Boulder raiders, packed full of guys with guns, appeared on our back trail. They're just sitting there getting wet. And then it started to snow."

"What do they think they're going to prove?" Sam asked with a yawn. "Pickups and motorcycles against a JLTV and a Humvee?"

"Yeah, well, Breeze says we're going." Tully hooked a thumb in the direction of the Jayco. "Go catch a bite. It's hot. Not exactly an epicurean banquet, but it'll fricking well do in a pinch. As soon as you and the last rotation chow down, we're rolling."

Sam's leg had fallen asleep. He took a moment to pluck up his Marlin where he'd laid it on the floor. The leg was tingling as he climbed gingerly down, but somehow, it didn't buckle under him as he eased to the ground. Tully climbed up, slamming the driver's door behind him. With a hitching limp, Sam rounded the big blade up front, found Jackie waiting for him on the other side.

Her eyes full with anticipation, she gave him a shy smile, asked, "Sleep all right?"

"Better than nothing," he told her. "When did the snow start?"

"Maybe five minutes ago."

"It's just the middle of September," Sam said warily, aware of how close she was walking. The intent look she was giving him from beneath the hood of her oversized sweatshirt.

"Nothing's the same. We're all going to have to live differently. Make new arrangements. I mean, like you. I know how it must feel. Losing Shyla. Like I lost David. Having someone to talk to. Someone who's been there. Knows the hollow and hopeless feeling."

From inside the hoodie, she was giving him a calculated stare.

"All this"—she waved one of her oversized sleeves— "means the old rules don't count. I didn't get that until you said, 'own it.' We have to, Sam. I mean, what they did to me? I need to know that isn't the rest of my life. That gang rape doesn't define me. I have to prove that I can be a whole woman again."

"Uh huh."

"People used to say I was pretty." She was glancing off to the side as they rounded the NPT truck where Margo Simone and Dennis Conchlen were shutting down the generators that powered the freezers.

"You are."

She shot him that doe-eyed look again. "I don't feel pretty. And words are just words, Sam. You could say the sky was yellow. Wouldn't make it so."

How did he answer that? *Have no words? Utter no words.* Now there was a motto he could live with.

They walked up to the Jayco, Jackie turning, blocking access to the door. She fixed on Sam, the wounded look in her large eyes. "I'd really like it if I could believe you. If there was a way you could prove it to me."

Sam saw the frown lines in her forehead, the way the snow was landing on her hood, melting. Maybe she wasn't as stunning as his Shyla had been, but men would notice her when she walked into a room. The way she was focused on him had his full attention.

"Hey, look. Any man would be lucky to have you in his life. Don't sell yourself short."

"Any man?" she asked herself, a flicker of satisfaction in her expression as she turned and opened the Jayco's door. Sam watched her climb into the motor home, a saucy sway to her hips.

Well, maybe what happened at Lyons Junction wouldn't leave her scarred for life.

Inside, the Jayco was warm, filled with people in wet ponchos as they stood crowded, each eating out of a bowl. These were all Guard, men and women who'd learned how to wolf a meal on The Line. In the rear, Noonan—eyes closed and face pale—was in one bunk, the wounded Biotek guy, Jim Perry, arm in a sling, in the other. Both looked miserable.

"Four bikes, eight guys, and two pickups filled with rifles?" Torpedo Hays asked. "Against us?"

"Yeah," Paco Vermijo said through a mouthful. "What's Breeze worried about?"

"Getting our asses shot off?" Deana Capriolli asked. "I tell you, the girl's got her shit together. Call it a sixth sense. Line riders who didn't have it, got really dead, really fast."

Shane Goggles, wedged in by the driver's seat, said, "I'm with Breeze. Let's get the hell out of here."

"I could use another twenty hours of sleep," Brylan Jones mumbled as he yawned wide, exposing half-chewed food.

Sam tried not to look. Took his bowl as it was handed to him and let Private Matisse squeeze past on the way out. In the process, Sam came within a whisker of having the "ration stew" spill down his front. Gratefully, he attacked the bowlful, aware of the odor of wet clothing, too many unwashed bodies, and the smell of food.

Might not have been the finest cuisine—as Tully had warned—but hungry as he was, it sure hit the spot. One by one, as the Guard soldiers left, the Lyons women were climbing back in, shedding their ponchos. Slipping past, they took seats at the table and in the back. Wet from standing guard, they were shivering, bedraggled.

He and Jackie were the last ones, the dishes having been collected and stuffed into a black plastic trash sack. Capriolli had settled in the driver's seat, flipping on her battle com, and announcing, "We're ready to roll."

Sam got another look at Noonan, laid out in the back. To Sam's way of thinking, the corporal didn't look good. Blood was seeping through the bandage swathing his right shoulder.

Hell, yeah. Time to roll. Dead tired they might all be, but lives were hanging in the balance.

To Jackie, he said, "Why don't you stay here. Be easier and a hell of a lot more comfortable than riding in that rocking horse of a wrecker."

She pulled her hood up. Covered blonde hair that gleamed in the motorhome lights. Fixed that unsettling blue gaze on him. "I'll stick with you, Sam." A flicker of a smile. "Call it destiny."

His teeth slightly on edge, he opened the RV door, stepped out into the falling snow.

The stuff came down in large wet flakes. A lot of them.

Hard to see more than a couple of hundred yards. Made him wonder what the guys in the backs of those pickup trucks must have been thinking. Like him, he doubted they were dressed for the cold and wet. Unlike him, they were stuck in the open. He had a nice warm snowplow cab. With Jackie.

As he led the way past the Excursion, Simone was standing in the passenger door. Something in her posture made her look compressed. The vehicle was already running, windshield wipers clearing the melting snow as rapidly as it fell. Behind the glass, Avery stopped whatever he'd been saying to Simone. It hadn't been kind. He looked pissed. Something about the set of his jaw, the hard black gleam as he locked eyes with Sam.

*Not my problem,* Sam thought.

At the plow—already idling and ready to go—Sam waited while Jackie climbed up, opened the door, and clambered inside. Sam made a face, feeling the stitch in his ribs as he made the climb. Damn. His chest hurt. Like it was just getting worse. He braced the Marlin and slid into the seat to slam the door behind him.

The plow's wipers were going, Tully staring at the gauges. "New order of travel. Breeze is going first in the JLTV, then us, then the NPT, the scientists, and Jayco, the MTV, Brylan in the second plow, and Paco's Humvee to cover the six."

Where the battle com was taped on the dash, Breeze's voice announced, *"All right. Let's go home, people. Headlights on. Move out."*

Tully shifted the plow into drive, feeding throttle to the big diesel. The Mack started forward as Tully rolled them out onto the pavement behind Breeze in the JLTV. Craning his neck, in the mirror Sam could see the rest of the convoy following. Matisse had the NPT truck close behind.

Tully exhaled wearily. "It's only about sixty miles back to The Forks. The road's clear. Even if we only average twenty miles an hour, that's three hours to a nice warm bed."

"Right," Sam told him. "It's snowing. Where you going to find a nice warm bed at The Forks?"

Tully gave him a calculating sidelong look. "Right in front of that big fireplace in the main room. Even if I have to build the fire to make it happen." Then, "What about you, Jackie? Got any plans for when you get across The Line?"

She gave Sam a sly smile. "Let's just say that I'm checking out my options."

Sam averted his gaze, frowning out at the snow. The woman wasn't right in the head. Not that anyone would have been after what had been done to her. But, damn it, how did he explain that he wasn't the man she needed? Didn't matter how kindly he'd try and phrase it, she'd blame any rejection on the rape. That she was somehow sullied, forever unclean and untouchable.

Sure, he had Shyla to fall back on. He could say, "Sorry, I'm still reeling after the death of my wife."

She'd throw his own words back at him, "Own it, Sam. Move on. That's your advice, so move on to me. Here I am. Prove you meant it when you said I was still attractive."

And then what would he do? Turn her down, and it would add to her injury.

He ground his teeth as the JLTV crossed the dam; down below, the ruined marina appeared ghostlike behind the veil of falling snow. Tully was humming under his breath as the JLTV passed through the gap where the Black Zone had once had a roadblock.

Brake lights flashed on the JLTV as it clattered across something that lay across the road. It looked silver and gleamed wetly. Like a foot-wide strip of something spanning the entire width of the asphalt.

"What the...?" Tully cried, slamming on the binders, the plow rocking forward with momentum.

"*Shit!*" Breeze's voice came through the dash-mounted com. "*We just ran over a spike strip!*" A pause. "*On deck, everybody!*"

"What's a spike strip?" Sam asked.

"Cops throw them down," Tully told him as he brought the plow to a stop, the gleaming silver band with its sparkling lines of spikes looking deadly in the lights. "Won't hurt the JLTV. Not with those honking-thick treads. I mean, it'll chew them up, but it won't puncture..."

The *snap-slap* of a bullet hitting the cab brought Sam upright and grabbing for his rifle.

"Oh yeah?" Tully bellowed. "Watch this, assholes!"

Tully reached out, worked the little joy stick that lowered the blade, and stomped on the throttle. The big blade banged onto the pavement, sent a jarring vibration through the truck. Then came the grinding sound as the blade scraped over wet asphalt. Sam barely heard the spike strip's metallic clatter over the noise, saw the gleaming steel with its spikes whip out in a vicious curl as the blade flipped it off to the right.

Tully reached out and thumbed the broadcast button on the dash com. "We're through! Road's clear. Stupid pricks didn't think a snowplow could be used for something besides snow?"

Sam, one hand on the barrel of his Marlin, caught sight of the shadowy figure who darted in from the side. Something trailing yellow flames flickered in his hand as he hauled off and lobbed it. The object, a liquid-filled bottle, cartwheeled in an arc and hit the right side of the JLTV. The pop of breaking glass was barely audible. Flame spattered and spread across and down the JLTV's side.

"Molotov cocktail!" Tully screamed, foot still on the throttle. "By God, you piece of shit! I'll show you!"

Sam grabbed for a hold as Tully swung the truck after the fleeing figure. In the falling snow, the headlights illuminated the thrower. He'd just pulled what looked like a whiskey bottle from a low pack that hung at his waist. Was flicking a lighter, trying to light the rag stuffed in the bottle's neck. Too late, the guy looked up, eyes wide as Tully roared down on top of him. He dropped the bottle, turned to run. The guy disappeared beneath the blade as the plow ran him down. Sam never even felt the impact.

Jackie screamed, hunched down in the seat, and placed a hand to her mouth. Shaking her head, she closed her eyes, expression anguished.

The pinging sounds, intermixed with the popping of guns, finally made sense in Sam's reeling brain as Tully slammed the plow to a stop just short of the drop off to the lake.

A *pock!* was accompanied by a bullet hole in the windshield not two inches from the one received at the cannibal fight.

"Show you, you pieces of shit," Tully howled, slamming the plow into reverse. Backing up, the ruined body emerged. Looked like the guy had fallen. Caught between the sharp blade and the ground, what remained barely looked human.

A flicker of fire came tumbling through the falling snow. Hit the front right corner of the big blade and burst in a shatter of glass and flames. While most of it ran down the blade, a smear of fire was thrown across the Mack's hood and right fender. Bullets kept making *pang!* sounds as they hit the truck.

*"Go! Go! Let's move it people!"* Breeze's voice came through the battle com. *"We've got a hole! Keep moving!"*

As Tully slung the plow around, Sam caught sight of the JLTV. Fire ran in streams down its side as it picked up speed. Another figure leaped up from the roadside, arm back. In a wide lobbing arc, he threw another of the flaming bombs.

*Breeze! No!* Sam raised off the seat, heart in his throat.

Followed by a flaming trail, the bottle dropped, caught the JLTV's hood at an angle, and rolled across. The bottle broke as it hit the pavement to spew fire. The JLTV continued past. Behind it, the NPT truck veered wide of the flames, trying to close the gap.

In the same instant, the angry *pang pang pang* of bullets rattled on the plow's cab. From instinct, Sam reached out, caught a fistful of Jackie's oversized sweatshirt, and shoved her down onto the floor. The pangs turned to pocks as glass was blasted out of the windshield. Sam, head bowed, was showered in glass.

"Pieces of mother fu…" Tully's voice cut off in time to the smacking of a bullet hitting home. Nothing else made that meaty snapping sound in bone and flesh.

From his angle, ducked down behind the dash, Sam watched Tully Harmon go limp in the driver's seat, head banging into the side window where yet another bullet hole had appeared. Tully's eyes stuck out from his face, blood starting to leak from his nose and ear.

The plow, still in reverse, rolled to a stop.

Even as it did, a firebomb smacked and burst against the plow's dump bed, fire running down the side of the box to stream over the tandem dual tires.

"Let's go!" Jackie was sobbing. "Please! Let's go!"

"Tully's dead!" Sam shouted, heedless of the pinging of bullets whacking into metal.

On the road, convoy vehicles were rolling past. A shadowy figure tossed a fire bomb against the side of the Jayco. It hit, but the heavy wine bottle didn't break. Only dropped to the road, the gas-soaked rag sputtering.

What the hell did he do? Just sit here holding Jackie down? Tully was dead.

Sam glimpsed arcing fire as one of the attackers tossed a Molotov cocktail into the back of the MTV. It landed intact, only to roll awkwardly down the dip where the protective tarp covered Daniels' and the other bodies. It dropped. When it hit the metal bed, the burning rag popped out, spilling gasoline. Fire, in streamers, flowed around the inside of the bed. Flames began climbing the tarp.

Jackie continued to scream as Sam grabbed her by the shoulders, physically dragged her across him with all his might. Which was when something let loose in his chest. He felt the snap, the instant agony. For a second he froze, paralyzed by the pain. Stunned. Unable to breathe. Unable to think.

A bullet smashed through the windshield, made a high-pitched flutter past his ear as cracked into the cab behind him. Brought him back to reality.

He screamed as he muscled Jackie out of the way. Shifted to her seat, got a grip on Tully's body. Tried to pull him out from behind the wheel.

Pain left him weak, feeling like he had to throw up. Couldn't. It just hurt too fucking much.

"For God's sake, Jackie!" he screamed. "Help me!"

He could see people running through the snow. Some dropped like broken dolls as the M249's chattering sent streamers of 5.56 rounds

through them. The MTV was burning brightly where it had run off the
road and pitched into the far-side ditch. Leaping flames gave way to a
sucking whoosh as the fuel cans in the rear went up. Fire made a mushroom of molten yellow mixed with black and orange. Then the first
explosion blew fire, burning tarp, cartwheeling boxes and cases of
ammunition into a fountain fit for hell. The concussion sent attackers
tumbling.

A second detonation ripped the ground sheets from the bodies up
forward, tossing the remains of Lieutenant Daniels, White Eagle, Clegg,
and the rest into the air.

"Help me!" Sam screamed again, averting his eyes.

He cried against the pain, braced his foot on the driver's door, and
grabbed Tully's body. Figured he'd never bear it...and began to pull. He
continued to scream at the tearing in his chest; tears welling, he clamped
his eyes. Pulled. Felt something else snap inside him. His vision blurred,
silvered. Couldn't breathe. The pain...

And then, there was a body next to him. Jackie, sobbing like a child,
yanking.

Together, somehow, they got Tully's body out of the seat, past the
blade controls, and flopped shamefully onto the passenger floor.

Sam climbed painfully into the seat, kicked Tully's foot out of the
way of the accelerator, and fed it throttle. In the melee, the plow
appeared to have been forgotten. As it began to move, however, two of
the attackers turned his way. One, a bottle in his hand, pointed. Then the
guy reached back. No more than fifteen feet in front of the plow, no way
was he going to miss.

*Fuck. Here it comes.*

The guy's arm went back. He put all of his might into launching the
bottle, using his whole body. Too much. The burning knot of cloth came
loose from the neck, spilled burning gasoline over the attacker's arm,
shoulder, and side. The guy dropped the bottle in mid-throw. It bounced
off his shoulder, splashing more fire down his chest and landed at his
feet. Engulfed in flames, the guy twisted, jerked, thrashed, seemed to
dance in the blaze pouring from the bottle at his feet.

"Jesus," Jackie cried. "Oh, God! *Oh, God!*"

A bullet whacked into the blade, made a ringing sound.

*"What's the status of those pickups?"* Breeze's voice came through
the com.

*"Can't see them through the snow,"* Paco's voice replied. *"What do
we do about the MT..."* The rest was lost as the M249 let loose with a
burst.

*"Leave it! We've got to go, people! Mission first."*

*"What about those pickups, Breeze?"* Paco asked again.

Sam reached over, pressed the send button. "Tully's dead. I've got them."

*"Sam?"*

"Breeze! Go! Trust me. Now, go! Go! Go!"

Sam struggled, trying to get his breath. Fuck it! Felt like his entire chest was torn in two.

"What I'd give for carfentanil." He shifted into drive, whimpering as he cranked the wheel around and accelerated. A motorcycle, resting on its side stand, came into view. Looked like a nice bike. Orange and white with aluminum saddle bags.

Sam ran it over. Heard the snapping and banging as blade knocked it over, then the tires crushed it.

He headed back through the gap. As he did, Jackie was weeping, trying to stay as far from Tully's bleeding body as she could. Breeze's voice was crackling through the com, telling him to respond.

He glanced in the mirror, saw fire burning along the side of the box; flames illuminated black smoke where the tires on the left side were burning. Well, hell, he guessed it would be a short trip.

*"Sam! Damn it! Respond!"* Panic could be heard in Breeze's voice.

Sam reached over and flipped the com off. Hell, he had enough problems just trying to see through the bullet-shattered windshield.

And there, just for the moment, he could see *Nynymbi* dancing in the flames that flickered and died on the hood.

# SURVIVORS

*I stand by the window in the governor's office. Beyond the glass, the first of the rain begins to fall. The drops are black. Really. Soot carried down from the clouds. Probably wind-born toxins from burning cities and forests around the world.*

*Agar is going over state geological maps with Dr. Holly. Something about Wyoming's incredible deposits of rare earth elements. REEs for short. They're some sort of metals. I'd never heard of neodymium, let alone praseodymium. Turns out there's a lot of it in northeastern Wyoming. It's used for super magnets. And then there's lanthanum and samarium. A huge deposit was apparently in something called a pluton under the Medicine Bow Mountains. Oh, and don't forget the boron that could be extracted from hot springs in Yellowstone.*

*Right. As if I could care.*

*All I can think about is Breeze and Sam. I'm still trying to delude myself into thinking I can commandeer a motorcycle and bust down south. In my head, I'm whipping the bike past roadblocks, outrunning raiders, and flying up canyons to find my friend.*

*And do what? Show up at the last minute, slide the bike to a stop in time to whip my M4 around and shoot the looters as they rush the Fallen Eagle convoy.*

*Like one woman on a bike would save the day when a bunch of armed WNG veterans, a chain gun, and SAW wouldn't?*

*As Agar and Dr. Holly plot how to transition Wyoming's coal mining expertise to excavating and processing REEs, I'm imagining Breeze holed up behind shot-up vehicles. Shooting, screaming, as Fallen Eagle is overrun by a horde of looters.*

*Daniels, White Eagle, and so many others are already dead. They lost a Humvee. My worst-case scenario brain watches it all unfold—over and over.*

*A sort of twisted replay of Custer's destruction on the Little Bighorn.*

— Excerpt from Lauren Davis' *Journal.*

# CHAPTER THIRTY-EIGHT

BREEZE SLAMMED a fist into the JLTV's dash. "Damnit, Sam! What the hell are you doing?"

Nothing. The com was deathly in its silence.

In the driver's seat, Shane Goggles was shooting her a measuring glance. He had one hand on the wheel, his foot hovering over the brake. Fire was flickering and dripping from the JLTV's side. Fortunately, the vehicle had been designed for such things. But it was sure as hell going to need a new paint job when it got back to Cheyenne.

"Sam! Damn you, answer me!" she tried again.

*"Breeze?"* Paco's voice came through. *"Tully's plow's on fire. I just saw it drive back through the gap headed south."*

"What's he think he's doing?" Goggles asked, his dark eyes flashing toward Breeze.

She ground her teeth, hammered her fist into the dash again. "Same thing he always does. Clark Ranch all over again. He's buying us time."

*"Orders?"* came the query through the battle com. *"Want us to go back in support?"*

Breeze ground her teeth, every fiber in her being desperate to shout, "Hell, yes!"

But what if they had another fifty-caliber rifle back there? What if they were planning another, more successful attack? Her command vehicle was on fire. She'd just lost the MTV, and maybe Tully's plow. Behind her, the NPT truck's headlights were glaring as it crowded close behind, as if for protection.

"Paco? Who else is missing?"

*"Torpedo's out of the MTV. He jumped just before the back went up. Never knew he could run that fast. Avery's car, the Jayco, they all made it. Molotov cocktail broke on the back of the wrecker. No telling what the fire took out. It's still got stuff burning back there. Bet it'll need a new seat cushion on the operator's chair."*

*"Breeze?"* Jennifer Fields' voice broke in. *"We'll do whatever you say. Remember, I'm counting on you."*

Yeah, to get the lab back in one piece. To save her wife's life. And so many others.

Memories of Sam played through Breeze's head: Him on Old Tobe, riding with all the grace of a sack of rice as they headed down the trail for Clark Ranch. That pensive look he got. The pain behind his expression as they crawled out of the *Puha* Cave. How he'd been so stoic as she changed the binding on his ribs after he'd come back to the ranch. How he got that special little smile when he was thinking of Shyla.

*Think he'll ever think of me with that same devotion?*

"Hey, Breeze?" Goggles said, that hope-I'm-not-out-of-line tension on his face. "We're down a Humvee, the MTV, and maybe a plow. Sam said Tully's dead. But so are the LT, the Sarge, Makelroy, Clugg, Kran..."

Yeah, yeah, the mission. That's what really mattered. She took a deep breath, blew it out. Realized that the snow was letting up. That the convoy was inching along as her lead JLTV idled down the road.

"Paco?" she asked into the com, "What's your assessment of the looters' strength. How many survived the fight back there?"

*"My call? I think we smoked the ones at the pull out. When Tully turned off to chase that first one. The rest sort of tossed their loads and fixed their attention to the plow. One turned himself into a human torch, and I think I capped the last one standing with the SAW."*

So, if they turned back...?

Sam's words, "Go! Go! Go!" echoed in her head.

Breeze closed her eyes, told Goggles, "Shane, let's go. We've lost enough on this mission. Get us home."

Yeah. Sure. Lost enough.

*"Hey,"* Matisse, driving the big wrecker, called. *"I saw the MTV go up. Breeze, we got dead back there. I mean, shouldn't we go back? See if we can collect the LT, the Sarge, and the rest?"*

To the com, in a wooden voice, she said, "We'll get them, Steve. Just not today."

As the JLTV, still dripping fire, accelerated down the ribbon of blacktop, Breeze leaned back in the uncomfortable seat, watching the wipers slap across the bullet-streaked windshield as the snow turned to a light rain.

An image of Sam's smile lingered in her memory. He'd been lucky at Clark Ranch. That sort of shit never happened twice. Against all those men with rifles? No way.

Being in charge sucked.

# RESIGNATION

*Tyrell had talked about it, of course. Tried to tell me what it was like to hold the lives of his team members in his hands. How they trusted him to use them responsibly, knowing that he might have to sacrifice some members for the mission, for the good of others.*

*That's what Agar had done when he put Breeze and Sam at risk in the desperate gamble. If it paid off, tens of thousands would live. If it failed, people I loved would die and irreplaceable equipment would be lost.*

*I know now that whatever's going to happen is going to happen.*

— Excerpt from Lauren Davis' *Journal.*

# CHAPTER THIRTY-NINE

PASSING THROUGH THE GAP, the snow let up. Sort of like the parting of a curtain. In the driver's seat, Sam gasped for breath, his right hand on the steering wheel. His left he cuddled around the searing pain in his chest, as if doing so would protect it.

Every rocking bounce the plow made added to his misery. Left him half-stunned and blinking from the pain.

Bullet holes made an irregular pattern of frosted white stars in the windshield. All of them spider-webbed together. Made it tough to look through. But sure enough, there were the damned pickups. Not fifty yards ahead, coming on at low speed. The white three-quarter ton Ram was in the lead, a throng of guys wearing hats, holding rifles, crowding up close behind the cab. Even as Sam got their measure, they were leveling rifles over the roof.

At the first muzzle flashes, Sam said, "Jackie, you might want to get down."

"What the hell are you…" She left off the rest, ducking down on top of Tully's body as the first *ping! ping!* of bullets hit the blade. Another made a *pock!* as it blew away one of the rotating emergency lights on its stalk over the cab.

"The blade's going to take most of the fire," Sam told her, wincing as he pressed the accelerator hard. The big diesel emitted its throaty roar, the plow rocking forward. "Got to get the blade set right."

Sam, ducked down as he was, scowled at the blade controls. Okay, how had Tully used the little joy sticks? The right one was the up and down, was the left the tilt and angle?

Reaching for the wheel with his left arm, he gritted out a hearty

"Fuck!" against the pain it caused his ribs. With his right, he started fiddling with the blade controls.

Down on the floorboards, Jackie cowered into a ball as a bullet *pock*ed the windshield and rapped the back of the cab. "You're *attacking* them?"

"Yeah." Sam heard a grinding as the blade kissed the pavement. Wrong way. He eased the control back.

Sounded like some kind of perverted hail as the bullets clanged, smacked, and splattered on the plow.

There! That was the one he wanted. From under the brim of his hat—as if it provided any protection from bullets—he could see the blade straightening.

He kept his jaw clamped against the spearing agony in his chest. Memories of *Nynymbi* dancing in the fire filled him with premonition. This wasn't going to end well. He'd try and make Breeze proud.

*Concentrate. Gotta get this right.*

Easing the control, he swung the blade square with the front of the truck. Figured that the height didn't matter.

*"I want the fuck out of here!"* Jackie screamed as another bullet blasted through the windshield. Powdered glass glittered as it settled on her blonde hair.

"Still think I'm the man of your dreams?" he asked absently, checking the speedometer. Thirty-five and accelerating.

Up ahead, the white Ram had slammed to a stop, pitching the guys in back into a knot against the cab. Good. They were too crammed together to shoot. One had even lost the grip on his gun. It went sliding across the cab, down the hood, to clatter on the wet road.

"You're fucking *insane*!" Jackie screamed, staring up at him with desperate eyes. Her fists were knotted, tears streaking down her cheeks.

"Gotta understand," Sam told her. "That lab? Avery and his bunch? That's life for tens of thousands of people." He shot her a quick glance. "Get it?"

"Fuck no!"

"It's easy math," he told her. "Stay down. Brace yourself."

The driver in the Ram had thrown the pickup into reverse, now he hammered it. The tires spinning on wet pavement; too late, the pickup leapt back. In doing so, it pitched four guys out of the back. Sent them sliding over the roof, down the windshield and hood to flop in a tangle on the pavement.

"Sorry, guys," Sam whispered.

*"Please,"* Jackie whimpered, sinking down on Tully's body.

Sam barely felt plow crush the four on the road. Through his little slice of windshield, he could see the guys in the Ram. The driver was screaming, fists knotted on the steering wheel. Doing forty-five, the plow slammed into the white pickup. When it did, more of the guys in the back were catapulted over the cab. Looked comic the way they flew, arms flapping, legs...

The impact tossed Sam onto the steering wheel. Pain stunned him. Wouldn't let him breath.

Seemed endless.

Couldn't have been more than seconds.

Jackie kept screaming.

Metal was grinding, squealing, and crumpling as the diesel thundered.

Sam caught the bizarre image of people tumbling from the sky. One —a blond guy, bearded, with blue eyes and wearing a green coat and black wool cap—flew over the top of the blade, smashed into the hood, and vanished into the gap between the blade and grill.

Sam got his eyes to focus, could see arms and legs sticking up above the top of the blade, the Ram's crumpled cab mostly hidden.

 For some insane reason, he glanced instinctively to the mirror, could see smoke boiling out of the tires as they spun on the wet asphalt.

Then the Ram smashed into the second pickup. Sam got a glimpse of more airborne bodies and tossed rifles as impact blew human beings up to somersault out of the Ford's bed. Caught in the instant, the Ram's rear flipped high, was thrust over the Ford's hood and cab.

Stupidly, Sam tried to let off the accelerator. Couldn't.

Realized that Tully's lower leg was pinning his foot to the throttle.

Kicking it back, the diesel slowed, the world filled with the screech of popping and rending metal.

And then it stopped. The only sound the idling of the big MP8 diesel and Jackie sobbing on the floor where she was crumpled atop Tully's corpse.

All Sam could do was gasp at the pain. He slumped onto the steering wheel, trying to find a position that didn't hurt.

Blinking through what little he could see through the shattered wind-shield, he tried to make sense of the scene: A foot. White Nike running shoe over a brown wool sock and a bit of ankle stuck up above the top of the blade. So did a twitching arm, the fingers fluttering in the rain. Behind it he could see the crumpled remains of the Ram, its ass end poked up and twisted. In what was left of the bed, two bodies writhed, limbs akimbo.

"Damn," he whispered through the tears and hurt.

Jackie, still sobbing, climbed painfully from the floor. With a sleeve, she wiped at the frosting of bullet-crushed glass on the seat. Like a gopher from a hole, she lifted her head to peek over the dash.

"Oh, my God," she whimpered.

"Yeah," Sam admitted wearily. To his surprise, tears were spilling down his cheeks.

Grunting, he reached for the shifter, slipped the transmission from drive to reverse, and gave the Mack throttle. He could feel the truck vibrating, glanced in the mirror to see the smoking tires spinning. Would have hammered the steering wheel and cursed, but it would have hurt too much. Hell, he could hardly breathe as it was.

"We're hung up," he admitted, letting up on the throttle.

Jackie climbed wearily up onto the seat. "Great. Good planning, Sam. Now what?"

Sam frowned down at Tully's crumpled body. "He'd know what to do."

"So?" Jackie tried to carefully whisk glass from her sleeve. "What would he do?"

Sam frowned, wished the fucking pain would go away long enough for him to think. Like back at the roadblocks. Tully would always add that lift of the blade that flipped the cars off to the side. Sort of like pitching...

"Okay, let's see." He gave it some throttle and toggled the joystick that lifted the blade. The hydraulics strained, metal squealed; the leg sticking up rose eerily, and the thrust-up arm seemed to be waving. The blade pulled free and the big plow rolled back. Something fell with a crash, the leg vanishing.

As Sam backed away, he got a good look at the carnage. Crushed bodies, wadded metal, broken glass, and twisted bodywork. Could hear and feel the plow's wheels crunching over bodies as he glanced in the mirror. Be just stupid to back off the road and fall down the mountain now.

He backed into a pull off, whimpered as he spun the wheel, and managed a three-point turn. Taking a look back at the wreckage, he could see some of the looters that had been thrown free. The sight would stay with him. Haunt him. The way they lay broken on the pavement, writhing, squirming. One staggered to his feet, took a step, and collapsed.

"Damn, Sam," Jackie whispered.

"Yeah, don't I know," he said through a pain-tight throat. Fought the need to throw up.

Pulling the wheel around, he rolled back onto the highway, headed toward the gap where a column of smoke rose from the burning MTV. Something wasn't right with the steering. The plow kept pulling first to the left, then to the right. Which kept the pain in his chest in a constant scream. Then came the flapping sound from behind. Looking in the mirror, he could see one of the burned tires was coming apart, shedding chunks of smoking rubber as they went.

# SALVAGE

*Supper that night was a slice of "mountain pie" pizza. New York style, Italian style, Chicago style were well known. Along the Rockies, a super deep dish pizza was baked in cast iron frying pans. Two inches thick, filled with sauce, ground beef or bison, mushrooms, Canadian bacon, pepperoni, black olives, and several kinds of cheeses, one slice was a meal in itself. Ours came from a little hole-in-the-wall restaurant down at the historic Union Pacific depot.*

*We ate at the coffee table, Agar, Ragnovich, and Dr. Sampson Healey from the University of Wyoming. Healey was head of the Molecular Biology department. Looking uncomfortable, he was sitting across the table, and kept shooting worried glances at Pete.*

*"So, we're talking worst case scenario. Assuming the truck carrying the lab equipment is looted," Agar continued. "What can we salvage? I mean, a lot of that equipment had to be loaded by forklift, so it's not like the looters can just toss it out on the highway."*

*Ragnovich kept giving the professor skeptical glances. The guy had dripped pizza sauce on his shirt and tie, seemed a bit overwhelmed.*

*"It will depend," Healey said. "But, honestly, anything you can bring back, we can use. It's not like Globe, Scilogex, QIAGEN, or United Scientific can send parts." Healey made a face. "But I know that Jim Perry down at BMB made a lot of his own equipment. Cutting edge stuff. Given a choice, I'd take him, and his brain, before all the PCRs, microscopes, and sequencers in the world."*

*Agar, chewing a piece of pizza, studied Ragnovich. Swallowed. "Harry, put a couple of armed Humvees at Ted's Place to control the junction. Send along an MTV. Be prepared to move on the Poudre*

*Canyon road within the next couple of days. Put together a salvage column to go down and collect whatever's left. Be ready to roll in forty-eight hours."*

*"Yes, sir."*

*"What about Jim Perry?" Healey asked.*

*Agar told him, "If he's still alive, we'll get him. But if they shot him and the rest of Avery's team, that wonderful brain isn't going to be of much use."*

— Excerpt from Lauren Davis' *Journal.*

# CHAPTER FORTY

As EXHAUSTED AND depressed as she'd ever felt, Breeze watched the cluster of deserted vehicles at the side of the road appear out of the growing gloom and misty rain. They had reached the junction with Highway 34 and the turn that would take them east to the Masonville Road.

Abandoned cars. Almost as good as a road sign. Go down to the first bunch of abandoned vehicles, take a right. At the next cluster, take a left. Then take a left at the Masonville cluster. Straight through the bunch at Stove Prairie, then right at the T intersection. A left at the abandoned cars at Ted's Place, and next stop, Wyoming!

Breeze leaned forward, hit the com. "We're going to stop just past the junction. Let's get a look at the damage. Take stock. After this, I want to run straight through to The Forks."

A collection of *"RT's* and *"Roger that"s* answered through the com.

"Guns up when we do," she reminded. "No telling who might be skulking in the weeds."

Goggles made the right, rolled for about a quarter mile, and stopped in the middle of the highway on the double yellow line. Why not? It wasn't like he was blocking traffic.

Breeze stepped out, slung her M4, and pulled the Surefire from her pocket. She flashed it around, seeing nothing but wet grass in the barrow pits, a dripping barbed-wire right-of-way fence, and a dark cherry orchard beyond.

The NPT truck pulled up behind her, the brakes squeaking. Dennis Conchlen dropped out of the cab, taking his own time to look for threats before walking back to check his truck. Along the line, Avery's bunch, the Jayco, the wrecker, and finally Paco's Humvee rolled to a stop.

"What do you see?" she asked Goggles, where the private was flashing his light on the JLTV's charred sides.

"Most of the gas dripped off before it could burn through the door seals" he told her. "Would have been a different story if one of those Molotov cocktails had broken on the turret up top. Come pouring down inside. Not just dripping fire on us, but setting off the rounds in the Bushmaster's magazine." Then, he bent down to shine the light on the tires. "Looks like the tires are all right. That spike strip chewed through maybe an inch? Inch and a half? Should be another full inch of rubber between us and the road."

"Let me see how the others are doing." She turned, walking back to where Conchlen was fingering a bullet hole in the side of his NPT truck's van.

"I think I'm golden," he told her. "Tires are good. Got a bullet hole in the windshield but nothing critical." He indicated the bullet hole. "This is a 5.56. There's another here. Probably used up most of their energy before they hit the cargo. Want me to check?"

"Nope. It is what it is." She tapped him on the shoulder with a finger. "You're the most important person in this convoy, Dennis. No matter what, get this load to The Forks. The rest of us? We're just here to see that you do that."

The guy gave her a sloppy smile. "You got it, Breeze."

At the Excursion, Avery rolled down the window. "Now what?"

"Taking five to check battle damage," she told him. "Make sure nothing's about to blow up. Then we're rolling."

"Thank God. You people take more breaks than Congress," he muttered, rolling the window up. In the passenger seat, Simone was giving the guy a disgusted look.

"Asshole," Breeze muttered as she crossed to the right side of the Jayco. She kept looking back, half desperate to see Sam's headlights back at the junction. Instead, there was nothing more than darkness. And rain.

She found Capriolli shining a flashlight on the side of the motorhome. "What's the report?"

Deana pointed at a mar on the side. "Bastards tagged us with a Molotov cocktail. Made a hell of a bang when it hit us. When I looked in the mirror, it was just landing on the road. Looked like a champagne bottle to me. I mean, who uses a champagne bottle for a fire bomb? How dumb can you get?"

Breeze squinted. "Aren't those bullet holes?"

"Yeah." Capriolli cocked her hip, thumb in her belt. "Couple of close calls, but nobody hurt. I hollered for the girls to lay on the floor. I think from here on out, the bathtub's gonna leak and a couple of the cabinets have ventilation." She paused. "Breeze? Noonan's not doing good. He's fevered. That wound's starting to turn. Whatever we're doing, we need to do it fast."

"Yeah, I hear you. Just five minutes to check things."

Capriolli caught her furtive glance back toward the junction. Told her, "I didn't get it at first. Couldn't figure out what you saw in Sam Delgado. Thought maybe it was some wounded sparrow kind of response, like you had to take care of him 'cause of some maternal instinct."

"Huh? Maternal instinct? What are you—"

"But I get it now," Capriolli continued, her own eyes fixed on the dark junction. "I'll say a rosary for him. Pray he's alive and on the way."

"Didn't think you were Catholic."

Capriolli's lips curled into a smile. "I didn't think you were, either."

"I'm not."

"See? Guess I'm the smartest one here after all." She hooked a thumb. "Go check your convoy. But, Breeze, for Noonan's sake, don't take too long."

At the wrecker, Torpedo and Matisse were shining lights on the still smoking back of the six-by-six M1089. They were fixed on the two big equipment boxes aft of the outriggers.

"What have you got?" she called.

"Put the last of the fire out," Torpedo called down. "Hydraulics lines burned through, caught the fluid on fire. Cooked the electrical wiring. In short, Breeze? Hope we don't find so much as a dead fly in the road. Without an overhaul and rebuild, we can't lift a mosquito."

"But is it roadworthy? Can you make it back?"

"Yeah," Matisse called down. "But let's not pick any fights, okay? After the shit we've hit so far, I wouldn't want to take on a five-year-old girl wielding a whiffle bat."

She gave him an evil grin. "Aw, I'd put you up against a five-year-old any day of the week. But if, say, she were seven? I'd consider you toast."

Matisse flipped her the finger.

Brylan Jones was looking over the remaining snowplow. He stuck thumbs in his belt as she walked up. "Hey, Breeze. I don't know why, but I can't find so much as a bullet hole."

"Good. Listen, when we roll, I want you to pull out and take Tully's position behind me." She glanced back at the dark junction again. "If we hit obstacles, they will probably be in front of us."

"Roger that, Breeze." He, too, looked back past Paco's Humvee. "Um. I didn't want to say anything on the com, but you oughta know. Tully's plow? It took the brunt of the fight back there. The guy was like a maniac. Saw him run down one of the looters, cut him in two with the blade. Sent a bunch of them scurrying. Broke up their whole attack. They pretty much turned their attention on Tully's plow. Tried to take it out. Bought time so that Paco could hose the ones left standing with the SAW."

"Got it." She was looking back at the junction. *Come on, Sam.*

"And, Breeze?" Brylan was scuffing his boot on the wet pavement. "I don't know when Tully went down. There was a bit there, in the middle, when the plow was just stopped. Maybe long enough to change out drivers. But in that time, it was pretty well shot up. Got smacked by three Molotov cocktails that I saw. I mean, that truck was burning when it started back up the road. Most of the fire was in the back. Tires in flames."

He pursed his lips. Frowned. "Since nobody's chasing us, I guess Sam took it to them, but if you ask me? That truck was on its last legs."

She closed her eyes, clamped her jaws so that her lips wouldn't quiver. Lowered her hat brim so he couldn't see her face.

Turning on her heel, her heart dropped like an anchor in her chest. Her voice had gone hoarse. "I want you in second place. We're rolling."

At the JLTV, she couldn't help but glance back at the junction. Blacker than the pits of hell, no lights—like from a battered plow—cut the inky night.

# REFLECTIONS

*Agar cancels his evening appointments, has Kace bring the Suburban around, and to my surprise, we are deposited at the hospital's front door. Kace hands my crutches out of the back, saying, "It's a long walk. We don't have to put on appearances here. This isn't exactly what you'd call a publicity opportunity."*

*Agar leads the way through the lobby, waving at staff, and seems to know where he's going. Second floor. Turns out it's to the nurses' station where he walks up to the window. Behind the desk, a middle-aged woman looks up, eyes widening. "Governor?" she asks. "What can I do for you?"*

*"Just wanted to walk the ward, Nel. How many do we have tonight?"*

*"Sixteen. Four critical." She pulls the glasses from her round face. "Three on the watch. Be a miracle if they make it until morning."*

*"I'll try not to disturb them." Agar motions for me and Kace to follow.*

*Halfway down the ward, I stop dead. "What are we doing here?" I ask.*

*My anxiety is building with each step, and I don't know why. It's like a black tsunami is rolling toward me inside, and I know I'm going to be crushed.*

*Agar says, "We set up this ward as a sort of hospice. Most want to die at home, but not everyone has family. And sometimes even family can't deal with the consequences." He stops at the first door. "So, let's go look people in the eyes. Remind ourselves what it means to die because you can't get the drugs that would keep you alive."*

*I lag behind, fighting off the overwhelming flood of fear and grief filling my chest. Every open eye in this place is hollow and seems to beg me for help.*

*By the time Kace turns around to check on me, I'm shaking so hard I can barely stand and tears are soundlessly streaming down my face.*

*Without a word, he walks back, takes my arm and supports me while he leads me to the exit.*

*Afterwards, I pray like I'd never prayed in my life that Breeze and Sam are headed north down some dark highway, and that every mile brings them closer to safety.*

— Excerpt from Lauren Davis' *Journal.*

# CHAPTER FORTY-ONE

WHEN SAM ROLLED through the gap, he stopped beside the burning MTV. Would have collapsed over the steering wheel. Instead, he shifted the tranny into park, staring woodenly at the sprawled bodies where the looters had been shot down. Three of the motorcycles were still resting on their stands at the edge of the pullout.

He glanced to the side where the MTV sent roiling black smoke billowing up into a stygian sky. A faint drizzle now fell, making the bullet-pocked remains of the plow's windshield into an opaque comedy. On impulse he flipped on the plow's warning flashers. Strobing yellow and blue flashed in the drizzle. Didn't seem very bright. Looking in the mirrors, the ones in the rear were dark. Only the one atop the right side of the cab seemed to be working.

Well, hell. What a letdown.

"What are we doing?" Jackie asked. She perched in the passenger seat, face somber in the glow from the instruments. She had her feet pulled up onto the seat so they didn't rest on Tully's corpse.

"Guess we'd better call Breeze, let her know..." He started to reach for the battle com where it had been mounted to the dash. Would have turned it on, but its casing was cracked, bent up. The bullet hole in the glass behind it was proof why. When the hell had that happened?

"Or not," Jackie told him. She was in the middle of the I-gotta-puke shakes.

Sam could relate. He'd always had the shakes after a fight. What was different this time?

*Maybe I'm just too numb and hurt to care anymore.*

"Gotta check the truck," he told her. Glanced down at Tully where he lay wadded on the floorboards like a pile of old rags. "See what's wrong with the steering. Maybe check what's left of the MTV. If there's anything we can salvage."

"Okay." She opened her door. Stepped out into the night.

Sam would have loved nothing better than to have taken a deep breath, but his ribs sent a stitch of white-hot agony through him at the slightest movement.

Reaching for the door, he climbed slowly down, delicately, like a ninety-year-old man. That last long step left him gasping, half hunched. The good news, if there were any, was that the snow had all melted. The other good news was that, peer around in the shadows all he wanted, he could see no sign of *Nynymbi*.

First thing, check the truck. He limped around, squinted. Only one of the headlights worked, as did the clearance light in the left fender. In the rotating flash of the one working warning light, he got a look at the blade. Where it used to sit forward a couple of feet, the mounts and hydraulics had been pushed back almost flush with the bumper and grill. Bent up as it was, the miracle was that it had lifted at all.

Jackie walked around, hands pulled into her too-long sleeves, head cocked. "See anything wrong?"

Sam squinted at the big front tire, not that he could see much in the dark. At least it wasn't flat. Same with the one on the right when he checked it. Good. He didn't have a clue where the spare might be. Let alone how to change it. But in the back, where the firebomb had burned the paint off the box and set the wheels on fire, both outside tires looked worse than blackened toast. Mere chunks of charred rubber were hanging from the rims, the steel belting like shredded rags. Despite the pain, he reached in as far as he could. Ran his fingers over the sides of the inner tires.

"I think the inside tires didn't burn," he told her. But in the dark, that was really more of a guess.

"So the truck's okay?" she asked, head canted to stare into the inky recesses beneath the bed.

"How the hell do I know?" Sam asked. "Hey, I'm not a car guy. Didn't have a car until I went off to college. When it broke, I took it to the repair shop."

"Oh."

"Yeah, oh," he told her sourly. Then, in the rhythmic illumination cast by the rotating flash of the warning lights, he made his feeble way to the MTV. The driver's door hung open, so Torpedo must have made it out. At least, no scorched body perched on the smoking remains of the seat.

Hitching around to the back, to his amazement, he found Breeze's boogie bag where the explosion had tossed it clear. Chuckling, he crouched down, loosening the draw strings. Sure, it hurt to reach inside, but feeling around, he cried, "Yes!" and pulled out her flashlight.

Flicking the beam on, he played it around. Ground his teeth. There, among the still smoking Humvee tires they'd salvaged, were the bodies. The tarps they'd been wrapped in had been blown away, of course. The dead now lay sprawled and broken in the most undignified of manners. Think of Halloween gone wrong.

"Jackie, I need your help. Got to lay our people out straight."

She gave him an owl-eyed stare. "They're dead, Sam. What do they care?"

He bit off a curse. "You want a ride to Wyoming, or take your chances here?"

"What's that mean?"

"It means you're going to help me. Get it? That, or I'm leaving you."

She closed her eyes. "God, you're a nasty shit."

But she did it. Helped him drag the corpses, one by one into a line. As they pulled Krandal's body down through the mountain mahogany, Sam tripped over something long. Used Breeze's flashlight to illuminate Jelly Roll's big fifty-caliber rifle. The Bamba, he'd called it. The gun had landed in thick brush. Looked to be in one piece, even the oversized optic. Someone had taped the two remaining cartridges to the stock.

When they'd finished with the bodies, Sam went back. Almost shed tears as he lifted the heavy rifle. Thing had to weigh thirty pounds. Somehow he carried it back to the plow, was stowing it behind the seat when he glanced down at Tully. Really? Just leave the guy to bleed and stiffen on floor?

This time, Jackie didn't demure, dragging the dead soldier unceremoniously out to tumble down to the pavement.

Lit by the strobe light's eerie flash, she leaned her head back, flickering face lifted to the light drizzle. "I just want to break down and cry. I mean, it's not like I really knew Tully. And we're dropping him like he's nothing more than a box of bruised apples?"

Sam looked down at the man's bloody head, the eyes still popped from the bullet that stopped in his brain. "He'll understand, Jackie. And we'll lay him next to the rest. We'll come back. Get them all. Bring them home." He paused. "I'd do it now. Take them with us. But hurt like I am? No way we could lift them into the back."

"Just...leave them?" She sounded numb. "What if someone comes along? Does something to them?"

"What?" He gave her a gallows smile. "You think this country's short on corpses?" Hand to his throbbing chest, he bent. "Come on. Tully's the last one. If I keel over dead in the process of dragging him over, just leave me next to the rest of them."

"You're really hurt that bad, huh?"

He blinked. "I think I rebroke my ribs."

But somehow, with Jackie doing most of the work, they got Tully laid out next to Krandal.

Something about the line of them, strobing blue, white, then yellow by the flashing warning light and the still-burning MTV. The absurdity struck him. As did the pathos. Pulling himself as straight as he could, Sam raised his hand, snapped off a salute. "Rest in peace until we're back."

The misty rain was picking up.

"What next?" Jackie asked, pulling her hood over damp and curly hair.

"Let me take one last look, then we're on the road. At twenty miles an hour, we'll be back in Mishawaka by midnight. The Forks by maybe one. Two at the latest."

He stowed Breeze's boogie bag. Flashed the light around, found a couple of boxes of rations, just in case. A set of goggles, an AR 15 that looked serviceable. A pack of loaded magazines. And over there...

Sam chuckled hollowly. Saw his pack lying in the brush. He walked over, grabbed a strap, and lifted. The pack disintegrated—the back of it burned out. Partially charred, what was left of his clothing tumbled onto the wet dirt. When they did, a glitter caught his eye.

Reaching down, he picked up a long sliver of shapely glass: a piece of his precious cognac bottle. The one he and Shyla had drank from the night they first made love. Sam swallowed hard, the grief knot pulling tight under his tongue. He turned, limped numbly back toward the plow where Jackie was waiting.

The thought went through his head. Seen so clearly. He could extend his wrist. Use the long sliver with its molecular edge and slice right down to the bone. Switch hands...slit the other. Two minutes? Three? And the pain would fade, blend with the night. And he and Shyla would be...

For long moments he stood there, the glass gleaming in the rain. He extended his wrist, laid the sharp edge on the skin.

Movement.

Sam glanced out to the side, using his hat brim to shade his eyes from the snowplow's brightly flashing warning light atop its stalk.

*Nynymbi* danced in the shadows, his concentric eyes fixed on Sam, the three-fingered hands waving.

Stifling a sob, Sam pitched the long sliver of glass into the darkness and started the painful climb up to the driver's seat.

# HEARTBREAKING

*Lying in my little twin bed, I stare up at the ceiling. That tour through the ward was terrible, haunting. I'm more afraid of the dark now than ever before. Of the sixteen, twelve were dying of diabetes for lack of insulin, the others of cancers for which no medications remained.*

*Insulin was one thing. One that we could begin to address if Breeze got Fallen Eagle back with its refrigerators full. Not that it would save any of the people I'd met. It was too late for them. But for others who were failing, it might mean they'd never find themselves in one of those beds. Then, depending on how long it took to set up the lab, the Biotek people could begin the mass processing of pancreas glands from cattle and swine.*

*Any hope for cancer meds, however, was a long way off.*

*Good news? If you could call it that, was that way more people in Wyoming had diabetes than cancer.*

*It all made me think. My heart ached for the dying, but at the same time, we were killing people in Colorado who were trying to kill our people who were retrieving a lab that would save tens of thousands of other people.*

*Is there really such a thing as morality? Good or bad? Right or wrong? I doubt it.*

*When a nation of laws collapses, morality becomes an illusion.*

*Or it could simply be that God just doesn't give a damn.*

— Excerpt from Lauren Davis' *Journal.*

# CHAPTER FORTY-TWO

BREEZE RODE with her foot pulled up on the edge of the JLTV's passenger seat. As she stared at the rain-damp road illuminated by the combat vehicle's lights, she felt absolutely foul. Granted, the seat was an improvement over the canvas ones she'd endured in the Humvees; it still hadn't been designed by the ergonomics geniuses at Bentley, Maybach, or even Cadillac.

The narrow road north through the Buckhorn Valley with its vacant farms, lightless houses, and overgrown fences seemed as black as her soul.

*I should have gone back for Sam.*

This wasn't Clark Ranch. No Jeep with twin-mount fifty-caliber M2 machine guns was poised to blow her away. They'd foiled the looters' attack. One that—except for a few shortcomings—should have worked. But for the JLTV running first, the spike strip would have stopped any of the other vehicles. Tully's quick decision to drop his blade had saved the day. Otherwise, they'd have been sitting ducks for the Molotov cocktails.

Any way she cut it, luck, and the quality of her people, had saved their asses at Carter Lake.

She slammed a fist onto the console between the seats.

Goggles gave her a look from the corner of his eye. "Sam knew what he was doing," he said. "The guy could be Arapaho. He's a warrior."

"Yeah, well, he's got a Shoshoni spirit helper."

Goggles lifted a shoulder in a half-hearted shrug, right hand resting on the shifter where it stuck up beside the wheel. "Nobody's perfect."

"Ah, hell, Shane." She ran fingers along the com where it was mounted on the angled dash. The heater vents blew warm air where they were mounted in slits just below the windscreen.

He said, "A heart has wings like a hawk, when it's in a cage neither wings nor a heart can beat."

She gave him her don't-fuck-with-me glare. "Is that supposed to be some profound ancient Arapaho wisdom?"

"No. I think I saw it posted on the internet with a picture of a bird." The corners of his lips twitched.

"Well, I don't know what the hell you're getting at." The tears caught her by surprise. She *hated* women who cried. Bent her head so that, even though it was dark, her hat brim hid her face. Tried to surreptitiously wipe the tears away. Wasn't sure that Goggles was fooled.

They rode in silence through the deserted remains of Masonville, rounded the corner past the three forlorn Larimer County Sheriff's cars, and started up the Buckhorn Valley on the Stove Prairie Road.

And all the while, the ache in Breeze's heart grew from a pang to a hard knot.

Images of Sam kept surfacing in her mind. Times he'd been so serious as a New Yorker out of his depth. That twinkle in his soft dark eyes. How she'd fit so perfectly into the hollow of his shoulder as they slept together outside the Biotek lab. The way she'd reveled in that feeling of security, like all was right with the world.

That image of her hat fitted so perfectly into his. What it implied. That she and Sam could...

"Fuck!" Goggles growled, hitting the brakes.

Breeze fought her way out of the memories and heartache, fixing on the log laid across the road in front of them. She placed herself by the irregular tangle of cars that had been pushed off into the borrow ditch. Remembered it as their own work from the last time they'd passed this way.

Gallagher Ranch.

Goggles had rolled to a stop. Behind the JLTV, the lights of the convoy added to the illumination of the humped dirt where they'd filled the trench with logs and packed it down on their last passage. Behind the scar, a single Ponderosa log had been dragged across the pavement. Off to the side, a faded blue New Holland backhoe was parked in the ditch. To the right, an older model F 250. It reminded her of how vehicles were left at the end of the day in the middle of a job.

"You know, the LT told them," Breeze almost spat the words.

*"What's the word, Breeze?"* Corporal Fields' voice came through the com.

"Stay frosty, people," Breeze ordered into the com. To Goggles, she said, "Let me check this out. Meanwhile, I want you on the chain gun.

Cover me. I've got the com on. If I give the word, take out anything that looks like a threat."

"Roger that." Goggles gave her a hooded look. "Breeze, I know you're mad and hurting. Don't do nothing stupid out there."

She clamped her hat down tight, brim low over her eyes. Swinging the door open, she stepped out. The lightly falling rain pattered on her poncho as she held her M4 at the ready. Step by step, she approached the log, staring around in the glow illuminated by the convoy headlights. Her boots sank into the loose soil where the trench had been bridged.

"Far enough!" a voice called from the 2008 vintage F 250. The pickup was canted at an angle off to the side.

"Gallagher?" she called.

The doors to the Ford opened, Jason Gallagher emerging from the passenger side, Marge from the driver's. Both now wore wide-brimmed felt hats and were shrugging into rain coats. Each carried an AR 15 at the ready as they approached.

"What the hell is this?" Breeze gestured at the log.

"Well, young lady"—Marge strolled up with authority— "you let us talk to the lieutenant, and we'll let you know. Now, go ahead. You scuttle off and find her."

Breeze, heartbeat hammering in her very bones, shifted, squinted. "Bunch of looters killed her outside of Boulder. I'm in charge."

A flicker of smile was barely hidden on Jason's lips. "Well, that sort of changes everything, don't it? Our agreement was with Lieutenant Daniels." He waved a hand in the direction of the convoy. "You could say anything you wanted about what went on down south. For all we know, you and your accomplices might have shot the lieutenant yourself. Decided you'd take the loot for yourself."

"Now," Marge chimed in before Breeze could vent her outrage, "we're not unreasonable. We've been in some binds ourselves, and it's a dog-eat-dog kind of world these days. So, we'll make you a deal. Cut us in on the take, and we'll set you up for a couple of days. Feed you all real beef, let you get your thoughts together before you take this here lab equipment north. Maybe you'll even come to think of this place as a base of operations for your scavenging forays."

Breeze struggled to keep her wits when every instinct urged her to shoot them both down.

As if reading her mind, Jason wiggled a chastising finger at her. "Now, now, we're not stupid. You're covered by four different shooters out there in the dark. Don't do nothing dumb. No, indeed. You be a smart girl, and you and your friends can come out of this with a real nice deal."

"If you think I'm..." She stopped short as a figure appeared out of the night from the right.

A long-legged man, thin faced, that she recognized as Phil Collins came trotting through the drizzle. "They're not all here," he announced as he pulled up, maybe ten feet out. "They're missing one of the Humvees, that five-ton cabover, and one of the snowplows. But they got a motorhome and what looks like a big SUV they didn't have last time."

Marge smiled, glancing at Jason. "Things must have been interesting down south. Who're the new people."

"Refugees." Breeze tightened her grip on the M4, wondering if she dared whip it up, shoot Jason and Marge, and hope she could drop flat before the snipers in the dark could tag her.

Jason turned, shouting, "Willy! Bring the swather down."

Breeze heard a starter whine; a diesel turned over a couple of times before the bark of exhaust. Lights flashed in the darkness up the road, and a Massey Fergusson swather puttered into the glow cast by the convoy's headlights. Puffing white smoke from cold exhaust, it came churning down, the sixteen-foot mower spanning most of the roadway. Pulling up behind the downed log, the driver killed the engine, allowing the silence to settle.

"Now," Marge said reasonably, "that ain't moving 'til we have a deal."

"Might as well meet us half way," Jason said. "You make this hard, we'll oblige and cut your share until you got less and less."

In Breeze's ear bud, Fields asked, *"Breeze?"*

"Last chance," Breeze told them.

"Yours, too," Marge insisted stiffly.

"This guy, Willy? He important to you?" Breeze took a step to the side.

"Just one of the guys who had a little experience with ranch work." Marge was grinning, looking like she had the world by the tail.

"You can move that swather, or get him out of that cab, or lose them both." Breeze took another step to the side. Was she far enough? Out of the line of fire?

"Don't give me that shit," Jason told her. "You ain't gonna bullshit a bullshitter."

"Got that right," Breeze told him. Then to the com, she said, "Goggles, take out that swather."

As thunder split the night, she dove for the wet pavement.

# UNWELCOME MOMENTS

*Kace Adams stopped me in the hallway today to ask how I was doing. When I coldly told him I was fine, he hesitated, started to say something, then he seemed to think better of it and walked past me down the hall to the door that leads outside.*

*Every time we're in the same room, he watches me like a hawk, as though he knows, at some point, I'm going to lose it and open fire on everyone in sight.*

*He's wrong.*

*Well... Pretty sure, he's wrong.*

— Excerpt from Lauren Davis' *Journal.*

# CHAPTER FORTY-THREE

THE BUSHMASTER'S EAR-SPLITTING *BANG! Bang! Bang!* hammered Breeze's head. Didn't matter that she clamped hands to her ears, each concussion, followed by the crack of the bullets snapping overhead at over a thousand meters per second, felt like blows. Even through that, Breeze could hear the *pang* each time one of the armor-piercing rounds tore through the swather.

Huddled on the muddy pavement, Breeze glanced up as Goggles put the final round through the Massey Fergusson. Saw the machine jolt at the impact, chunks of metal flying out from the torn cowling behind.

In the aftermath, the silence could almost be felt, the light drizzle falling like glowing silver in the headlights' glare.

By some miracle, the driver, Willy, shoved the cab door open, wobbled out, and almost collapsed as he climbed down. The guy hit the ground, staggered, and stumbled his way off into the darkness, seeming to struggle for balance.

As Breeze stood, she could see the hole blown through the bottom of the cab. Goggles had put all five of the M242's rounds into a group the size of a grapefruit. The heavy slugs had punched their way between poor Willy's feet, then taken out the engine in the back. In the gleam of the headlights she could see oil, hydraulic fluid, and coolant leaking from the shattered block and hoses.

Jason Gallagher had cowered into a ball, hands to his ears. Marge was turned away, back curled where she clapped hands to her head. She was the first to straighten and shield her eyes from the glare as she took in the blasted swather.

Breeze stepped close, recovered enough to slap the AR 15 from

Marge's hand. "Don't even think of signaling your snipers. By now, my people have them spotted and targeted. We've got night vision. You don't. And I'll make you a promise: They shoot, and Shane Goggles is going to turn that autocannon on you and Jason. You think it fucked up the swather? You oughta see what one of those twenty-five millimeter rounds does to a human body."

Breeze gave the stunned woman a smile. "So, what's it gonna be?"

Fifteen minutes later, Breeze watched as Phil Collins—in the backhoe—used the hoe bucket to pull the Ponderosa log off to the side. Marge and Jason, shaken, had taken an unceremonious leave. They'd piled into the Ford pickup, started it up, and thrown mud and gravel as they backed around, circled the blasted Massey Ferguson, and vanished up the road accompanied by the blatt of loud exhaust.

Breeze, Goggles at her side, and Jennifer Fields off to the right, studied the remains of the swather. The thing looked pathetic where Collins had used the backhoe to shove it off into the ditch. It had stopped after rolling into the line of t-posts that had once been the right-of-way fence. Oil could still be seen leaking from the burst engine onto the wet grass.

"Five rounds left in the chain gun," Goggles noted. "It took all the self-control I had to keep from blowing that thing apart. I mean, that fricking Bushmaster? Shooting that thing is more fun than an orgasm."

Fields turned, eyebrow lifting as she gave him a skeptical gaze.

"Okay," Goggles said sheepishly. "It's *almost* more fun than an orgasm."

The backhoe roared, one big rear wheel spinning as the lugs slipped on the wet pavement. Then it caught, maybe when Collins locked the positraction axle. The log gave, sliding across the pavement with a hollow rumble.

Collins stopped, raised the hoe, backed, and rounded the log. He used the bucket on the loader to shove the log off to the side. Then parked the backhoe out of the way.

Breeze watched him step down from the cab, pulling gloves off his hands as he walked up.

"That's it," he told them. "You're clear all the way up to the north end. There's a spruce log blocking the road there." He stuck thumbs in his belt. "My call? I'd say put the snowplow up front. Log's small enough you can just shove it out of the way. You won't even have to stop. And Mark and Tammy who are standing watch up north won't even think of getting in your way."

Breeze indicated the swather; punctured, twisted, and torn cowling showed where the heavy AP rounds had blown chunks of metal out of the engine. "Hope you got all the hay up. What's left of that thing won't cut a daisy, let alone grass or alfalfa."

He inspected the machine. "Yeah, well, maybe you haven't noticed, but there's a lot of equipment standing in fields and yards up and down the valley. And nobody left to complain if we drive off with it." A beat. "The good news? Most of it's a lot newer than this old two-by-twice crap Jason's been using."

"Yeah, well, that still leaves you without a bull for your last six cattle. And to tell you the truth, after what Marge and Jason tried, I doubt they're going to find a friendly reception should they come north of The Line looking for one."

Collins shot a skeptical glance at her. "Not sure but that you shouldn't have shot Marge and Jason when you had the chance. They can carry a grudge way past when it makes good sense." He gestured across the valley to where the burned house was hidden by night and falling rain. "Like with that Denver lawyer."

Breeze managed a half-shrug. "Not my problem."

"Well, it sure as hell is mine." Collins worked his jaw, water dripping from the bill of his cap.

Breeze tilted her head so he could see her face in the glow of the headlights. "Then think this through: It's the wild West. They're the bad big-time ranchers. Ever see the movie, *Open Range*? *The Sons of Katie Elder*? Or maybe *Crossfire Trail*? In the end, someone always has to take out the badass and ruthless kingpins." She slapped him on the sleeve. "Maybe it's about time you and the rest down here take matters into your own hands."

"Yeah," Collins muttered uncomfortably. "I've seen *Yellowstone,* too. Sometimes it don't pay to challenge the guys in black hats."

"Then I guess nothing's for sure, huh?" Breeze turned to go.

"Wait." Collins was looking back where WNG people were heading for their vehicles. "I haven't seen Sam."

Breeze stopped short, head tipped forward, water dripping from her hat brim. Her heart might have been a stone. "Like I said, Phil. Nothing's for sure. Sam didn't make it."

Phil pursed his lips. "Too bad. He was a good guy."

*Yeah, a good guy.* She ground her teeth, telling herself she'd grieve later.

Breeze turned for the JLTV, calling, "Let's get a move on, people."

# REGRETS

*I saw a dog today...*

*Black and white, lying outside the hospital door with his big head resting on his paws.*

*I sat down on the bench a short distance away and called to him, but he refused to budge. His gaze was fixed on the door as though his very life depended upon watching every person who came out.*

*After a few minutes, he leapt up and barked while he furiously wagged his tail, clearly watching someone inside coming toward him, but when I leaned forward to look through the glass doors, the corridor was empty. The dog whimpered and charged for the automatic doors, which opened to allow him inside.*

*I started to rise to go and catch him and bring him outside again, but the dog was running forward to meet someone who was not there. In the empty hall, he started leaping into the air and barking, his head tilted back, looking up as he trotted back. The door opened at his presence. The dog came out with his tongue dangling and his tail swiping the air.*

*I watched him happily trot away down the sidewalk—as though walking at someone's side.*

*I've thought about the dog all day.*

*I know he met the person he was waiting for.*

*...And I wonder, why I am so afraid of the dark?*

— Excerpt from Lauren Davis' *Journal.*

# CHAPTER FORTY-FOUR

TULLY'S WORDS might have been prophetic when it came to their rate of travel. The big Mack snowplow could only be driven at a maximum of twenty miles an hour. Any faster, and the steering got way too squirrely; a shimmy would start that tried to whip the wheel back and forth until it strained Sam's pain tolerance past breaking. The truck was happier wobbling along at fifteen. Happier still at ten., And it still goddamned hurt! The effect was like someone was using a Sawzall with a bent blade inside his chest. He'd have to stop, try and suck air without breathing.

Yeah, try that some time. Lots of fun.

To make matters worse, their strobing flashing warning light had quit. The single headlight that still worked might have provided enough illumination, but trying to see through the bullet-shot and spiderwebbed windshield was nigh on to impossible. Every reflected glow from the dash instruments glittered along the thousands of cracks like a screen of light separating them from the night.

At the junction with Highway 34, Sam stopped. Glanced at Jackie. "I can't do this anymore."

"Want me to drive?" She was giving the steering wheel the kind of stare that let him know that driving was about the last thing on earth she wanted.

Sam resettled himself. "Reach around behind the seat. There's a ballpeen hammer there. It's sort of down behind the butt of that big rifle."

"What's a ballpeen hammer?"

He pulled his hat off and ran a sleeve over his brow. "A hammer.

Wooden handle. The only one there." As she reached around behind her, he added, "It has a round knob on one end."

"What's it used for?" she asked as she handed it to him.

"Either balling or peening?" He took the hammer, studied the rounded head. "I don't want to get into balling, so let's just say peening. Whatever that is. Look, I worked in a restaurant. Want a world-class enchilada? I'm your guy." He reached back, swung, and whacked the shattered window. A white-hot spear of pain shot through his chest. Glass flew. "And, okay, I guess I'm your guy when it comes to knocking holes in windshields, too." He smacked it again. It hurt each time. "Gotta love new career opportunities."

Sam had never broken out a safety-glass windshield. It was a hell of a lot harder than it should have been.

Fifteen minutes later—his chest feeling like it had a thousand razor blades slicing through it—he and Jackie finally pushed the flaccid sheet of plastic and crumbled glass out onto the truck's hood. He had wrapped his hands in rags for protection against cuts. She'd found gloves. What was left of the windshield slid off to the side and hit the pavement with a crackling slap.

Sam opened his door, eased his way to the ground, and stood beside the truck. Panting, he stared off into the darkness where abandoned cars lined the side of the intersection.

Meanwhile Jackie perched on the step and was using a cloth to wipe as much glass as she could from the dash and blood-caked floor. "You know, it's going to rain again. You can smell it on the wind."

"Yeah, I know."

"We just broke out the windshield."

"Yeah, I know."

"So, how are you going to drive?"

Sam tried to grin. Felt it die on his face. "I've got Breeze's boogie bag."

Jackie whisked the last of the glass from the floor; he could hear it tinkle musically on the pavement. She gave him a speculative look. "I didn't know that boogie bags could drive."

"They can't. But there's goggles in there somewhere."

Ten minutes later—goggles protecting Sam's eyes from the wind, the brim on his battered Resistol providing some protection from the misty rain—they made the turn onto the Masonville road. Didn't take long before Sam was soaked.

Not everything was a disaster; the heater worked great. Jackie was now curled down behind the dash, out of the wind blast, in front of the heater's open vent. Sam thought his face was freezing.

"We could have died back at Carter Lake," Jackie called against the wind.

"We could have." Sam had his head turned, was trying desperately to hide behind the Resistol's brim. The goggles allowed him to see despite the water droplets. Cold numbed his jaw and blew down his wet shirt. He'd started to shiver, which hurt like hell.

"I've never been so scared." Jackie huddled into a tighter ball.

He tilted his head to glance down through the rain-spotted goggles. God, had he ever been this cold? "You have to turn your mind off. Concentrate on what has to be done. Oh, and it helps if you accept that you're going to die. Or that you don't care."

She'd fixed her wide-eyed gaze on him. "How many people do you think we killed back there? In those pickup trucks?"

"A lot. Fifteen. Maybe twenty."

She looked off to the side, opening her damp sweatshirt so the heater vent shot hot air inside. "A lot of them were alive when we drove off. Really hurt."

"Uh huh."

She made a face. "God, I'm just trying to get a handle on this. On what to do. Who to be."

"We all are."

He tilted his head to the side where the heater vent was angled to shoot hot air up. It helped. He just couldn't drive for long with his head at that angle. Doing so aggravated the agony in his chest. Their single headlight cast its glow on the blacktop with its white lines, illuminated the brush, grass, and right-of-way fence. Here and there, the blazing red or yellow of a reflector gleamed where a vehicle had been abandoned. Didn't matter that they were passing farms and orchards, not a single light burned in the dark houses.

She said, "Funny isn't it? When this started, I thought nothing could be worse than when my iPhone stopped working. Like, the total end of the world. That Saturday, David and I went downtown to Maxwell's in Fort Collins for his birthday dinner, and they were closed. Like, I'd made the reservations myself. I was incensed. Livid. How goddamn dare they? Then the order came to shelter in place. But after a couple of days of that David told me a friend of his had said the best thing was to head for the mountains. David thought if we could get to Tim's cabin outside Estes Park, it would be okay. If things got really bad, we could shoot a deer."

"Ever shot a deer before?" Sam asked.

"No. You?"

"Breeze made me. Then Pam showed me how to cut it up."

Jackie shifted to get a better angle on the heater. "The way David talked, I thought killing a deer would be, like, the worst thing in the world." A pause as her gaze went distant. "And then we hit that road-block. It was so quick. They walked up and shot David dead on the spot. Not even a warning. He just...dropped. Flopped there, eyes wide...

mouth open…but gone. I went into some kind of shock. Couldn't think. Couldn't breathe. Then there's like…a blank, you know? I remember hands, them grabbing me. Dragging me…"

Sam reached up to wipe water from the goggles. Tried to keep from shivering. God, that hurt so much he wanted to cry.

Jackie's voice had dropped to a whisper. "Nothing could have been worse than seeing David shot, right? But the worst thing in the world just kept getting worse and worse."

He cast her a measuring glance as he steered around a pile of trash in the road. "Maybe we ought to make t shirts that say, 'If you think this is bad, wait'll you see what comes next.' We'll make a fortune."

He actually got a sliver of smile in return.

She gave a weary sigh. "It wasn't being fucked by all those men. I mean, that was bad. But you just turn your mind off. Imagine you're somewhere else. Send yourself outside of your body until it's over. It was being made worthless. They crushed out Jackie Feeley the way you would a cigarette butt. I wasn't a person. Just meat to be fucked."

Sam worked his jaw where the cold was making it ache. The oscillations in the steering wheel felt like someone was sawing his chest in two with a dull blade.

In the dash lights, tears streaked down Jackie's face. "You know the worst part?"

"No."

"After the shock faded, I went along with it. I told myself to let go. Just do what they wanted, that I'd live longer that way."

"They had you chained to the floor," Sam reminded.

"Isn't that Helsinki complex, or whatever they call it? Where you become an accomplice? Can you believe? I thought if I was the best fuck on that floor, they'd reward me. Maybe give me a blanket? A little extra food? A soda instead of water?"

"Jackie, you do what you have to do." Sam glanced down. "The rules are different now."

"I should have fought," she said bitterly, tucking her long sleeves under her chin. "I should have made them kill me." A pause. "Like you just said. It helps if you accept that you're going to die."

Sam wished the heater could be set higher. He slowed, rounding the curves as the road dropped down, crossed the creek, and wound through Masonville with its dark, abandoned, and haunted houses. All black as pitch.

"Who taught you that?" Jackie asked. "To accept that you're going to die?"

"Shyla, I guess."

"You know what makes me enraged?"

"I suppose the list is about as long as—"

"The fact that no one told me. Not my parents. Not society. Not Snapchat or YouTube. Not my friends. Nobody. They made me believe that all I had to do was be pretty and people would keep me safe. Guns are bad. The police will protect you. And that's the lie that led me right to that mattress and that chain."

Sam shifted the goggles, bent his head closer to the heater vent in spite of the way it hurt his ribs. "That's how we all thought."

She shifted, seemed to have forgotten the clotted blood she sat on. "A big fucking lie."

"Jackie, the 'civilized' world lived in a self-delusional web of lies. Believed the myth we told ourselves that it could never happen here. Sure, we had our aberrant individuals, but they were mentally ill, economically deprived, or from disadvantaged homes. The statistical outliers of a progressively genteel and enlightened society."

Sam laughed bitterly, face tingling from the wet and cold wind blowing through the cab. "When my Dad told me I'd have to fight all of my life, he meant work. The struggle to make ends meet. Buy a house. Be able to support a wife and raise a couple of kids." He shook his head at the folly of it. "Not in his wildest dreams did he figure I'd be killing people just to keep breathing."

Down on her floor, Jackie bowed her head. The woman's shoulders were convulsing as she wept. He figured it would be best if he just let her cry it out.

Sam tried to keep his face from freezing. Wished he had a warm coat. And, damn, every time he started to shiver, it was like knives in his chest. Every now and then, he could feel something grinding in the midst of the agony. Had to be a broken rib. Maybe two.

It might have hurt worse to stick his hand in a blowtorch's flame. But not by much.

Wondered if it would be worth it to stop, just let the heater warm him for a time.

Two more hours, Sam promised. He just had to hold on for two more hours.

The cold helped. Kept him focused.

Reflectors glowed as the line of cars, trucks, and RVs came into view. He knew those pillaged vehicles; they'd made it to the Gallagher Ranch. Keeping a grip on the shimmying steering wheel, he stuck his right hand in front of the heater vent, trying to get feeling back in his fingers. A log had been laid across the asphalt. In the glow of the plow's single headlight, it barely stood out from the dirt-laced pavement.

Behind it, a blue backhoe was parked in the center of the road. Off to the side, and tipped into the ditch, was one of those big mowing machines the Tappans called a swather.

Flexing his fingers, Sam fought a gasp as he pulled up his Marlin and let off the throttle.

"Why are we stopping?" Jackie asked, scrambling up from the floor.

"Gallagher Ranch," Sam explained. "I wouldn't say we had trouble here on the way down. But I wouldn't call it real friendly, either."

As he braked the plow to a stop, the backhoe's cab door swung open. And, yeah, that was Phil Collins—still wearing his John Deere cap— who stepped down. Blinking, left hand up to shield his eyes from the single headlight's glare, Phil carried one of the ubiquitous AR15s in his right hand.

"Stay here," Sam said. Nerved himself and opened the door. He pulled the goggles off, laid them on the dash, and swung his feet out. The pain—as he gingerly climbed down—left him gasping, senses reeling. Somehow, when he got his wits back, he was still standing, but braced against the plow, trying to breathe without making it worse.

"Hand me the rifle," he said. And took the Marlin as Jackie handed it down.

*Got to think. Clear my head.*

Sam walked out past the plow's bent blade, trying to look normal. Couldn't. It hurt too damned much, so he eased his way up to where Collins stood, calling, "Hey, Phil. It's Sam. What's with the log?"

Behind him, over the Mack's idling diesel, Sam could hear thumping and banging up in the cab, like something heavy was being moved. It hurt too much to turn to see what Jackie was up to.

"They said you were dead." Phil's eyes shifted to the idling plow, and he lowered the brim of his cap to shield them from the glare.

"Yeah, well, things got a little Western. I guess if there's a lesson to be learned, it's don't bring a pickup to a snowplow fight."

"You don't look so good."

"You oughta feel it from my side." Sam cocked his head. "I need to get through. I'm, for sure, the last."

Phil shifted the AR, the muzzle centered on Sam's gut. "I've got orders," Phil told him uneasily. "From the Gallaghers." He inclined his head toward the snowplow. "That's a valuable piece of equipment. Everyone thinks you're dead. And that means—"

"No one will miss me, or the plow," Sam put it together. Blinked against the pain in his ribs.

The AR didn't waver as Phil's thumb flipped the safety to the "Fire" position.

# THE GAUNTLET

I'm sitting on the bench out front at the governor's residence, looking at the trees and gardens, letting the cool air soak into my face.

It's a strangely silent day. There's no traffic on the road beyond the fence, no sign of enemy jets shooting across the sky, just the faint conversation of the two guards standing at the gates. Kace's deep voice carries, but I can't make out his words.

I desperately long to return to the Tappan Ranch where I don't have to control myself, slice myself in half, and push the rest of me away. Here, I am a Pretender. And it's getting harder and harder to pretend that I'm okay.

Then I remember that the sheriff told the governor to take me away. That I killed Coretta Kapital. That it's the Wild West in the Bighorn Basin. So I probably can't go back now even if I want to.

Feeling lost, I lower my face into my hands and close my eyes.

He moves so quietly, I don't know Kace is there until he sits on the step beside me, and says, "You need to get that darkness out into the light, Davis. You have to talk about it."

"With you?" I ask in a hostile voice. "I barely know you."

He frowns and bows his head. "Not necessarily with me, but..." There's a long pause. "I was in Afghanistan right up to that cluster fuck at the end. I left friends...people who'd saved my life, to die. I spent eight months in a military psychiatric hospital. The grief and guilt were just too much to process. I couldn't breathe or think. I wanted to kill the whole world. Myself most of all. So, I have some exper—"

"Why didn't you?"

His blond hair falls over his unemotional blue eyes, partially hiding *them. He looks away as he says, "I always felt like I was two people. One walking ahead. The other following with a gun, guarding my back. I decided to turn around and face him."*

*"And what happened?"*

*"I got to see myself from the outside. That who I thought I was inside wasn't who I had to be." A faint smile. "And once you realize that, you can begin to accept that you're not really the monster you had made yourself into."*

— Excerpt from Lauren Davis' *Journal.*

# CHAPTER FORTY-FIVE

BREEZE HAD ORDERED the JLTV to take the lead after Brylan had used his blade to push the log out of the way. They hadn't seen hide nor hair of anyone as they passed through the Gallaghers' northern blockade. Then they threaded through the maze of abandoned vehicles at the Rist Canyon junction in Stove Prairie; Breeze sat sideways in the seat, propped by the door, back braced and head forward.

Half drowsing, she couldn't get Sam out of her mind. The guilt about not going back.

*Your first concern is the lab. Tens of thousands of people are depending on you.*

Yeah, bought with Sam's life.

Could he be alive?

She sucked her lips in, mulled it over.

Brylan said Tully's plow had been pretty shot up, that it was on fire. The tires had been burning. Not only that, but the Boulder looters had been too damned good. Their plan to take out the lead vehicles as they left through Boulder Mountain Biotek's front gate would have worked if the Guard hadn't taken the initiative. The same with the attack at Carter Lake: it, too, had been competent. Only the JLTV, with its tough tires, and Tully's quick reflexes when he dropped the blade on the spike strip had saved the day. If the NPT truck had rolled over those razor-sharp points, they'd have flattened every tire. With the trucks unable to move, they'd have been sitting ducks for the Molotov cocktails.

Sam's plow had been damaged to start with. Burning. The cab had been anything but bulletproof. Maybe he'd disabled the attackers, maybe he'd just blocked the road with the burning truck before they killed him.

She felt the grief knot tighten under her tongue. Fought the tears.

*When did I start to love him?*

Not until after they'd come down from the *Puha* Cave. But somewhere along the line she'd fallen for the guy. Maybe it had been during one of their conversations in the cabin at the ranch? In some shared moment as he'd talked about his Shyla? How the glow had filled his eyes, that wistful smile on his lips? How he'd always just been so easy to be with?

*But what the hell could I do?*

Water Ghost Woman's eerie face formed in her memory, along with the reminder of her supposed power over men.

"Yeah," she whispered under her breath as the JLTV bounced over a pothole and jostled her uncomfortably. "I could have seduced him."

Right. And Sam would have tortured himself afterwards, drowning in guilt and remorse for being unfaithful to his beloved Shyla.

"Couldn't do that to him," Breeze confided to herself, and wondered when she'd become such a pillar of morality.

*Should have,* the voice in her head told her. *At least you'd have something to remember him by.*

She let herself drift, imagining what it would have been like to have made love with Sam. How gentle he'd be, how perfectly their bodies would fit together in the eternal rhythm of...

Breeze didn't remember drifting off.

"Hey, Breeze?" Goggles' voice brought her upright, startled out of fractured dreams. She blinked awake as the JLTV slowed. Goggles added, "We might want to take a break. You might be getting your beauty sleep—not that you need it—but I'm blinking and nodding off. Need a hit of fresh air. And I bet half the people in our wayward expedition have to pee."

She caught her bearings, seeing the burned Forest Service truck where it had been pushed into the ditch. Remembered where they were: the T intersection with Highway 14.

"Yeah, good idea. But let's go down the road for a bit. I remember there were guys here that we chased up the hill. I mean, getting your ass shot off while taking a whiz doesn't read well when it's etched on your tombstone."

"Got a point there," Goggles told her as he made the corner and accelerated onto the highway.

Breeze hit the send on the battle com. "Take a break in five, people. Bathroom stop and a chance to stretch our legs. But make it fast."

*"Roger that*s" answered on the com, along with Tortilla's *"About goddam time!"*

"Thank God," Goggles muttered. "My molars are floating."

"Up ahead," she told him. "River runs right close to the road on one side, mountain goes straight up on the other. No cover for anyone who might want to ambush us."

"Yeah?" Goggles muttered. "And no bushes for privacy, either."

She gave him a dead stare. "I don't really give a flying fig. Men can pee up front, women in the rear. I'm not taking any chances on losing anyone else. Even if it looks like there isn't another human being within miles."

"Roger that, LT."

"Shane, I'm not a lieutenant."

He gave her a sidelong look through bloodshot eyes as he pulled the JLTV to a stop and shifted it into park. "You are to me."

She gave him a playful punch to the shoulder. "Yeah, well don't mention it in front of Ragnovich. He'll figure he can give me orders."

Lifting the mic, she called, "Stay frosty, people. Don't take chances. We're just stopping long enough for a stretch and bathroom break. Don't wander off. We're rolling in five."

Again the chorus of "*Roger that*" could be heard.

Breeze opened the door, grabbed her M4 from the rack, and stepped out into the soggy night. The smell of pines, river, and rain hung heavy in the air.

Behind her, the convoy had pulled up close; Brylan's heavy blade stopped a few feet shy of the JLTV's rear. The NPT truck nosed in close behind. As Breeze walked down the line, it was to see tired people as they climbed out of their vehicles.

At each, she called, "How you doing?" and "Stick with it, we're almost there" getting weary responses, smiles, and the occasional thumbs up.

At the Jayco, Jennifer Fields climbed down from the RV's steps. Most of the Lyons Junction women were stretching arms and legs, complaining about the rain, and running back for the Jayco's shelter as it became apparent that being outside was wet and cold.

"How's Noonan?" Breeze asked.

"Hanging on," Fields told her. "You ask me, it's a miracle he's still breathing. The guy's in misery. The lab geek, Jim Perry, he's all right. In pain, but I don't think he'll lose his arm."

Breeze glanced up at the falling rain, felt it pattering on her face. Wondered what kind of toxic pollution it carried. "Unless we hit something unexpected, we're less than an hour out. Only chokepoint I can think of is at Ted's Place. When I get back in the JLTV, I'll radio ahead. Have an ambulance waiting."

"Hope he lasts that long, but I'll tell him. Maybe it'll keep him alive." Fields gave her a nod. "And, Breeze, you're doing a hell of a job. Daniels couldn't have done better."

*Yeah, for all but Sam.*

Breeze gave the woman a halfhearted smile before she continued on her inspection. The Excursion had all four doors open. Rymart Avery had vanished somewhere, and Margo Simone appeared from behind the big SUV, zipping up her pants as she stepped into the headlights.

"How's it going?" Breeze asked.

"We're not armed," the woman told her wearily. "Otherwise, we'd have shot Ry and left his corpse by the roadside."

Breeze cocked her head, seeing the woman's disgust. "Maybe that's the cost of being brilliant."

"Yeah, brilliant."

"Margo, you don't say that like you mean it."

The woman led the way to the side as Jenna Blix and Kathy Goodrich rounded the Excursion's rear, fastening their pants as they hurried for the Excursion's protection from the icy drops falling from the cold black sky.

Out of earshot, Simone said, "Oh, he's brilliant, all right. Especially when it comes to selling himself." She kicked at the gravel on the shoulder. "Sure, he was golden when it came to marketing, grant money, contracts. I mean, the guy can sell himself all the way to the moon. Hell, you're living proof. You're here, aren't you?"

"How's that?"

"Ry talked the Governor of Wyoming into sending a whole military convoy just to get us. That's what he's brilliant at."

"If you ask me, he's an asshole."

"He is. But hey, without him, we'd never have been able to break our contract with CU. He got us the initial funding, brought in sponsors so we could pursue promising lines of research. Each time we made a breakthrough, he sold it to the accounts, handled the business. And, I mean, sure, we were turning out one hell of a good product line. Cutting edge medical patents, new syntheses for catalysts and reagents, innovative pharma. You know what I mean? If Rymart didn't sell the stuff we were developing, how could we stay in business?"

A shiver ran through Breeze's spine. "Now, tell me the truth: You guys really can make insulin, right?"

Simone nodded, flicked at the rain dampening her hair. "Insulin? Piece of cake. And that's just the start of what we can do."

The way the woman said it, like it was no big deal, sent a wave of relief through Breeze. "Good, because we've paid a hell of a steep price getting you here."

*Sotto voce*, Simone said, "We know, Breeze. And don't think that Jenna, Jim, Kathy, and I aren't thankful." She hesitated, gaze focused just past the NPT truck.

"But what?" Breeze asked, seeing Rymart Avery as he came striding down from the front of the convoy. The man was holding his coat over his head for protection.

"Hey!" he called as he reached the driver's door. "Let's get this show on the road! We're wasting time, and there's a hotel with a hot shower and fancy bed waiting for me in Laramie. Then, by God, we can get down to business."

"Business?" Breeze called, rounding the front of the Excursion.

The guy paused, giving her the eye from beneath the shelter of his coat. "You got the radio, right? Why don't you call ahead and tell your governor that as soon as I have a good night's sleep, I'll be ready to dicker."

"Dicker?" Breeze asked mildly.

Avery gave her a cat-like smile as he pointed at the NPT truck where its clearance lights glistened wetly in the dark. "You don't think that all comes for free, do you?"

Breeze stiffened. "Mister, people have died getting you out of that lab down there."

"Yeah, Soldier"—his voice had gone airy— "and tens of thousands more are at stake, right? Now, why don't you get us up to Wyoming so your governor and I can figure out exactly what those people's lives are worth."

# THE DARK OF NIGHT

*It's four in the morning, and I'm in the back seat of the Suburban beside Agar. Bill is driving and Kace is sitting in the passenger seat. It's darker than the pits of Calcutta. We're headed down Central Avenue to the Capitol. That phone call was from Dudley Gardner. Something about a late night heads up from Jerry Finger. A story about to break. Did Pete want Dudley to drop by with a briefing?*

*"No," Agar had told him. "I'll be in. Meet you in my office in a half hour."*

*I don't dare glance Kace's way when then vehicle passes under streetlights. Too much chance that he might look in the rearview mirror at just the wrong instant and read something in my expression.*

"You are, and always have been, more."

*I may have been more once.*

*But not now.*

*Underneath this blurred half-real mirage that others call real life, the past is not past. I exist on the hazy edge of The Line with each heartbeat. Every few moments, for a split second, I walk out of the pole barn at Marsy Ranch, hoping to give the people locked inside those bullet-riddled depths a chance to escape...and I have to win or my friends will die. Again. And again. That's my real world. Fight. Win. Every few moments. The rest of the time the splintered reflection of me sleepwalks across the mirage, waiting for "reality" to come again. That's what I am. That's all I am.*

*If Kace thinks I'd see someone else when I look back at myself, he's crazy.*

*Dear God, nothing is guaranteed. Not even survival itself, let alone that puny little Wyoming is going to be the burning beacon and last hope of civilization. I mean, the end of the world is usually accompanied by plagues and epidemics...and we don't even have penicillin. And there's the climate to think of. It's a hell of a lot colder than it should be at this time of year. The crops are dying in the fields, about a third of the expected harvest is coming in.*

*To fight is to survive.*

*From somewhere inside me, I hear Thomas Star's voice say, "...non-violence is not the shield of a coward, it's the supreme virtue of the true warrior."*

*I didn't realize until now that he was saying the same thing Kace is. Sheath the blade. Kill the other me that follows behind with the gun, and have the courage to go on alone without her.*

*I wish I could believe that.*

*Today, I heard a rumor that two of the Chinese armies have pushed into Nevada and Idaho...*

— Excerpt from Lauren Davis' *Journal.*

# CHAPTER FORTY-SIX

SAM SHIFTED, cocking his head to get a better look at Phil. As bad as his chest hurt, he wondered if he'd even feel the bullet. Not that Phil's heart seemed to be in it. Sam figured that he could thumb the hammer back, try and lift the Marlin in a single fluid motion. But, debilitating as the pain in his chest was, he couldn't count on speed or accuracy.

And all Phil had to do was pull the trigger.

"Why are you doing this?"

Phil indicated the swather, and in an almost-whisper, said, "Breeze didn't exactly leave Jason and Marge in a happy mood. Shot up the swather. She humiliated them. Scared them. Shouldn't have done that."

"Is there a problem, Phil?" the call came from the side, and Sam shifted to see Jason Gallagher walking up from where a Ford pickup was parked in the darkness off to the left. The man was carrying a rifle, wearing a cowboy hat and slicker.

"Mr. Gallagher," Phil called back, "Sam, here just wants to pass. And that plow looks really shot up. Might not be worth the—"

"Shoot the son of a bitch, and let's get on with our business." A pause. "Or do you need a little lesson in discipline."

"That's the problem with Phil," Marge called, stepping into the light from behind the shadowed swather. "The silly bastard's never had his heart in it. But don't shoot him now, Jason. We need someone to drive that plow back. After we rebuild the barricade, I'll be in the pickup, you have to drive the backhoe, and someone has to drive the plow."

"I don't think they like you," Sam told Phil as the man's jaw clenched and he tightened his grip on the AR.

"Sorry, Sam," Phil told him. "I don't have a lot of choice here."

Sam swallowed hard as Phil made a face, his finger finding the trigger.

"*Fucking stop! Or I'll shoot!*" came the shrill cry from the Mack's cab. "Don't think I won't!"

"What the hell?" Jason asked as he came stomping up.

"Who's that?" Marge had a hand up to shield her eyes as she tried to look past the headlight's gleam. The misty rain had strengthened, filling the air with silver haze.

"I got a really big gun on you!" Jackie's voice was strident. "Don't make me use it!"

"Yeah," Sam said, stepping back from Phil's AR. "She's behind a fifty-caliber rifle. The one we took from the looters down in Boulder. Hell of a thing. They took out a Humvee with it. Figured we'd need it for a situation like this."

On a hunch—given the shot-up swather—he called, "Jackie? They hurt me, and you shoot the backhoe. Right in the engine. Second bullet is for this guy in the cowboy hat. Third one goes in Mrs. Gallagher, here. Then you can shoot Phil and anybody else who might want to…"

It happened so fast.

Jason snapped his rifle to his shoulder—aimed into the darkness behind the plow's headlight. The muzzle blast flashed fire in the night— the *bang,* painful to the ear, made Sam jump and stabbed pain through his head.

Ears ringing in the stunned silence that followed, Sam eared the Marlin's hammer back and shot from the hip. It wasn't more than five feet. Maybe he couldn't miss from that distance, or just got plain lucky. Jason Gallagher went down harder than a felled oak.

Sam asked Phil, "You in or out?"

"Fuck!" Phil was backpedaling, the AR forgotten in his hands. He was staring at where Jason was quivering and gasping on the muddy pavement. The wracking sounds Gallagher was making caused Sam to grind his teeth. So did the way the man was twitching and jerking in panic and agony.

"Jason?" Marge gaped incredulously, mist glowing where the light haloed her head.

Sam took another step back. "All we want is to get by. Let us go. This doesn't have to go any—"

"*Bastard!*" Marge screamed, whirled, raising the AR that had been held muzzle-down by her side.

It hit Sam like a thrown brick. Should have levered another round into the Marlin. Fast as he tried to work the lever, he was too late. In the plow's headlight, as if in slow motion, Marge leveled the AR. Sam could see her thumb as she flicked the fire control. Was settling her head behind the red dot sight.

*Shoot, Jackie! Shoot!*

Instead of the big fifty's deafening boom, it was a sharp *crack! Crack! Crack!*

The muzzle flash off to the right blinked, each report like an icepick through Sam's already ringing ears.

Straight-legged, Marge landed flat on her butt. Hard. Her AR clattered on the wet pavement. The woman's face—illuminated in the drizzle—looked shocked. Wide-eyed. Her mouth worked, and she blinked. Tried to take a breath, and toppled onto her right side, head hitting the pavement with a hollow smack.

Sam stared, struggling to make sense of it.

"Guess I'm in," Phil said in a tired voice as he lowered his rifle. "When you see Breeze, tell her the Gallaghers weren't nearly as tough as the Duttons."

"Huh?"

"She'll understand." Phil pulled his John Deere cap off, beat the water from it, and tugged it back on his head. "Give me about five minutes, and I'll pull this log back. There's a radio in Marge's pickup. I'll call up to the north end. Have Mark and Tammy open the road for you. Don't even stop. Just go, Sam. And keep going."

Sam studied the man, could see the confusion and disbelief. "Thanks, Phil. Anything I can do for you?"

"Find us a bull? Without one, we really don't have much of future down here."

"If I have to rustle you one, I'll do it."

# DIDN'T SEE THAT COMING...

*Kace holds the door as I stride through, avoiding his questioning gaze. Attentive as he is, he knows I'm struggling.*

*He insists we take the elevator.*

*The light is on in Agar's office. Randy, yawning, is already at his desk, which means that whatever it is, Dudley has called in the team.*

*"Morning, sir," Randy calls, getting to his feet and following us into the governor's office.*

*Dudley rises from where he's been waiting on the couch, glances uneasily at me, and then announces, "We've got a problem."*

*"Let's see,"—Agar starts ticking off on his fingers—"there's the Collapse, a nuclear attack, possible starvation, shortages of...well just about everything, the—"*

*"Jerry Finger wanted you to know that Bruce Edgar is booking ads on KCHY. Now that the station is up and running, he's demanding that elections be held. And he's making the point that you're term-limited. That the time's come for new leadership. Says that if you don't lift your emergency suspension of the state constitution, he's going to file suit."*

*I saw the slight frown deepen on Agar's face. He stops at his desk, fingertips tracing the fancy wood. "I sure didn't see that coming."*

*"Me either." Dudley crossed his arms. "Now, Jerry Finger's always enjoyed playing both sides against the middle if it means ratings. You know he's looking for leverage."*

*Agar says, "Bruce Edgar isn't smart enough to—"*

*"Okay, but if we deny the people an election, understand that it will look like a power grab and be meat for Edgar's burger machine, and maybe even start an internal rebellion."*

— Excerpt from Lauren Davis' *Journal.*

# CHAPTER FORTY-SEVEN

BREEZE FIGURED there was no reason to stop at Mishawaka. Not given Noonan's condition. And, truth be told, she was fuming after her latest encounter with Dr. Rymart Avery.

As they passed the vehicles pulled into a defensive formation around the Mishawaka Lodge parking lot, Breeze was grinding her teeth, thinking up different ways that she could murder Avery. Arrogant prick really thought that it was all about him? Oh, she could make it that way, all right. She could toss his ass out on the side of the road so he could bask in the pleasure of his own company while he walked all the way to Wyoming.

The JLTV's lights illuminated the narrow strip of asphalt as they rounded the curves, sometimes glowing on the conifers that lined the right-of-way, sometimes shining on brush-thick mountainside, the reflector posts passing like markers.

Breeze lifted the mic from the radio set and thumbed the button. "Cheyenne Actual, this is Breeze Tappan with the Fallen Eagle convoy. I need to talk to Captain Ragnovich."

As she waited, Goggles told her, "It's just after five in the morning. If the captain has any sense, he's sound asleep at home in his own bed."

"Yeah, well, I've got a bad—"

"*Fallen Eagle, roger that. This is Cheyenne actual.*" The signal must have been going in and out, the voice fading. "*We've got a call in for Captain Ragnovich. 10-3.*"

Breeze glanced at Goggles. "What's ten three mean?"

He gave her disapproving look in return. "Stand by."

They had just come in sight of the cannibals' fancy Venetian motorhome when Ragnovich's voice scratched from the speaker. *"Fallen Eagle, this is Ragnovich. Over."*

"Hey, Captain. We're just passing the cannibal camp." She stared woodenly at the confusion of vehicles they'd shoved off the road on the way up. Thought about all the things she'd have done differently if she'd known Sam wouldn't be coming back. "First off, what's the status of the ambulance at The Forks?"

*"Should be one on station. I take it you have wounded?"*

"Two. Corporal Noonan's in pretty bad shape. The second's one of the Biotek scientists, Jim Perry. GSW to the arm. Noonan's critical, Perry's just hurting."

*"Roger that."* A pause. *"Sit rep?"*

Breeze took a deep breath. "Cap, I think we've got a problem."

# AND THE HITS KEEP COMING

Behind closed doors, Agar's in the middle of an urgent meeting. It's a little after six, and I'm worn out, lounging in a comfy chair outside the door where he asked me to wait in case he needed me to bring 'a touch of hope' to the meeting.

Me. Hope?

That's where I am, lost in terrifying dreams when the voice calls, "Lauren?"

I crack an eye and see Harry Ragnovich in his usual rumpled uniform. With bags under his blood-shot eyes, he looks like he's slept even less than me. I'm sure that whatever has kept him awake was a hell of a lot less fun than my excuse.

"What's up, Captain?" I ask, stifle a gasp as I straighten in the chair.

Ragnovich turns worried eyes toward the closed door. "I need to see Pete. I just got off the horn with Breeze. We may have a real problem with the Biotek bunch."

I exhale my relief. "So, Breeze is okay? God, I've been worried."

Ragnovich's lips twitch. "I swear, even if that girl was trapped in Hell, she'd steal the Devil's pitchfork and fight her way out." He started for the door.

"Sit down for a few minutes? The governor's in a private meeting with his top advisors," I tell him.

"This can't wait," Ragnovich reaches for the door.

"Unless Breeze and Fallen Eagle are about to be wiped out, don't. Heavy shit's coming down in there."

*Ragnovich stops short, heaves a weary sigh, and drops into the chair next to mine. "That bad, huh?"*

*"I guess. General Kyzer usually doesn't show up without warning."*

— Excerpt from Lauren Davis' *Journal.*

# CHAPTER FORTY-EIGHT

SAM WAITED in the falling rain, his body braced against the Mack's scorched front fender. It hurt too damn much. Brought tears to his eyes if he tried to stand straight. Whatever was wrong with his ribs and chest, it wasn't good. As much as he wanted to slump in the plow's seat and try to sleep, the sooner he was gone from here, the better. The only help for him lay across The Line in Wyoming.

If he could last that long.

In all, it might have taken Phil fifteen minutes to drag and shove the log out of the road. Despite the differential lock, the blue New Holland's tires kept spinning on the wet pavement; the rain fell like silver darts in the machine's lights. It beat in a gentle patter on Sam's water-logged hat.

While Phil attended the log, Sam stared thoughtfully at Jason and Marge's bodies lying broken and bleeding in the lights. The drizzling rain had begun to soak through their clothes, adding to the pathetic effect.

*I just shot another human being.* Sam bent his head, water trickling from his old gray Resistol. He looked down at his hand, wet where it held the Marlin. Remembered that he hadn't thought. Just turned and shot from the hip. Purely instinctive.

The way Jason had fallen replayed in Sam's head. As did memory that the man hadn't died right off. Might have taken five minutes as he gasped for breath, kicked, and flailed with his arms.

*I should have ended it.*

But he hadn't. Which made him...what?

"It's not like the movies," Sam told himself. He could hear Jackie crying up in the cab. She hadn't taken it well either.

In the movies, the killer always said, "I can see their faces. Every one."

Sam lifted his hand again, spread his fingers. He should have had the shakes. Felt that sick need to puke. Instead his hand was steady as a rock. And as to the faces? When he tried, he could remember shooting Earnest Tubb. And a couple of the men he'd shot at Clarke Ranch. The three bullets he'd put into Edgewater's chest. And then…? And then…?

They sort of became a blur. Like a haze of murky events.

Just flashes of images. Fragments of memory.

*Am I even human anymore?* he wondered.

The backhoe's exhaust brought him back to the present. Phil had shoved the log clear and now spun the machine around, lowered the bucket, and slid it up to Marge's body. Sam watched him step down from the cab and roll the woman's limp remains into the bucket. Climbing back into the cab, Phil wheeled the backhoe around and did the same with Jason's corpse. When he'd finished, Phil raised the bucket, heedless of the one leg and the two arms that stuck out.

Phil opened the cab door, calling, "You're all clear, Sam. I'll hold you to that bull!"

As simple as that.

In reply, Sam gave him a thumbs up.

His broken ribs like liquid fire, the pain made him whimper as he forced himself to climb up to the cab. Opening the door, the dome light illuminated Jackie, huddled down in the passenger seat on the other side of the big AR 50. The gun's butt was braced against the seat back, the barrel extended out through the missing windshield where the forearm-mounted bipod rested on the scorched hood.

"You all right?" Sam grimaced as he eased into the driver's seat. Damn, he was tired.

"That guy shot at me," she whispered. "I mean, the bullet wasn't even close. Like, I think it hit the top of the cab."

"Hey," he told her softly. "You did all right. They were going to kill me." He emphasized it with a dry chuckle. "They had no clue we only had two rounds for the big fifty."

Her expression went fragile. "I tried to kill Phil, but when I pulled the trigger the gun didn't fire." A pause. "Didn't matter how hard I pulled."

Sam shifted the Mack into drive, starting them forward. 'Did you take the safety off?"

"There's a safety?"

Sam shot a quick glance at the AR 50's butt stock. The two cartridges were still taped in place. "You didn't load it either."

Jackie ran the sleeve of her oversized sweatshirt under her nose. "How do you do that?"

Sam couldn't help it. Didn't matter. The laughter hurt so much he had to scream.

# CALCULUS

*I'm alert enough to hear the door open as Randy Meyer exits, followed by Governor Agar's staff: Margaret Bates, Clete Wolf, Nels Curley, Dudley, and Randy. And finally, General Kyzer.*

*They pass silently, each giving me a respectful nod, as though in deference to my reputation.*

*After they troop out into the hall, I realize that Captain Ragnovich—sprawled in the over-stuffed chair—is too sound asleep to notice. I place a hand on his arm and gently call his name.*

*He wakes and drags himself up in the chair. "Thanks."*

*As he stands, he futilely tries to straighten his rumpled sleeves before he walks into the governor's office, and I hear him say, "Pete, we have to talk. My people are buzzing with the news..."*

*Ragnovich closes the door, and his words fade.*

*I study the hall in complete boredom for another twenty minutes.*

*When Ragnovich walks out of the meeting, he looks dead tired.*

*I ask, "Did he confirm the rumors? He's got to hold an election and step down?"*

*Ragnovich stares at the far wall for a while, before he answers, "Governor needs to see you, Davis. And don't argue. Just do it."*

— Excerpt from Lauren Davis' *Journal.*

# CHAPTER FORTY-NINE

LOOKING UPWARDS through the missing windshield, Sam began to discern the faint outline of the mountain to his right. Dawn was coming. His face had gone numb, the pain in his chest—now a constant fire—throbbed with each jolt as the truck bounced over potholes in the road. The truck's wobbling front wheels continued to jerk the steering wheel back and forth, adding to the agony. Seemed to be worse.

*Just got to endure. I can do this.*

And, the heater be damned, he was cold to the core, shivering.

Didn't matter that the goggles he wore protected his eyes from the wind. Pain brought tears to his eyes. The constant twenty-mile-an-hour blast having flattened the brim of his Resistol to his forehead.

The valley was narrow here, and he'd barely caught a glimpse of the gate where the dangling bodies had discouraged trespassers. Fact was, he was closing on the junction with Colorado 14.

*That's all I've got left.*

Just reach that goal. Nothing else mattered.

As he had told himself when they passed the Rist Canyon Junction up in Stove Prairie.

All the mattered was the next step, the next goal.

This time, however, he wondered if it would be the last.

Damn it. He just hurt too much. Was too tired.

He let himself drift, seeing Breeze's face. Her slight smile. How those remarkable Tappan eyes could mesmerize him. And, truth be told, he loved to just look at her. Watch her move. She had a tiger-like suppleness to that lithe and muscular body. Call her the perfect package.

And when Breeze was on a horse the effect was magical. A melding of grace and balance. She and Joker made the words "poetry of motion" into something tangible. And she did it effortlessly, without a single realization of what a miracle it was.

Breeze was walking toward him, smiling, her arms out to enfold him into...

*"Hey!"* Jackie screamed.

Sam jerked awake, yanked the steering wheel back to the right where he was headed for the ditch. Pain, like a hot spear through his chest, made him gasp.

Sucking shallowly for breath, he blinked, trying to concentrate.

"You all right?" Jackie demanded where she huddled in a cramped ball next to the heater, her hood pulled down tight, wind whipping strands of blonde hair this way and that.

"Sorry," he mumbled.

The big fifty caliber AR 50 shivered and rumbled where they'd tied it in place with paracord. The butt they had wedged into a slit Sam had cut into the seat back. And he'd talked Jackie through the process of loading it clear back at Gallagher's. They might only have a round in the chamber, and one more taped to the stock, but it sure as hell looked mean where it stuck out over the Mack's hood.

"So, you really love her, huh?" Jackie asked as Sam let the plow roll to a stop.

For the moment, all he wanted to do was lay across the wheel, see if the hurt would stop. Maybe close his eyes for a couple of minutes.

"Who? Shyla?"

"No, Breeze, you dummy."

"She's just a friend, Jackie."

Didn't matter that he'd closed his eyes; he could feel Jackie's stare, so hot it might have been infrared.

"Guess there's no chance for me." Her voice carried a wounded note.

"Huh?" He tried to think through the agony in his chest.

"Don't blame you," she added. "I guess you'd never forget all those other men. Laying where they laid. Thinking of them shooting their—"

"Hey!" Sam cracked an eye. "God, Jackie, give it a break! That's not what loving someone is about. It's about partnership and trust. Sharing, you know? Enjoying each other's company. That special way that you and she just fit together." *Like Breeze and I when we were sleeping outside the lab that day.*

"Sort of like stacking hats," he added. "You know what I mean? How you can fit a smaller hat into a larger one?" The image of Breeze's hat in his came so clearly, her Rand's inside his Resistol, how they'd looked on the parking lot that afternoon.

Jackie had fixed her wide eyes on his. "I could do that for you."

Sam would have sighed, but it hurt too much. "Listen to me. Pay real close attention here. When I'm done, think about what I'm telling you."

"Okay."

"You've lived all your life in Fort Collins, right?"

"And Loveland. But, like, I went to California for a couple of months when I got out of high school. And once to Paris for—"

"Right. What did your parents do? I mean, how well off were they?"

"Daddy was a full partner in Thompson, Fitch, Rawlingford, and Hanson. I mean, they were like the most badass attorneys in F.C., and Mom, she sort of had this trust, you know? Like a check came every month. Mom called it her 'gravy' money."

"Shit," Sam muttered, trying to just breathe. Wishing the steering wheel would turn itself into a feather bed. He grimaced as he shifted. "You don't have a frigging clue about real life. You've never had blood on your hands. Never had to make the hard decisions. Someone's always been there to do it. Your folks. That guy Dave. And I'll bet there have been a string before him."

He cracked an eye to see if she was listening. "So, Jackie, if we make it to The Line, maybe you'll find another sugar daddy who will take care of you because you're pretty, and you'll figure you can justify your existence by screwing the daylights out of him. But my guess is that you'll be miserable for the rest of your life, because you'll be tossed from man to man."

"What the hell do you know about me?" she spat the words.

"I know you got a choice." Sam groaned. "You can play Cinderella and fool yourself with delusions of princes, or you can make the hard choice and figure out just how strong you are. Build a new you that someone can really love."

"David loved me," she insisted.

Sam fought for air, wished that, if only for a minute, the pain would let him draw a full breath into his lungs. "Men don't cherish women like you. They use them...at least until they get tired of them. Is that the kind of woman you want to be?"

"God," she snapped, "you're a nasty mother fucker!"

"Yeah," Sam whispered. "I probably am."

"And if you're so strong, why are you laid out over the steering wheel like a wimp? Huh? Think your precious Breeze would give you so much as a glance? You look pathetic, you piece of shit."

In Sam's mind, Breeze's Tappan eyes narrowed. He could hear her. *Come on, Sam. Gut it out. You're almost to the junction.*

Gritting his teeth, Sam still whimpered as he straightened, blinked the tears from his eyes. The world seemed to sway, dizzy. Vision going glassy. He ground his teeth and let off the brake. As he accelerated, the steering began its rhythmic slapping back and forth. Each one like a hot knife in his ribs.

# CONFESSIONS

*With the KCHY TV truck following Agar's black Suburban, we speed west on I-80, passing the Harriman Road exit. For me, the trip is fraught with painful memories. This stretch of road played such an important part in my days on The Line. Desperate days. When people's lives hung in the balance. Where, just down there, we'd captured the Chinese pilot.*

*Nothing has changed. People's lives still hang in the balance. This time it's a truckload of lab equipment, medicine, and the people who know how to make it.*

*I glance back through the rear window, not that I expect Jerry Finger to do anything but hang close.*

*"Worried?" Agar asks.*

*"Hell, yes. I don't know what to say." I lower my voice. "This is a really bad idea."*

*Fact is, I'm more than worried. I'm scared stiff. Me, Hero of The Line, wanting nothing more than to run away. Doesn't matter that I said I'd do it in the governor's office.*

*If I could have any wish, it would be that a raider might appear out of nowhere, ambush Jerry Finger's TV truck, and get me off the hook.*

*Agar frowns out the window. "Just tell them the truth. There are a lot of rumors circulating. Stay focused. People need to believe in heroes. Don't answer any questions where you have to speculate."*

*Exhaling a long breath, I say, "And when are you going to tell them the truth?"*

*He squints slightly, still looking out the window. "Long before they're ready to hear it."*

— Excerpt from Lauren Davis' *Journal.*

# CHAPTER FIFTY

IN THE GRAY MORNING LIGHT, Ted's Place appeared out of the haze. The rain had stopped, the sky growing lighter. The buildings, service station, and businesses remained dark, and this time no people came trickling out from the campers and lash-ups in the parking lot. Everything seemed quiet.

*Yeah, and I can live with that,* Breeze thought.

"Hey," Goggles told her. "Look."

She followed his pointing finger to the junction. A couple of Humvees were parked in the wide intersection at Ted's Place. One, dominated by an M2 fifty-caliber machine gun, the other with a turret-mounted M249 SAW. Behind them an MTV was parked, recognizable by the cab-over design and the tarped load on its cargo deck. Two figures in uniform stood guard.

"Think they're ours?" Breeze asked cautiously.

"Best hope so." Goggles gave her a worried look. "That fifty caliber could really fuck up our day. And we'd have to tag them with the chain gun before they blasted us. You want to wiggle around and charge the Bushmaster?"

"Sure," Breeze told him, contorting her way between the seats and into the back. Once again, she was thankful for being fit, limber, and wiry. Poking her head up into the modified Cockerill turret, she powered up the chain gun.

She'd had a crash course on the Bushmaster, checked to see that it had a round chambered, and that the dual feed and chain drive was clear for the pitifully few shells that remained. If this turned into a fight, it was going to be fricking short and sweet, and she'd have to put each and every shot right on target.

Breeze got her sight picture, snuggled into the autocannon's fire control. Through the optic, she could see the guys at the junction. And, yeah, they were ready. A head and shoulders were visible behind the M2 on the lead Humvee's roof. Her first round would have to blast its way through the Humvee and the shooter. Then a follow up just for insurance. Then she'd swing to take out the SAW-mounted Humvee.

*God, help me to make the shot.* Breeze's heart began to hammer against her breastbone, her mouth going dry.

Just as she was sure she was going to have to shoot, somebody in an ACU opened the driver's door on the lead Humvee, stepped out, and stuck his thumbs in his belt.

Breeze took a deep breath and blew it out in relief. A belligerent wouldn't pose out front like that. This was someone who wanted to talk.

"I think they're friendly," Breeze called to Goggles. "Pull up, and I'll go see who these guys are."

"Don't need to," Goggles called back. "That's Harry Doveman. I'd know that crooked-assed stance from a thousand yards. They're WNG. Welcome home."

When Goggles pulled the JLTV to a stop not more than ten yards from where Doveman blocked the way with his Jolly Roger buccaneer's stance, Breeze opened the right rear door and dropped to the pavement.

"Hey, Breeze!" Doveman called. "Long time, no see."

"You still going out with sheep just so you can say you been on a date?" Breeze asked, walking up and hugging the tall and gangly Doveman.

He patted her on the back. "Sheep? When I have so many women hot for my bod that they got to take a number? By the way, if you want one, I think number five thousand fifty-eight is available."

"You kidding? I wouldn't take number one, even if it came with a hundred bucks, a bottle of good wine, and dinner at the Hilton."

Doveman grinned. "Good to see you. Captain Ragnovich sent me down, and…" He cocked his head at the sound of a vehicle approaching from the north.

Breeze turned, seeing the headlights. The vehicle was a square, white… Yes, an ambulance.

"'Bout time," Doveman told her. "And, just as soon as we get Noonan transferred, we'll be on the way." Then he gave Breeze a flinty look. "Whatever that last message to Ragnovich was, you've got a shit storm brewing. I'm told that Governor Agar's on his way. I'm to make sure that you get that NPT truck to The Forks, and not a moment to lose."

Breeze glanced back. From behind the line of vehicles, Rymart

Avery had stepped out of the Excursion to see what the holdup was this time. The man had a hand to his forehead, as if to shade his eyes despite the gray overcast.

"Yeah," Breeze told him. "I think there's gonna be fireworks, and it doesn't matter that it's not the Fourth of July."

# THE SPOTLIGHT

*They have me posed in front of a Humvee with a turret-mounted M2 Browning. Jerry double checks that he has The Forks in the frame. Makes sure that guys in ACUs are walking in the background. He says, "There. Makes you look like you're in your element."*

*Sadistic son-of-a-bitch.*

*Agar stands off to the side, arms crossed, while Kace stands about five feet away, watching the crowd with one hand on his slung rifle. When Jerry starts the interview, asking what it's like to be a hero, I can't find any words, so I just give him a cold glare. He seems to do a double-take, stutters, and instead asks about my escape from Colorado, which catches me by complete surprise. He asks how I made it to Cheyenne.*

*The interview kind of fades, because I'm back there, reliving it all. Honestly, I don't make a conscious decision. I just fall into the memory. As I do, I hear my voice. Like it belongs to someone else. The words just roll out without thought.*

*I don't realize how quiet it's gotten as I talk about Buffalo Camp, about The Line, about what it all means. Even Agar's expression slackens while I speak. I can tell that all the Guard and Militia people gathered around are seeing it again, too, trying to understand what the Collapse has cost us as human beings. At one point, I break down and sob, and the crowd goes absolutely silent.*

*Jerry gives me a few moments, before he continues: "And how did you get to Marsy Ranch?"*

*"In a beet truck," I tell him through a long exhale. "With a bunch of Militia. A lot of good people died there."*

*I go on to talk about the terrified children, the dying horses, and what it meant to cower in that barn, under fire."*

*I am in tears. To my surprise, so is Jerry Fingers as he blinks and holds the microphone in my direction.*

*"Do you understand?" I ask, wiping at my cheeks. "This is the price I have to pay."*

*Jerry Fingers nods sympathetically. "Yes, Lauren. I think now, we all do."*

— Excerpt from Lauren Davis' *Journal.*

# CHAPTER FIFTY-ONE

SAM HAD STARTED to wonder if the Colorado 14 Junction would ever be reached. Didn't realize he'd slowed to a crawl. The pain in his chest just kept getting worse. He was driving slower and slower, trying to ease the sawing of the steering wheel. To save himself the agony, he was barely making five miles an hour. Was having trouble keeping his eyes on the narrow canyon road as it wound down toward the Poudre. He'd been getting ever more light-headed, the shivers worse.

Hell, his vision kept going hazy, watery and narrow, like a gray tunnel was closing in. He'd blink, grind his teeth and squint to get the road to come back into focus. Half the time he felt like he was either floating off the seat, or that parts of his body were getting too heavy to hold up. And, damn it, what he'd give to just surrender. Float away.

How much more of this could he take?

He shook his head to clear his vision again, fighting off the drifty feeling. As he forced his eyes wide, it was to see *Nynymbi* dancing on the charred hood. The little concentric-eyed spirit helper leaped from one three-toed foot to the other, his arms waving back and forth like seaweed in a tidal current. The wavy-lined headdress swayed back and forth as *Nynymbi*'s head rocked. The way the spirit's fingers wiggled was like casting a spell.

"What do you want from me now?" he croaked hoarsely.

Memory tried to take him back to the *Puha* Cave. Back to the visions he'd had of him and Breeze. How side-by-side they'd walked in the Spirit World while terror and disaster surrounded them. Through it all, their only strength had been the union of male and female Power. A reconciliation of opposites that allowed them to face the fear and abomination.

A unity of souls. A joining of the bodies that...

His head dropped, and he jerked awake, blinking behind the goggles. Jackie was watching him through worried eyes.

To Sam's relief, *Nynymbi* no longer danced on the hood.

But as the morning brightened, the narrow gulch widened, opening into the larger Poudre Canyon, and there, beside the road, was the burned out Forest Service pickup. Beyond it, the stop sign and green directional road signs that pointed toward Rustic left and Fort Collins on the right.

Sitting right in the middle of the T intersection, partially blocking the highway, were a dark-blue Chevy Suburban of recent make and a hulking four-wheel-drive Chevrolet Silverado 3500 HD. The latter a white, crew cab, long box dually. A knot of men, all armed, some dressed in hunting camo, others in denim, stood around a pathetic figure of a man, long-haired and dirty. The guy knelt in the road, hands behind his head. Looked like they'd taken him prisoner.

At the sound of the plow, they all turned.

The guy on his knees pointed a trembling finger in the plow's direction, seemed to be pleading. A big guy wearing brown Carhartt overalls leaned down, shouted something.

At the prisoner's nod, the guy in Carhartts extended a pistol and shot the kneeling man in the back of the head.

"What the hell?" Sam croaked, slowing as the knot of men spread out, weapons raised. The corpse of the ragged man flopped face-first onto the pavement.

"Now what?" Jackie asked as she climbed up from her warm lair next to the heater.

She hadn't said so much as a word. Just seemed to be sulking. Not that Sam cared. He was too sick and hurt. Reeling from the dizzy spells. Feeling weak.

The guy in Carhartts walked out ahead of the others, waving his arms. As he did, the white Chevy dually started up, rolled past the prisoner's skinny corpse, and took up a blocking position in the middle of the road. The Suburban pulled into the dually's place in the center of the interchange.

Sam slowed, close enough now he could make out the man's face with its blond beard, big nose, and pinched-looking eyes.

"Think we ought to just ram them like we did those others?" Jackie asked.

"I don't know if the plow can take it," he told her. "I almost can't steer as it is."

Sam eased to a stop, shifted the plow into park, and took small panting breaths as he tried to ease his chest. World took a half spin, leaving him on the verge of throwing up.

The guy in Carhartts led the way. The others followed, a collection of rifles held at the ready.

"Where'd they come from?" Sam asked. "These aren't the guys from Mishawaka."

Then he remembered how Mark Leskowski had asked them to accompany them up to Rustic to take out some bad actors and clear out the canyon.

Carhartts had raised his arms, voice carrying over the idling diesel as he called, "We just want to talk! We know you're clearing the roads. Figure we can make a deal."

Sam tried to fill his lungs to shout back. It hurt too much. To Jackie, he said, "Tell the guy to let us pass. No one's gotta get hurt."

Jackie cupped her hands, her shrill voice repeating Sam's words.

Carhartt laughed. "Hey, we got a lot more rifles, and, looks to me like you don't have much to hide behind up there. Now, let's deal with this in a civilized way, all right?"

Jackie had bent down to fish Sam's Marlin from the floor.

"All right," Sam whispered. Damn it, all he felt was exhausted, sick, and defeated. "This is gonna hurt like hell."

"What are you doing?" Jackie asked, worried blue gaze flicking Sam's way.

"I'm taking out their truck," he told her. "Maybe that will get their attention."

His yip of pain caught him by surprise as he shoved up in the seat. Somehow, he got his fingers around the AR 50's pistol grip. Almost passed out from the blinding agony in his chest. He just needed to keep his wits as another dizzy spell made his head spin. He got an eye aligned with the rifle's scope. Shoved on the butt enough to fix the crosshairs on the big Silverado's grill. Couldn't push it far enough to quite center it.

In the scope, he could see Carhartts' image off to the side, see the man's widening eyes as he realized what Sam was doing.

Yeah, well, the son of a bitch would get the full effect of that seven-hundred grain bullet whizzing by his elbow at close to three-thousand feet per second, too.

Sam flipped the safety and triggered the rifle.

The recoil was like being kicked through space. Hurt so bad he barely heard the thunderclap of muzzle blast. His vision caught the instant: The guy in Carhartts blew apart. His rib cage splayed wide as lungs and heart vaporized. The left arm and part of the shoulder flying up and cartwheeling over the guy's head; it, too, blown upwards by the impact. Bits of tissue burst out in fragments from a misty red haze where the guy's chest had been.

The instant passed. Eviscerated meat and bone, what had been Carhartt dropped in a pile while bits of lungs, meat, and tissue sailed in an arc to pepper the guys to either side and spatter the front of the white Chevy in patterns of red.

Sam had the barest image of the surviving raiders running, the white Chevy flying backwards, slamming into the Suburban. Men sprinting... flinging the pickup doors wide...

Unable to comprehend, incapacitated by the pain, Sam watched them swing around, tires smoking as they took off up the road...

Vision swayed and went watery. Every nerve on fire. He couldn't breathe, couldn't move.

God, the pain.

Jackie, shouting in his face.

And then a soft haze as the terrible agony faded...

# THE EMPTY VESSEL

*For long moments, my heart hammering at my chest, mouth gone dry, I stare into the camera lens. That big, wet black orb seeming to suck my soul away into…where?*

*Jerry Finger sucks in a full breath. Asks, "Did you expect to die when you walked out to confront the raiders at Marsy Ranch? I mean, you knew it had to be suicide."*

*I blink hard. "It was the only thing left. I had to buy time for the Militia to escape." I gesture around. "That's what we're doing here. Buying time. Trying to hold the monsters at bay while we save what's left of our way of life. You focus on me, but look around. These people, the Guard, the Militia, and especially Governor Agar…we're all willing to do what we have to to save each other."*

*In the corner of my eye, I catch Governor Agar's twitch of a smile, a glint of victory in his dark eyes as he turns and walks back to the Suburban. Kace opens the door for him before Agar climbs in.*

*Jerry Finger says, "Before the Collapse, you were engaged to a lieutenant in Delta Force. Have you heard from him? And, how do you feel about…"*

*I'm panicking. I can't go there. Not now, not in front of all these people.*

*I draw a breath to tell him to go fuck himself when someone down at the roadblock bellows, "Trucks coming!"*

*I mean, it's over. Just that quick. Everyone rushes away. Jerry, the cameraman, all of the soldiers. But I'm still in my head. The empty vessel. Locked in that barn at Marsy Ranch, hearing children scream, seeing friends hiding behind hay bales, and bleeding to death on the floor...*

*As I turn away and walk toward the Suburban, Kace keeps step beside me with his rifle cradled in his arms as if to guard my retreat.*

*Then someone shouts, "Hey! It's the Fallen Eagle convoy!" and I whirl breathlessly to watch the line of approaching vehicles. "Breeze?"*

— Excerpt from Lauren Davis' *Journal.*

# CHAPTER FIFTY-TWO

THE FORKS HADN'T CHANGED. Most of the same vehicles were parked in the same rows; the only difference Breeze could see was that some of the Militia pickups were different, and the parking lots were now dotted with puddles left by the recent rains. Oh, and there was the TV truck. That was new, and its presence made her anything but happy.

A crowd had gathered to greet them. Maybe a hundred people in ACUs and the assorted ranch and outdoor wear the Militia tended to.

The JLTV now followed one of the Guard Humvees from Ted's Place —the one with the 5.56 SAW. Doveman had stayed behind to guard the MTV with its supplies. His job was to control the Ted's Place junction with its strategic access to the Poudre Canyon in preparation for a relocation of The Line farther to the south. With control of Colorado 14 west to Walden, in Jackson County, Wyoming could cut the number of OPs and personnel needed to guard the border on the Third Quadrant by about half.

If nothing else, Fallen Eagle had proven the feasibility of that.

Goggles had a silly half smile on his lips as he drove past the checkpoint's lifted barrier. One hand was on the wheel, the other on the shifter. He lifted a thumbs up as calls, shouts, and applause broke from the WNG and Wyoming Militia who'd come out to watch Fallen Eagle's arrival. Now people lined the way, whooping, laughing, clapping hands high as the vehicles passed.

Where the Livermore Road split off, the familiar black Suburban was parked to the side. Captain Ragnovich, arms crossed, leaned against the front fender. He now straightened, walking out into the road. Behind came a guy in a suit and another in Dockers and a sweatshirt, his eye glued to a camera.

The escort Humvee pulled off to the right, allowing the JLTV to roll up to where Ragnovich waited.

Goggles braked to a stop, shifted into park, and killed the engine. "Looks like we made it."

"Yeah. Hell of job, Shane. Thanks."

He gave her a fist bump. "Thank you." His expression sobered. "I mean, yeah, a bunch of us would have probably fought our way back through Carter Lake and Gallagher Ranch. Not sure we'd have gotten the NPT truck through. Or the scientists."

"Sure you would." She gave him a saucy wink. "I'm just along as window dressing, remember?"

"In a pig's ass," Goggles muttered. Gestured at her door. "Go meet your adoring fans. Ragnovich is starting to look anxious. And I don't want the good captain taking too close a look at the scorch marks and bullet strikes. He might get ideas that it's my fault."

Breeze opened the door, and stepped out, feeling the chill in the morning-damp air. Behind her, Brylan's plow had come to a stop, and then the NPT truck. The rest of the vehicles, including the Excursion, M1089, and Jayco pulling in with her tail-end Humvee in the rear.

The guy with the camera was hovering obnoxiously close, dancing back and around to catch her and Ragnovich in the frame.

"Hey, Captain," she greeted, and pointed back at the NPT truck. "There's your lab. Got the scientists to run it. Best of all, we've got a couple of refrigeration units full of insulin ready for distribution."

Ragnovich—God, the guy looked tired—studied her thoughtfully, and said, "Guess it was a little rougher than we expected. Breeze, once again, I don't have the words to express what this means."

"Daddy tells me that I leave people speechless." She tried to ignore the fucking cameraman and the guy in a suit who hovered too close with a microphone. "But, damn, I think we're all reeling and in need of rack time. We're running on fumes and asleep on our feet. What these people did? They'll tell you it was nothing, but line each and every one up for a medal."

"Who's in charge here?" a shrill voice demanded as Guard and Militia were swarming the vehicles, slapping Breeze's people on the backs as they climbed down.

She turned, seeing Dr. Rymart Avery as he pushed through the press, a hand up and waving for attention.

"I need to speak with whomever is in charge," Avery insisted. Breaking free of the crowd and stalking up, he fixed on Ragnovich. "You! Are you in charge?"

Breeze said, "Captain Ragnovich, sir, this is Rymart Avery."

"*Doctor* Avery," Rymart insisted. "You're Ragnovich? I want you to know that this was about the most slip-shod excuse for a rescue I could have imagined. We barely made it. One delay after another. And most of it was because of Ms. Tappan, here. If Lieutenant Daniels had been in charge—"

"Go fuck yourself." Breeze accented her words with a stiff middle finger and stalked off before her anger could get the better of her. Bad enough she'd lost it in front of the camera. She took refuge where Goggles had taken position just behind the JLTV to watch.

"There! Do you see what I had to put up with?" Avery launched into Ragnovich. The guy with the camera was zooming in on Avery's face. The Captain, hands in a calming gesture, was trying to get a word in edgewise.

Slipping through the crowd came Margo Simone and Kathy Goodrich, looking remarkably relieved and giving people weary smiles. Questioned if they were the scientists, they answered that, yes, they could make medicines.

Seeing Breeze, Simone excused herself, hurrying forward. She took in where Avery was outlining demands, one by one, and slapping a hard two fingers against his palm with each one. The guy seemed to have swelled up to twice his size in front of the camera. Breeze could hear stuff about salary and expected housing.

"See you haven't shot him yet," Simone greeted.

"It was close," Breeze muttered. "But that damn camera made me reconsider."

Jenna Blix wiggled her way through the crowd, saying, "All's well. I just checked the refrigeration in the back of the NPT truck. Got the generators started. Another fifteen minutes, things might have gotten critical."

"Why didn't Avery attend to that?" Goggles asked. The guy kept yawning. Now that they'd made it, he was wilting faster than a desert flower.

"He'd tell you it wasn't his responsibility," Kathy Goodrich said. "Not that he'd know how to monitor the system in the first place."

"Whoa! Holy shit," Breeze cried. "That's the governor." She watched as Pete Agar ambled forward in his natty three-piece suit.

Then she saw Lauren limping along in the governor's wake. She'd pulled her dress jacket back, and one hand was on her pistol Something about her eyes, she looked like she'd been crying.

"Lauren?" Breeze called.

"Who's Lauren?" Simone wondered as Kathy Goodrich sidled up.

"Like Breeze," Goggles said. "A living legend."

"This I gotta hear." Breeze started forward as Agar walked up to where Avery was still outlining his demands to a now red-faced Harry Ragnovich. The camera guy stepped back to get them all in the frame.

"...And, of course, the electricity, water, and other utilities will be paid by the State of Wyoming. The same with any of the maintenance expenses for the building. I'll expect a driver, and of course, security. Especially after—"

"Perhaps I could help?" Agar said, stepping in and offering his hand. "I'm the governor. While the captain here has my full trust, your requirements fall outside of his expertise." Agar's smile went falsely placid. "Ragnovich is better at firing squads and executions...if you get my drift."

Avery missed it completely. Turned to Agar. "Good. You will no doubt have a better grasp of the value of my work. Now, as to the lab—"

"Anything you need. After the Collapse, we've got a surplus of warehouse and commercial space. I've been discussing it with my team, and we'll be placing your facility in Casper. Center of the state. Easier distribution."

"I see," Avery frowned. "I was thinking more of setting up operations in Jackson Hole, but I'm sure once the lab is running, I can work remotely." A pause. "I assume that after the present difficulties, there is also a surplus of, shall we say, upscale residences in Wilson? Along the Snake? Or perhaps on the national park boundaries? Something with a view of the Tetons?"

Breeze caught Lauren's incredulous look. Shared a 'what-the-fuck?' stare with her old friend. Breeze slipped up next to her saying, "Let me guess, you want to kill him as bad as I do?"

Lauren's brows lifted as she looked Breeze up and down, taking in the wrinkles, the dried blood. "You look like shit. Tough one, huh?"

Agar, a curious, almost amused smile on his lips, told Avery, "Oh, to be sure we've got estates by the dozen in Jackson these days."

"Good. We'll discuss this more as soon as I've had a good night's sleep, a long hot shower, and a proper meal. Um, I do hope that you have a driver? Perhaps a limousine? A more suiting ride for someone of my value to the state?"

"Is he out of his mind?" Lauren asked, fixing her stony gaze on Avery.

Simone, who'd walked up behind, said, "That's been suggested more than once. But it's like something snapped down at the lab. Maybe, when all of a sudden, he realized it didn't matter who he was. That he could die just as easily as the rest of us."

Breeze chewed on her thumb, and all the while, Lauren was incredulously evaluating Avery.

Breeze took a breath, asked, "Margo? Kathy? That lab, the notes and files in the Excursion...?"

"Yeah?" Margo shot a wary look at Kathy.

"Something you said back on the road... That Avery was the public face of the company. How much of the actual science was his?"

"Not much," Kathy said. "But he's the guy who put us all together. I mean, he was smart enough to recruit each of us for our individual expertise. Jim with technology and design, Jenna with biochem and genetics, Simone—"

"I think I'm getting the picture." Breeze strode forward, hand on her pistol.

Lauren, reading her expression, shot her a warning look. Gave a slight shake of the head.

"Lauren, he's conning us."

Lauren's gaze had thinned, her predatory eyes fixed on the cameraman and the guy who was slipping his microphone as close as he could to catch it all. "Let me handle this." A beat. "But you can come along for the fun."

Breeze, not sure what Lauren was up to, stayed a step behind.

"This is bullshit." Lauren interrupted Avery in midsentence.

All eyes turned on her.

"Double bullshit," Breeze agreed, tapping fingers on her pistol.

"Get this woman out of my sight." Avery crossed his arms, a satisfied smile adding to the delight in his twinkling eyes. "She's a—"

Breeze hit him hard in the chest with a balled fist, knocked him back a half step. "Shut the fuck up, or I'll slap you silly." To Agar, she said, "The arrogant piece of shit's using you, sir."

Lauren was giving her a disapproving look. "This is how you let me handle it?"

"I know," Agar told her. "I'm willing to endure a little bit of using if it will mean the lives of my people."

Avery blurted, "Governor, this Tappan woman has already cost the lives of your people through her..."

Breeze didn't think. The pistol came up so smoothly, it just seemed to appear in her hand. She shoved the muzzle hard into Avery's breastbone, bulled him backward against the scorched side of the JLTV. Was staring into those wide, totally terrified eyes. The man's mouth was working, making a puckering O as he struggled for breath.

Somewhere behind her, Lauren was saying, "Stand back! Let Breeze handle it."

She was barely aware of the camera poking close, that lens shining like a wet dark eye.

"Too many of us died for you, you piece of walking excrement. Daniels, White Eagle, Kran, Clugg, and rest. Sam Delgado sacrificed himself to get that lab back across the line. You get it, you overblown bag of wind? *Died!*"

"Breeze," Ragnovich was shouting. "Stand down! Now, soldier!"

"Hear her out," Lauren snapped. "That's Breeze Tappan, the hero of The Line. When she speaks, everyone listens!"

*What the...?* But Breeze kept her pistol hard in Avery's breastbone.

Agar's calmer voice said, "Wait a minute, Harry. If Lauren says to hear Breeze Tappan out, we're hearing her out."

Breeze was vaguely aware that she was center of attention for the entire crowd, that you could have heard a mouse fart from thirty meters. That squirrely looking dude in the suit had the microphone shoved at her.

"Breeze says this guy's a con," Lauren said reasonably, and the camera switched to her. "Jerry, we were just talking about the price Wyoming has paid in blood and tears, and now this piece of shit wants to hold us up for a Jackson Hole estate?"

The Guard and Militia surrounding them began jeering, shouting. Someone bellowed, "Shoot the son of a bitch!"

Agar had stepped back, a cunning light in his dark eyes, which were mostly fixed on Lauren.

Breeze watched the sweat begin to bead on Avery's forehead as she raised her voice. "Simone? Kathy? Jenna? You're the brains behind Boulder Mountain Biotek, aren't you? I mean, it's not like good old Rymart here ever got his fingers dirty in the lab, right? You said he was just the business head? The salesman?"

Simone stepped forward. "I guess you could say that. But, I mean, we wouldn't be here without him. He insisted that we leave town. Wait it out at the lab. Otherwise, God knows what would have happened to us."

"But you can make anything we need?" Agar asked, catching on. "Without Avery here?"

"Wait! I—" Avery choked it off when Breeze shoved the muzzle of her pistol painfully into his breastbone.

Simone, looking cowed, glanced back and forth between Kathy and Jenna. The look they shared was answer enough, but Jenna said, "And Jim, don't forget him. But yeah, that's why Rymart was so desperate to save us. Even back at the lab, he wouldn't let us take chances. That's why we're the only ones left."

"Ms. Tappan?" Agar asked softly. "If you're going to shoot him, let me know so I can step back. Getting a suit cleaned of blood spatter is so much more difficult these days."

The guy with the camera swiveled on his heels to get Agar in the picture.

Breeze glared into Avery's horrified eyes, could feel the man's fear through the pistol, the quaking muscles, terror in his frantic heartbeat. "You kept them together for us. I guess that's worth something."

She stepped back, re-holstering her HK .45. "Now, get the hell out of my sight. You're done. Finished. Wyoming's obligation to you is over."

"You heard her." Lauren raised her voice so the Guard could hear. "He gets to go. Breeze Tappan says so."

As Rymart Avery sank to the ground, back sliding down the JLTV's scorched fender, Breeze turned her back. Needed to get away. She barely realized that the crowd parted before her aimless path.

*God, Sam. You saved us all. And tens of thousands more.*

Her vision had silvered, tears hot.

Now she could grieve.

# AFTERWORD

*We're headed back up US 287 toward Laramie, passing the burned out houses and ranches around Tie Siding. Escorted by WNG Humvees, the NPT truck and the scientists' Expedition are ahead of us.*

*Agar has been thoughtful, considering me with appraising eyes. Now, he says, "You did a marvelous job out there today. That interview was the perfect preamble to the arrival of the Fallen Eagle convoy. Then you and Breeze taking Dr. Avery down?" A beat. "It reinforced, once again, what heroes you both are. We're going to need heroes, Davis."*

*I think I grunted. I'm too worried about Breeze. I've seen her weary and disheartened, physically exhausted, dirty, and mentally drained. But to see the grief in her eyes today? If Sam is dead, she'll never get over it. She's probably off somewhere right now, alone, wondering if any man she falls in love with is gonna die.*

*The governor interrupts my thoughts: "By tonight, if I'm lucky, you'll be the focus of the entire state, which will ameliorate the things I must say in my press conference."*

*I narrow my eyes and look across the seat. "You're going to suspend elections?"*

*He pauses to take a deep breath and seems to hold it far too long.*

*Finally, he answers, "We have maybe a month before the war reaches us. What would you do?"*

— Excerpt from Lauren Davis' *Journal.*

# CHAPTER FIFTY-THREE

THE SLEEPING BAG might have been the Hilton's finest mattress. Breeze had walked into the first tent she'd had come to with a cot and flopped onto it. Fully dressed, wearing a coat she'd found, she went out like a flipped switch. The tent was the standard heavy canvass military issue, olive drab, with a slight odor of oil and mildew. But it would be proof against the rain, which looked threatening in the low black clouds.

That was the thing about the end of the world. It might just be September—usually the driest month in Wyoming—but apocalypse was turning out to be a soggy process. Meant the alfalfa cuttings would be at risk of molding. And God knew what it would do to the wheat and sugar beet harvest. At least she had a coat now. Borrowed, but warm.

In her dreams, Sam was cooking on the little heat stove in the guest cabin back at the ranch. Something with black beans, lots of diced jalapeños, and little squares of cube steak sautéed with onions to be wrapped in corn tortilla. He kept grinning at her, talking about how food for the senses made sex incredibly fulfilling.

*I mean, enough talking. Get on with it!*

But as much as she wanted him to lay the spatula down, lift her from the chair, and rip her clothes off, the guy just stood there, back to her, talking about food.

She wanted to scream.

Behind her chair, Water Ghost Woman was making *tsking* sounds, shaking her head and clearly disappointed with Breeze Tappan when it came to the expression of her feminine wiles. So much for the misuse of her ability to seduce men.

*Got to do it myself.*

Bracing herself, Breeze tried to lift her weirdly ponderous weight out of the chair. Like, wow. She could barely move…like her arms and legs were solid lead. Struggling, slowly rising. Each limb lifted in slow motion and she just couldn't…

"Damn it, Sam!" she shouted. "Will you come help?"

Meanwhile, unaware, he kept chatting as if…

"Hey! Breeze!" The words intruded into her dream, jarring, out of place for…

The kick to her feet brought groggily awake.

Dark and smelly army tent. Laid out on a cot, in an unknown sleeping bag, wearing a stranger's coat. She was at The Forks. Had stayed behind with the rest of the Fallen Eagle squad as Lauren, Governor Agar, Ragnovich, the NPT truck, the Excursion with the scientists, and the Jayco had headed for Laramie.

"What the hell?" She rolled over to blink sleep-bleary eyes at Goggles, a silly grin on his face.

"Come on, LT. Got a surprise for you."

"I'm not a lieutenant, Shane. I'm not even—"

"Oh, will you stop that! All the rest of us, we know what you did. Daniels, on her best day—and she was good—couldn't have done what you did. And, wow! Talk about being a legend? You oughta hear what they're saying about you pulling that pistol on Avery. You're going to be on TV! It's like a whole new level of herodom."

"Herodom isn't a word."

"Maybe not in scrabble, but it sure describes you. I mean, you took that asshole down right in front of Agar. You know what kind of balls that takes?"

She lifted a cross eyebrow. Figured she didn't need to give him a lesson in anatomy. At his age, he should have figured out who had what for himself.

Goggles reached down, pulled her to her feet.

"If this is some silly prank, like you and the rest are pulling off a surprise party? Maybe going to make me an honorary lieutenant, douse me in Gatorade, or some other sophomore idiocy when I could be sound asleep? Gotta tell you, I'm pissed, exhausted, and I have a round chambered in my Heckler and Koch. See, it's right here on my hip."

Goggles didn't seem to take the hint, that stupid smile bending his way-too-Arapaho lips into a curl as he found her old Rand's hat and slapped it onto her head. It was all Breeze could do to keep from stumbling, still sleep-logged, as he dragged her out into the day.

Outside, Tortilla Gomez and Paco Vermijo waited. Paco cried, "Good! You got her." And Tortilla added, "We played rock, paper, scissors to see who'd have to go in to wake you. Shane lost. We were waiting to hear the gunshot."

"Don't count it out...yet," Breeze growled, eyes narrowed, hand on her pistol.

"'Bout time," Paco said, looking off toward the highway.

Breeze yawned, fought to clear her muzzy senses. The cool air helped, a slight misty rain starting to fall as they wound though the Militia pickups.

Her three tormentors led the way to the intersection, past the Humvees, to where a crowd had gathered at the barricade. All eyes fixed on her as she approached. And, damn it, Shane had been right. The glowing worship, the way they all went silent as she walked among them, it was eerie. Like she was some sort of divine luminary.

"Should have seen her..." was whispered by one.

"Walked right in front of Agar and shoved a pistol in the guy's mouth!" hissed another.

Mouth? she wondered. Where in hell had *that* come from?

"I mean," another told his companion, "Agar didn't raise a finger."

"Shit," the companion answered, "that's Breeze Tappan. If you were governor, would you?"

"Don't forget, Davis was there backing her up. Would you mess with *her?*"

"Oh, for crap's sake," Breeze snapped as she turned on them. "I was just too tired to think it through."

Didn't seem to cow any of them. They just nodded, that unsettling gleam in their eyes. Like it wouldn't have mattered if she'd said the sun was green.

"All right"—she stopped short in the middle of the highway—"what the hell is going on?"

"That." Tortilla pointed to the south.

Breeze turned, followed his extended finger.

"Got a call from the OP at Ted's Place," Goggles told her. "Thought you'd want to be here."

She could hear the engine now, a low rumble. Could make out the approaching truck. The blade didn't look right, bent, cocked at a just-wrong angle. Behind it, the hood was a mottled almost-camo-pattern of scorched black patches on Highway Department yellow. The windshield was missing, as were all but one of the stalks for the flashing hazard lights that stuck up from the cab. What Breeze recognized as the big long-barreled AR 50 was resting on the hood. And, damn if only one headlight was burning, the other shot out. Worse, the big truck was wobbling back and forth, the front wheels, bent out and oscillating. Looked like at any second, they'd come flying off to bounce and careen into the ditches.

Breeze sucked for breath. Couldn't help but lift a hand to her throat. Impossible, but here it came.

"Dear God," she whispered as the plow slowed. It passed the uplifted barricade pole, shook itself slowly to a stop. Steam was rising from behind the grill, wheezing out around the seams in the scorched hood. Breeze got a good look at the bullet holes, realized the dump bed on the back was totally charred. Worse, the tandem sets of rear duals on the driver's side…well, the remains of three of the tires were mere rings of burnt rubber held on the rims by their wire beads. The battered Mack had been limping along on a single inside back tire, and it was half flat.

In the cab, Jackie used an elbow to knock out the bullet-shattered driver's side window. It hit the ground with a splat, diamonds of glass shooting out. The woman looked hollow-eyed, bone weary, and her hoodie was splotched with dried blood.

As the Mack's engine stuttered to silence, Jackie called down. "Sorry about the glass."

"What the hell did you do to my truck!" One of the highway department guys raised his hands to his head in disbelief as he stared the plow's twisted metal. "Holy shit! The frame's bent to hell and back. And there's a fricking *dead* guy squashed behind the blade. He's half-way through the grill!"

"Where's Sam?" Breeze called as she climbed up on the step below the bullet-riddled door. "How the hell did you get here?"

"Sam's in the passenger seat," Jackie told her wearily. "Hope you got an ambulance, 'cause I'm not even sure he's alive anymore."

# EPIPHANY

*I met my other self that afternoon when I least expected it. I did it in the home theater room at the governor's residence.*

*By myself.*

*Sitting in one of the fancy movie chairs.*

*The "me" I encountered was on the large screen as it played the Jerry Fingers television interview I'd shot that morning.*

*There I was, standing in front of that Humvee at The Forks, all those Guard and Militia crowded around. And this stranger. I mean, I'd never seen myself on television. Never heard my voice over the air. Would have loved to declare that whoever that hard-eyed and haunted woman was, she sure as hell wasn't Lauren Davis. That woman up there on the screen has cracked-glass, tan eyes wary as a wild animal's, but something about her posture, the hand propped on her pistol, sent a shiver through me. She looked dangerous. Tough.*

*For the first few seconds, as Jerry asked his questions, I could see her reluctance, that she'd rather be anywhere else, doing anything else. But when she started talking about escaping from Colorado, something in her voice went through me like a fiery arrow. I listened, transfixed. In that honest voice, I heard courage, pain, and remorse. But in addition, hidden among the syllables and intonations, was an iron resolve and reflection. One that bespoke a young woman who'd been pushed beyond her limits and who had paid a terrible price to overcome and survive.*

*It wasn't anything I could put my finger on. That young woman with the cracked-glass gaze seemed to reek of resilience. Vulnerable, yet tempered. Strong. Like she'd looked into Hell, and could stare the Devil, eyeball to eyeball.*

*Through the entire interview, I had to ask:* Is this who Lauren Davis really is?

*I mean, couldn't be me.*

*Took me five viewings to realize the answer was yes.*

— Excerpt from Lauren Davis' *Journal.*

# CHAPTER FIFTY-FOUR

SOMEONE HAD LAID a sack of cement on Sam's chest. Had to be. The weight was just too heavy to let him breathe. And it fricking-well hurt! Never being able to catch a full breath left him in a constant state of panic. Took all his concentration to suck just a little puff. If only he could fill his lungs. Just once.

That he couldn't, kept distracting him from what Breeze was saying. She was tucked snuggly against his shoulder, like she'd been that day down at the lab. His arm was around her, reassuring, warm. He reveled in the feel of her, solid and completely his. Dependable, tough, and everything a woman should be for a man.

They sat on a high point. On a resistant basalt outcrop above a field of grass, lupines, asters, and larkspur. Had to be somewhere up in the Absarokas. The sun was shining on the distant snow patches and the thrusting, irregular, and ragged grey peaks where they clawed at the cerulean sky.

Sunlight! Sam leaned his head back, could have sat like that forever, but for the dragging weight on his lungs.

"You gotta see, Sam," Breeze was telling him. "We can't keep doing what we're doing. I mean, what's the point of being married if we're just going to have to keep killing one Cole after another from here on out? And it's not like we're going to run out of them. They breed like rats."

"I don't want to kill any Coles. I don't want to kill anybody."

She twisted around until they were chest to chest, blocking the bright sunlight. Reached out to place her hands on either side of his face. God, her hands were so soft. He was staring into her tan Tappan eyes as she kissed him sensually on the lips.

He vaguely heard her say, "There's a way to end this, but I've got to go now." Then her head was beside his, her voice whispering in his ear. *"In case this doesn't work, you need to know. I love you."*

And then she rose, floating up into the sky, drifting into the sunlight, which, in turn grew darker and darker until nothing but black remained...

Out of a haze, he came to. Alone, with the weight pressing down on his chest. But when he tried, he could conjure visions, wraith-like, of Breeze. Her hair flying as she rode bareback across a spring-green field. Seeing her walk toward him across the ranch yard, her body supple, thin, and long-legged. She flipped her hair back, giving him an intimate smile that hinted of delights to come. He dreamed her, stepping into his embrace, her arms slipped around his neck, her gaze fixed so intently on his.

Sometimes Breeze shape-shifted, becoming Shyla. Those intense Tappan eyes turning green, only to fade back into Breeze's as they made love in the little guest cabin. As the erotic dream faded, he was left to wonder which woman he'd been locked with.

*"It's all right,"* Shyla whispered as she backed slowly away and faded into a silvery mist.

The way she vanished left Sam with a terrible ache that expanded to his throbbing chest.

...And then he was back. Home in Hempstead. And, to his astonishment, Breeze walked through the swinging silver doors into The Yucateca kitchen. She had a stack of dirty plates in her muscular arms. A cloud of steam rose from his sink—thick and filled with the odors of corn tortillas, carne picado, and Mom's special red chili made with Sandia and Guajillo.

"Well, hurry up," Breeze chided as she added her dirty dishes to the towering pile of plates waiting to be washed. "We've got hungry people out there. You expect them to eat on paper towels?" Then she turned, flipped her hair over her shoulders, and looking back, winked. "Bet you can't live without me, huh?"

His heart sank as she vanished out through the swinging doors. Around him, the stacks of dirty dishes were higher. Didn't matter how many he washed; the stacks just kept growing.

*"In case this doesn't work...you need to know...I love you."*

Dreamlike, the words whispered through him...

Sam?" The voice brought him awake.

He blinked, realized everything was blurry. Tried to reach up, but his arm was trapped.

That set off a panic. He jerked, tied to suck a breath, fought to... *Damn! That hurt.*

"Sam!" Lauren Davis snapped. "Hold the fuck still. Ease down! You're all right. You're in the hospital. You're safe."

He tried again to breathe, felt like an iron band was clamped around his tortured ribs. "What the hell? Lauren?"

She used a warm cloth to sponge his face, saying, "Relax, cowboy. Your eyes are filled with protective goo. There, is that better?"

He blinked, still sucking for breath, and fixed on the ceiling overhead. Acoustical panels, the fluorescent lights. And, yeah, there was the usual bedside monitor with its screen reflecting his pulse, heartbeat, and blood pressure. He was partly propped in a hospital bed, rails on each side. An IV was in the back of his hand.

He blinked at Lauren. "God, it's great to see you."

She took his free hand and held it. "They've had quite a time with you. Said you were pretty much dead when Breeze pulled you out of that plow. Guess the way Jackie stuffed you down on the floor saved your life. Something about your legs being elevated after you landed on the floorboards. You remember any of that?"

Sam returned the slight squeeze of the hand she gave him. "Last I remember was shooting at a guy blocking the way." He frowned. "I was aiming at his truck. Hit him."

"Jackie said you blew him in two." A pause. "Did you think to check the zero on that rifle?"

"Huh?"

"Well, the guys in the Guard who ended up with it, say it must have taken a hell of a wallop. It shoots way right of where the crosshairs align on the scope." Her eyebrow lifted. "But then, as I remember, you have a reputation for aiming one place and hitting another."

To change the subject, Sam asked, "What happened to me?"

"They say you went into something called distributive shock caused by fatigue, intense pain, and intercostal bleeding where you'd pulled a bunch of your healing ribs apart. You lost consciousness, then your organs started to shut down."

"I can barely breathe."

"Been there, done that. Still got shrapnel in my lungs." Lauren let go of his hand and pulled up the single chair, regarding him thoughtfully. "The places you'd broken your ribs and popped the cartilage apart were pretty messed up. So they went in and sort of stapled and wired your ribs back to together. Being a celebrity, the whole state is keeping track of your recovery."

"Why am I a celebrity?"

"Jackie told the whole story." That skeptical eyebrow was raised. "All about your burning snowplow and the Carter Lake battle, your gun battle at Gallagher ranch. Blowing that looter into pieces with the AR 50. You're like an old-time gunslinger, buddy."

She paused. "Oh, by the way, when the story got out about you shooting that rancher, a bunch of people got together and crowd-sourced. Then sent that guy, Phil, a bull. In your name, if you can believe. Jerry loved it."

"Who's Jerry?"

"Jerry Finger. Runs the news at KCHY TV. He and Jackie are quite the hot couple. He's got her dolled up and hanging on his arm like a fixture."

Sam sighed as much as he could without adding to the hurt. "Guess that's all she can be. The woman is living a Greek tragedy worthy of Aeschylus."

"Who?"

"Never mind." Then, heart in throat, he asked, "Where's Breeze?"

Lauren gave him a probing look. "Tell me something straight, Delgado. Do you love her?"

"Yes. And it fills me with guilt."

"Shyla's dead." Lauren leaned forward. "Breeze is alive."

He took a shallow breath. "Thing is, I don't feel like I measure up, you know? I never rodeoed. Never broke horses or fed livestock in blizzards." He would have laughed at the futility, but it hurt too much. "Hey, I just washed dishes in a *mas o menos* Mexican restaurant in a suburb on Long Island."

Lauren started to say something, looked mystified. Then she gave a slight shake of the head, sighed. "Okay. It's now an established fact that you're an idiot. Guess Breeze will just have to find herself a real man."

Lauren got up to leave.

"Wait. Where is Breeze?"

"She's probably in Hot Springs by now." Lauren paused at the door to look back.

"Doing what?"

"She's going to settle things with Corwin and the Cole family. Said she'd do it no matter what it takes."

Sam panicked. Tried to sit up, realized he was strapped in the bed. "Well, don't just stand there, help me!"

"To do what?" A half smile had bent Lauren's lips. "You're held together with staples and wires."

"Doesn't matter. I can't let her face him alone. I gotta have her back!"

"Don't measure up, huh?" Lauren shook her head. "But you're not getting out of that bed. No matter how much of an idiot you are."

# CATHARSIS

*There he is.*

*"I've been looking for you," I say as I slowly plod across the lawn of the governor's mansion to where Kace Adams stands in the trees. The Wyoming wind is blowing his blond hair around his face. He carries his rifle slung over his left shoulder.*

*"What do you need?" he calls.*

*I stop about three feet from him and spread my feet to brace my aching knees. Uneasily, I say, "Funny thing. Had an encounter with the other Lauren Davis. The one who follows behind. I got a really good look at her. Saw how the rest of the world sees her. How there's her, and the me that's inside. How she's strong and tested, and the inside me is frightened and tenuous. You were right all along. About who I am."*

*"Tough coming face to face with yourself, isn't it?"*

*I chew my lip, glance up at the giant spruce trees that give the spacious yard a parklike appearance. I think about Sam Delgado, who has no clue that he's delusional. I think now that I am just as much of an idiot as he is.*

*The wind makes a soft roar in their needle-thick branches. I say, "Given what's coming. I mean, if the offer is still good... If you're ever off duty, maybe we could go get something to eat and I could just..." I clench my fists at my sides and force myself to go on. "I need to talk to someone who doesn't expect me to pretend I'm okay."*

*His face is expressionless, then a slight smile touches his mouth. "I can do that. I'm off at seven. Burger?"*

*"Yeah," I answer through a relieved exhale. "Burger is good."*

*As I turn back to the portico and the residence's front door, a sliver of smile curls my lip. Suddenly, tomorrow isn't nearly as frightening as it had been.*

— Excerpt from Lauren Davis' *Journal.*

# CHAPTER FIFTY-FIVE

BREEZE FIGURED the hospital was as good a place as any to face Corwin and Sandra Cole. If this went south—and anyone survived—medical care would be rendered on the spot. Not that medical care was what it had been before the Collapse. Supplies of anesthetics, antibiotics, needles, plastic tubing, and all the myriad of little sterile packets medical services had once had at their disposal were gone. Rather, hospitals now had become a pastiche of twenty-first century mixed with the 1930s. Homemade glucose and saline were dispensed from glass bottles that could be sterilized in the autoclave or boiled. Needles and syringes were laboriously cleaned and reused. Where anesthetics had once eased pain, people now gritted their teeth and suffered.

But there was hope. The NPT truck had made it to Casper, was being set up in a warehouse on B Street. The contents of the refrigeration units that Fallen Eagle had kept running were being dispensed to the most desperate of patients.

Dr. Simone and her team would be up and running in weeks. Not without issue, of course. Labs run on chemicals that would have to be synthesized locally. Building a pharmaceutical industry from scratch would come with bumps and starts. Substitutes would have to be found for raw materials that had been sourced from around the globe.

Breeze sat back in the visitor's chair and pulled her leg up as she inspected the sleeping child. He lay supine, covered with a sheet. His sunken eyes, sallow expression, and breathing left no doubt of his serious condition. Kid was only eight, after all.

Something was seriously wrong with the world when a kid like him had to suffer so. It wasn't like the little boy had lived long enough to make the kind of bad choices in life that would merit such misery.

But then, looking at the monitor, the boy's blood pressure was up, his respiration less labored. Since Breeze's arrival just before midnight, she'd seen the kid's improvement.

Closing her eyes, she was drifting off when the sound of boots could be heard in the hall. Breeze glanced up, saw it was a little before six.

"...hope he's not suffering. I should have been here." Sandra's voice could be heard as she approached the door.

"You got animals to care for. A ranch to run. I know Doc's doing everything." Bradley's voice carried the strain of a worried man trying to sound strong.

And then Sandra led the way into the room. She was wearing worn Levi's, boots still muddy from the corral. She had on Scotch cap and a blue felt shirt, a wild rag around her neck. Her Carhartt coat hung open. Bits of hay were clinging to the sleeves. She'd come straight from feeding the cattle. At sight of Breeze, she stopped short. Her eyes went wide, then filled with hate. "You!"

Corwin was through the door, hot on her heels, his jaw tightening, eyes narrowing in that tunnel vision a man got before going in for the kill. He took a hard step forward, reaching for a pocket where the outline of a pistol could be seen.

"Hold up!" Breeze said, rising from the chair to drop a hand to her own pistol. "I'm here on a peace mission." Her smile thinned. "Besides, shooting up the hospital would be in bad form."

"*Get out!*" Sandra hissed the words through locked jaws, fire in her eyes.

"I said I'm here to make peace," Breeze said mildly.

"How?" Corwin had stepped right up to her; the man was trembling in rage.

"I'm reaching in my pocket," Breeze told him, literally eyeball to eyeball. "I took a life from you. Now I'm giving one back. So, don't do anything until you hear me out. Deal?"

Corwin's mouth was working like he was about to spit into her face, but he jerked a slight nod.

Breeze slipped her hand into her pocket, pulled out the little vial, and raised it between them. "This is from Sam and me."

Corwin raised a hand, as if ready to knock it out of her fingers. Warily asked, "What is it?"

"Insulin," Breeze told him. "Oliver got his first injection just after midnight. He's stabilized. He's going to make it."

Sandra had rushed over to the bed, was staring down at her son. "Ollie?" she asked softly, too much hope in her voice.

The little boy yawned, blinked his eyes open and, voice weak, said, "Mama?"

Breeze was forgotten as Corwin bent over the bed. "Hey, kiddo! How you doing?"

She took a deep breath, placed the vial on the bedside tray, and started for the door.

"Tappan?" Corwin called. "Is this for real?"

Breeze looked back. "Yeah. I brought enough to keep Oliver stabilized. Doc Willson says you're going to have to be really careful until production can be ramped up."

"You and Delgado did this?" He was looking confused. "For us?"

"For everyone." She slapped the door frame. "Listen. What's between us can't be washed away. I'm not asking for forgiveness, just a truce. We've got too many other things to deal with in the Basin."

Corwin's expression pinched, twitched, like he was struggling through it all. Then he nodded. "Yeah, I guess we can live with that."

"That's all any of us can hope for these days," Breeze told him before walking out the door.

# A LOOK AT: DARK INHERITANCE

## By W. Michael Gear and Kathleen O'Neal Gear

**W. Michael Gear and Kathleen O'Neal Gear, international bestselling authors of *Dissolution*, present a gripping, thought-provoking contemporary thriller in the tradition of Michael Chrichton's *Jurassic Park*. Here a project of cutting-edge genetics might lead to a better world—or a waking nightmare.**

For thirteen years—since he became one of several scientists chosen to raise apes bred by the pharmaceutical giant SAC—Dr. Jim Dutton, his young daughter Brett, and the bonobo ape Umber have been a family. For Umber is far more than a subject or pet. She types, reads, speaks sign language, favors psychedelic clothes, and even contemplates the nature of God.

Then a colleague forces Jim to confront the reality he's tried to ignore: Umber and the other SAC apes are too intelligent to be pure bonobos. They are "augmented" apes, more like early hominids than to anthropoids. And when SAC abruptly demands Umber's immediate return, it becomes vital for Jim to discover why the corporation created this new species.

The quest for answers will take Jim and his family to Africa, to a SAC facility that fronts as a preserve dedicated to helping once-captive chimps. But the grounds also hide a covert genetics lab, a missing band of blue-eyed apes, crude buildings decorated with skulls, and, deep in the shadows, human corpses savagely hacked to pieces...

Now the struggle to uncover SAC's secrets becomes a fight for survival. Suddenly Umber, Brett, and Jim find themselves hunted by beings who are fiercely territorial, brutally aggressive, and far stronger than any human.

And like humans they can be utterly, and murderously, psychotic...

*AVAILABLE NOW*

# ABOUT THE AUTHOR

W. Michael Gear is the New York Times and international bestselling author of over fifty-eight novels, many of them co-authored with Kathleen O'Neal Gear.

With seventeen million copies of his work in print he is best known for the "People" series of novels written about North American Archaeology. His work has been translated into at least 29 languages. Michael has a master's degree in Anthropology, specialized in physical anthropology and forensics, and has worked as an archaeologist for over forty years.

His published work ranges in genre from prehistory, science fiction, mystery, historical, genetic thriller, and western. For twenty-eight years he and Kathleen have raised North American bison at Red Canyon Ranch and won the coveted National Producer of the Year award from the National Bison Association in 2004 and 2009. They have published over 200 articles on bison genetics, management, and history, as well as articles on writing, anthropology, historic preservation, resource utilization, and a host of other topics.

The Gears live in Cody, Wyoming, where W. Michael Gear enjoys large-caliber rifles, long-distance motorcycle touring, and the richest, darkest stout he can find.

Check out the Gears' website at: www.gear-gear.com

Made in the USA
Coppell, TX
10 June 2023

17902034R00239